DAUGHTER OF TIDES

OTHER TITLES BY KIT ROCHA

The Beyond Series

Beyond Shame

Beyond Control

Beyond Pain

Beyond Temptation

Beyond Jealousy

Beyond Solitude

Beyond Addiction

Beyond Possession

Beyond Innocence

Beyond Ruin

Beyond Ecstasy

Beyond Surrender

Beyond Doubt

Beyond Forever

Gideon's Riders

Ashwin

Deacon

Ivan

Mercenary Librarians

Deal with the Devil

The Devil You Know

Dance with the Devil

Bound to Fire and Steel

Consort of Fire

Queen of Dreams

DAUGHTER OF TIDES

KIT ROCHA

Montlake

This is a work of fiction. Names, characters, organizations, places, events, and incidents are either products of the author's imagination or are used fictitiously. Otherwise, any resemblance to actual persons, living or dead, is purely coincidental.

Text copyright © 2025 by Kit Rocha
All rights reserved.

No part of this book may be reproduced, or stored in a retrieval system, or transmitted in any form or by any means, electronic, mechanical, photocopying, recording, or otherwise, without express written permission of the publisher.

Published by Montlake, Seattle

www.apub.com

Amazon, the Amazon logo, and Montlake are trademarks of Amazon.com, Inc., or its affiliates.

EU product safety contact
Amazon Media EU S. à r.l.
38, avenue John F. Kennedy, L-1855 Luxembourg
amazonpublishing-gpsr@amazon.com

ISBN-13: 9781662523625 (paperback)
ISBN-13: 9781662523618 (digital)

Cover design by Hang Le
Cover images: © Andrei Armiagov, © Android Boss, © Dolucan / Shutterstock

Printed in the United States of America

To Akeisha, Lee-Sien, Megan, Helena, Alyssa, Shivani, Sara, Cal, Devin, Candace, and LB. $1,021,023 for voting rights. You did that.

Our hopes have always shaped the world. The whispers of our hearts are candles set afloat on the rivers of eternity, all flowing inexorably toward the Everlasting Dream. The Dream surrounds us. We are born from it. When we die, we return to it. And when we reach out in fear and longing, the Dream provides.

When time was new and the world barely formed, the Sheltered Lands cried out for a protector. So the Dragon appeared from the flames, and the Siren rose from the depths of the seas. A handful of others followed, gods who could hear the whispers of the world itself.

They were the Dreamers, and where they walked, the world thrived.
When they Dreamt, the world changed.

Then they fought, and the world broke. And, in darkness and fear, our nightmares formed the Endless Void.

The War of the Gods
Author unknown

Chapter One

> *And what exactly is Akeisa, you might ask? It is the northernmost kingdom in our Empire, and the last to come under the benevolent rule of His Imperial Majesty. Due to an oddly frigid current in the strait between Akeisa and northern Kasther, the climate on the island is significantly colder than the rest of the Empire, even during the summer. A fitting home for the Ice Queen.*
>
> Akeisa: A Comprehensive History (Volume One)
> *by Guildmaster Klement*

The queen was nervous.

Aleksi watched as she pushed food around her plate, then abandoned her cutlery in favor of draining her ornate goblet of wine.

He pondered her unease as a silent servant stepped forward and refilled the queen's goblet. Aside from the servants, he and Anikke were alone in the private royal dining room, so this could be a simple case of awkwardness. The conversation *had* lulled a bit. And though he had a standing invitation as honored guest and dined often at Castle Roquebarre these days, it was always in the main hall. Those long tables, filled as they typically were with courtiers and visiting nobles, bustled with conversation. It was a handy way to avoid the silences that tended to crop up with only two diners present.

The pressure to maintain a steady flow of engaging conversation could tax even the most outgoing of wits. Except . . . this private dinner was happening at Queen Anikke's behest. With a snap of her fingers, she could beckon said courtiers and nobles to her side and end her torment.

It had to be something else.

Before he could ask, Anikke smiled. "How is your quail?"

"Delicious, as always," he answered honestly. "Your head cook is a genius. I've frankly considered trying to steal her from you."

"You already have all the poets and painters," Anikke protested. "The musicians, too."

He shrugged lightly. "That's the curse of being me. The god of love itself always seems to be the first muse toward whom any artist gravitates."

She laughed. "You *could* leave some genius for the rest of the country."

"Very well. But only because you asked." At least the girl was smiling now. "Have you heard from your sister?"

Her smile widened. "She visited me last night."

"All the way from Akeisa?"

"Through my dreams." Her wondering tone left no doubt how much she admired Sachielle's power to travel into a person's consciousness as they slumbered.

It didn't matter one whit to the queen that Sachi, formerly of Castle Roquebarre, was not truly of royal blood. It didn't even matter to her that Sachi wasn't human at all, but the primal force of Creation itself. Sachi and Anikke were sisters at heart, and that was the one tie nothing could sever.

"She gave me this. A gift from the island kingdom." The girl raised her arm and pulled back her fitted velvet sleeve. Beneath, a bracelet of carved shell and driftwood wrapped around her small wrist.

"It's exquisite." It wasn't a fancy piece, made of precious metals and stones, but Anikke clearly treasured it. "How are they enjoying their diplomatic mission?"

"Sachi likes this sort of work." Anikke bit her lip. "These are the kinds of skills my father taught her for show, you know, and never expected her to use. There's a satisfaction in that, I think."

"A very wise observation." Aleksi tilted his head. "And Ash and Zanya?"

"I believe Sachi's exact words were, *they're savoring the opportunity to immerse themselves in the island's culture.*"

Which meant they both hated being on unfamiliar, potentially enemy territory, and were eager to get back to the sorts of fights they recognized. But they would stay by Sachi's side, fiercely protective, guarding her from any and all threats.

Poor old dead King Dalvish II. Anikke's predecessor—and father—never saw this particular twist coming, did he? Two decades ago, he'd taken in two orphans, but his intentions had not been benevolent. He'd taken on Zanya, a child gifted in shadow magic, shining darkly with the power of the Void itself, as part of his household staff, and had adopted Sachi, who looked enough like him to pass as his heir.

And then he'd begun to put his scheme into motion. The bare bones of it were simple: every one hundred years, the Mortal Lords owed the Dragon a sacrifice. Not one of blood and pain, but of marriage. The current ruler was obligated to send their heir to serve as the Dragon's consort, tying the royal family to him—and their fates, in a very real way, to the well-being of the land itself.

In this way, the arrangement created even more obligations for the royal family. Having their fortunes bound to the land prevented them from exploiting it for their own excessive gain. Dalvish had sought to free himself from this check on his greed by sending Sachi and Zanya—a false heir and an assassin masquerading as her handmaid—to murder Ash in his bed.

Instead, the two women, who had already loved one another with an intensity that had glowed brighter than their respective magics, had fallen in love with Ash. And their joy was incandescent.

Perhaps no one could have foreseen it, not even the most gifted seers in the Sheltered Lands. There had been only one path to a happy ending, and the three of them had somehow stumbled down it. That alone would have pleased Aleksi to no end. The fact that Ash was one of his best and oldest friends only added to his pleasure.

"Sachi also said that Grand Duchess Gwynira—" Anikke faltered and frowned. "Is she still a Grand Duchess, now that the Betrayer's Empire has fallen?"

Who the hell knew? "My advice? When you're attempting to cultivate a foreign power as an ally, afford them every honor and courtesy you can without giving up any of your own."

"Of course." She nodded eagerly, and Aleksi could practically see the gears turning in her head as she processed that information.

The girl was young, but she cared about her people, and about using her power as their queen to protect them and better their lives. With the Siren serving as her mentor and the rest of the High Court guiding her, she would grow into a formidable ruler and salvage House Roquebarre's legacy.

A servant entered the main door, carrying a covered dish. He placed it before Aleksi, then lifted the lid with a flourish and a bow.

On the ornate silver tray lay a single rose. Its green leaves curled around a delicate stem, and the deep-red color of its petals gave way to a lush violet near the outer edges. White streaks reached up the body of each petal from the calyx, slowly swirling into the red and purple.

Aleksi smiled. "It's beautiful."

"It's yours," Anikke answered in a rush. "A new cultivar. The *Queen's Protector*, named in your honor."

"I'm touched." He picked up the bloom. The stem bore shorn spots where the thorns had been painstakingly snapped away, and the petals felt like silk. "I do love flowers. And to have one named for me? This is a precious gift, indeed."

"This is nothing," Anikke countered. "Certainly not enough. My lord, you saved my life."

He had bestowed his blessing upon her, and that blessing had protected her from an assassination attempt when her court had been infiltrated by a spy from the Empire. He had done it because she was in danger, and because he had seen the kindness that dwelled in her heart. If she had not earned his protection on her own merits, she would not have had it.

But it was nice to be appreciated. He inclined his head. "The Sheltered Lands need their queen."

Her cheeks flamed, and she leaned forward in her chair, her hand sliding across the table toward his. "They could also use a king."

Oh. Oh, *no*. "Anikke—"

"I know that I'm young," she blurted in a rush. "It would have to be a long betrothal. But if you're willing to wait . . ."

In retrospect, it felt so obvious. After the situation with the Imperial spy, the girl had gazed at Aleksi with starry eyes filled with something akin to hero worship. She'd endowed him with an actual title, for fuck's sake—Queen's Protector—and given him a standing invitation to visit her home as he pleased. And he was, after all, the god of love. A manifestation of the Dream in this realm, the tiny bit of it that nurtured the growth of all things.

Including infatuations.

Still, it might have ended there, with a harmless crush she would outgrow with time. Except that Anikke had just watched her sister, a woman she perceived as being only slightly older than her, marry an immortal god.

Fuck.

Aleksi's fingers clenched around the stem of the rose. An errant thorn that had escaped the gardener's notice pierced his thumb, and he bit back a hiss. He had to say something. The deflection had to be gentle enough to spare her tender feelings, but firm enough to leave her in no doubt of his lack of romantic interest.

He could do this. He'd had thousands of years of practice.

The silence had lingered long enough to grow teeth. Anikke's hopeful smile dimmed a little, and Aleksi damned himself for his shocked silence.

But before he could speak, one of the pages stepped into the room. "Another visitor, Your Majesty."

Naia walked in, her dark hair and light-brown skin gleaming in the candlelight. Her deep-blue robe, almost black under the flickering flames, floated around her like the nighttime ocean as she dropped into a low curtsy and bowed her head. It was a solemn courtesy the nymph offered freely, though her standing as the Siren's newest godling made her more or less Anikke's equal.

Then Naia looked up, and her nearly black gaze focused on the rose in Aleksi's grasp. "My sincerest apologies, Your Majesty, for interrupting your dinner."

Anikke waved away Naia's words and gestured to the table. "You are always welcome. Would you like to join us?"

"I wish I could, but I'm here at the behest of the Siren." Naia finally straightened, a warm smile for the child queen curving her lips. "I've come to fetch the Lover back to Seahold."

Aleksi frowned. "This very moment?"

Naia's smile didn't waver. "It is a matter of some urgency."

"Very well." He turned to Anikke. "Our conversation—"

"Can wait," she told him firmly as relief softened her expression. After his telling hesitation, she was as eager to be free of this moment as he was. "Please, give my regards to the Siren, if you would be so kind."

"Of course." Leaving the rose behind felt like a slight, so Aleksi carried the bloom with him as he took his leave.

Naia walked silently at his side as they navigated the darkened corridors of Castle Roquebarre. Instead of heading toward the courtyard that led to the main part of the structure, she turned toward the back, past the kitchens, and descended to the sheltered private dock built on the very edge of the bay. From here, it was a straight shot across the bay to the docks at Seahold.

A small skiff, flying Dianthe's standard, awaited them, and they climbed aboard. Despite the lack of sails and the still, glassy water, the skiff began to drift across the bay—Naia's influence, no doubt. She communed with the waves like they were old, cherished friends, and they responded to her in kind.

Finally, she spoke. "Things seemed a bit . . . fraught back at the castle," she whispered over the murmur of the water splashing off the skiff's hull. "Are you all right?"

Damn. He'd hoped she wouldn't notice. "The queen has romantic ideas."

"Designs, you mean. On you." Naia's nose wrinkled. "That's awkward. We can't really blame her, though."

"We can't?"

"Not one bit." Naia winked at him, soothing and teasing all at once. "You're a tremendous catch."

Aleksi knew better than to take her words seriously. Naia liked him, he had no doubt of that, but fun, harmless flirtation was the extent of her interest in him. Or perhaps it was merely the extent of what she could conceive—unlike the Mortal Queen, with her starry eyes and romantic ideas, Naia clearly could not imagine the god of love falling in love *with her*.

Aleksi should not imagine it, either. Because the young nymph had developed a fondness for monsters—at least, for one in particular.

And all the better for her.

Naia leaned over the side of the skiff and dipped her hand into the water. Droplets swirled up her arm like a waterspout, then broke away to dance around her head in a glittering halo. She laughed, the water arced back into the bay with a splash, and the skiff began to move faster.

She was fascinating. At home here, on the water, the way Aleksi was in his vineyards. And powerful, somehow as ancient as she was young. Already, the whispers had begun—that she was Dianthe's heir apparent, second in power only to the Siren herself when it came time to call the water.

"Do you know what Dianthe wants?"

"No," Naia answered, then hesitated. "But I think they need us."

The rest of the High Court had been in the Empire for weeks, sorting through the chaos left in the wake of the Betrayer's defeat . . . but they had left Aleksi behind. Ostensibly, he had been charged with helping Dianthe to guide the new queen and keep peace in the Sheltered Lands.

But everyone knew the *real* reason. The final battle against the Betrayer had been difficult and painful for everyone—physically, mentally, and emotionally—but it had been a special kind of hell for Aleksi. The Betrayer's witch had cast a spell that had temporarily severed their connections to the Dream. For most of the High Court, it had been an inconvenience, an indignity through which they'd had to fight. They had all been human once. They knew how to cope with being alone in their minds. In their hearts.

Aleksi had never been human. He wasn't born of parents, of a small, exquisite communion of life, but of the Dream itself. That day on the battlefield was the first time he'd ever felt . . . absence. *Blankness.* A complete and utter lack of love.

It had wounded him in a way the others all saw, but could never comprehend. They had considered leaving him behind a kindness. But until he faced this fight instead of running away from it, that wound would never heal.

"It's about time," he growled.

Dianthe met them at the dock, her beautiful face drawn into a serious expression that hewed dangerously close to a frown. Instead of her usual flowing clothing of glittering teals and deep blues, she wore dark pants and a bodice made of braided leather straps that reminded him of armor. She'd captured her long black curls in a twist on top of her head, revealing the golden tattoos that traced her deep-brown skin and shimmered even in the scant moonlight.

"Thank you for coming so swiftly." She reached out a hand to steady him as he stepped onto the dock. "I would have waited for your return, but I didn't want to risk missing the tide."

If they did, they'd have to wait days for the next tide high enough to allow a ship of any considerable size to dock. Even Dianthe could only do so much to counter the pull of the moons. "What is it? Has something happened?"

"Sachi, Zanya, and Ash need someone to take over the negotiations in Akeisa. So they can join the others in the Empire."

Were they still trying to protect him by keeping him away from the fighting in the Empire? It was possible, though Aleksi had to admit that, aside from Sachi, he *was* the most qualified person for a diplomatic endeavor. "Understood."

Dianthe had clearly been braced for him to argue. When he didn't, she grasped his shoulders and smiled. "Naia will accompany you. These people are islanders who honor and fear the sea. Her powers will command their respect."

"When do we leave?"

"Almost this instant. Your trunks have already been packed, and the Kraken should arrive shortly."

Naia, who had been beaming at Dianthe's vote of confidence, suddenly found the water lapping against the dock utterly fascinating. She stared at it, her cheeks growing pink with heat.

Adorable.

"Don't worry about us, Dianthe." He offered his fellow Dreamer his most reassuring smile. "I'll watch over your charges."

"They're meant to watch over *you*, Aleksi."

Normally, he would have insisted breezily that he had no need of such close and clever guard. But he glanced down at his thumb, where he'd suffered the angry prick of the rose's thorn. It was a nuisance, a scratch that should have healed almost instantly.

Instead, the small hole still bled sluggishly.

Perhaps his wounds ran deeper than even he had realized, and he could very much use this protection, after all.

Chapter Two

> *The ancient name of the island, still used by some of the more remote villages, is Rahvekya. Upon its surrender and entry into the Empire, the land was named in honor of the strategic genius who led the campaign, General Leeshyn Akeisa. The General also served as its first Grand Duke.*
>
> Akeisa: A Comprehensive History (Volume One)
> by Guildmaster Klement

The Kraken was coming.

It wasn't that Naia possessed any particular knowledge of this fact. Rather, it was more of a sense, the fine hairs on her arms and neck lifting at his approach. She could simply *feel* him. She always could. It was a tugging sensation, low in her belly, one that she hadn't recognized at first but now understood.

Arousal.

She clenched her hands into fists and stared out over the harbor, her cheeks still hot and her body pulsing gently with anticipation.

Damn him, anyway.

Churning water heralded a disturbance deep in the bay. The tiny waves that lapped at the docks turned to swells that frothed and splashed. Everyone on the dock froze in unison as a massive wooden monster stabbed out of the waves. The waters of the bay shuddered as the prow of a ship followed it, slicing up from the depths as if carried forth on a giant swell.

The Kraken revealed itself in pieces. Dark-black wood and shiny gold portholes and massive green sails that emerged from the water improbably dry and immediately filled with a wind that touched nothing and no one else.

Except for Naia. It sighed through her skirts and lifted her hair as the ship raced toward the docks, water still sluicing off its deck and hull.

Only one person stood on the deck, gripping the ship's wheel with an assurance that spoke of confidence and experience—Einar, captain of the vessel.

The Kraken himself.

On the surface, he vaguely resembled the man standing beside her. He and Aleksi shared the same coloring—dark hair and eyes, golden skin. They were even about the same height.

But that was where the similarities ended. Aleksi was broad through the shoulders and lean everywhere else, with a lithe sort of strength that screamed speed and grace. And his gorgeous face had inspired countless songs and sculptures and paintings, all of which had endeavored in vain to capture the full glory of the Lover—the elegant slash of his brows, his long lashes, his luxurious mouth. He *was* a work of art, perfect and untouchable.

Einar wasn't elegant. He wasn't even beautiful. His nose was crooked, and his craggy features were rough. But something about their asymmetrical arrangement pleased Naia, especially when he smiled.

And when he laughed . . .

She tore her gaze away from him as the ship shuddered to a stop alongside the dock. The deck abruptly swarmed with crew who tossed ropes to waiting dockhands and lowered a gangplank. Einar was the first person down it, ignoring the awed gazes and excited murmurs of the small crowd as he strode directly to Dianthe and bowed in a way that somehow married arrogance and reverence. His dark hair was shaved on the sides, but the top spilled rakishly over his eyes as he glanced up at her with a wicked smile. "My queen."

Dianthe sighed with exasperated fondness as she ran her nails through his hair and then tugged, pulling him up. "Save the dramatic obeisances, Einar. It is enough that you came so quickly."

Einar transferred that wicked smile to Naia, and her stomach clenched. "How could I not, with such precious cargo to be conveyed?"

Naia inclined her head. "Captain."

Behind him, shouts sounded as a second gangplank hit the deck. Nimble sailors scampered up, carrying crates of supplies and heavy trunks. Einar winked at Naia before pivoting to face Aleksi, who received a much shallower bow and no mischievous grin. "My lord."

"Einar." Aleksi glanced at Dianthe. "Do you anticipate trouble in Akeisa?"

Einar's smile faltered. "Akeisa?"

"Our destination," Naia explained. "Do you know it well?"

His smile returned abruptly, too bright. Too forced. "Can't say I've ever visited. I don't imagine its ruler would have welcomed a ship from the Sheltered Lands."

"Well, Gwynira is ready to welcome you now." The Siren's beautiful face hardened. "And while I don't *anticipate* trouble, given the mess the Betrayer left behind . . . I plan to prepare for it."

Naia quelled a sigh of relief. If trouble did arise, at least the Kraken and his crew could effect a ready escape. Not that she was frightened. She'd fought in the final battle against the Empire; surely she could handle a little diplomacy. But she was young, and it sometimes seemed as though the entirety of her existence had been . . . *bigger* than her.

Her first mission for Dianthe had been to escort the Dragon's promised consort from the capital to his keep, high in the mountains. That consort, Sachielle, had turned out to be the Everlasting Dream itself. And Sachi's lover and companion, Zanya, was the manifestation of the Endless Void.

Naia considered them *friends*, which barely made sense even in the confines of her own mind. And now, Dianthe was trusting her to accompany two elder Dreamers, the Lover and the Kraken, on a vital mission.

The god of all things that grew and a terrifying sea monster.

In this company, who *wouldn't* be a bit intimidated?

Aleksi touched her arm, a gentle graze she could have imagined if not for the way it lingered. "You'll be fine, Naia. Better than fine. You were born for this."

She flashed him a grateful smile, and there was no more time for doubts. Dianthe bade her farewell with a kiss on the cheek, and then Einar's large hand found the small of Naia's back and gently steered her toward the gangplank. "You'll have to settle for plain old wood this time."

How did he manage to make that sound filthy? "If I recall correctly, you found my water bridges insulting to the dignity of your ship."

He only chuckled, a low, dark sound that shivered up Naia's spine. She shrugged free of his touch and hurried up the gangplank unaided.

The moment her feet touched the deck, a wave of sense memory rolled over her. She closed her eyes and listened to the sounds of the crew bustling around, laughing and calling out with questions and orders. The scents of salt water, wet rope, and pitch surrounded her. Enveloped her.

the net drapes across her lap, damp and slick, but all her attention is on the tear to be mended, the netting shuttle heavy in her hand, her fingers slipping effortlessly into grooves worn into the bone

leaning over the carved edge of the canoe, watching the shallows for the telltale flash of fish scales in the slanting afternoon light

he climbs aloft to trim the sails, worn boots balancing on the footropes, hands tight around the jackstays, don't look down, don't look—

Naia gasped in a breath. The memories were both hers and not, moments that she had not lived, but that belonged to her now, all the same. They had come from the minds and hearts of fishermen and sailors and divers, from lives spent in tiny villages and out on the open seas. They were a part of the ocean, and Naia had brought them with her from the Dream.

"Steady, now," Einar rumbled in her ear, a caress every bit as tangible as his fingers on her arm. "You good?"

The familiarity sparked something hot in her chest, a gentle pain that felt suspiciously like longing. "I'm not a fancy lady who's never been on a proper ship before, Captain."

Laughter spilled over her, deep and low. "Proper ships, eh? My sweet goddess, there is nothing *proper* about the Kraken."

She bit her lip to hide a smile. "A hull, several decks, a crew . . . It all seems proper enough to me."

"That's because they're all being responsible now. Wait until we're sailing under a starlit sky and they've found their way into the brandy. Whatever you do, don't gamble with any of them."

So he hadn't *completely* figured her out. Not yet. "I am not afraid of a good-natured wager."

"No, I imagine you're not." His fingers teased over her arm as he released her. "Be sure you know the stakes when you bet against a pirate, though."

"Why? Is someone going to take advantage of me?" She met his sparking gaze, held it just long enough to turn the words into a challenge, then looked away. "It's a beautiful ship, Einar."

"I know," he growled.

The deck seemed to vibrate under Naia's feet, as if it was grumbling right along with its captain. Sometimes, it was difficult to tell where the god ended and his vessel began.

A tall, wiry woman with a sun-weathered face and wild gray hair appeared from belowdecks, dusting off her hands. "Supplies are almost loaded in. We'll make the tide."

"Good." Einar turned, but the woman planted both feet and cleared her throat, looking pointedly at Naia. After a moment, he pivoted back. "Naia, meet my first mate, Petya."

"A pleasure," the woman said warmly as she held out a hand. "We didn't get a chance to meet on the trip to the Empire, but I saw you fight. You're a formidable young lady."

It should have sounded like an idle compliment, but the sincerity shining from the woman's eyes had Naia smiling as she shook her hand. "You honor me. Is there anything I can do?"

"Do?" she asked.

"To help, of course."

Petya shook her head. "You're a sweet girl, but the crew has their rhythms and it's best not to disrupt them." The old woman turned as Aleksi joined them on the deck. "You are welcome, my lord."

"Petya." He took her free hand and kissed the back of it. "Stunning, as always."

Her weathered cheeks flushed. "Flatterer."

A small, sleek black cat curled around Petya's legs before approaching Naia with a plaintive meow. Naia picked her up and smiled when the cat curled into her arms and began to delicately lick one paw.

"That's Ceillie, my cat," Petya said. "Is she bothering you? Here, let me—"

"No." Naia leaned away slightly. "No, it's fine. She's beautiful."

Aleksi sighed. "That is not a cat."

Naia was torn between confusion and indignation. "Excuse me?"

"She's a higher intelligence *shaped* like a cat," he explained. "That's what happens after a thousand years or so."

"After a thous . . ." Feeling almost faint, Naia trailed off and peered down at the cat in her arms. Ceillie stared back, her green eyes assessing. "This is an immortal cat?"

"Don't worry. You're perfectly safe. She likes you." Aleksi plucked the cat from Naia's arms and stroked her head before handing her off to Petya. "Are we off?"

Einar inclined his head respectfully to Aleksi before turning back to Naia. "Petya can show you both to your cabins, if you'd like to settle in." His eyes lit with that wicked challenge again. "Or you can join me on the quarterdeck."

A cabin was simply a place to sleep. And since the real excitement on a ship happened everywhere else, Naia intended to spend as little time in hers as possible. She opened her mouth to say so, but Aleksi slid into the silence with a wide grin.

"Oh, there's plenty of time for all that. I think we'd both rather stay and admire the competence of your crew." He arched a brow at Naia. "Am I mistaken?"

"No, you're not." He was, however, up to something. She could feel it, tickling along the top of her spine like a whisper.

Einar seemed to feel it, as well. But he only waved for them to follow him up a short flight of stairs to the raised quarterdeck. The massive wheel stood proudly, painted ebony and deep green, with each spoke tipped with burnished gold. Einar touched it almost reverently before raising his voice. "All hands, ready to cast off!"

A deep bell pealed, the sound piercing the overcast evening sky. In unison, some members of the crew retracted both gangplanks, while others hauled in the heavy ropes that had been secured to the dock cleats.

"Stand by to make sail!"

The crew melted across the deck, hurrying to man their stations. Petya had been right. There *was* a rhythm to this, one Naia remembered in her bones, and the Kraken's crew kept impeccable time.

"I usually coax the ship past the breakwater before I raise the sails," Einar said. Beneath them, that familiar magic rippled through the ship and out into the bay. He glanced at Naia, his brown eyes snapping with heat—and more challenge. "If you still want to help, you could always ask the seas to be sweet to me."

The way he said it made it clear he thought she wouldn't—or even couldn't. And though she told herself not to take such obvious bait, the idea of letting him think she was too weak to answer his challenge was unbearable.

Or, worse, too timid.

So she closed her eyes and reached out, gathering the attention of the rocking waves. *He thinks we can't,* she whispered silently. *Would you like to prove him wrong?*

The waves surged, and droplets sprang from their surface in an eager spray. The reply vibrated through Naia, no words, just the rumbling, rushing sound of the impatient water.

The vessel shot forward, tripling its speed in the span of a heartbeat. It was reckless to do while still in harbor, but Naia felt every molecule of the bay beneath them and knew the water would carry them safely to the open ocean.

What she hadn't considered was the fact that Einar was so wholly a part of his ship that he was already *in* the water. Heat poured through her as her magic met and mingled with his, and her eyes shot open.

Einar stood tall and proud at the wheel of his ship, his strong hands gripping polished wood. But his gaze was locked on hers.

His normally brown eyes had turned blue. Not the clear blue of a summer sky, but a deep, luminescent teal that reminded her of glowing sea creatures. They shimmered with awareness and curiosity, full of promise and all the things only lovers can ever know. Nighttime murmurs and startled laughter and soft, appreciative sighs.

And hunger. *That* was the heat sliding through her veins, prickling over her skin and making her nipples ache. Out of sheer desperation, she broke eye contact, but her attention merely shifted to his fingers flexing around the handles of the wheel, and that only made things worse. She could feel his hands, sure and determined, sliding down the center of her body. The contact was inevitable, less like a fantasy and more like the memory of something that had already happened.

"Good girl." Aleksi's growl broke the spell, and Naia looked at him. He was close, so close, his softly curving mouth only inches from her ear. "Teach him that you're not to be trifled with."

"I'm not." A breath shuddered out of her, but she felt . . . *bold*. Like this moment was a bubble that would burst at anyone else's careless touch, but not at hers. Never hers. "You'd best not forget that, either, my lord."

The sea breeze carried his soft laugh off into the night. "Trust me, love. I never do."

Chapter Three

It is undeniable that the island of Akeisa is home to a stunning variety of life seen nowhere else in the Empire, including a species of fish whose oil burns green, a distant cousin to Kasther's popular gooseberry known as the tealberry, and even a hardy strain of tundra cotton with natural aquamarine fibers. One suspects the overabundance of this particular hue has some still unknown scientific basis, but if you ask a local they will all agree—teal was their goddess's favorite color.

Akeisa: A Study of Flora and Fauna
by Guildmaster Klement

Einar was twelve hundred years old the first time he heard the shanty about how he had cut out his own heart and buried it deep in Dead Man Shoals, causing the islands to freeze as solid as the lover he'd lost to the North Sea's icy depths.

The supposed identity of that first lover had been lost to time, but over the next thousand years he'd heard a dozen variations of the song, with every generation bringing it back and adding to the legend. Where, why, and how he'd carved that vital organ away changed, but the refrain never did.

No lad, no lass, no lover fair,
can hold him past the dawn.
There's nothing in this world he loves,
for the Kraken's heart is gone.

It was true enough that Einar had never found a dalliance so compelling that he couldn't walk away come morning. But the songs and the legends had always misunderstood why.

This was what he loved. The weathered wood of the deck beneath his boots. The taste of brine on the wind. The night sky stretched out above him, each endless star a cherished friend who had guided him across distant seas and safely back to port.

He loved the feel of the ocean when he gripped the wheel, the way the waves caressed the hull of his ship, playful and adoring. He might not have the Siren's gift for air and water, but when he stood at the helm of the Kraken, there was always wind enough in his sails and welcoming seas to speed his journey.

"Brynjar said you sent him to his bunk and took his watch," said a chiding voice behind him. His second mate stepped up next to him, her boots thumping on the deck. "You know we need you fresh tomorrow."

True enough, but Einar still found himself reluctant to relinquish the wheel. Sleep had been an elusive lover of late, and the thoughts that kept him awake were hardly pleasant company. "What, am I suddenly so old that I can't handle a single night on watch?"

"Age has nothing to do with it," Jinevra replied with a knowing grin. "But you *did* take us down this morning, and you may have to do it again if things go wrong in the Empire. You've earned a good night's sleep."

Another truth. Einar's most precious gift was his ability to travel vast distances in a matter of moments, carrying his ship and all its passengers with him. But it was no small feat of power to traverse the Heart of the Ocean, and Jinevra was right—he had to be ready to do it again at the first sign of peril. That was why Dianthe had entrusted him with Aleksi's and Naia's safety, after all. The icy island nation of Akeisa might be half a week's journey away under favorable winds, but if its frigid ruler turned on them, Einar could return them all to the Siren's doorstep in the time it took to pour a cup of tea.

Reluctantly, he released the wheel and let Jinevra take his place. "You'll call me if anything happens."

"I'll ring the bell at the first sign of trouble." She offered him a jaunty salute. "You might ask Lady Naia if she'll put in a good word for us."

The words were casual, teasing. Most of the crew had seen how easily the young water god seemed to get under his skin, how effortlessly she coaxed him into conversation, and how cheerfully she argued with him.

None of them knew the way the touch of her power in the sea stirred a longing in him so deep even the ocean couldn't contain it. *That* was a secret he still held close. "Just keep an eye on the horizon. You know how fast the weather can turn out here."

"Yes, Captain."

There was nothing but earnest agreement in her voice, but even the most superstitious of his crew would admit that trouble seemed unlikely tonight. This stretch of the North Sea saw its share of dangerous swells and deadly storms, but there was no whisper of warning in the water tonight. In fact, as he descended from the quarterdeck and drew in a deep breath of the night air, the only things he tasted were salt and a too-familiar sweetness that haunted him.

The crew couldn't sense that power as it hummed around them, caressing the ship like teasing fingertips grazing over skin, but they sensed the difference as the Kraken skimmed the water.

Einar might be able to feel the pulse of a storm and ride its towering waves, bringing both ship and crew safely to port, but the ocean had never gentled itself for him. Not like this, with a mirror calm that reflected the stars in an unbroken expanse despite the strong wind that filled their sails. They would reach the eastern edge of Dead Man Shoals by dawn, far ahead of schedule.

The reason for it all was perched at the bow of the ship, adorable and ethereal. Naia's white gown and dark hair floated in the same breeze that sped their way, as if it was flirting playfully with her.

Einar couldn't blame it. He wanted to run his fingers through those silken strands, too. The compulsion was nearly overwhelming, and he *wished* it ended with the urge to wrap those glorious locks around his fist as their bodies rocked together with the rhythms of the sea.

Lust was simple. He'd been sating it for years with those who wanted nothing more than the thrill of bedding a pirate god. Some few had yearned for more, but he'd always meticulously avoided those, knowing that no good could come from false hope and empty promises.

Now *he* was the one pining for something beyond his reach. Naia was the Siren's golden child, the heir to the throne that ruled the sea. Even if he knew the first thing about courting her, she stood as far above him as the untouchable stars.

And she'd been maddening him from the first moment of her existence.

He'd *known* the instant she came into being. After twenty-two centuries of life, he could always taste a new Dreamer's influence in the sea. Unlike the other members of the High Court, who might have one or two protégées at a time, Dianthe's court at Seahold fairly teemed with power. Those who sought their fortunes at sea knew the power of the ocean and those who controlled it. Their belief fed back into the Everlasting Dream, strengthening the Dreamers. But most of the young gods who followed Dianthe were quiet eddies in the waves, whispers of sound like a song heard from another room.

Not Naia. She had exploded into being, a bright and giddy melody that wove playfully around the Siren's powerful song. And the taste of her in the water . . .

Sweet. So, so sweet.

"Are you going to stand there and stare at me, or say something?"

Her voice was as sweet as the rest of her, haunting and musical. Einar imagined plenty of sailors would follow that teasing melody into the teeth of a gale or straight into rocky shoals, and slide down into the depths without regret. He liked to think he had a little more self-control. "Why would I say anything when the view is so pretty?"

Naia turned her head and smiled at him over her shoulder. "Because it's polite?"

He choked back a laugh as he stepped up next to her to rest his elbows on the wooden railing. "I've been accused of being many things in my life, Lady Naia. *Polite* isn't often one of them. Nothing polite about war."

"Is this war?" she asked lightly. "I thought you were flirting with me."

"Oh, I am," he agreed readily. They were so close that he needed only to nudge his elbow to the side, and their arms brushed. The glancing contact prickled over his skin, and he savored her tiny shiver. "But it doesn't change the fact that I've spent most of my life at war. It's who I am."

"Fair enough. Though, by that token, I suppose I could say the same," she added somberly. "I have also spent most of my life at war."

Truth, and the contradiction of it had only deepened his fascination. He'd watched her in the final battle against the Betrayer, channeling her gifts with a deft confidence that usually came only with centuries of practice. How could the ethereal creature who stared up at him now with guileless eyes be the same woman who'd faced the bloodiest battlefield he'd ever seen without flinching? Even when they'd been surrounded, doomed by impossible odds, she had not faltered.

He had seen soldiers with twenty years of fighting beneath their belts crumple where she'd stood strong. Where had that steel *come* from?

Her gaze turned dreamy as she stared out over the water. "But I've known other things, too. I've seen the full moons glinting off a thrashing fish on a longline. Weathered gales of legend, felt my joints ache with the cold. Told outrageous tall tales, and come home to the eager arms of faithful wives. I wasn't just born of the sea. I carry its Dreams in my heart."

It was his turn to shiver, a wonder twisting through him that he hadn't felt since the first time he'd knelt before the Siren and felt her power wash over him. He'd been a mortal man on that day, one who'd spent almost every day of his thirty years on one ship or another. Respect for the ocean and its dangers had been bred into his bones, and Dianthe represented the pinnacle of that power.

But even she had been mortal, once. Naia had simply . . . *become.* Newly born and yet achingly ancient. A manifestation of the Everlasting Dream, a god born of the hopes and wishes and sweetest imaginings of thousands of hearts. Apparently, she'd brought with her bits and pieces of them, the precious scraps of memory that made up a life.

Did she carry some part of *him* inside that pretty head? He hoped not. After twenty-two centuries of waging a very personal war against the Betrayer, he had far more grim memories than soft ones. Surely her eyes wouldn't sparkle with that innocent wonder if she saw the brutality and death of the Empire's worst excesses every time she closed them.

He was staring at her. But she simply stared back, her assessing gaze roaming his face. No self-consciousness, no fear, just an open curiosity that taunted him. *Tempted* him. How easily he could answer the questions she barely seemed to realize she was asking with those big eyes. She was ravenous to experience a life she'd only known through other people's memories.

He was ravenous for *her.*

The wind teased a lock of hair across her face. He reached out before he could stop himself, catching the wayward strands with his finger. His knuckle grazed her cheek, the softness of her skin making his own calloused finger feel too rough. It didn't stop him from savoring the slide of her hair over his hand as he leaned closer. "What's your favorite memory, then?"

"I don't know." Her long lashes fluttered as she tilted her face to his touch. "There are so many, and they're all special in their own ways."

He could do it. Seduce her, sate this impossible hunger, and hopefully carve the weakness it represented from his chest. As long as he was distracted with wanting and wondering, he couldn't keep his mind on the task ahead—the Empire and its scattered armies, broken but not yet defeated. Once he'd satisfied his curiosity, he'd be able to walk away.

And surely she knew what she was getting into. If she carried the Dreams of the ocean in her heart, she understood exactly what Einar was.

> No lad, no lass, no lover fair
> can hold him past the dawn . . .

He ignored the mocking refrain as he traced his thumb over her cheek and let it ghost across the full curve of her lower lip. "What do you remember about me?"

"I have no memories of you," she whispered. "But I'm not naive, Einar. I know what you're about. It's all anyone at Seahold can seem to talk about."

> There's nothing in this world he loves,
> for the Kraken's heart is gone.

Every word she spoke caressed the pad of his thumb like a teasing kiss. So easy to imagine those lips elsewhere—parting beneath his as he tasted her mouth. Open in a gasp against his throat as he slid his hands under her clothing and over her skin. Glistening in the candlelight as she sank to her knees and—

He didn't know if the growl that rattled his chest was hunger or frustration, only that the answer to satisfying both stood before him. "Then come to my cabin with me. I'll make it good for you, sweet Naia. So very, very good."

An answering heat flared in her eyes, only to be quickly replaced by wistful longing. "And then what? It's over? And you spend weeks pretending not to see me when our paths cross so that you don't have to have any awkward conversations?"

"It doesn't have to be awkward," he rumbled. "One night of pleasure, freely shared. Once we arrive at our destination, you'll have your duties and I'll have mine."

"That's what *you* want." Naia shook her head, finally breaking the contact between them. "I'm looking for something else. Something that's just mine."

The loss of her warmth beneath his fingertips nearly snapped the leash on his sanity. He curled his fingers toward his palm and jerked his hand away before he could reach for her again. But he couldn't stop the words that spilled free, the arrogant Kraken at his best—or worst. "Your loss, sweet goddess. When the ache of wondering what you missed grows too deep, come and find me. I promise to soothe it."

The longing in her eyes slowly faded, and gentle reproach took its place. She opened her mouth, then shook her head again and dropped into a curtsy. "Have a good night, Captain."

All the warmth was gone, leaving a politeness so chill it burned in a different way. And then *she* was gone, quick, certain steps carrying her down the deck. Einar stubbornly turned his back on her, but the part of him that grasped hungrily for any trace of her listened for the whisper of those footsteps even after they'd faded.

Soon enough, a familiar, confident tread replaced them. "I should slap you silly and toss you overboard to cool off."

He didn't want a lecture right now. *Especially* not from Petya. "Do you honestly think you could?"

A hand thwacked the back of his head, more of a warning than anything else. "Don't try that high-and-mighty Kraken bullshit with me, boy. It does not impress."

No, it wouldn't. Petya had known him *far* too long.

He growled rather than dignify her with an answer, hoping she'd go away. She didn't. Instead, she leaned against the railing in Naia's place and stared out over the placid water with its glittering starshine. The sight brought him back to his childhood, watching her stand at the bow of their fishing schooner, her gaze fixed on the horizon, her expression intense as she listened to some inner prompting that always seemed to guide them to safe waters and plentiful fishing.

No one who crewed the Kraken truly aged, so long as they didn't stray far from its decks, but time had all but passed Petya by, even before he'd manifested his power and extended it to his crew. Her reddish-brown hair had already been mostly silver in his earliest memories, and her freckled skin had always been lightly tanned by the sun and weathered by the sea. And in all the intervening centuries, she'd never lost a warrior's sleek muscle and captivating grace.

No, Petya was every bit as dangerous as she had been the day she'd fled an invading army with a sword strapped to her back and an infant Einar bound to her chest. She might not be his mother by blood, but she was the one who had raised him. That bond earned her the right to chide him over any damn thing she pleased, even when he was being an asshole.

Especially when he was being an asshole.

But that didn't mean he had to like it. "You should be asleep."

"So should you. Instead, you're out prowling." There was a long silence, filled only by the gentle creaking of the ship and the water lapping against wood. Then she lowered her voice to a whisper so soft that a breeze could have stolen it away. "I heard that we're headed to . . . the island. Are you worried?"

He noticed she didn't name the kingdom. Akeisa. A name bitter with learned hatred, but for Einar the tales that inspired the emotion had been only that—stories. For Petya, Akeisa would never be a place. No, Akeisa was a *person*—the brutal general who had stolen everything from her. She'd sooner cut her own tongue from her mouth than let that cursed sound cross her lips.

And she wouldn't insult Rahvekya, the island she had once loved, by calling it by the name of an enemy.

Einar lowered his voice, as well. "I should be asking *you*. You're the one with the memories."

Her sudden bark of laughter held more pain than humor. "They burned all of the places I knew to the ground over two thousand years ago. There's nothing left of the land I protected but dreams."

That was what Einar was counting on. Perhaps he should have warned Dianthe and Aleksi of his connection to the island, but what connection was there, really? He'd told the truth. *He'd* never set foot on it, unless you counted the first weeks of his life. And he didn't. He had no memories of Rahvekya, and chances were good that Rahvekya had no memories of him.

But Petya was different. For her, this mission would *hurt*. "If it becomes a problem—"

"It won't," she cut in firmly. "Because I won't be leaving the ship. Someone needs to guard against treachery. Your task is to befriend the snake. Mine is to hold our escape route open for when she inevitably tries to bite you."

Einar hid a wince. If that was how she thought of Gwynira, it was probably best if she stayed on board. He'd have enough of a struggle managing his own temper without having to worry that Petya would upset diplomatic relations by finding her way into the Grand Duchess's chambers to murder her in the middle of the night. "The Siren thinks we can make peace," he reminded her—and himself. "So does Lady Sachielle."

Petya only snorted. Then she turned to him, her gaze unexpectedly serious. "Be respectful toward Lady Naia. And don't underestimate her. Memories can fade, but faith dies more slowly. When I look at her . . ."

She trailed off, letting the gentleness of the waves give voice to what words could not encompass. Even with Naia gone, the Kraken still glided smoothly forward, as if carried by loving hands. She wasn't even actively using her magic now, not like when she'd sped them out of Siren's Bay on joyful swells, but it didn't matter. The water hummed for her, and power caressed the planks of his ship. Tonight, he'd dream of her fingertips ghosting over him, stroking him everywhere as he drowned in the taste of her.

"Do you still believe?" he rasped. "In the old religion?"

In response, Petya tugged at the leather cord around her neck, freeing a small bronze medallion that bore faint ridges lightly raised in an elegant spiral. Her thumb brushed its worn surface, as it must have thousands upon thousands of times. What had once been a charm cast in the shape of a seashell had been worn smooth over the centuries, but she had resisted all offers to replace it.

"Like I said," she murmured. "Faith dies slowly."

He'd have to take her word for it. Einar might love the sea and his ship, but as much as Petya had tried to instill in him a fervent belief in the old ways, Einar's only religion was war. His temple was this ship and his crew. His only sacred rite was fighting the Empire until its citizens knew freedom and safety.

He was a monster in every way that mattered, but if centuries of watching the Dragon had taught him anything, it was that being a monster made him perfect for the job at hand.

Naia and Aleksi could try to make peace. Let one single Imperial noble so much as *breathe* too strongly in their directions, and Einar would make war.

Chapter Four

Many wonder why Akeisa lacks the comforts of civilized life seen throughout the rest of the Empire. The truth is that the common folk of the island prefer the rustic traditions of their ancestors. However, you can see some modern innovations in science, transportation, and entertainment in cities such as South Harbor, which remains a popular destination for those Imperial citizens willing to brave the cold weather in search of adventure.

Akeisa: A Comprehensive History (Volume Three)
by Guildmaster Klement

Aleksi was in the midst of a *lovely* dream—rough hands and silky hair, both flowing over his body like water—when Sachi interrupted it with a whisper.

"Aleksi."

He turned away from the sound, much preferring the low, laughing growls and soft sighs that beckoned.

"Aleksi."

The tugging in his midsection grew, and grew, until it hauled him straight out of his dream and into . . .

The Dream. Not the beautiful, surreal garden he knew as the Heart of it, but a cozy sitting room with a crackling fire. Sofas and cushions were arranged in a semicircle around the merry blaze, with each spot just close enough to enjoy the warmth of the flames without any danger.

Not that any danger existed, not here. The fire would not sear his flesh, and the candles that cast a dim glow around the rest of the study would never burn low and sputter out. Everything here existed only in the realm of the imagination, and it was all created and controlled by the smiling woman in front of him.

It was, in fact, part of her.

"Sachi, darling." He greeted her with a kiss on the cheek. "You knocked instead of slipping straight into my dreams."

"After what happened last time, it seemed prudent."

"Aye, fair enough." He would have owed Sachi and her lovers more than a heartfelt apology if she'd wandered into *this* dream. "Though if you think Ash and Zanya might be interested . . ."

"Careful." She patted his jaw. "When your flirtation gets too desperate, it begins to look suspiciously like an attempt at distraction."

Aleksi growled. "Go and fetch them, will you?"

Sachi was still smiling when the room *shifted*. It didn't waver, not exactly. It simply held two occupants in one moment, and four in the next.

"Aleksi!" Ash rushed forward and enveloped him in a bone-crushing hug.

Relief broke through the low level of fear that had lurked in Aleksi's gut since Dianthe's abrupt summons. "Ash. You're well?"

"As well as can be, given the circumstances." Ash leaned back, keeping hold of Aleksi's shoulders as he studied his face. "You?"

"I'm on a ship in the middle of the North Sea," Aleksi told him dryly. "I'm freezing my ass off."

Zanya stood several feet behind Ash, a silent, watchful shadow. She wore a frown, an expression comprised less of displeasure than of readiness.

Combat readiness. Aleksi held out a hand and smiled at her. "Zanya, love."

The frown twitched, and one corner of her mouth rose. Then she broke, reaching out to clasp his hand with a welcoming smile. "Big brother."

He lifted her hand and kissed the back of it. "How has the island been treating you?"

"Gwynira has been very generous with her hospitality," Sachi interjected.

"And that," he pointed out, "is not what I asked. Zan?"

"It's a mess," Zanya said bluntly. "Gwynira might be generous, but her court makes the Mortal Lords seem friendly."

"They're Imperial nobles. If you professed to like them, I would not believe you. You barely like *me*, and I'm adorable."

Zanya pretended to glower at Aleksi, but her eyes glinted with amusement. "I like you just fine. When you're not annoying me."

"I make no apologies. Now . . ." Aleksi grasped Ash's arm. "We're here, in the safe silence of the Dream. Tell me everything."

Ash's warm smile faded as he scrubbed a hand over his face. "Elevia sent a message. She's encountered a . . . situation. Something she can't handle on her own. She needs Sachi and Zanya."

"What in blazes can *Elevia* not handle?"

Sachi looked almost somber. "It might be more accurate to call it something unfamiliar. A phenomenon she's never encountered before."

Elevia was even older than Aleksi, one of the more ancient Dreamers of the High Court. The customs and superstitions that had led to her manifestation were tied to some of the first activities of mankind—hunting for food, defending their homes. Searching for knowledge.

The only thing scarier than something Elevia couldn't handle was something she'd never even *seen*. "I understand. But I do have to ask—if the situation is so dire, why waste time on this ocean voyage? Why didn't one of you just come and fetch me? Preferably Sachi." Aleksi threw Zanya an apologetic smile. "No offense, darling."

Zanya only grinned at him. "None taken. Trust me, I find carrying you through the Void as uncomfortable as you find being carried." She stroked her fingers protectively over Sachi's golden hair. "But that's a trick she's not ready to reveal."

Sachi blushed. "There's no hiding the fact that Zanya can use shadows to step through the Void. Everyone witnessed her doing it during the final battle against Sorin. We . . . have not been so forthcoming with Gwynira about my ability to use light to travel through the Dream."

Aleksi barked out a laugh.

"What?" she demanded, her lips trembling in a clear effort not to curve into a smile. "It seemed wise not to expose *all* our secrets."

So typical. Everyone was terrified of Zanya, who commanded the Endless Void and swam in shadows and would merrily stab you in the face. But in their haste and ignorance, they often overlooked the threat that Sachi posed. He'd never seen her stab anyone in the face, but she *could* quietly plot no fewer than six paths to your utter ruin before she'd finished her morning tea.

"Sachi, love?" He drew her close and kissed her forehead. "Have I told you lately how very glad I am that you're not evil?"

"Yes, in fact. You have." She stretched up on her toes, kissed him softly, and smiled. "But it's always nice to hear."

It was Ash's turn to stroke Sachi's hair with a fond smile. "Secrets are all well and good, but we had a more strategic reason for calling for the Kraken. Gwynira *seems* welcoming, it is true, but we could not leave you here without at least the option of a swift retreat. If the Grand Duchess turns on you, Einar will take you to safe harbor."

"A prudent decision," Aleksi allowed. "The mood at the Akeisan court?"

"Vaguely desperate," Sachi answered. "Gwynira bears no lingering love or loyalty for Sorin *or* his Empire. She fought hard to maintain her distance, even kept her people free of the spell that drained the dreams of those on the Imperial mainland. She needs allies as much as we do, if not more. But she doesn't trust her own nobles. She certainly isn't ready to trust us."

"Give me a week. I'll change her mind." A strange vibration around Ash drew Aleksi's attention. A part of him seemed . . . *dark*, almost hidden. Secretive. "But what are you not telling me?"

Ash's shoulders slumped. "You see me too well, old friend."

"I know."

Ash met Aleksi's eyes, and the discomfort in those dark depths bordered on fear. "What Elevia found is a creature who menaces an entire valley. She thought it was a Terror at first, but it isn't. At least, not like one she's ever seen before."

"What does that mean?"

The three of them looked at one another, but it was Sachi who answered. "It wasn't born of the Void at all," she said slowly, "but of the Dream. A newly awakened god."

Aleksi arched an eyebrow. "But Ash called it a *creature*."

"Yes," he said evenly. "I did."

"Something has . . . twisted it. *Transformed* it." Sachi shook her head. "A particularly violent awakening, perhaps?"

Aleksi could hear unspoken words hovering on her tongue. "Or?"

"Or this was something that was done to them," Zanya growled. "Purposefully."

Was that possible? They'd all encountered new horrors as a result of Sorin's treachery, but this seemed unimaginable. Belief was the only force strong enough to change reality, and that took more than a single moment—or a single person's will—to effect.

Then again, had Sorin not possessed even greater power when he'd created his shadow court of dukes and duchesses by pulling them straight from the Dream? Compared to that, was it really so unfathomable that someone could hold the ability to fundamentally alter another being?

Sachi sighed. "So now you see why we must make haste."

"When?"

Daughter of Tides

"Tonight," Ash rumbled. "We would stay to greet you and make all the proper introductions, but we cannot delay."

Aleksi quelled a laugh. The last time he and Grand Duchess Gwynira had seen one another had been on the field of battle, when they had both been swept up in the dark spell that had torn away their powers and left them defenseless. Bereft.

What introductions were necessary after such a moment of bloody vulnerability?

"Go," he ordered, "and do not fret. Your mission in Akeisa is safe in my hands."

But Sachi hesitated. "Take care, Aleksi. This island . . ." Her usually clear blue gaze clouded over. "Its past is hidden from my sight, and its future I cannot discern."

"What an ominous thing to say, darling. Very well, I shall sleep with one eye open."

"Aleksi, I'm serious," she said gravely. "This place has *secrets*."

Do not we all?

Chapter Five

The green scanty is a fish commonly found in large numbers in cold oceans. Its taste is so pungent that those of the Empire have only ever used it as bait for more palatable fish. But one of the most popular Akeisan dishes is a stew made from green scanty that has been dried and preserved. While the taste is decidedly unique, I must caution you that it can be overwhelming for the more refined palate.

Akeisa: A Study of Flora and Fauna
by Guildmaster Klement

Einar couldn't remember the last time he'd had the captain's table set for guests.

Most of the time, he was happy enough to eat in the mess with the rest of the crew. On the rare occasions when he needed to have a serious—and private—discussion with his officers, they brought their food to his personal dining room with little pomp or fuss.

Tonight, the table was *all* pomp and fuss.

"Was all of this truly necessary?" He tugged at the edge of the tablecloth his cook had spread out over his perfectly acceptable Witchwood oak table. The deep violet was the same color as the banners that flew above the Villa and at Dragon's Keep whenever the Lover was in residence. There had been no warning that Aleksi would be joining them, and no time to take on custom supplies in Seahold, which left Einar wondering if Harlen had been hoarding tablecloths in the colors of the entire High Court, just on the off chance he'd have the honor of serving them at Einar's table.

Harlen swatted Einar's fingers and smoothed the fabric back into place before casting a judicious eye over the entire spread. "I won't have it said that my galley doesn't know its duty to the High Court," he grumbled as he leaned forward and laid his hands on either side of a metal tureen. The air shimmered, and a cool breeze tickled past Einar as Harlen drew heat from the air and transferred it to the dish.

The strong smell of salted fish and herbs rose on the steam from its contents, a scent that took Einar back to his childhood. "Is that the stew I asked for?"

"Yes. And it took *hours* to get enough salt out of that dried fish to make something palatable from it."

Einar imagined so. There had been no fancy cooks to delicately prepare the dried fish on that first tiny fishing boat. There had only been Petya and Jinevra and Einar himself, not quite ten and already learning the trade. There had been weeks where they'd had nothing to eat beyond what they could catch and what they'd dried and stored. The salty fish stew had been a staple of Petya's youth, and sometimes she still enjoyed a bowl. Elevia, who always showed great respect for Petya when she visited Dragon's Keep, had prepared the dish on their last visit—much to Einar's dismay.

And much to Naia's *delight*. At the first taste of it, she'd rolled back her eyes as if caught on a wave of pure nostalgic bliss. Now he understood why—she might have dozens of memories of it from people just like Petya, people who associated it with warmth and home and love and the pleasure of a full belly.

In that moment, Einar had come very close to envying a *stew*. But Naia's enjoyment made it the perfect peace offering. Perhaps Naia would savor the dish enough to forget his unkind words from the previous night.

"Well." Harlen adjusted two more serving dishes before polishing a fork on his apron. "If that's all you need . . ."

It was a cue to express his fervent gratitude, which Einar would do without reservation. He might grumble over the table settings, but he couldn't risk actually irritating Harlen. The man might decide to finally accept one of the many generous and prestigious postings he'd been offered over the centuries. No one—least of all Einar—wanted to go back to Jinevra's culinary experiments. "It looks fit for the High Court," he said with honest appreciation. "I'm sure Lady Naia and the Lover will appreciate the time and effort you put in."

"I can only speak for myself," Aleksi said from the doorway, "but I certainly do. Harlen, you set a lovely table."

Harlen beamed, his pale cheeks flushing at the praise as he bowed. "My lord, it is an honor to serve you. Especially now. I have a special menu planned tomorrow in your honor."

"You shouldn't have. This feast is more than enough."

"Ah, but it's no trouble." Another bow, this one even lower, and Einar began to worry that his cook would bob himself into an outright swoon. "The crew expects it. The Siren and the Huntress may be the captain's particular patrons, but we hold faith with the entire High Court on this ship. We always celebrate the first day of a new moon."

Einar gave Harlen an encouraging pat on the shoulder. "And we are grateful to you for making those celebrations possible. If you need extra help preparing for tomorrow, have Petya assign you a couple of assistants. She'll know who can be spared."

"Yes, Captain." Harlen made it two steps toward the door before bowing again. "My lord Lover."

"Have a good night, Harlen."

When the cook was finally gone, Einar rubbed a hand over his face and sighed. "I'm sorry if they pester you. But they are *very* excited to have you on board. And Lady Naia, as well."

"Your crew's manners are *delightful*, Captain." Aleksi tilted his head as he sank into a chair at the table. "It makes me wonder what happened to yours."

Had Naia complained to him? Or did the Lover simply *know*? His worshippers would certainly ascribe that power to him—to know of every romantic entanglement or lustful proposition, as if his will alone dictated success or failure. Einar had known the High Court for long enough to winnow truth from myth most of the time . . . but Aleksi's perception could be as uncanny as his wit was cutting.

Einar pulled out the carved chair at the head of the table and sat. "I find pretty manners can get in the way of getting things done."

"It can seem that way," Aleksi agreed. "If you view courtesy as a sort of prescribed ceremony, unique to circumstances rather than people."

Einar frowned and waved a hand at the table, with its endless silverware and truly ridiculous number of glasses, each of which had come with a stern lecture from Harlen about what liquids they could or must not hold. "What else would you call it? All the trappings are just there to remind some of us that we grew up rough and never had a chance to learn all the rules."

Aleksi plucked a fork from the table and twirled it between his fingers. "Would it bother you if I ate the meal tonight with my hands?"

"I mean, the stew might be a little awkward, but even that works with a bit of bread." Einar shrugged. "It's how I'd be eating it if you weren't here, more likely than not."

"I'll take that as a *no*, even though you didn't actually answer my question." Aleksi held up the fork. "You wouldn't be offended, but there are others who would be miserably uncomfortable watching me do that. So I would never do it in front of them. *That* is the key to courtesy."

Discomfort cracked the perfect armor of Einar's confidence. "And if it makes someone miserable to sit at a table and be judged for not knowing which fork to use? Most of the fancy lords I've met wouldn't care if they were making someone uncomfortable."

"Because they're discourteous, Einar. Pay attention." Aleksi leaned forward. "Knowing your companions and demonstrating care for their feelings—that's all it is. Anyone who tries to make it about forks or what someone's wearing is perverting the very simple concept of thoughtfulness."

There was little Einar could say in response to that well-placed verbal slap. And he'd certainly earned it, though he'd turn the table on its side and risk Harlen's wrath before admitting it.

"But you know exactly what I'm talking about." Aleksi gestured to the tureen of stew. "You had Harlen prepare this dish, even though you loathe it and it rather smells. Why? Because it's one of Naia's favorites."

Oh, he'd do worse than upend the table before confessing to *that.* He'd toss this entire disastrous dinner into the sea first, and let the fish have joy of it. How Aleksi had known—or guessed—his dislike of the damn stew . . .

No. Thinking about it would only risk revealing more. Reaching for a bottle of wine—the regular kind, *not* the Lover's vintage—Einar poured himself a glass and took a sip. "The stew is a favorite of Petya's." His easy drawl sounded *almost* casual. "Don't make something out of nothing."

"You're an abominable liar." Aleksi's smile softened the sting of his words as he held out his own empty glass. "So. You and the nymph. It's predictable, but there's a certain charm in that, I suppose."

He *was* a terrible liar, so he busied himself filling Aleksi's glass before bluffing with the truth. "Only a fool would have designs on Dianthe's protégée."

"We are all fools when it comes to love."

Einar snorted and thumped the bottle of wine back on the table. "Fools, maybe, but I still have *some* survival instincts. Anyone who wounds Naia's heart will find themselves in a watery grave so deep, even I couldn't survive it."

"Then the trick, I imagine, will be not to wound her." Aleksi retrieved his glass and raised it in a jaunty salute. "Lesser men have done right by their lovers. So can you."

Einar accepted the unsubtle jab and responded with a teeth-baring smile. "Haven't you heard the songs? Most of the people who write and rewrite them make their home at your villa, after all. You should know that the Kraken has no heart."

Aleksi's next words were low, earnest, with no trace of amusement. "It is never too late to teach them a new song."

The flicker of yearning in Einar's chest was as unexpected as Naia's sudden arrival. She hurried into the cabin, snow still clinging to her hair, dressed in a warm gown with long quilted sleeves and a plain skirt. The fabric was light teal, the color of seafoam, and double-woven with hints of midnight blue peeking through the top layer. The combination made the colors shift with every movement, until Naia's dress seemed to ripple like water.

"Sorry I'm late. Petya was teaching me how to do a chain splice, and I lost track of . . ." She trailed off, and her cheeks turned a deeper pink as she took in the formal table settings. "Should I have changed for dinner?"

With Aleksi's lecture on manners fresh enough to sting, Einar shoved his chair back and rose. "Not at all. My cook is just happy to have someone to show off for. Take a seat."

She met his overtures with a brilliant smile. "Thank you."

Once she was settled in a chair, Einar poured her a glass of wine before resuming his place at the head of the table. Candlelight danced over the dozens of dishes and threw sparkling rainbows from the tiny crystal glasses waiting for him to pour the Lover's special vintage. It was as elegant a presentation as anything seen at Seahold, and Einar felt awkwardly out of place presiding over it.

Aleksi and Naia simply looked at home.

Well, that's why *they* were the diplomats and he was the hired muscle sent to protect them. But this was *his* dining cabin on *his* ship.

No amount of frippery or number of forks could change the fact that the Lover and the nymph were now in his domain. On the Kraken, only one master ruled.

Lifting his glass, he wrapped the monster around him like armor and gave his laziest smile. "Dig in. If you don't enjoy your dinner, Harlen will be heartbroken."

Naia's smile turned mischievous. "Does that mean he's finally forgiven me for beating him at dice?"

Einar felt his eyebrows fly up before he could stop them. "You were dicing with the crew?"

She avoided his gaze. "A lady never tells."

"I believe that applies to something other than gambling," Aleksi pointed out.

"Hush."

Einar pulled the cover from the dish closest to his elbow, unsurprised to see large shrimp swimming in a spicy chocolate sauce. "Did anyone warn you about the final day of the Witching Moon, Lady Naia?"

"No." She leaned toward him, her chin resting on her hand and her eyes sparkling. "Tell me."

He tilted the dish toward her, letting the decadent smell fill the air between them. "It's all about chocolate. I assume you've had some?"

"I *did* visit the Witchwood during the consort's progress."

The one place you were guaranteed to see chocolate no matter the time of year. Einar had never been to the fanciful palace deep in the woods, but he'd heard plenty of stories. "Well, outside of Inga's domain, most people only have chocolate for one moon out of the year. We eat it on festival days during the Witching Moon. But my cook assures me that it is bad luck to have any left when the new moons rise on the first day of the Lover's Moon, so . . ."

"Bad luck on a ship? We can't have that." Naia turned to Aleksi. "Well, my lord? Are you up to the task?"

"Of eating too much chocolate? Always." He grinned rakishly. "I helped Inga perfect it, you know."

"You invented chocolate?"

"I *helped.* I was her last resort, you see. Elevia thought it was frivolous, Dianthe salts everything, Ash kept burning it, and Ulric can't eat the stuff." He lowered his voice to a seductive rumble. "I was her only hope."

Naia's bright laughter filled the cabin, and Einar worked to keep his expression even. Aleksi probably wasn't even trying to flirt; the Lover couldn't help if everything he said came out sounding suggestive. Einar *certainly* shouldn't give in to the unpleasant stirrings of competitiveness.

There was no hope for him and Naia. She wanted more than he had to offer, and breaking her heart could well break his relationship with Dianthe—or worse. Flirting would be disastrous. He should not think about how her dark eyes sparkled by candlelight, or how the flush of pleasure in her cheeks made him wonder where else she might flush if he—

"There's also soup," Einar rumbled, nodding toward the dish he'd placed to the left of her seat. "Fish stew."

She gasped. "Is it . . . ?"

"The same," Aleksi confirmed, betraying Einar cheerfully and with obvious enjoyment. "Einar knows how much you love it, so he had Harlen prepare it just for you."

Her smile softened, and her expression was almost shy as she met Einar's gaze. "Did you really?"

Oh, no. Those soft, sweet eyes were the *last* thing he needed. He'd learned a thousand years ago to avoid anyone who looked at him like some sort of hero out of myth—those were the lovers who built dreams out of a single night and gave their hearts too recklessly. He didn't *want* to hurt anyone, and he certainly didn't want to hurt Naia.

But after last night, it felt so good to see her smiling. And he swore that he could *feel* the shift in the sea itself, as if a door she'd closed against him had cracked open. The water caressed the hull of his ship again, teasing and playful. Her power, so vast and so deeply a part of her she probably didn't realize she was doing it.

He couldn't tear his gaze away, not even to cast Aleksi an irritated glare. And he couldn't be cruel to her again, not with the song of her humming in his blood. "It was nothing," he said gruffly. "I remembered that you enjoyed it. Petya does, as well. It's based on an old family recipe of hers."

"I've missed it," she whispered. "So thank you."

Something funny twinged in his chest. Not quite a flutter, not quite an ache, somewhere in the vicinity of his supposedly absent heart. He cleared his throat and looked away. "The flatbread is good, too. Another of Petya's favorites. Harlen is a much better baker than she is, though."

"I won't tell her you said that," Naia offered as she dished the stew into her bowl. "But you'll owe me a favor, and I *will* collect."

Einar quirked a teasing eyebrow at her as he began to fill his own plate. "First you gambled with my crew, now you're blackmailing a notorious pirate captain."

"And I'm just getting started."

"Who knew Naia would turn out to be such a knave." Aleksi smiled over his glass of wine. "How does our journey progress, Einar?"

"We're making better time than expected." Einar didn't point out why—either Naia was aware of what she was doing already, or the acknowledgment might make her self-conscious. See? He could be courteous. "We should be traversing the Western Wall within days. If the weather is nice, it'll be a good time to come up on deck."

"Will we finally see the arctic whales that Harlen promised me?" Naia asked.

"Hopefully." He smiled, imagining her joy at watching the majestic creatures surface. "Most people imagine the Western Wall to be barren, but undersea mountains tend to have thriving populations of smaller creatures. That attracts the large predators, of course. You could see a few sharks as well."

"Perhaps we'll be lucky and see them all." Naia winked at Aleksi. "After all, we have the Lover on board for the dark of his moon. That is lucky, indeed."

"Don't let the crew pester you too much," he warned Aleksi. "We've never been able to make it to the villa for the first day of the Lover's Moon, so they're very excited to have you here."

"I'm sure they'll be fine."

If anyone knew how to deflect the attentions of an adoring mass, Einar supposed it was Aleksi. The Lover might be the most beloved figure on the High Court, the only one who attracted veneration untouched by fear. So he accepted Aleksi's assurances and let the matter drop. "Once we're past the Western Wall, we should be able to catch the northern current. We may make it to the island within a few days after that, if the weather holds."

"Good." Naia unfolded her napkin across her lap. "I'm looking forward to seeing Sachi and Zanya again."

"Unfortunately, you won't," Aleksi told her quietly. "They've already decamped for the mainland."

"Oh." Naia tilted her head, the speed of her whirling thoughts clear on her face. "So it's serious, then."

"I think we can assume so."

The mission ahead took on a new weight. "And the situation in Akeisa?" Einar asked.

Aleksi met his gaze, but he did not smile. "I suppose we'll see, won't we?"

Einar's conscience twinged again. If there had ever been a time to confess the truth of his history with the island, it was now. The proper thing to do was to arm Aleksi with every available bit of information possible. Even if the island had forgotten its own history, there were people on this ship who remembered. Maybe some scrap of knowledge from Petya's or Jinevra's childhood could—

No. If there was one thing at which the Empire excelled, it was obliterating the past. The Ice Queen and her Imperial Court would have their own religion, their own customs. Their own *world*, one where Einar meant less than nothing.

The secrets of his past had no value here. The best thing he could do was look forward. Ash might be forgiving enough to believe that a viper raised to leadership in the Betrayer's Empire could be an ally, but Einar knew the truth.

You could not trust an Imperial noble. Sooner or later, they'd betray you.

Einar's job was to make sure that betrayal wouldn't prove fatal.

Chapter Six

While fishing has always been one of the main industries on Akeisa, the island has a long history of trade. Its fine tundra cotton is especially prized, but other unique items include intricate driftwood carvings and brass jewelry. But by far their most precious resource is their knowledge of the sea. The sailors of Linzen and Kelann might protest, but no one knows the ocean like an Akeisan captain.

Akeisa: Customs and Culture
by Guildmaster Klement

Naia had made an unlikely friend at Seahold—a master shipwright who specialized in small vessels. Stefan constructed each craft himself, painstakingly planing every plank and sanding every board, judging everything by look and feel alone. Naia would visit him near the docks sometimes, and they would chat as he began construction on a crab boat or put the finishing touches on a dinghy.

    He would ask her questions about boats, questions she could only answer if she said whatever came instantly to mind, without stopping to think about her words. Whatever seafaring knowledge she'd brought with her from the Dream was buried in her borrowed memories, and the key to accessing it seemed to be instinct. In this way, over the months, her friend had been able to benefit from the wisdom of other masters he had never met, both far-flung and ancient.

In return, Stefan would tell Naia about his family. Often, his wife would bring them lunch, and Naia would chat with her while Stefan crooned softly to the rounded swell of her stomach—and the child growing inside of her.

Inga had explained to Naia that babies in the womb could purportedly learn to recognize the cadence and timbre of certain sounds. They could be born recognizing their parents' voices.

Being on the Kraken felt like that to Naia.

It was simply something she recognized in her bones. Not the people—she was still learning their names—or even the anatomy or logistics of a ship like the Kraken. But she had heard the cadence and timbre of it all, long before she came into being.

Sometimes, the mood on the ship was all business . . . but not tonight. They had been out at sea long enough to fall into a routine where there was less constant work to do, and more time to laugh and play.

After dinner, Petya set a skeleton crew. Nearly everyone else gathered in the spacious quarterdeck cabin to drink, play cards, and simply *be*.

Naia looked around at the faces she had slowly started to recognize. There was the second mate, Jinevra, who also served as the ship's quartermaster. She wore her black hair in braids decorated with carved beads that bounced off her smooth brown cheeks as she shook her head, laughing at one of Silvio's off-color jokes. Finally, she waved him away and went back to her book, still chuckling. Her wife, Arayda, sat beside her, light glinting off her blue hair as she bent her head over a pile of velvet. She was pulling lush golden thread through the lapel of a jacket.

A gift, she had said, for their captain. Her accent was soft, elegant, something that Naia vaguely recognized. She had heard that Arayda was a runaway princess from some far-off land to the east, which certainly explained her skill with a needle . . . and her familiarity with formal clothing.

Brynjar was a bull of a man, with reddish hair and a full beard. His wife, Bexi, was quiet, a skilled fighter who was good with her hands. He liked to brew things—"all sorts of things, so mind your head," Einar had warned her—and Bexi was fond of wood carving.

She was working on a piece now. It was a shard of wood, part of a plank from a sunken vessel. Naia had thought, perhaps, that she'd just found the piece, but apparently she'd held on to it for more than ten years. Waiting until the wood whispered to her what she should carve in order to properly memorialize the fallen ship's history.

Naia had brought enough memories of dockside taverns with her from the Dream to know that Silvio was a gambler. He was tall, with dark, shaggy hair and a charming, flirtatious smile. His hands were constantly moving, shuffling through decks of cards or rolling coins across the backs of his fingers. He had abandoned his jokes in favor of arguing with Solorena, a solemn-looking woman with pale skin who was very serious, but still somehow pulsed with an otherworldly, almost mystical energy.

Naia didn't know them well, but just like their work on the ship, there was a rhythm to this. Being isolated and in close quarters, out to sea for months or years at a time, either made for the bitterest of enemies or the closest of friends.

Or it made a family.

Harlen, the cook, was a large man with a jolly disposition. He wore an apron even when he wasn't busy in the galley, and he somehow managed to keep it pristine at all times. He pressed a tankard into Naia's hand. "Brynjar's latest. Try it."

It smelled like mead, sweet and fruity with a hint of spice. Naia took a sip, and the rich flavors of cloves and currants washed over her tongue. "It's delicious."

Brynjar beamed at her. "I'm honored, my lady."

"Lucky is what you are," Silvio drawled before winking at Naia. "Sometimes his experiments turn out so odd the captain won't even let us throw them overboard. Doesn't want to scare away the fish."

Naia smiled. "You're exaggerating."

"*Yes*, he is." Nusaiba smoothed a piece of paper out on the table before them. Then she pulled a silver flask from her hip pocket, unscrewed the cap, and poured a small puddle of black ink onto the corner of the sheet.

"Better put that away," Brynjar rumbled, "before Silvio decides to sneak a drink. He's done it before."

"Scandalous falsehoods," Silvio declared.

Bexi snorted. "The truth of it was all over your face, Sil—literally. It took you a week to get the ink stains off your lips."

"Shh," Petya urged. "Don't distract Nusaiba when she's trying to work."

The young woman placed her finger lightly on the very edge of the paper. Then she looked at Naia—no, she *gazed* at her, with a searching look that seemed less like she was studying Naia's face and more like she was peering into her soul.

Slowly, the ink began to spiral up from the puddle, forming lines that stretched through the air, bending in on themselves. Naia had seen her do this once before, just before the battle against the Betrayer, when Nusaiba had used her abilities to sketch an intricate map of Sorin's hidden fortress. This time, the lines swirled into a tiny, perfect replica of Naia. Not sitting at the table, but standing at the bow of the Kraken with the wind in her hair and both moons hanging overhead in a sky strewn with stars. Slowly, the ink sank back into the paper, holding fast to the lines Nusaiba had drawn in midair.

It was a beautiful process, even otherworldly, and it took Naia a moment to speak past the lump in her throat. "That's lovely. You have a rare gift."

"Thank you, Lady Naia." Nusaiba slid the paper across the table to her. "I enjoy having an excuse to create something other than navigational charts."

Curiosity gripped Naia. "If you don't mind my asking, how does it work? You're clearly not limited to things you've seen with your eyes. Do you see them some other way?"

The young woman tilted her head. "In a manner of speaking. I need someplace to start, like the notes the Phoenix brought me about the Betrayer's stronghold. But I've always been good at putting the pieces together in my mind, and if I can see it there . . ." She grinned and waved to the paper. "I've always had a vivid imagination."

It seemed too simple to be true, but Naia wasn't rude enough to press for more details. Besides, people's secrets were their own— especially on a pirate ship. "I appreciate the gift."

"Your turn for a magic trick, Solorena." Silvio gestured toward her as he opened his fiddle case and prepared to tune the instrument. "Do one of your readings for the lady."

"If she likes." The woman hummed and tilted her head. "Do you wish to know what I see, Lady Naia? Consider the question carefully, for not everyone does."

Naia bit her lip to hide a smile. "I am not afraid."

"I did not speak of fear." Solorena lifted her hands from the table as Harlen slid three small, delicate glasses of water to rest in a line in front of her. "Shall we make the others leave?"

"Not at all. Anyone is welcome to hear what you have to say to me."

"Very well." Solorena reached for Naia's hands and held them loosely in hers, their arms forming a complete circle around the trio of glasses.

Slowly, the water in the glasses began to shimmer. Lines drifted up from nowhere to float on the surface, multicolored and glistening like an oil slick. They came together to form identical but abstract images in each glass, almost like a language that Naia could not read.

Solorena peered down at the glasses . . . and frowned. "Intriguing. The glasses represent your past, present, and future." She blinked at Naia. "Yours are all the same."

"Is that . . . strange?"

"Exceedingly." She continued to stare at Naia until Silvio struck the first notes on his fiddle, then finally released her hands. The water in the glasses cleared immediately, and Solorena lifted one glass absently to her lips. "Fascinating."

Harlen held out his hand as Silvio started playing, silently inviting Naia to dance.

She took his hand gladly, and laughed out loud when he began to move. For a moment, he and Naia simply danced to the lively beat—at least, as much as they could in the relatively small space of the cabin. Then Jinevra joined them, and the three of them laughed and danced through song after song.

Then, when Naia had just started to think that Silvio's hands would never tire, the music abruptly stopped. Naia turned, following all the other gazes to the door.

Einar stood there, his hands resting on the top of the jamb. His face was fixed in a stern expression, but his eyes twinkled with mirth.

Naia shivered.

"So," Einar growled. "You lot decided to throw a party, and no one invited the captain?"

Solorena frowned, looking thoroughly confused. "Did you need an invitation?"

Einar's lips twitched as he dropped his hands from the jamb and strolled into the room. "Probably not," he admitted. "But it's rude to have this much fun without me."

"Acknowledged."

Silvio had set aside his fiddle, but Harlen retrieved his concertina and struck up another song, this one slow and soulful.

Einar looked at Naia, who was rooted to the spot, unable to move. He walked over to her slowly, his hand outstretched, one eyebrow raised in a silent question.

Dancing with him was a bad idea, all things considered, but she took his hand anyway. She didn't even decide to, just laid her hand in his.

She had to *say* something. "You're late," was all she managed.

"Am I?" He smiled wickedly and pulled at her hand. A sudden sway of the ship left her pressed against his chest. "I'll have to make up for it, somehow."

She fell silent again. Perhaps words weren't necessary at moments like these. A thousand of them, after all, couldn't affect her as much as the gentle pressure of Einar's fingers through her tunic.

The ship swayed again. Their feet weren't even moving, but it still felt like they were dancing, and Naia blinked up at him.

"This is the Kraken, Naia," he whispered. "When you dance with the captain, you dance with the ship."

She could feel it as she rested her hands lightly on his shoulders. At least, that's what she *tried* to do, but she wound up clutching at his shirt anyway as a hint of magic vibrated up through the wooden floor.

Einar's eyes had gone teal. His gaze dropped to her mouth, and she knew—she *knew*—that he was imagining a kiss. How it would feel for her lips to part beneath his, for her tongue to touch his and shyly dance away.

His hand slid around to the small of her back and pressed her closer.

If she didn't draw the line here, she never would. She would be lost—and she almost remained silent anyway. "I meant what I said before, Einar," she whispered, thoroughly regretting every syllable.

His hand tightened on her back, but he stopped moving. Even the swaying of the ship ceased, leaving her feeling oddly disoriented. The vivid teal drained away from his eyes, leaving the usual brown staring down at her in frustration.

Then he released her and backed away. "I apologize for overstepping."

"No, Einar. You—"

He bowed sharply, then smiled. Gone was the open friendliness *and* the heat, leaving only the arrogant Kraken behind. "Don't stay up too late." It was half order, half announcement, directed at the entire room. "There's hard sailing ahead."

Then he was gone.

Naia stood there awkwardly and silently cursed herself, though she wasn't sure exactly why. For holding on to her convictions? For her inability to stay away from him, despite those convictions?

For her silly, stupid need to be *loved*?

"Come." Jinevra slung an arm around her shoulders and pressed another tankard of mead into her hand. "We're putting together a game of Damned Lies. Silvio has far too much coin in his pockets, and I intend to win it all tonight."

Chapter Seven

I was chosen in the summer of my twentieth year. The day I met her, I asked how I might best serve her. Her response was to correct me. I did not serve her, she insisted, but the people of the island.

"How might I best serve the people of the island, then?" I asked.

"Hmm." And then the goddess took my hand. "Let's go find out."

from the unpublished papers of Rahvekyan High Priestess Omira

Einar did not always sleep well on land, but that lack had never followed him out to sea.

It had tonight. The gentle rock of the ship wasn't soothing him, and every time he closed his eyes he could feel Naia in his arms. He swore the intoxicating scent of her still lingered in his clothing—some maddening combination that made him think of tropical flowers on distant shores and the breeze over crystal-blue waters on a sunny day.

Ludicrous. He scrubbed a hand over his face, as if that could wipe the whimsical fantasy away. He was the Kraken. The Western Wall. The nightmare that had haunted the Imperial nobles for generations beyond counting. He was a warrior and a pirate with a heart of ice so legendary, they'd sung of it in taverns for a thousand years.

He did *not* moon about like a lovesick boy.

Groaning again, he swung his legs over the bed and sat up. The moment his feet touched the wooden floor, he felt the tremble of the ship beneath him. The restless energy within him sharpened into a familiar buzz.

If he hadn't been so distracted by Naia, he would have felt the signs before now. A storm was coming—and judging by the nervous roll of the waves against the ship, it would be a ferocious one.

Einar pulled on his boots and strode through the captain's dining room and out onto the deck, which already buzzed with the practiced industry of a crew who knew how to meet a storm. The wind whipped past Einar's face, bringing the scent of rain and that sharp, metallic warning that promised lightning forking across the sky. He caught a glimpse of it flashing in the distance before he stomped his way up the steps to where Brynjar manned the wheel. "Someone should have woken me."

His third mate quirked an eyebrow. "We've ridden through enough storms in our time. We know our work."

Einar couldn't argue with that. All but one of the sails were already secured, and the hatches and doors shut up tight. There was little else that had to be tied down or stowed away—Einar didn't allow loose gear on the deck, knowing that they might be forced to dive at any time. His crew could prepare the Kraken to survive a trip through the Heart of the Ocean in their sleep at this point. A storm was nothing compared to that.

Distant thunder rumbled as Einar watched Bexi perform a final sweep of the deck. She offered Einar a jaunty salute and blew a kiss to her husband before disappearing belowdecks, leaving only the two of them to face the storm.

Brynjar slapped a big hand against Einar's shoulder. "There's no need to worry, Cap. The Kraken has seen worse. Besides, we have Lady Naia aboard. The sea will be sweet to us. You can go back to bed."

"I wasn't sleeping anyway," Einar grumbled.

The burly man grinned. "Distracted by something, hmm?"

Einar twisted his face into his fiercest Kraken scowl, but his third mate's grin only widened. The crew who had sailed with him for centuries might still walk softly around the High Court, but they knew their captain too well to fear him.

"Go plague your wife," Einar ordered, placing one hand on the wheel.

"If you insist."

Brynjar relinquished the helm, and Einar took his place, barely noticing his third mate's departure. As soon as he gripped the wheel with both hands, that restlessness within him stilled. The roil of the waves lost their nervousness, and instead became teasing. Taunting. Like the ocean wanted to play with him.

Bright forks of lightning streaked across the distant sky. Thunder rumbled again, louder this time. Einar stroked a thumb over the polished wood of the wheel. "You want to play rough tonight, don't you?" he murmured. The air sizzled with the warning that this storm would be angry. Einar sank his power into the ship until he could feel every plank and join in his bones, giving warning before trouble arose.

Instead of trouble, he found Naia.

Her magic still whispered in the water where it met his ship, but the bright joy of it had muted. The melody twining with the growing waves was sad.

Fuck. He'd made her *sad*.

He was an ass.

He never should have asked her to dance. They'd been coexisting peacefully since the dinner in his cabin, any awkwardness put firmly aside—mostly through Aleksi's efforts in smoothing over any conversation. There was a reason they'd made the man a diplomat, after all.

But then he'd seen her there, with his crew. Dancing. *Laughing.* So much a part of the joyous chaos of this odd little family he'd created from the outcasts of a dozen lands that her presence felt natural—felt *inevitable.*

He'd lost his grip on sense. That was the only explanation for it. He didn't dance. He didn't even know *how* to dance—not that what they'd done had been dancing. No, they'd been swaying to an ancient rhythm better put to more carnal uses. Her body pressed all along his had been maddening and perfect.

Small mercy that he hadn't propositioned her again. He'd been moments from doing just that—a reckless decision he never would have made under normal circumstances—when she'd pulled away. She'd made it clear she wanted more than he could give, and Einar was not in the business of breaking hearts.

But he would make a fool of himself over her if he wasn't careful. At best. And at worst—

The first fat drops of rain fell to the deck, hitting his hair and running down his spine like an icy claw. A warning of what the Siren might do to him if he hurt her beloved protégée. A swift death in the merciless deep would be a blessing compared to facing Dianthe's wrath.

"Standing alone against a storm?" Aleksi's gently amused voice broke through Einar's preoccupation. "Aren't there better ways to punish yourself, Einar?"

The Lover stood a few paces away, balanced gracefully in spite of the increasing roll of the waves. The rain had already slicked his dark hair, and left his shirt plastered to his impressively built chest and arms. Einar had stopped wondering how the Lover could look elegant and alluring in the most absurd circumstances—but he did envy it. It made his muttered reply sound grumpier than he intended. "It's not punishment. It's my duty as captain."

"To stand alone?"

"Why should everyone else get drenched clothes and chattering teeth when the cold doesn't bother me?" Einar fought for a firmer tone this time. "This is going to be a rough one, my lord. You might prefer to be snug in your cabin."

Aleksi only arched one perfect eyebrow before taking an easy step forward, moving with the swaying of the ship. "So this is for their benefit, not so you can brood in peace. I see."

The Lover's perceptiveness could be a true aggravation. Lying never worked with the man, so Einar made the truth into a joke. "I could have brooded in just as much peace in my cabin. But I prefer a dramatic backdrop. I look much more impressive like this."

"That you do." The wind tugged at Aleksi's hair as the rain began to fall in earnest, pelting the unbothered god with the force of the gusting wind.

Well, a little frigid rain was unlikely to seriously harm a member of the High Court. And while Einar didn't share the same awe of the Lover as the younger Dreamers did, he didn't *quite* have the temerity to order the man belowdecks. "If you want to stand out here and brood with me, I won't stop you."

"It seems wrong, somehow, to leave you as alone as you obviously wish to be." Suddenly, his brow furrowed, and he looked over at Einar. "Are you worried about what we'll find on the island?"

Einar's fingers flexed against the wheel. Aleksi couldn't know the island held a very personal—and tragic—place in his heart. A single wrong word to the Lover could reveal far more than Einar intended to. So the truth, again. Simply not the whole truth. "How could I not be? I have no love for the Imperials, and you know *they* have no love for me. And given the chaos in the Empire right now . . ."

"You need not concern yourself that we're walking into the same situation as the others," Aleksi told him gently. "The harsh awakenings to the Dream and the Void that are happening on the mainland do not trouble Akeisa."

That was news to Einar. "How can that be true?"

"Because Gwynira did not let Sorin's greed touch her part of the kingdom." Aleksi inhaled deeply. "It's a mark in her favor, certainly. And it gives me hope. She protected her people."

Lightning forked dramatically across the sky, drawing the Lover's gaze. Thunder cracked overhead, loud enough that Einar felt the vibrations in his bones. Hopefully the combination would distract Aleksi from the storm of conflicting emotions inside Einar. Hearing the people of Rahvekya referred to as *Gwynira's* people grated at him, but he couldn't help but be grudgingly relieved to know that the horrors seen in the Empire might not be happening to the descendants of Petya's family and friends. He'd tell her as much tomorrow, and hope it eased her heart a little.

"The storm's getting worse," Aleksi observed, still seeming more curious than concerned.

"We're headed toward the heart of it now," Einar agreed. "Are you sure you don't want to seek the safety of your bed?"

For the first time, Aleksi had to raise his voice to be heard over the whipping of the impending gale. "I'm not leaving."

"Then brace yourself, my lord." Einar widened his stance as the bow lifted, the ship climbing its largest swell yet. "You're in for a hard ride."

The Lover smiled in anticipation.

So be it.

It was effortless to sink his power into the ship again, to feel the surge of the water against the hull. On the ships of his youth, the deck would be swarming with anxious crew as they sailed into the wind, hoping to find that terrifying balance of hurtling forward fast enough to top each wave but not so fast that they lost control. In the earliest days on the Kraken, when he'd been a mere mortal sailor, it had been like that too.

No longer. As his legend had grown in power, so had the ship, until it seemed to defy the ravages of age and the elements as easily as he did. Wood on the ship didn't rot. Metal didn't rust. The Dreamers who chose to sail with him found their powers enhanced when they stood on her decks. Even those mortals who made their home on his ship seemed changed by it—stronger, more robust. They healed more swiftly and didn't age. Over the years some had left his crew to settle down and live normal lives, and age had renewed its gentle grip on them. But for those who stayed . . .

The Kraken protected its crew from the very rhythms of time. How could a mere storm compare?

A fresh gust of wind whipped at his hair—a warning not to be complacent. The Kraken might ride the massive waves of this storm like a lover, but only a fool failed to respect the ocean's moods. He could feel the power of it in the tension on the wheel, and the strength it took to hold their course steady.

But even now, with the rain falling hard enough to sting the skin and thunder an ominous roar above them, that sweet, sad song was still there. Naia's power, sliding through the sea, whispering to the waves. Perhaps that was why even the largest swells carried them gently forward to the next, and towering waves only broke once they were past.

In the heart of one of the angriest storms Einar had seen in a long time, the sea still gentled itself in the face of the awesome power that flowed from Naia.

Lightning flashed directly above them, illuminating Aleksi's face in profile. The Lover had closed his eyes and tilted his head back, lifting his face to the storm as if the furious rain was nothing more than a gentle mist. He was as oblivious to the crack of thunder and the howl of the wind as he was to the deck pitching and rolling beneath his feet.

Something about the Lover seemed primal in that moment, a whispered reminder that Aleksi wasn't simply the god of desire, but in a very real way the god of life itself. He might not be able to summon the rain like the Siren, or hold dominion over the earth like the Dragon, but where he walked he left fertile ground, and when the rain sank into the dirt and found that spark, flowers grew.

Aleksi opened his eyes, and Einar sucked in a breath at their color—not their usual rich brown, but a deep, glowing violet that was another reminder. Magic sizzled through the air, the pulse of the Everlasting Dream all around them. This was the difference between a regular Dreamer—even one like Einar, who had seen over two thousand years—and a member of the High Court.

Power.

Some ancient instinct stirred in Einar, the Kraken recognizing the threat of a far more dangerous predator. His skin itched with the need to shed his mortal form and wrap the armor of the deepest ocean around him—

Lightning slashed through the night sky, close enough to raise the hair on the back of his neck. The boom of thunder made the ship vibrate beneath his feet. The wheel jerked, fighting him. The Kraken listed to starboard, and Einar tensed his arms and put all of his immortal strength into righting it.

The wheel creaked beneath his hands, loud enough that he could hear it over the wail of the storm. He'd never worried about the wood cracking in the face of a storm before—every part of his ship, from rudder to mast, seemed to defy all but the worst damage—but there was an anger to this storm that felt personal. Vicious. As if it wanted to punish *him*.

Einar caught movement at his side out of the corner of his eye, and suddenly he could *feel* the Lover next to him, the weight of so much power like the feeling when he slipped too deep into the ocean, with water pressing in all around him.

One warm hand covered his. Aleksi's fingers wove between his, gripping the wheel. Adding his strength. A second hand followed, the sensual glide of fingertips across the back of his hand like heat tearing through the frigid rain.

The Lover wasn't trying to seduce him. There were no coy glances, no suggestive smile. Aleksi simply lent his formidable strength, and when his fingers slid across the polished mahogany of the wheel, something . . . sparked.

The ominous groan of wood stressed to the breaking point softened. The wheel seemed stronger in Einar's grip. The planks beneath his feet felt . . . firmer. As if the very ship itself was a living thing, and the Lover had whispered to the heart of it, to the parts that had once been proud trees stretching branches toward the sun. Even the wind seemed softer, the storm gentled.

When you dance with the captain, you dance with the ship, he'd told Naia. He hadn't told her that the reverse was true, as well. Aleksi's magic wound through him along with the ship, coaxing life and strength and *vitality.* Arousal swelled within Einar, hardening his cock and awakening a hunger to touch. To taste. To fall into this man as he hadn't in over two thousand years—

No. *No.* There was a reason he didn't dally with the Lover the way the rest of the High Court did so readily. A reason he avoided those infamous joining-day celebrations, the joyous parties where pleasure and ecstasy were traded between all who were willing.

It was the same reason Aleksi had been sent on this damned mission to begin with. Desire might be bait in the Lover's trap, but his most dangerous weapon had always been his ability to find his way through the protections you built around your own heart. No labyrinth was too complex for him to navigate, no wall too great for him to scale, no rage too deep for him to soothe.

Einar liked his rage. *And* his walls. His frozen heart had served him well over the centuries. It kept him sharp, kept him focused. It kept him fighting the Empire that had taken everything from him, and let him keep the people who trusted him safe.

As soon as he'd delivered Aleksi and Naia safely home from their mission, Einar would have to remind himself why he fought. A nice, clean battle would wash away this distraction, and help him rebuild his walls.

Because this was all he needed. This ship. His crew. His fight against the Empire.

Maybe tomorrow, with some distance, that wouldn't feel like a lie.

Chapter Eight

Until recently, information about the so-called High Court of Dreamers said to rule over the primitive continent to our west was difficult to obtain. Imperial scholars all agreed that whatever powers these so-called gods might possess, they paled in comparison to the might of the Imperial Court. Having now met the Lover, I must state definitively that Imperial scholars were gravely mistaken.

*Untitled Manuscript in Progress
by Guildmaster Klement*

Naia had the nicest cabin on the ship.

It was spacious, as far as these things went, and well-appointed. A large berth fitted with a soft feather mattress lined one side of the room, while a desk and chest of drawers, both of dark, exquisitely carved wood, sat on the other side. The walls had been covered with thick paper in a rich blue hue striped with gold leaf, and the little luxuries scattered about were of a quality—and quantity—usually reserved for the captain of a vessel.

Or *very* important guests. This was the cabin Dianthe used when she traveled on the Kraken. The Siren's sigil, a cresting wave, was everywhere—carved into the head of the berth, inlaid into the top of the desk in mother-of-pearl, embossed onto the leather cover of a handbound journal that rested on one of the shelves. It was even embroidered on the corner of the bed's coverlet.

Naia had counted fourteen tastefully discreet uses of the sigil throughout the room, and she was fairly certain she'd spotted them all, since she'd mostly remained in this room for the last two days.

She wasn't *avoiding* Einar. She simply wasn't seeking him out.

The lie drew her gaze back to the bed. The maddening sailor had managed to proposition *and* reject her in the same breath. It shouldn't have seemed possible, yet he'd done it several times now. Einar was like that—one moment, he would casually invite her to join him for a romp in his cabin, and the next, would be so carefully solicitous of her comfort that it felt like being singled out with special regard.

And so it went, up and down, back and forth. He could be cool toward her, detached. Then he would serve her favorite dish at dinner— though she suspected he didn't much care for it. A less charitable person might have proclaimed that Einar was a changeable wind, blowing hot and cold.

For her part, Naia was mostly confused. A little dizzy. Who was he, truly? A ne'er-do-well pirate who lived only for the simple pleasures of cold drinks and warm bodies? A dedicated servant of the Siren, waging unflagging war against the Empire and all its evils? Achingly competent commander of the greatest ship—and crew—to ever sail the North Sea? Perhaps he was all of those things . . . and none.

And what did he want with her? *From* her? There was what he professed . . . and then there was the way he looked at her sometimes, with a softness and wonder that she recognized not from her own experience, but from the memories of others. From eons of distantly remembered longing and love affairs.

No, that would not do. Ascribing to Einar desires that he had not expressed was folly. He had told her what he wanted, *all* he wanted, and she had no choice but to take him at his word. In Einar's mind, the undeniable physical attraction between them merely warranted a bit of carnal indulgence—enjoyable but ultimately ephemeral, and quickly set aside.

And she was tempted. Oh, was she tempted. There was nothing wrong with exploration, with casual pleasure motivated only by lust and curiosity and fondness, unencumbered by doubts and expectations for the future. But when Naia contemplated sharing a single night with Einar, one emotion thrummed in her chest more strongly than the others, a caged bird beating its wings against her bones.

Sadness.

That *really* wouldn't do. But it was all Einar seemed capable of offering her, hence the reason she'd spent the last few days staring at the walls of her fancy cabin . . . and trying very hard not to ponder its soft bed and silk sheets.

Had he given her this cabin because she was serving as Dianthe's emissary? Or had he been thinking about Naia and those damned sheets?

She had just returned to pacing the plush carpet when the muffled sound of a bell drifted down from abovedecks. It had happened several times during the voyage—once, when a passing ship's captain hailed them to deliver news from the Empire, and again when the third mate had spotted a pod of whales and thought everyone might like to see them.

Naia grabbed a thick woolen cloak. She was already dressed more warmly than usual, in heavy layers of embroidered velvet, but the sea air had been especially frigid ever since they'd passed Dead Man Shoals. If she were human, even the soft wool might not protect her from the cold.

She hurried up to the foredeck. Aleksi stood there, his arms crossed, the chilly breeze tousling his hair. Naia followed his gaze out—and stopped where she stood.

They had reached Akeisa. Its icy shores spread out before them, rocky and barren, dotted with cliffside dwellings as well as fishing huts.

In the distance, the incongruously delicate spires of the Grand Duchess's palace rose from the snowy landscape to pierce the clear blue sky.

The parts she could see were built of white stone, enormous columns topped with ornate domes that had been painted or otherwise decorated with bold colors and delicate panes of glass. It was breathtaking, and she would have strained to see more.

Except that a wall of ice stretched in front of the ship, blocking the mouth of the harbor.

"A warm welcome," Aleksi observed dryly.

"A warning," Einar rumbled behind them. "The Empire has always liked its ruthless displays of strength. The Imperial lackeys will make us wait on their pleasure just to teach us our place."

Aleksi seemed to ponder that, then turned to Naia. "What do you think?"

She thought both Aleksi's sarcastic observation and Einar's assessment were accurate. Worse, she thought the Empire's assumption was that the ship would have no choice but to wait. That this new representative of the Sheltered Lands would be powerless in the face of such might.

And she didn't like that one bit.

"There are several possible explanations," she said finally.

"A circumspect answer," Aleksi shot back. "Very diplomatic."

"Very *honest*." Naia shrugged. "It could be an oversight. We have made excellent time, and are arriving ahead of schedule. It could also be a slight, a display of power wrapped in a sly insult directed at you. Or . . ."

His eyes gleamed. "Yes?"

Naia's pulse quickened. "It could be a test."

"All valid interpretations, and ultimately unimportant." He pursed his lips. "The real question is . . . what will you do about it?"

Startled, Naia very nearly took a step back. "Me?"

He hummed. "Yes, you."

Her heart continued its lively dance, driven not by surprise or fear but . . . anticipation? Because Aleksi was right. *Why* this wall stood before them was incidental. They could never truly know the answer, nor could they change it. All that was left was to decide their next move.

"We mean to enter the harbor, yet a wall of ice blocks our way," she answered. "So we should remove it."

"Tear it down?" Aleksi asked lightly. "Just like that?"

Naia met his gaze. "Just like that."

He stepped back, gesturing to her with a flourish. Einar clenched his fingers and opened his mouth, but said nothing when Aleksi laid a hand on his arm.

Naia swallowed hard as she stepped forward. Indignation burned in her middle, a hard knot that tempted her to lash out in anger. Instead, she breathed deeply, held her arms out to her sides, and called the water.

It rumbled and roiled, rolling up the sides of the ship until it washed past the railings and onto the main deck in sheets. The crew's protests died as Naia drew the water closer, keeping it away from the vulnerable hatches and the others standing on deck.

She closed her eyes as the icy water converged on her, surrounding her in its freezing grasp. Instead of waiting for her whispered instructions, it washed over her, caressing her skin, the way one might embrace a beloved friend. The droplets seeped into her, until she had become one with the sea.

The ice imprisons us, she murmured. *Wash it away.*

The water surged back over the railings, leaving behind dry wood and Naia, alone and bereft, as it swirled back into the sea.

For a moment, nothing. Then a chorus of dull crackling noises filled the air, punctuated by sharp pops. Naia opened her eyes in time to see cracks begin to form in the ice wall, dark shadows snaking up its length until great sheets of it began to break apart. Waves buffeted the ship as those giant chunks of ice slipped beneath the water's surface, once more subsumed by the sea.

Silence reigned as the unobstructed harbor revealed itself.

"Well," Aleksi breathed. "You *are* handy to have around, aren't you?"

Naia tried to exhale, but her breath left her on a shuddering sigh. The power of the ocean still flowed through her, trapped by flesh and bone too restrictive and delicate to contain it. It *seethed* within her, desperate in a way she couldn't understand, couldn't control—

"Relax." Aleksi's fingers slid into her hair and cupped the back of her head, comforting and commanding, all at once. "And breathe."

It took several moments, three pounding heartbeats that she counted off in agonized silence, before she was able to nod in his grip. "I'm fine."

Two more heartbeats, and he released her. "Good."

The sudden crack of Einar's voice shattered the quiet. "What possessed you to do something so reckless?" he snarled, stalking closer with a wild look in his dark eyes. "The sea is too powerful! She could sweep you away. You should not endanger yourself like that just to make a point!"

The fear in his voice felt like biting on metal, and Naia's chest ached as she reached for him. She touched his face, stroking away his stormy frown. But the ache only *bloomed*, replacing everything else with a sweet, familiar pain.

Her voice echoed in her ears as she soothed him. "You always worry too much."

"I don't—" He froze when the words brushed his lips against her fingertips. His entire body went rigid, and something stirred behind those eyes—not so dark anymore, but electric, the way they looked when he used his power.

The way they looked when she tested his control.

The moment ended as he shuddered and tore away, jabbing a finger in Aleksi's direction. "Keep her from getting herself killed," he growled, already storming off.

Einar shouted orders, instructing his crew to take them into harbor as he once more took the wheel. Naia stood, unsure of what to do until Aleksi grasped her hand.

"You scared him a bit, love," he murmured. "Doesn't mean you did anything wrong. Now—are you ready to face the Empire again?"

The words worked as he so obviously intended—to remind Naia of the stakes of their mission. She squared her shoulders and looked up at him. "This? Is just a friendly visit."

"Precisely."

Grand Duchess Gwynira waited for them on the docks, which were constructed of white stone and weathered gray wood. She was flanked by a smiling man with pale-blond hair and refined clothing and a hulking man, handsome but severe, clad in leather and metal armor.

A diplomat and a guard, no doubt. There were others on the docks, workers and a handful of courtiers that whispered as the gangplank was lowered and Aleksi, Naia, and Einar disembarked. Only Gwynira stood, unmoving, her face frozen in an expressionless mask.

Like stone, Naia thought. *Like ice.*

She did not come to meet them, instead forcing them to cross the entire distance from the end of the docks. Only when they reached her, making their bows and curtsies, did she finally speak.

"Welcome to Akeisa." Her voice rang out like the cracking of the ice wall. "I hope the rest of your sojourn on our lovely island will not be as needlessly aggressive as your arrival."

Naia tensed. *Shit.*

But Aleksi only smiled warmly. "My apologies, Grand Duchess, for the dramatic entrance. I was led to believe we were expected."

"You were." A pointed silence. "In several days' time."

He shrugged. "What can I say? We enjoyed fair winds and calm seas for the duration of our journey."

"Of course." Gwynira smiled, a chilly, scant movement of her lips, and turned to Naia. "I remember you."

The last time they had faced each other had been on the battlefield, during the High Court's final confrontation with the Betrayer. Gwynira had been the first of Sorin's court to take to the field for close combat, and Naia and Einar had fought *hard* to keep her ice magic from overwhelming the others. It had taken all of their combined might to keep her distracted and at bay. "I remember you, as well, Grand Duchess."

Gwynira tilted her head. "It seems you've been practicing."

"Yes. I realized I needed to improve my skills." She paused, then gave credit where credit was due. "*You* taught me that."

This time, Gwynira's smile thawed a little, and she chuckled quietly. "Fair enough. Lord Aleksi, Lady Naia, and Captain Einar, all of the Sheltered Lands. This is Sir Jaspar Astile, my seneschal. And Arktikos, my personal guard." Her introductions complete, she turned for the palace courtyard. "You'll be wanting to rest, of course. Sir Jaspar will show you to your rooms."

She vanished through an archway, trailed closely by her guard, leaving her seneschal to smile broadly at them. "Shall we?" He offered Naia his arm, and she took it without thought.

Sir Jaspar led them through another entrance, and Naia seized the opportunity to study the architecture more closely. The stone exterior gave way to wooden beams and hammered metal. These items seemed to be used decoratively as well as part of the structure itself, creating a uniformity that she had not expected but found pleasing to the eye.

Then Naia did a double take. What she'd assumed from a distance were panes of glass were actually sheets of ice. They had been placed into the curving casements just like windows, and Naia had to marvel at the amount of sheer *power* it must have taken Gwynira to do this. Not to create the ice, but to have it persist without constant conscious effort.

She shivered.

"Are you cold, Lady Naia?" the seneschal asked, though he did not wait for a response. "I'll have the steward arrange for ample fuel in your quarters, and extra furs for your bed."

"Thank you, Sir Jaspar."

"Just Jaspar, please." His smile widened. "We shall be great friends, with no need to stand on ceremony."

Judging from the slightly dazzled way he was looking at her, becoming Naia's *friend* wasn't necessarily his primary goal. Still, he kept his attentions respectful, even when he covered her hand with his and patted it lightly.

Behind them, Aleksi smothered a cough. Einar simply glowered.

"Now," Jaspar murmured. "Tell me about yourself."

"What would you like to know?"

"Everything, of course."

This time, Aleksi's muffled sound was definitely a *laugh*.

Naia shot him a sharp look. As she did, she noticed two young women outfitted as maids hovering at the end of a cross hall, whispering to one another. When they saw they'd drawn her notice, they paled and broke apart, vanishing out of sight.

Why had Naia immediately chosen the boldest, showiest option when faced with that damnable wall of ice? Now she had to deal with whispering servants, a starry-eyed admirer, and—worst of all—a suspicious hostess.

A grand start to their diplomatic mission.

Chapter Nine

Some have referred to the goddess as ruler of Rahvekya, but nothing could be further from the truth. A queen, even a benevolent one who wants only the best for her people, still controls what they do. How they do it.

The goddess was never this island's ruler.

She is its mother.

from the unpublished papers of Rahvekyan High Priestess Omira

The Seneschal of Akeisa was practically humping Naia's leg.

Aleksi could hardly blame him for his interest. She'd already deftly and decisively demonstrated her abilities to the people of this island. Of course a man as obviously ambitious as Sir Jaspar would not be able to resist her. Not when an alliance with a god could elevate his entire family for generations.

And the fact that Naia was also beautiful certainly did not hinder Jaspar's regard.

Down, boy, Aleksi thought ruefully. Then he glanced over at Einar, who was absolutely plotting the man's untimely demise, and resolved to intervene. Naia was handling the handsome young seneschal's attention with aplomb, but if Einar threatened him—or *worse*—

"Here we are," Jaspar announced. "The Lover's chambers. Now, if you'll follow me this way, Captain Einar . . ."

The man undoubtedly planned to unload his unwanted cargo, then take his sweet time showing Naia to *her* room—while possibly attempting to coax from her an invitation into its intimate confines.

I don't think so. "Where are their rooms?" Aleksi asked, deliberately inserting an edge of steel into his otherwise easy voice.

Jaspar blinked. "Down the hall, just around the corner. But—"

"We can find our way." Naia dropped a low curtsy. "Thank you for your assistance, Jaspar."

To his credit, he recovered quickly. "I am at your disposal." He took her hand and kissed the back of it. "Night falls so early this time of year that we dine at the eighth chime. May I claim a seat next to yours?"

Naia demurred. "The seating arrangements are not mine to dictate."

"Surely you could—"

"We'll see you then." Aleksi clapped the man's shoulder and spun him to face back down the corridor. "And trust that you'll handle everything to your mistress's satisfaction."

Sir Jaspar obviously wanted to linger, but his manners and position overcame his reticence. He dropped one last short bow, then turned to walk away.

"Was that necessary?" Naia asked. "I was *managing* him."

"Yes, but now you don't have to," Aleksi shot back. "And we don't have to watch him drool on you, so everyone wins."

He pushed through the heavy double doors and into his assigned chamber. It was spacious, featuring ornate carved stone walls and marble floors. It could have been a cold, sterile space, if not for the large stonework fireplace, the thick rugs, and the richly woven tapestries that hung in smooth spaces between the wall carvings.

Alcoves were set into the far walls, little spaces dedicated to activities like reading and bathing. Folded screens sat beside each one, barriers that could be set out for the sake of privacy. Even the bed, a monstrous, fur-laden affair that took up nearly a third of the cavernous room, had curtains hung around the massive frame that could be dropped to enclose it.

A necessity, since the windows were bright and wholly uncovered. Aleksi stepped closer to the nearest one, reaching out toward it, and shivered when his fingertips brushed ice instead of glass.

Was the climate of the island an artifact of Gwynira's icy powers? Or did its condition predate her arrival? He'd have to ask. The response could do much more than answer his query. The real, valuable truths were always to be found in the shape of a response, in the precise *ways* people chose to convey information.

"This is cozy," Naia observed. "Ice and all."

Einar hovered just inside the closed door, his face still tense. "I don't like that they've separated us."

Aleksi raised an eyebrow. "I wasn't aware that you were prepared to share a bed with either of us." A lie, but only a small one.

If anything, Einar's glower deepened. "I don't trust that seneschal. If you think he won't find an excuse to visit Lady Naia in the middle of the night . . ."

Her laughter rang out like a bell. "If he were so brazen as to attempt such a thing, he might find his attentions met with cold steel in place of a warm embrace."

"As I should hope to see any unwanted advances met." But Aleksi shook his head. "No, he wouldn't dare. Naia has power and connections. The qualities he most covets about her—aside from your loveliness, of course, my dear—are precisely the ones that render coercion impractical. He shall have to *charm her* instead."

A blush colored her cheeks. "You mean he shall have to *try*. I am not easily won."

Einar stared at her so long that her blush deepened. Then he looked back to Aleksi. "I still don't like it. I don't like the way this palace feels."

"Nor should you, I fear." Aleksi gestured to a plush sofa in one corner. It was shaped like a nearly complete circle, with a small stone table built into one end. "Sit."

Naia slid onto the cushions, tucking her legs beneath her. Einar perched gingerly on the edge, boots planted firmly on the floor and his elbows resting on his knees.

Aleksi remained standing. "The Empire is in shambles. You both know that. Hell, you *saw* it after the final battle. People lost, frightened. Awakening to the Dream or the Void with no idea what was happening to them, much less how to manage it. Absolute, utter chaos. That is what Ash, Sachi, and Zanya have gone to deal with. And, in doing so, they've left Akeisa to us."

"To you," Naia corrected.

"No, to *us*." Aleksi finally sat, dropping to face his two companions. "It is true that I represent the High Court, but your influence here cannot be overstated. You've faced Gwynira in battle, and now you've seen the respect she affords that experience. Beyond that, you are both creatures of the sea. You belong here in a way I never will. So when I say *us*, trust that I mean it."

Einar shifted uncomfortably on the velvet. "This sort of thing . . . Diplomacy? It isn't one of my skills. And considering the way most Imperial nobles feel about me, I might do more harm here than good. I'm better as a bodyguard."

"The nobles don't have to love you. In fact, it's better that they don't." Aleksi opened the decanter that sat on the stone table and sniffed it. Water. He poured three glasses and handed one to Einar. "*I'm* here to be liked. *You're* here to be feared. Not too much, mind, but just enough. Sorin has told them all that we're weak. Part of our mission here will be to correct that misapprehension."

Naia looked thoughtful as she accepted her glass. "Sachi said that Gwynira helped her when the Betrayer was holding her captive, but only once she realized that Sachi wasn't soft."

"Of course. She was hedging her bets. It would have done her no good to needlessly expose herself as Sorin's enemy." Aleksi drained his glass. "She had to be sure. Just as she must be sure now."

Einar huffed and drank half his water in one gulp. "Well, if we need strength, I'll just lurk behind you both and scowl." A sudden, wicked smile curved his lips. "I know how to play the monster."

"*Careful.*" Naia's voice was singsong as she stretched out one leg and nudged Einar with her foot. "Gwynira might take a shine to you."

"Ha!" Einar's hand shot out to catch Naia's ankle. "Something tells me I'm not the type to melt the Ice Queen's heart."

"Then perhaps *I* should test those chilly waters."

Her words echoed strangely, and Aleksi's vision blurred. He blinked, but it didn't help. Naia and Einar kept up their banter, their flirtatious words distant, almost beyond his perception.

Because all he could perceive was *light*, a dazzling array of colors that swirled around the room. He saw lingering hints of the room's previous occupants—Ash's earthy red mingled with Sachi's glittering rainbow and Zanya's darker hues, three vastly different auras that shouldn't have melded together but *did*, and in such gorgeous harmony.

And right in front of him, so vivid it almost hurt his eyes, *blue*. Naia's lighter tint, warm shallows and gentle waves. And Einar, deep and cold, the darkest abyss. A shade that Aleksi had never seen before, in or out of the Dream, surrounded them both, hewing close, as if to block out the rest of the world.

Other colors seeped into his consciousness, rendered dull by lack of familiarity. A cluster of deep green, envy distilled into its purest, harshest form. A jovial pop of jonquil yellow. A bustle of cherry blossom pink too busy to be bothered.

"Aleksi?" Naia frowned. "Aleksi, are you—?"

The emotions hit him next, a tidal wave of nervousness and joy, melancholy and bone-deep fear. Love and desperation and hatred so intense that he was glad to be sitting, else his knees would have buckled. The room spun, and he shut his eyes tight against the dizzy whirl.

But it was the whispers that finally threatened to drive him into the darkness. Idle musings and secrets and wishes, silly fears and existential panic. Thoughts meant only to be entertained in the silence of the mind, never spoken aloud.

—what will I make for dinner—

—did she notice me—

—why would they—

Aleksi gritted his teeth as one vow rose above the rest, resonating with the fervent devotion of a prayer.

I will end them, this heart whispered. *For the glory of the Empire.*

Then it was over. The haze cleared, and the noise that filled Aleksi's head subsided. Strong hands gripped his shoulders, and he opened his eyes to find Einar holding him upright, concern carving deep lines into his stony face.

Naia hovered just behind him. "Are you well?"

Aleksi unclenched his jaw. "Perfectly. Why do you ask?"

"Why do I . . . ?" Her eyes widened in disbelief. "Because you were swaying as if you were about to fall over. Einar had to *catch* you."

Aleksi examined his empty glass. It was certainly possible that it was poisoned, or even another substance entirely, only masquerading as water. That might explain his momentary loss of control. But Einar and Naia had also partaken of it, and both seemed unaffected.

Which meant this wasn't a problem with the drink. It was a problem with *him.*

He considered Einar and Naia. Though the haze that had blurred his vision had abated, they still seemed . . . dark. Muted. The dark-blue velvet of Naia's dress looked almost black now, as if the color had been leached from it.

"I'm tired," he said finally. Truthfully. "The entire journey came as somewhat of a surprise, and I had not the time to properly prepare myself for it. I will be fine after a nap and a bath."

Naia relented, but Einar released him with reluctance, both hands hovering for a moment on either side of Aleksi's shoulders, as if poised to catch him again. "Are you sure?"

"Go," Aleksi urged. "Dinner will come soon enough, and we have to be ready."

Einar stepped back, still alert. When Aleksi didn't immediately slump to the floor, the Kraken nodded shortly. "I'll escort Lady Naia to her quarters."

Naia gazed back at him over her shoulder, even as Einar guided her away with a protective hand at the small of her back. Aleksi managed to stay on his feet until the door finally closed behind them, and he felt free to collapse back to the sofa.

He had to consider the hard, cold facts of the situation. First, there had been the prick from the rose's thorn—instead of healing immediately, it had taken hours—and now he'd experienced a loss of control. The former was concerning, but the latter . . .

Aleksi did not lose control. The very core of who he was demanded absolute self-discipline. Love without consideration and restraint was not love; it was something dangerous, a viper waiting to strike. Not since the earliest days of his existence had he done anything so shameful as read people's emotions without due cause, much less without meaning to do so in the first place.

But what did it mean? As far as he was aware, this had never come up amongst the members of the High Court, had never been an issue. Once they mastered their abilities and learned to govern themselves, it took a truly ruinous circumstance indeed to shatter that control.

No, Aleksi had never heard of anything like this before. But he understood intuitively, as only someone so centered in *life* as he was could, that these things were only a hint of what was to come. That they could and would get much, much worse.

He was sick.

He was . . . fading, and fast.

He had never heard of this happening before because it never *had*. All members of the High Court knew what it was to have their power wax and wane with the passage of centuries, as the people's beliefs either grew or subsided. Even as they evolved into something entirely new. But those changes were excruciatingly gradual, like a tree slowly adding ring after ring to its trunk as the years passed. Aleksi had never witnessed a sudden decline. And it begged the question: could a member of the High Court weaken and die this way, from illness rather than catastrophic injury?

He shook himself and poured another glass of water. What he'd suffered during the battle against Sorin, being torn away from the Dream? That *had* been catastrophic. But he'd assumed it had resulted only in damage to his psyche, an emotional and mental blow that he had to work through and overcome. And then it would heal.

A silly notion, when his very existence was based on the power of thought. Of the High Court, he alone had been born of emotion, and now it seemed he might die the same way. Suddenly, like a crop of wheat destroyed by a freak summer hailstorm. Like a child's first cry also being its last.

Like a heart breaking.

It was uncharted territory, but that was fine with Aleksi. In a way, he had always stood apart, even amongst his fellow gods. He would navigate this new ending with as much grace as he could muster. With any luck, he could complete his mission and escape back to his villa before his decline became too marked to mask.

He didn't want the world to see love die.

Chapter Ten

Work never frightened the goddess. She tilled fields, built walls, dug ditches. She did all of these things with hands that bled but never faltered.

A question haunted me: why did she not use her magic for these menial tasks?

She laughed and told me that magic would not spare the people of this island from the rigors of hard work. So it would not spare her.

from the unpublished papers of Rahvekyan High Priestess Qmira

Gwynira's seneschal was insulting Einar.

It wasn't subtle, either. The servant who had brought in the outfit had been deferential enough—maybe *too* deferential, gazing at Einar in nervous awe as he smoothed nonexistent wrinkles from the heavily embroidered jacket—but the words shoved into his mouth by that too-pretty bottom-feeder were pure spite.

"My Lord Seneschal offers this small token of his appreciation." The man's voice was rendered raspy by reluctance. The words that followed seemed dragged from him at the tip of an invisible sword. "In the event you felt unequal to the task of dressing for the Grand Duchess's table."

The insult delivered, the servant braced himself as if expecting to have repayment for the slight visited upon him. It told Einar all he needed to know about the nobles of Gwynira's court, but the rage surging through him like the rising tide would only terrify the man more.

Remember, these are still your people.

Petya's final words to him before he'd left the ship. He'd accepted them without comment, not having the time to dispute the claim. Petya might imagine him to be a great leader with an important duty, but she of all people knew that Einar had been raised on a humble fishing boat, not within the walls of a palace. He'd worked with his hands every day of his life—honest work. *Hard* work.

His only people were the crew he had gathered to him. The only kingdom he'd ever ruled had been his ship. That was enough.

It *had* been enough.

Fear all but trembled in the servant's eyes. Einar tightened his grip on his temper and made his voice as gentle as he could manage. "Thank you. I can dress myself."

He waited until the relieved man had bowed his way from the room before turning to face the clothing spread out on the bed. It truly was exquisite quality—the shirt and trousers of a pristine white that only someone with servants to clean it would ever want to own, and the elaborate calf-length overcoat covered in such intricate gold-on-ivory embroidery, he imagined the thing could stand up on its own.

The seneschal had obviously hoped to trigger his pride—or his legendary temper. No doubt the nobles of the Empire expected a barely leashed monster to arrive at their table. The brutal beast from their nightmares, who sank their warships and captured their rich cargo vessels any time they dared to smuggle goods to and from the Sheltered Lands.

The Kraken of their imagination would have his fists in this elaborate costume already, destroying it just for the satisfaction of hearing it shred apart. Einar should thwart the bastard seneschal's foolish little game and appear arrayed in their best finery, as civilized as any of them could want. He should sit at their table and smile in their terrified faces, while Naia and Aleksi made friends of those who had once been enemies.

But the idea of putting on the trappings of the people who had conquered this island turned his stomach.

Biting off a curse, Einar strode to the wardrobe and yanked it open. It was filled with all the finery that had been in his trunk, no doubt carefully unpacked and pressed by the same servant who'd presented the formal clothing. Most of it was his casual wardrobe—fine fabrics cut for simple comfort and the demands of an active ship captain—but Einar hadn't spent over two thousand years watching Dianthe use fashion as a weapon without learning the value of having one outfit that warned the world that you were not to be underestimated.

Einar's one outfit happened to be infinitely appropriate for dining with the greedy interlopers who ruled this island.

He dressed like he was preparing for battle—heavy black trousers tucked into shiny, knee-high boots, a black silk shirt that slid over his skin like a caress but still gaped just enough at the throat to flash a teasing hint of a tanned chest and dark hair. His vest buttoned with shiny gold buttons, but even they seemed dull next to the thick gold embroidery that wove ancient patterns across the rich black fabric. A wide belt followed, fastened in place with an intricate golden buckle shaped like a kraken, with tentacles that curved around the stamped leather and eyes that glinted a deep teal by candlelight.

The same color flashed as he shrugged into his finest jacket, the stiff unrelenting black lined on the inside with an expensive silk that shone teal or midnight blue, depending on the way the light hit it. Dianthe had told him once that when he moved in it, he looked like a vengeful god rising from the depths of the ocean.

Maybe that would make the seneschal mind his damn manners.

The final touches rested in the small chest on his vanity. Hammered gold earrings, a handful of thick golden chains, heavy rings with sapphires that sparkled from the deep blue of the frozen North Sea to the teal seen on the southern coast of Seahold. A touch of shimmery dark powder from a jar the Witch had gifted him completed the look, outlining his eyes in smoky darkness.

His mirror told him that he looked every inch the terrifying pirate king. But when he stepped out into the hallway, it was Naia's widened eyes he found truly gratifying.

"You look . . ." But she merely trailed off, as if words had failed her.

She had donned clothing provided by their host, but the rich fabrics and intricate stitching barely registered. Naia had dressed for battle, too—a battle waged with guileless eyes and charming smiles and an unshakable sense of her own power that made her glow. He'd seen that nimbus of power around others a few times before—Princess Sachielle was like a rainbow of light, and Dianthe fairly seethed with the deep blues of her ocean—but Naia was like the sparkle of sacred glass on a sunny day, or the crash of crystal waves against a sandy shore.

Brilliant. Seductive. Genuine reverence filled him as he reached for her hand, prepared for the shock of her skin against his and still nearly undone by it as he bent over her hand and let his lips brush her knuckles. Temptation beckoned, the urge to part his lips, to taste her skin, to see if she'd gasp if he let his tongue—

No. Over twenty-two centuries of life, and she had him acting like an anxious boy trying to steal his first kiss. He forced himself to straighten, to flash the Kraken's wicked grin as he murmured, "You look exquisite, too."

A flush darkened her cheeks as she lifted a hand to her ornate metal headdress. "I look *fussy*," she murmured. "I don't think Imperial fashion suits me."

"On the contrary," Einar said firmly. "*Anything* would suit you."

Aleksi chuckled. "He may dress like a scoundrel and a pirate—though a prosperous one—but he speaks the truth."

Belatedly, Einar turned to face the Lover—and was immediately glad he hadn't tried to wear the Imperial clothing.

Aleksi was stunning. The stiffly embroidered jacket that would have felt like the enemy's chains to Einar flowed over the Lover's lean body as if grateful for the honor. Even the familiar scabbard hanging at his side could do nothing to diminish the elegance of his figure. Aleksi had walked the world for too many centuries to have the same glow as Naia—the one reserved for those fresh from the Dream or deeply connected to it—but his presence was so much larger than a few scraps of fabric and thread. His dark hair framed a face immortalized in tens of thousands of paintings and sculptures, and even the bronze stitching on his coat seemed faded compared to the rich glow of his light-brown skin.

Einar and Naia may have prepared for a battle, but Aleksi would never have to. Einar expected he could have appeared at Gwynira's table wrapped in a burlap sack with frayed rope for a belt, and made every person at the table frantic to find a tailor who could replicate it.

Aleksi laughed again. "Speechless, Einar? I'm flattered."

Einar covered his self-consciousness with a rude noise. "Don't pretend you don't know exactly how pretty you are. Who wouldn't stare?"

"Who, indeed?" Aleksi offered Naia his arm. "Shall we?"

A servant waited just on the other side of the door, her head bowed. "Begging your pardon. For you, my lady."

Instead of a missive, the woman handed over a small cloth sachet, then hurried away without another word.

"A gift?" Aleksi hummed. "From your admiring seneschal, perhaps?"

"Perhaps." Naia's nimble fingers made quick work of the ribbon, and out slipped an exquisite piece of teal sea glass strung on a leather cord. She gasped and held it up to the light. "It's gorgeous."

It swung from her fingers, somehow catching the light in spite of its cloudy surface. *Goddess-touched,* Jinevra had always said, every time she pulled hers from beneath her vest and let the sun illuminate it. No other sea glass looked quite like it, because the rare bottles from which it came had been lost to the depths of the Northern Channel millennia ago. The sea gave it up with great reluctance, and only a handful of precious fragments washed ashore every year.

As a child, Jinevra had scoured the beaches every day in search of treasure. She'd been one of the lucky ones, blessed by the goddess's bounty, and the necklace had nestled safely beneath her clothing, resting against her heart, for two thousand years. If she'd stayed here, on the island, it would have become a beloved family heirloom, as this one surely was.

And someone had just given it to Naia.

"Your admirer has impeccable taste," Aleksi teased.

"Oh, hush." Naia laughed. "You know very well he did not give me this. It isn't *fancy* enough for Sir Jaspar."

"Too true."

If only they knew.

"But I love it." Her eyes shining, she held it out. "There's no way it will fit over this headdress. Will you, Aleksi?"

"Of course." He untied the leather cord as Naia turned away from him, still beaming. He draped the pendant around her bare neck with excruciating gentleness, retied it, and smoothed it against her skin in an innocent gesture that was somehow still painfully sensual.

Somehow? Oh, no. There was no *somehow* with the Lover. Einar knew that firsthand. The way he touched Naia was *inevitably* sensual, for all its casualness. Even thousands of years later, Einar could still remember what it was like to feel the Lover's caress, so the sweet flush in Naia's cheeks was no surprise . . . but the confused tangle of wanting *was.* Einar managed to catch his sudden growl before it could rattle its way into his chest, but the sight of Aleksi's clever fingers sliding over her hair as he coaxed it back into order snapped his self-control.

The Lover wasn't the only one who knew about sensual touches. Einar stepped forward and caught the leather cord with his finger, tugging it gently into place until the glass pendant nestled in the deep vee left by her fancy gown. His knuckle grazed the softness of her skin just above the swell of her breast.

Naia drew in a sharp breath . . . then smiled. "Does it suit? Better than the silly clothes, I mean?"

"It's perfect for you," he said honestly. "A treasure of the sea, for a creature of the sea."

"I'm never taking it off."

"You shouldn't." He could only hope that Jinevra was right, and that the pieces held the blessing of the island's ancient goddess. Considering whose table they were about to sit at, they could use it. "I suppose we have to go to dinner."

It was Naia's turn to laugh. "My dear captain, it is a meal, not a tribunal. You will be fine."

She reclaimed Aleksi's arm, and Einar fell in behind them, wishing he could share her confidence. Wishing he believed that the chill down his spine was simply this frigid castle and its icy windows.

A servant stood at every hallway intersection to guide them in the right direction. Each one bowed deeply at Naia's approach—and each one seemed to have some familiar bit of ancient lore Einar recognized from Petya's and Jinevra's stories. Some wore woven rope fiber studded with wave-smoothed driftwood clasped around their wrists. Others showed hints of sea-frosted teal on their fingers or at their throats. Shiny brass seashells that mirrored Petya's beloved charm dangled from earrings. One or two sported tokens that looked eerily like the emblem on Einar's sails—the ancient silhouette of the kraken.

And none of them looked at Einar with fear in their eyes.

Petya would be thrilled to see how well the old religion thrived, even after all this time. Einar kept his eyes focused straight ahead and hoped Aleksi's observant eyes were busy lingering on Naia—though *that* thought made him uncomfortable in different ways.

Finally, they reached a pair of grand doors that stood thrown wide, and the three of them entered to formal announcements and polite applause. It was the kind of courtly ceremony rarely, if ever, seen in the homes of the High Court. They tended to operate more casually, leaving all the pomp and circumstance to the Mortal Lords.

Still, Aleksi and Naia moved through the hall as if they were both accustomed to such fanfare. They walked, their backs straight and heads held high, to their places at the high table—Aleksi on Gwynira's left, and Naia on his.

Whispers buzzed at the far end of the table as Einar took his seat next to Naia. The fear he'd expected from the servants was *here*, gathering in the eyes of Gwynira's assembled nobles as they snuck disdainful and horrified looks at him. He'd been the monster of their legends for thousands of years—the cruel and rapacious pirate who supposedly preyed on their merchant ships and attacked innocent sailors.

Einar had never been above taking a little of the Empire's wealth to help those desperate few he'd rescued from its shores, but his real crime had always been keeping these greedy nobles penned in and afraid, unable to pillage the bounty of the Sheltered Lands after they'd wrung their own lands dry.

So he bared his teeth in his fiercest smile and savored the dread in their eyes. It would only make him stronger, after all. And as long as they were busy being nervous about *him*, they'd have less time to plot mischief against Naia and Aleksi.

When everyone was seated, the Grand Duchess, from her central spot at the highest table, raised her goblet. "In Akeisa, we welcome strangers as old friends, for that is what they are destined to become . . ."

Subtle movement to his right drew Einar's gaze to Naia. Her graceful fingers opened another of those tiny cloth sachets. This time, a bracelet tumbled free—weathered shark teeth strung on a leather cord. A delicate driftwood carving of a whale joined it. A second cloth pack revealed a freshly cast brass seashell on a basic chain—the very image of what Petya's necklace must have looked like on the day she'd first put it on.

The symbol of the goddess who had once protected this island.

A soft smile tinged with confusion curved Naia's lips as she stroked her thumb over the gleaming brass, and Einar swore he could feel that touch on his skin. A hunger stirred that was totally unrelated to—and totally inappropriate for—the dinner ahead of them. He wanted to strip those endless layers of court finery from her body and bury himself in the feel of her skin, in the sweet and seductive scent of her—in her *magic*, which must shine as clearly to the servants here as it did to him.

They looked at her and saw a goddess remembered only by hazy myth.

He saw an obsession that only seemed to grow by the day.

Applause filled the hall, and Naia belatedly set the gifts aside to join in. Once it subsided, conversation began to fill the quiet left behind. Servers began to bring out the first course, an hors d'oeuvre of bite-size toasted bread piled high with lump crab and fresh herbs.

Naia leaned closer to Einar and held up the bracelet. "Do you think this is a local tradition? No one has brought gifts to you or Aleksi."

"We're not the ones who summoned the sea to bring down an ice wall," he replied dryly. It wasn't a lie. Neither were his next words. "I imagine any island nation would respect the power you wield."

She blushed, but her smile was short-lived. "Tell me you aren't still angry about that."

The painful earnestness in her eyes should have chilled his ardor. Whatever his flaws, and in spite of his reputation, he'd never been the type to deliberately lure innocents onto the shoals of romantic heartache. He wasn't cruel by nature, and Petya would have tossed him overboard if he'd made a habit of it.

But for some maddening reason, Naia's big, curious eyes only stoked his hunger. And the reminder of how recklessly she'd channeled the full power of the ocean lent that hunger a dangerous edge. "I wasn't angry, I was terrified. I've never seen anyone but Dianthe do something like that, and she's had thousands of years of practice."

Daughter of Tides

"I'm sorry. I didn't mean to scare you." She laid her hand on his arm, the bracelet of shark teeth still twined around her fingers. "I would never do that on purpose."

It was only imagination that he could feel the warmth of her fingertips through his layers of clothing, but imagination was enough. His body stirred, as impulsive as the youth he had not been in over two thousand years.

Across the way, from where he'd been seated on the other side of the high table, the seneschal's gaze fell on Naia's hand. His eyes narrowed for a split second before he lifted his goblet with a forced laugh. "What in the world is that?"

Naia stiffened. "A gift, Sir Jaspar."

"From one of the servants, I presume. It's far too rustic to have come from anyone else." He scoffed. "Such a superstitious lot."

Disdain fairly dripped from his voice, and his smile was so condescending Einar felt the overwhelming urge to punch it.

Aleksi stepped in smoothly—and saved the man's teeth. "Superstition and worship are but two sides of the same coin. The gift—of belief, I mean—is a considerable one." He lifted his cup to Gwynira. "In honoring your guest, your servants honor you, Grand Duchess."

Gwynira flashed him a tight smile over the rim of her own goblet. "Their religion precedes my arrival, my lord."

"Please—Aleksi."

She nodded. "Aleksi. As Jaspar has demonstrated, some of the Imperial nobles find the local beliefs provincial and silly. But I see no harm in them. Let them have their myths, their legends. It's all the same to me."

Naia set the bracelet aside. "Do you know much about it?" she asked Gwynira. "The old religion?"

"Just a bit. Like most other island nations, they worshipped the sea." She gestured toward her seneschal. "It's honestly more Jaspar's area of expertise than mine."

His condescending smile somehow grew even more smug. Einar gripped his goblet to keep from forming a fist as Jaspar leaned forward, his eager attention fixed on Naia. "It's actually quite fascinating. Most of the primitive religions encountered during the Empire's expansion faded away once the natives were exposed to proper civilization."

Einar thought of the stories Petya had told him. The poetry. The songs sung in a soft voice as the movement of the ship rocked them to sleep. Songs from a people who had loved the sea and known its rhythms in a way no *civilized* citizen of the Empire could imagine.

Jaspar's nauseating little speech continued. "But the natives of Akeisa clung to their goddess mythology, even after being brought under the grace of Imperial knowledge."

What a gentle way to describe a brutal war of conquest that had lasted three bloody generations.

"They even say that this goddess once walked among them, long before the founding of the Empire, though why she vanished is up for considerable debate. Convenient that she disappeared before anyone could verify her existence."

"How odd of you, to scorn the notion of a living god," Naia noted icily, "when you currently dine with several."

A wise man would have heard the warning in her voice, but Jaspar would not be put off, and his belittling laugh grated Einar's nerves. "Personally, I've always suspected they clung so hard to their goddess because their cowardly king betrayed them in the end."

Pain sliced through Einar, opening a wound he'd thought scabbed over since childhood. The goblet dimpled under his fingers as Jaspar continued his story in the voice of someone recounting a tremendous victory. "The Great General Akeisa had surrounded the island and demanded that the tyrant king submit to Imperial peace. Of course, the coward refused."

Soft fingers brushed Einar's arm. He looked over into Naia's concerned face, then followed her gaze to his hand. Wine had spilled over the edges of the crushed goblet, splashing down his hand to paint the white tablecloth like a puddle of blood.

He unflexed one finger at a time, forcing himself to release the goblet. To take the napkin Naia offered him. To wipe the wine from fingers that trembled with the force of his anger. It built and built, a pressure inside of him with no outlet.

And Jaspar didn't even notice. He was too tied up in the grisly details of the Empire's grand triumph. "The tyrant king and his queen spent the lives of their people recklessly, in order to buy themselves time to gather their hoarded wealth and flee."

Einar's rage boiled up, like the places deep in the sea where the earth cracked and scalding water bubbled, heated by the heartbeat of their world.

"It was pointless in the end, of course," the seneschal confided in a gleeful voice. "But their actions cost countless native lives."

"Actually, the queen died first."

The words burst from Einar on a cresting wave. Then it broke, and silence flooded the room. Every eye turned to him, where he sat with his wine-soaked napkin gripped in one fist.

Jaspar persisted. "I studied Imperial history at the Scholar's Guild in Kasther. I know the founding story of every kingdom in the Empire. I assure you, the rulers fled the island, forsaking their people."

There was nothing Einar could say. No reason he should know the truth—no reason that wouldn't cause a diplomatic incident, in any case. From the way Gwynira was studying him now, her gaze positively chilly, he might have already done so.

It hurt to grind out the words, but he forced himself to do it. "If you say so."

"On the contrary," Gwynira countered. "I'd like the version *you've* heard, Captain Einar. If you would be so kind as to indulge me."

Oh, yes. That was suspicion in her eyes. How many of the old stories persisted? Did she *know*? Petya had always told him that he looked exactly like his father, and if any paintings had survived . . .

He met Aleksi's eyes and saw the same curiosity Gwynira had professed echoed in their depths.

Perhaps it wouldn't matter, either way. The urge to correct the man's vile lies was too strong. Straightening in his chair, Einar stared directly into Jaspar's eyes. "There was no slaughter that day. No sacrifice of their people, though their subjects were willing enough. The king and queen ordered them all to flee. To hide. And, if the worst came, to survive the day's storms and live under the invader's rule if they must. But to *live*."

"Impossible," Jaspar snapped. "There was a battle. Hundreds of good Imperial soldiers gave their lives to liberate this island."

"Yes," Einar agreed evenly. "There was a battle. The queen was goddess-touched, like her father before her. She was stronger than any human soldier, and far deadlier with a blade. And she knew that the first thing any invading Imperial army intended to do was slaughter the ruling family. So she met the assassins at the gates of the castle."

The seneschal scoffed. "One woman? Against a hundred of the Empire's best soldiers?"

"One queen," Einar corrected in a deadly quiet voice. "One woman touched by a power beyond herself. *She* destroyed the invaders. To buy time."

Jaspar was actually flushed with outrage now. "Time for what? For the king to flee? I know for a *fact* that he was caught on a royal sloop, trying to escape with the bulk of the treasury."

If he closed his eyes, Einar would see Petya's face. The tears that came every time she described that moment. King Consort Vylanar, casting off from the docks one last time, charging Petya to obey her queen's final command.

Knowing that the order would be *his* final command.

Einar made his voice like ice, unwilling to share that pain with the nobles hanging on his every word. "Yes. The king boarded a ship marked with the family crest, carrying enough riches to distract any greedy general, and sailed directly into the enemy's arms. Hardly the actions of a man attempting escape."

Daughter of Tides

"I suppose you think it was some daring last stand." Jaspar sipped his wine, clearly trying to hide his anger beneath a display of haughty condescension. "You're as gullible as the locals. Perhaps I should direct you to one of their taverns. You'd probably find the company more to your tastes."

"Jaspar." Gwynira's single word froze the man's features. But she focused on Einar. "Tell us, Captain. What *was* the king doing?"

Einar was surprised frost wasn't covering the water glasses at the table. It was foolish to answer, but they were past the point of caution. "He was giving General Akeisa a target too tempting to ignore."

Movement at his side drew his attention to Naia. Her eyes had gone wide, and she stared at him with an understanding that ripped away any pretense. She knew, as they all soon would. Einar watched her as he spoke the words. "He turned himself into bait, because six of the Queen's Guard had taken the infant prince to a hidden cove and then sailed north, into the Storm God's Maze."

A few whispers rose from the diners closest to the high table, and even the other guests seemed to sense the tension. But silence descended around those closest to Einar, like a fog blanketing a harbor.

Naia reached for him, then stopped short, her hand hovering over his.

That near touch seemed to snap the seneschal's final hold on his temper. "Pretty words, but they're only that. It makes for a lovely legend, I'll grant you, but it has no basis in reality."

"Are you so certain, Jaspar?" Gwynira's voice remained casual, almost disinterested.

"Of *what*, Grand Duchess? That this . . . childish fantasy of heroes and rescues is just that?"

"General Akeisa mounted a brutal assault, that much is true, and the early years of his occupation were equally destructive. Half of the palace had been reduced to rubble by the time he was done with it, and the stewards who followed him were even worse. But a few of the royal family's possessions still remained by the time I arrived." Gwynira's gaze had grown sharp enough to sever an artery. "I wondered, you know. Why you looked so familiar."

A plate clattered. One of the servants started to drop into a curtsy, but another grabbed their arm and hauled them upright with a fearful look at Gwynira.

She pushed her chair back and rose. Her frozen gaze fell on Aleksi. "I believe we should discuss this in private. I'll see you in my personal receiving room."

Guards scrambled to open the massive doors as she swept toward the back of the room, with Arktikos towering protectively at her side.

Sir Jaspar *still* couldn't seem to stop talking. "If you think I'll accept your credentials as some long-lost barbarian prince—"

Einar's chair scraped loudly over the stone as he shoved it back and tossed down the wine-stained napkin. "I don't give a fuck what you do and do not accept."

The seneschal's face turned a furious red that did his elaborate clothing no favors. Einar ignored the whispers and stares and even Naia's plaintive voice as he stormed from the dining hall.

Einar only made it two steps before Aleksi caught his arm. *"Stop."*

Every muscle in his body tensed. The instinctive urge to tear his arm free was tempered by the knowledge that the Lover's lean body and easy demeanor hid the strength of a god who had walked this world for at least a thousand years longer than Einar. Aleksi could likely pin him face down on the floor with very little effort.

It was madness to want to test that, but at least a bruising fight might give the confusion and rage churning through him an outlet.

Aleksi's furious expression both invited and forbade such an outlet. "What were you thinking?" he demanded.

Naia stepped forward. "Aleksi—"

"No," he interrupted. "He owes us this conversation. In fact, he owed it to us before we arrived. You know how this *looks*, Einar—the exiled prince coming home right when Gwynira's at her most vulnerable. And to have the supposed diplomat bring you here?"

"I'm not a prince," Einar growled. "I've *never* been a prince. My parents' country died when I was weeks old. My first memories are of a fishing boat and an empty belly. It shouldn't matter."

"And yet you know it does. You saw Naia's gifts. The old religion lives still."

More strongly than he'd ever imagined, apparently. And the truth of that slashed through his anger. "Why?"

"Why what?"

"*Why* does the old religion still live? Because Jaspar is a sniveling little shit, but he was right about one thing. The Empire obliterates the local customs and cultures in every place they conquer." Einar turned to fully face Aleksi. "I thought they would have done the same here."

Aleksi shook his head. "What lives in men's hearts cannot be eradicated by force, and trying will only drive it deeper, right into the soul. It merely becomes *secret*, whispered but no less real."

"But it's *not* secret here." Einar waved a hand at Naia's necklace, where the frosted teal glass seemed to shimmer against her skin. "That's goddess-touched sea glass. The shark's teeth are for protection. The brass shell is the ancient sigil of the goddess. If I'd known it was like *this*, all out in the open—"

The words *I wouldn't have come* balanced on the tip of his tongue, but with the Lover's brutally observant gaze fixed on his face, he was terrified to speak them.

Terrified they would be a lie—one he wouldn't just be telling Aleksi and Naia, but himself.

Aleksi stepped closer, crowding out that broken silence, and reached for Einar. For his *face*, cupping it in his hands with a gentle care that belied his intensity. Aleksi stared into Einar's wide eyes for a moment, then leaned in to rest his forehead against his. The presence that had so overwhelmed the Lover's borrowed clothing could bolster, too. The *feel* of the other man curled around Einar, a power that transcended seduction, that went so much deeper than yearning.

When the Lover made you the center of his attention, it was as if the world itself embraced you—and you would give anything to cling to that feeling for just one heartbeat more.

"Tell me true," Aleksi whispered, the words singing in Einar's blood. "Did you come here in service of Dianthe, or to take back your home, no matter the cost?"

Einar couldn't even remember how to lie. Truth tumbled from his lips, and he was only grateful that the truth was what Aleksi wanted to hear. "My only home is my ship," he rasped. "I grieve the loss of what was because the women who raised me grieve it, but it was never mine. I'm here to carry you and Naia to safety if Gwynira turns on you. Which she may be about to do."

"No." Aleksi straightened. "Leave the Grand Duchess to me." Then he turned sharply on his heel and strode away.

The abrupt loss of the Lover's attentions made Einar's world tilt drunkenly. He slammed a hand against the wall and struggled to ground himself. But he was too far from the sea, too far from the source of *his* power. The only thing that lay beneath him was cold stone and frozen earth . . . and the bones of the parents he couldn't remember.

"Einar?"

He spread his fingers against the icy wall and drew in a shuddering breath. "I should have told you both."

"I don't give a damn about that." Her voice drew closer. "Are you all right?"

"I needed a moment to catch my breath." Einar forced himself to stand and face her, to weather the soft concern in those haunting eyes. "The Lover sometimes forgets his own strength, I think. Maybe the rest of us do, too."

"That's not—" She shook her head. "The *horrible* things Jaspar said about your family . . . I'm so sorry."

Something cracked inside him, a pain impossibly sharp and gone in the next moment. But it echoed through him, like the sound a glacier made when the ice began to fracture. Maybe it was his frozen heart, trying desperately to beat.

"I never knew them," he said hoarsely, and he could hear the lie trembling beneath the words, the grief and the rage. No amount of distance could diminish the fact that Jaspar's ancestors had slaughtered the family that Einar *should* have had. He cleared his throat and tried again. "I know what lies the Empire tells about the people they've conquered. I should have been prepared."

"For *that*? How could you possibly be?"

Because he was over two thousand years old. Because mortals with their swift, abrupt lives moved past grief, didn't they? It shouldn't still hurt like this. It *hadn't* hurt like this—the stories Petya had told him could have been any other ancient legend, tales of great heroes who might not even have existed at all.

But then he'd set foot on this island. He'd breathed in the sea air, heard the song of the waves against the sand. He'd seen the tokens of a goddess who should have been erased and yet somehow seemed to thrive.

"They were never *real* to me before," he whispered, the words escaping on a swell of raw honesty. "None of it was. But now . . ."

Naia reached for him. His entire body tensed, and he fought a brief war within himself—pull away from the kindness that would only deepen his vulnerability? Or take advantage of her compassion to learn the feel of her body against his?

A heartbeat later, it didn't matter. Her arms curled around him, surprisingly strong as she tugged him into her embrace. And it didn't matter that there were half a dozen layers of clothing between them, or that the thickly embroidered fabric of her gown was so stiff that he could barely feel the curve of her body against his, or that their skin wasn't actually touching anywhere.

She ran her fingers lightly up his spine, and the contact burned as hot as if they were naked. She pressed her cheek against his shoulder, and he barely noticed the jabbing pressure of that ridiculous headdress when the intoxicating smell of her hair surrounded him. He knew the scent must be something floral, something that had grown on the land, but he dragged her into his lungs and heard the roar of the sea and the crash of waves, felt the sun beating down on his bare back in the moments before he dove deep beneath the surface and the glorious chill of the ocean embraced him.

Naia was familiar to him in a way that defied logic or reason. It felt as if she'd been wrapping her arms around him just like this for centuries beyond numbering.

"What was it called?" she whispered. "Your home."

"Rahvekya," he rasped.

With the sweet kiss of her power curling around him, Einar didn't care about politics. He didn't care about diplomacy or the war or the Siren's likely rage or even the futility of trying to be a man who could stay beyond the dawn.

The woman in his arms felt like home, and he'd gladly drown in her and pay the price.

Chapter Eleven

There are many contradictory stories about the day Akeisa fell. Official Imperial history tells us that King Vylanar was captured while abandoning his people on a ship filled with riches. I suspect this to be an embellishment of General Akeisa's meant to demoralize the local population. However, local legends of the King's bravery are equally suspect. An objective scholar must acknowledge the most likely truth: the King and Queen were given ample time to agree to a peaceful resolution and the full benefits of Imperial citizenship, and in their stubborn shortsightedness condemned their people to a bloody and ultimately futile battle.

Akeisa: A Comprehensive History (Volume Two)
by Guildmaster Klement

Gwynira's study wasn't a large or particularly welcoming room. It was . . . generic. There were no personal touches, nothing to suggest that her preferences had in any way materially altered it. It featured a large fireplace, rather too large for the room, with several chairs arranged near it, an imposing desk, and shelves laden with books set into the stone walls. Everything was rather dull looking, though

Aleksi supposed that was more to blame on his fading vision than on Gwynira's listless attempts at decorating. A gargantuan fish with a vicious spike protruding from its head had been mounted and hung above the fireplace, and the main part of the floor had been covered with what looked like the skin of a North Sea tiger.

Or perhaps these poor dead animals *were* her bloodthirsty personal touches. That would certainly make his job—convincing her not to murder him and his envoy on the spot—a bit more difficult.

But Aleksi had always enjoyed a challenge. He spared the tiger's snarling face a grimace of commiseration, then cleared his throat. "Reporting as requested, Grand Duchess. We need to talk."

Gwynira turned, not moving from her spot before the fireplace. She was flanked by her guard, who glowered silently, and her seneschal, who was rather more vocal with his displeasure.

"You have some nerve," he spat as he stalked toward the door. "To come here and make *demands*—"

"No, he's right, Jaspar," Gwynira cut in calmly. "We *do* need to talk."

The guard spoke for the first time, his voice low and rumbling. "Your guest is armed, Your Grace. Unacceptable."

"But easily remedied. Arktikos, was it?" Aleksi unbuckled the belt around his hips and held it out along with his scabbard. "Please, take it."

The hulking man accepted the scabbard and examined it, as if it might explode in his mistress's hands. Finally, reluctantly, he bowed his head and presented it to Gwynira.

Rather than taking it, she pulled the sword from its scabbard and regarded it thoughtfully. Reflections of the firelight danced off the blade as she hummed. "Created by magic?"

"Merely enchanted," Aleksi answered. "The blade itself was crafted long ago, by the finest bladesmith in the Sheltered Lands. My friend Inga layered in spells to make it lighter and stronger, but the sword's functionality is unchanged. It is exactly as it appears—a sword."

"Inga," she repeated. "I know that name. She's also called the Witch." Gwynira's gaze flicked up to Aleksi's face. "Sorin had one of those."

"I remember." He managed to suppress a shudder, but his voice almost cracked, so he took a moment to steady it. "I believe we both do."

"Indeed." Gwynira placed the naked blade on the small table between the two chairs. "For your sake, I hope yours is nothing like Varoka."

Had that been her name? Aleksi had never even wondered, only referred to her in the screaming quiet of his mind as *the Betrayer's witch*.

"No," he said finally. "Inga is fascinated by possibilities, and her curiosity knows no bounds. But she's a healer, and she isn't cruel. She would never knowingly inflict harm on another without very good reason."

Gwynira tilted her head. "You don't believe Varoka had *very good reason* to harm you?"

"Of course she did. War is war, after all. But she did not seem to mind that you were also on the field of battle, and would be harmed by her strike." He shook his head. "Inga would never sacrifice one of her friends."

She laughed. "Presuming, of course, that Varoka and I fit in that category."

"Not a safe presumption, I take it?"

"Far from." She gestured to one of the chairs. "Do sit." As Aleksi complied, she turned to her seneschal and watchful guard. "Leave us."

Sir Jaspar protested at once. "Your Grace, surely you don't—"

"Why, Jaspar." She eyed him mildly. "If I did not know better, I might think you considered me unequal to the task before me and in desperate need of your particular assistance."

"Of course not—"

"Then perhaps you think I cannot fend off a single unarmed attacker." Her eyes flashed. "That I need your very human protection."

103

He blanched. "I would never—"

"Excellent. Then I will see you in the morning."

The man huffed with agitation—and pinned Aleksi with a vicious glare—but he did as she bade, leaving the room after a quick, almost violent bow.

The hulking guard was silent, but no less reluctant to quit the room. He simply stared at Gwynira with patent concern and did not move.

Finally, she sighed softly. "Go, Arktikos. It will be fine."

The gentle urging worked. He nodded once and followed after Jaspar, closing the door quietly behind him.

"It will be, will it not?" Gwynira asked as she retrieved two glasses and began to fill both with a rich red liquid from an ornate crystal decanter. "Fine, that is. Or have I lied most egregiously to my personal guard?"

At least Aleksi had the truth on his side. "I wish you no harm. Sachielle considers you a friend, and who am I to argue with the Dream?"

Gwynira passed him one of the drinks. "And what of your companion?"

"Einar?" The liquid, which turned out to be wine, was almost thick with cold, and Aleksi realized that the decanter was not crystal at all, but ice. "He has sworn to me that he came here only as a servant of the Siren. This is his family's homeland, yes, but not his. Not anymore."

She settled into the chair opposite his. "And you believe him? You *trust* him?"

"I do. On both counts."

His sword still gleamed on the table between them, and Gwynira's shrewd gaze lingered on it as she swirled the wine in her glass. "And your other companion? The nymph?"

"Naia? She is a young god, new born and—as I am sure you noticed—rather guileless."

"Or a truly superb actress."

Oh, Aleksi should have seen this coming. Einar may have had the might of tradition and birthright behind him, but Naia possessed the sort of sheer power that could challenge a god. "She means you no harm, either."

Gwynira tilted her head back and forth as she considered that. "Well, she *did* begin her diplomatic visit with a grand display of force."

Truth, Aleksi. "She was worried," he told Gwynira softly. "Anxious that she not appear weak, lest that weakness endanger her friends in the future."

"And you and the long-lost prince allowed her to take sole responsibility for your collective safety?"

"Not us," he corrected. "I mean her particular friends, Sachi and Zanya."

Gwynira laughed again. "And how exactly am I to harm Creation itself? Menace the very embodiment of Destruction?"

He sipped his wine. "Your former emperor did a fine job of both."

All traces of amusement fled, and Gwynira pulsed red, sharp and metallic, like biting a fork. Like blood. "Sorin created me," she said stiffly. "I never had a choice of whether to associate with him. Can *you* say the same?"

"No, I cannot." The memories had been somewhat dulled by the passage of thousands of years, but Aleksi could still remember Sorin as he had been—*the Builder*. Strong, capable. He had been good, once, back before envy and thwarted ambitions had twisted him into something violent and unrecognizable. "I'm sorry."

Gwynira blinked at him, startled. "For what?"

"I don't know," he admitted. "That you *didn't* have that choice, perhaps. Or that you never had a chance to know him . . . before."

She flashed red again, an emotion beyond anger or rage. Pure, bloody hatred. And she whispered her answer with the fervency of a dying prayer. "I wish I'd never known him at all."

There was a deep well of loss inside her, a chasm of pain so agonizing and endless that Aleksi wanted to turn away from it. Instead, he caught and held her gaze. "I don't blame you one bit."

For several long moments, silence. Then Gwynira looked away. "So. You have known betrayal—for that *is* what you call Sorin, yes? The Betrayer?" At Aleksi's nod, she pursed her lips. "Did you verify the exiled prince's claims, then? Peer into his soul and pluck the truth from his heart?"

"I did not."

She exhaled sharply. "No, I suppose you wouldn't. That's what I've heard, anyway—not without his consent."

He could not let *that* stand. "One cannot consent to such intrusion. The mere act of asking is tantamount to coercion. Only after a ready and eager invitation would I ever even *consider* it."

"I see. So if this scorpion *does* sting, he shall sting us both." She smiled. "Acceptable."

Aleksi wanted to argue, but thought better of it. He imagined this was precisely how Sorin's court had operated—through the security and threatened assurance of mutual annihilation. It would be familiar to her, comforting in its own way.

Satisfied, Gwynira finished her wine and leaned forward, as if to set her empty glass on the table between them. But her gaze snagged once more on his sword, and she froze as another wave of pain filled the stiflingly hot air between them. The furious red remained, only now it was streaked through with onyx sorrow.

"It's a lovely blade," she murmured. "Truly exquisite work. I've not seen its equal since . . ."

She lapsed into heavy silence, the kind that brimmed with confessions. Aleksi could almost hear their desperate wings fluttering against the cage of secrecy, and he held his tongue. Just in case.

But she only shook her head and reached once more for the frosty decanter. "Shall we drink more?"

Gwynira's pain was familiar, a place and a song and a feeling as fixed in Aleksi's memory as his own face. She had lost someone dear to her, the love of her life—just as he once had. But though Aleksi still felt his long-dead lover's absence, his pain had been transmuted by the years, had both deepened and mellowed into a bittersweet sort of ache. Gwynira's remained sharp, discordant. A jagged, freely bleeding wound that had not knitted up, much less healed.

But she said no more, and Aleksi followed her lead. He finished his wine and offered his glass to her with a nod. "Yes, let's."

Chapter Twelve

It might be easy to dismiss local legends of the island being a paradise before the "loss" of their goddess, but my colleagues interested in the study of the natural world tell me that the rings of the ancient fir trees at the heart of the island do indicate that Akeisa was not always the frozen world we see now.

Akeisa: A Comprehensive History (Volume One)
by Guildmaster Klement

The water was rising fast.

Naia huddled against the ribs of the hull as the water lapped around her calves, her desperate gaze locked on the closed hatch at the other end of the hold. To reach it would mean potential survival, but by the time she managed to draw in a single ragged breath, the water had reached the tops of her thighs.

Too fast for escape, but plenty slow enough for regret. She hated that her life would end this way—away from her family, in a ship that belonged to someone else. There were so many things she should have done, and now—

The water covered her mouth, surged into her nose. Filled her.

And now there was no more time.

Naia jerked out of the nightmare, her heart pounding and her fists clenched. She panted for breath as tears tracked down her temples and into her damp hair.

Not a nightmare. She'd had one or two of those after the final battle against Sorin, confusing tangles of fear and surreal danger from which she had struggled in vain to wake. Unlike those labyrinths of terror, this had felt *very* real.

A memory, then.

Her chest ached, and more tears leaked from her eyes as she closed them to whisper a small prayer for the drowned sailor. She didn't know who they were or when they'd lived and died, but she knew that their final moments had passed in paralyzing fear and aching solitude. That their last thoughts had been of a home they would never again see or touch or taste.

Sleep was an impossibility now, and she knew better than to try. Naia slipped from her bed. In the dim light of the nearly dead fire, she found her robe and slippers, but left the heavy cloak in the wardrobe as she reached for a lamp. She seemed to be acclimating to the frigid temperatures faster than she'd anticipated—not that she needed warmer clothing just to roam the halls of Gwynira's palace.

She hesitated just outside, her hand still on the latch as she gazed down the darkened corridor toward Einar's room. She longed to see him, but she couldn't intrude and possibly interrupt his sleep. He wouldn't mind, but he *would* make assumptions about why she'd come, and he wouldn't even be wrong.

The day had been too full of emotion to make rash decisions. They both deserved better. So she headed in the opposite direction, passing by closed doors and peeking through open doorways until she found a library.

She drifted in, taking in the shadowed space. It was a small, round room, dominated by a hearth and an arrangement of reading chairs. Every single bit of wall space had been built up with stone shelves, and the shelves were filled with books.

It was exactly the sort of place Naia required—cozy and secure, with a thousand tiny distractions at hand, just in case she needed them. She set the lamp on a small table and sank into one of the reading chairs. The leather was cool through the twin layers of thin fabric she wore, and she shivered.

Soft footsteps pricked her ears a moment before a flash of movement drew her gaze. A servant walked past, knelt before the hearth, and began to lay a fire.

"You don't have to do that," Naia protested.

"It's no trouble, my lady," he rumbled.

He actually sounded *sincere*, not at all as if he had to reassure her or potentially face his mistress's wrath. As the tiny flames began to take hold and grow stronger, another servant entered, this one bearing a shining silver tray. She placed an engraved carafe and a mug on the table next to Naia's lamp. Silently, she poured a measure of dark liquid into the mug and pressed it into Naia's hands.

The metal was warm to the touch, and the scent of spiced wine filled Naia's senses. "Thank you."

The woman nodded and stepped back, the now empty tray clutched in front of her like a shield. She stared at Naia with wide eyes until the other servant rose, his task complete, and joined her.

The silence grew heavy—not with expectation, as if they were waiting for Naia to speak again or offer them something in reward for their efforts, but with something even more profound. They stood there as if watching her *was* their reward, and Naia finally recognized the emotion hanging in the firelit room.

It was faith. The fervency of *belief*.

She thanked them again, her words falling into the dim room like rain onto upturned faces. "If I need anything else, I'll be sure to call."

The man bowed his head, but a bright, relieved smile curved the woman's lips. "We are honored to be able to give thanks for Her blessed intercession."

Naia could clearly hear the elevated importance placed on the pronoun: *Her.* But before she could ask for clarification of those cryptic words, if they spoke of their long-dead goddess, the two servants melted into the darkness of the hallway, leaving her alone with the fire and her thoughts.

She should have expected the dreams to surface here. She wasn't sure why some places seemed louder than others, almost closer to the Dream itself, but she could certainly feel it here. It had been the same in the Burning Hills, when they had camped at the Phoenix's Tower during Sachi's progress through the Sheltered Lands. Snatches of emotion had seemed to echo off those sun-scorched cliffs, battering Naia from all directions.

Perhaps this island was like the Burning Hills, and it simply held too many memories to be contained.

A low whistling echoed through the hall, and Naia turned just in time to see Aleksi saunter past the open doorway, looking rumpled but definitely in one piece.

The sound abruptly stopped, and he ducked his head back, a quizzical look furrowing his brow. "Naia? You're up late. Does your room not suit?"

"The room is fine." She shook her head. "I couldn't sleep, that's all."

"Ah." He entered the room, studying it as he crossed the stone floor. He pulled a hand from his pants pocket and indicated the chair closest to hers. "May I join you?"

"Of course."

He'd shed his jacket as well as his tunic, leaving him in a gauzy undershirt that resembled a shorter version of the garment Naia had been provided to wear under her dress. The fabric was finely woven but plain, unadorned even by buttons. Instead, it fastened at the neck and wrists with simple ribbon ties. It looked out of place with his formal gold-embroidered pants and the firelight glinting off his jewel-encrusted shoes.

He should have looked ridiculous, not handsome enough to steal a person's breath. But that was Aleksi, wasn't it? Even the scant few human foibles and flaws that the rest of the High Court retained did not seem to plague him. He was pure physical perfection, enticing and untouchable.

"Have you—?" Her voice came out too high, almost breathless, and Naia cleared her throat. "Did you just leave the Grand Duchess?"

"I did." He settled into the chair with a sigh. "We came to an accord."

Naia arched an eyebrow and waited.

The corner of his mouth quirked up. "We also drank quite a lot."

"Evidently." She wanted to press him for details, but that felt far too revealing, so she sipped her wine.

Aleksi changed the subject. "Why could you not sleep?"

"No reason," she deflected. "It's nothing."

But his dark eyes saw too much. "Bad dreams?" he asked gently. "Or perhaps memories?"

The question startled Naia into a nod. "Memories, yes. From the Dream."

"Tell me?"

Naia took a moment to order her thoughts. "They're always present, but usually . . . hazy. Like something I knew once but have forgotten." She swallowed hard. "Not here."

"Some places do bring them up more readily than others," he whispered. His expression softened until only the mere hint of a smile remained. "I remember. It was unimaginably difficult. Suffering the throes of longings and pangs of heartache that weren't mine, not really, but also—"

"Are a part of you, just the same," she finished, dazed. "You were never human?"

He hummed and shook his head. "No. I was born of the Dream, just like you. A being of belief."

Naia's heart thudded painfully in her breast. It had never occurred to her that he might not have come into his power like the rest of the High Court, in a violent manifestation during a low moment of very human desperation. She leaned forward, eager for . . . what? His advice? His tutelage?

Perhaps simply to connect with someone else like *her*.

"How did you learn to manage it?" she choked out finally. "All the feelings and memories that weren't yours?"

"Badly," he admitted. "My first few decades were a disaster. I was easily overwhelmed, and there were times I could barely hold myself together. But I had help, Naia. And so will you."

It should have sounded like a platitude, an empty reassurance that would amount to nothing of substance. But when Aleksi spoke, it was *impossible* not to believe him. Every aspect of his being screamed sincerity, as if he was made of the sort of honesty that could only be found in intimacy. His voice was a quiet conversation in the dark, sometimes painful and revealing but always, *always* full of absolute truth.

So she offered him the truth in return. "It helps just to know," she admitted. "That there's someone else who understands, I mean."

"I do." Then his smile reappeared in brilliant force, an expression that bolstered Naia's spirits just as much as his next words. "For the record? You're handling all this much better than I ever did."

It made so much sense to her now, why Aleksi had suffered so during that final battle against the Empire, when he and the others had been cut off from the Dream. Naia had escaped the same painful fate only through circumstance, because she and Einar had been closer to the ship than to the heart of the conflict at the time.

The other members of the High Court had managed to fight through it, perhaps because that removal was not new to them. They already knew what it was to understand the Dream as a distant concept rather than the very core of who they were. But the attack had nearly felled Aleksi, and no wonder. The Dream was all he'd ever known, and to have it wrenched away like that . . .

Currents of sympathy swirled around Naia's heart, and she started to reach out to him.

But suddenly, Aleksi's smile turned wicked. Mischievous. "You haven't asked about Einar yet. A supreme act of willpower."

A blush washed over her. "You said you and Gwynira had reached an accord. I assumed that meant—"

"Worry not, little nymph," he murmured. "Your lover is safe."

The word alone made Naia blush even hotter. "He is *not* my lover."

Aleksi arched one perfect, incredulous brow. "Are you suggesting that I wouldn't know? Am I not the expert here?"

There was no argument to be made there, nothing she could say to effectively deny his claim. What did *she* know of love? All she had were the vague memories of a thousand dead Dreamers . . . and a yearning that all too often left her weak-kneed and aching.

"He is your lover," Aleksi said again, "and I am glad of it. I would tease you mercilessly about taming the Kraken, but I cannot. It is good to see. Einar has been alone and lonely for *far* too long."

There was an almost wistful note in the observation, and it gave Naia pause. She'd underestimated Aleksi before—no, that was inaccurate. She had never discounted his power or his dedication or his sincerity. She simply had not considered his emotions, or even that he might *have* them. She had not thought of him as a person, but as an ideal, and the realization shamed her.

But she was a quick learner. Instead of dwelling on her mistake, she tilted her head and looked at Aleksi—truly *looked at him*—for the very first time. Pain bracketed his eyes as he stared into the fire, distant memories haunting his gaze.

And she found herself asking him the most ridiculous question. "Have you ever been in love?"

"Once." The word left his lips as a barely audible whisper. "Just once."

Daughter of Tides

How could that be? Not only was Aleksi thousands of years old, he was the god of love, a Dream-born manifestation of the emotion. Loving was not second nature to him. It was his first nature. His only.

But he had not said that he hadn't loved freely, eagerly, just that he had been *in love* only once. And it made a strange sort of sense. He was more than the Lover, after all; he was also a *man*, not through birth but through lived experience. And didn't the poets and bards often speak of the elusive nature of true and abiding love?

The pain in his eyes had not diminished, and Naia sucked in a breath. "You don't have to—"

But Aleksi was already speaking—softly. Carefully. "Her name was Alysaia. She was one of Ash's consorts. This was long before they learned to fear him as a matter of course, but Alys . . . was shy and nervous. So Ash asked for my help. Could I set her at ease so that they might get to know one another properly?"

"I see."

"Do you?" A wry smile twisted his lips. "It worked, of course. They got along famously. For a while, it was all good fun."

Naia's blush returned. She had been at Aleksi's villa during Sachi's progress, and had attended the Union Day celebration under the moons and the stars. She had watched as Aleksi had seduced Sachi, Ash, *and* Zanya by putting his hands and mouth all over the writhing, panting princess while her lovers drank in the sounds of her helpless moans.

Naia knew well how Aleksi defined *good fun*.

Aleksi huffed out a quiet laugh. "I see that look, little nymph. You may blush to recall my many debaucheries, but how did *you* spend that evening?" He leaned forward, bracing his elbow on one knee. "Naked between several members of the Raven Guard, from what I remember."

Yes, she had spent that night in a dizzying whirl of discovery. She had tasted desire, learned what it was to give and receive pleasure. It had been new and old, all at once, a familiar melody with words she had yet to hear.

115

Then the true import of his words hit her, and she met his gaze. She had not known he'd ever taken notice of her. Why would he? "You were watching me?"

He didn't look away. "My attention is often drawn to beautiful things."

There was that breathtaking sincerity again, only this time, it was wrapped in a low voice, potent and smooth, like spiced honey. It was a voice made for the deepest embraces in the quiet of the night, for secret promises and seduction.

Naia wasn't immune. His words shivered up her spine. For a moment, she remembered that night, the moons and the stars. Imagined herself in Sachi's place.

She shuddered. And still, Aleksi held her gaze, almost daring her to . . . what? Break first? Or never, ever look away at all?

Naia's skin felt too tight. The room was suddenly hot, the fire stifling, and she closed her eyes because she had to. Because she had no idea what would happen if she didn't.

"What—?" Her voice rasped, cracked. "What came to pass? Between you and Alysaia?"

He hummed, the sound rumbling through the still, close room. "We became fast friends. Somewhere, in the middle of everything, we became more. Before long, she had moved into my villa, and every day was just as good as the first. We laughed, danced. Cried." He paused. "It was perfect."

Naia's mind reeled at the revelation. "Was Aoh upset?"

Aleksi chuckled, more fondness than mirth in the sound. "Of course not. His heart is too big for that. No, he was happy for us."

"And then what happened?"

There was the grief again, wreathing Aleksi like smoke. "What always happens to humans. We had seventy-four years together, and she died in my arms."

His voice hitched on the final words, as if the pain had contracted around him, no longer distant or faded or vague but as fresh as a new, bleeding wound.

Naia *did* reach for him this time, wrapping her fingers tight around his. "I'm so sorry, Aleksi."

"Don't be, love. Not for me." He drew her hand to his lips, kissed the backs of her fingers. "It was worth every moment—before, during, and since. Even with the pain, I would not trade those years for anything in all the Dream."

The absolute conviction with which he spoke rattled Naia, made her hunger for something—*anything*—that unshakable. It was the very thing she'd longed for, this living devotion that still shone in Aleksi's eyes.

He kissed her hand again, this time with finality, and released her. "Good night. Do try to get some sleep, Naia."

With that, he left. Confused and flustered, Naia sat, tears burning her eyes, marveling at how cold the room seemed now, though the fire still blazed merrily in the hearth. Aleksi had spoken with such certainty, such boundless depth of emotion. And just one question kept circling in Naia's mind, slipping away only to form again almost instantly.

What would it be like, to be loved like that?

Chapter Thirteen

Of all the animals unique to this island, perhaps none is more spectacular than the giant reindeer of the northeast plains. Despite the Empire's best efforts to breed and raise these marvelous creatures in captivity, they thrive only here, on this frozen island.

Akeisa: A Study of Flora and Fauna
by Guildmaster Klement

Restless music haunted Einar's dreams.

Others might have called it the song of the Siren. Certainly that was what sailors imagined when the sea sang to them with an irresistible voice. When it curled around them, whispering promises of the ecstasy they could only know once the water closed over their head and they sank into the ocean's sweet embrace.

Einar knew the Siren personally. Dianthe was compelling, it was true. She was as glorious as the ocean—vast and untouchable, unfathomable and sometimes cold. But the Siren knew power in a way few others could. The waves rose and fell for her pleasure, and the wind spoke with her voice. Dianthe didn't coax. She didn't have to. Dianthe commanded.

The song that wove through Einar's dreams was something else entirely—a sweet caress almost like a lullaby. There were no demands in that gentle melody, just teasing laughter and soothing murmurs, and wrapped through it all was a steely protectiveness that promised safety.

Did Naia know that she reached out to him in her dreams? Was she even reaching out to *him* at all, or did her magic run so deep that it touched everyone? Perhaps it did, and Einar was simply more sensitive to it. He'd always heard the chorus of the tides more clearly than others, even when he'd been nothing more than a mortal fisherman.

Whatever the case, Naia's power was clearly growing. Hardly a surprise, here on an island where people looked upon her and saw ancient myths made real. Their belief thrummed through the palace, building as the stories grew. If Naia was already so strong now, still fresh from the Dream, in a few centuries she would be truly formidable.

And she wanted to protect him.

There'd been protectiveness in the note he'd received from Aleksi last night, too. In swift, elegant strokes, the Lover had reassured him that the situation with Gwynira had been dealt with, but that Einar should stay in his quarters—and away from potential danger—until they could strategize over breakfast in Aleksi's suite.

So much for his role as monster and fearsome bodyguard. Both of his charges seemed more determined to keep him safe. The question of whether he *merited* such protection after hiding the truth had apparently not occurred to either of them—a grace Einar wasn't sure he deserved.

It felt . . . odd. For endless centuries, *he* had been the one doing the protecting. Even Petya and Jinevra, the maternal presences of his youth, were now part of his crew. The power that flowed through him and his ship kept them ageless and strong, but it was the violence of the monster that stirred deep within him that truly brought safety to those in his care.

A monster that a sleeping Naia had curled around in her dreams and stroked into eager submission.

Shaking away the thought, Einar strode into his sitting room. Last night, he'd found the letter from Aleksi on an ornate bronze tray resting on a table just inside the door to his quarters.

This morning, the tray was scattered with tokens.

He paused to sift through the offerings. Some were like those gifted to Naia—precious bits of rare sea glass and brass seashells to honor the goddess. But even more of them held the painfully familiar sigil that flew over his boat. Hammered into silver, cast in brass, carved from driftwood, burned into leather, even molded in the dark, distinctive clay harvested from the beaches at the lowest tides . . .

All bore the fearsome silhouette of the kraken.

Eventually, he would have to explain why to Naia and Aleksi. He owed them the whole truth now. *Especially* Naia. But the emotional wounds from yesterday had barely scabbed over. He wanted nothing more than to fill his belly and figure out how badly he'd fucked up the diplomatic mission—and what he had to endure to make it right.

Naia and Aleksi were already seated at the table in Aleksi's receiving room, an array of silver dishes spread out between them, when Einar arrived. He claimed the empty seat on Aleksi's left and found himself staring across the table at a soft-eyed Naia, who smiled at him.

"Good morning," she greeted him. "How did you sleep?"

Did she know? He examined her face, searching for some hidden message beneath the simple words, but there was nothing there save earnest inquiry. He reached for one of the steaming ceramic pitchers on the table and discovered it filled with a dark tea that smelled strongly of cinnamon. It might have gone down better with a healthy splash of rum, but he poured himself a mug and sipped it before answering. "Probably better than I should have."

"And almost certainly better than *you* did, little nymph," Aleksi murmured.

Naia blushed furiously but said nothing.

"She was uneasy last night." Aleksi poured a small coffee and downed it in one go. "Worried about you."

Protective. Discomfiture was no match for the warmth unspooling within him. "Neither of you needs to spend your time worrying about me. I'm fine."

"Good to know. But I wish you'd said as much before I spent half the night convincing Gwynira that you didn't come here to kill her and usurp her throne."

Aleksi's voice was lightly teasing, but the words still needed to be addressed. "If you have questions . . ." He broke off. Took a deep breath. "I owe you both answers. I should have told you when I realized where we were headed."

"You don't *owe us* any more than we've already learned," Naia countered. "But we're willing to listen. Aren't we, Aleksi?"

He inclined his head. "Always."

He'd never actually *told* the story before—not even to Dianthe. He barely knew where to start. "It's never felt like my story. I was less than a month old. Petya and Jinevra, they're the ones who lived it."

"They've been with you since the beginning?" Naia asked softly.

"Twelve members of the Queen's Guard left the palace that dawn." He stabbed a knife into the tiny little bowl of jam hard enough to scratch it. "Only two survived to see midnight. There should be ballads about the ones who fell. They should be *remembered*. But this is what the Empire does. It takes away your history and your stories."

Aleksi's gentle gaze encouraged him to continue. So he did. "Petya and Jinevra tried to keep them alive by telling me stories. Stories about the island, about my parents and grandparents. About my great-grandparents, who were the first to fight off the Empire's attempts to conquer the land. So many stories . . . but that was all they ever were to me. Legends. Myths."

"This again." Aleksi smiled gently. "Truth can drift in the retelling, it's true. Stories change every time a generation starts and ends. But you had the word of those who were *there*, Einar. The only thing separating truth and myth here is time."

"Not just time," Einar rumbled, giving up on his meal. He wasn't hungry anyway. "There was a wide, endless ocean between the truth and me. Now I'm here, and . . ."

"It hurts," Naia finished for him.

He opened his mouth to agree, but a piercing sound tore through the silence—a horn so loud and deep it seemed to make the very ground tremble.

Naia half rose from her chair. "What in the world is that?"

"Some sort of alarm." Aleksi held out his hand. "Come. We'll see what's the matter."

By the time they reached the door, the hallway had filled with the sound of running footsteps. Servants darted by, arms overflowing with armor and voluminous fur cloaks. Einar fell in behind Aleksi as he and Naia followed the flow of people toward the Great Hall.

Gwynira stood in the center of it, already clad in pristine white trousers and an intricately embossed leather tunic in the same color. She held out her arms absently to allow a servant to buckle a thick woolen cloak around her shoulders, her attention fixed on Arktikos as he bent low to rumble something in her ear.

"Good morning, Grand Duchess," Aleksi greeted. "Or is it? There seems to be something amiss."

She broke off her conversation and turned, her chilly gaze sweeping ruthlessly over Einar before landing on Aleksi. "Nothing that need interrupt your breakfast. A nearby village called Jamyskar is under attack and has called for aid. When I've returned, we can resume our discussions."

"Nonsense. If aid is required, we will also give it."

The seneschal, dressed in armor so shiny Einar knew it had never seen real battle, stepped forward and cleared his throat. "Surely your assistance is not necessary."

Aleksi flashed him a tight smile and held his ground. "Oh, but it is. I insist. If the Grand Duchess rides out to protect her people, she will have the might of the Sheltered Lands behind her, as well."

Gwynira exchanged a silent look with her bodyguard, who appraised the three of them with something almost like approval before nodding once. "Very well," she said abruptly. "I have seen you fight, I won't turn away your help."

Jaspar opened his mouth to protest again, but closed it with a snap of teeth when Gwynira gave him a slashing look and gestured for more cloaks to be brought forward. Einar didn't bother to hide his smile of satisfaction at seeing the man so completely put in his place—especially when the seneschal's furious gaze raked over him.

That one would be trouble.

But not today. Einar pivoted away and fell into step behind Gwynira, who was marching down the length of the Great Hall. Wide double doors were thrown open ahead of her, and a long hallway lined with frigid windows of ice instead of glass gave way to a bustling courtyard.

Huge white reindeer bearing double saddles snorted and pawed at the snow-dusted stones. Naia gasped and approached the nearest one, her hand extended.

"Careful, my lady," Arktikos warned in a rumble. "They're wary of strangers and tend to bite."

But the enormous creature merely nudged her open palm and dipped its head. She stroked her fingers over its velvety muzzle, and it bumped against her, but only to rub its face against her shoulder.

"I wish I had a treat for you," Naia whispered. "Later, I promise."

Einar moved up beside her, unable to contain his own soft wonder as he reached out a careful hand. He froze as the reindeer huffed and cast him a baleful look of warning.

Taking the hint, he let his hand drop to his side. But he still marveled at seeing the giant reindeer from Petya's stories in the flesh. She'd claimed they were taller than a grown man at the shoulder and could outrun the wind, but it had seemed as fanciful as everything else—simply a story.

The truth stood before him, nuzzling Naia's hair.

"He likes you," Arktikos observed. "If you give me leave, I can lift you into the saddle."

Naia flashed him a brilliant smile. "There is no need." She grasped the saddle and the reins and nimbly climbed up, using small footholds that Einar hadn't even noticed. She looked *right* perched on the graceful creature's back, as confidently at home as any of the mounted soldiers— and this time it wasn't only the servants casting her sidelong glances and exchanging furtive murmurs.

Oblivious to the speculative looks, Naia transferred her smile to Einar and reached out. "Will you ride with me, Captain?"

Arktikos had already boosted Gwynira into the saddle and swung up behind her. Aleksi accepted the outstretched hand of a blushing soldier and climbed gracefully into the saddle. Einar's world narrowed to Naia's hand as he reached to accept it, braced against the shock of her skin sliding over his.

Oh, this would be a terrible mistake.

But it was too late to back down. Einar didn't even have a chance to find the footholds. He was still savoring the warmth of her touch when those deceptively slender fingers tightened around his in a stark reminder that no matter how delicate she looked, Naia was a god, born of the Dream, with the strength of a dozen mortals. She lifted him effortlessly, and a moment later he was settled in the saddle behind her, breathless as a schoolboy at the press of her body against his.

Somehow, he found his voice as he laid his hands on her hips. "You would think this isn't your first time at this."

"It's an island, Einar, and the sea has always lived close to the Dream." She laughed. "I brought more than an assortment of colorful seafaring profanity with me when I came to this world."

A chilly breeze cut through the courtyard, flinging the loose strands of her hair to tickle his face. He couldn't stop himself from inhaling, dragging that intoxicating scent of her deep into his lungs as he tugged her more firmly against him. The sweet curve of her ear was enticingly close, and he gave into temptation and brushed his lips against it as he lowered his voice to a rumble. "Then I put myself in your expert hands."

She shivered and started to turn her head. Then another horn blast sounded, higher and shorter, and the great beast beneath them leapt forward, its first mighty stride covering enough ground to steal Einar's breath.

And then they were running.

No, they were *flying*.

The reindeer's hooves must have been hitting the ground, but their gait was so smooth Einar couldn't tell. He couldn't hear it, either, not against the packed snow with the wind carrying Naia's delighted laughter.

Einar had ridden one of Elevia's specially trained messenger horses once, and the speed of that had rattled his teeth. This was faster. The world around him became a blur—everything but Naia.

Instinct had wrapped his arms around her waist. Her back pressed to his chest, and her hair whipped around his face. Her ass nestled sweetly in the cradle of his thighs, and he found a new appreciation for the sleek muscle in *hers*. She rode as if she'd been born in the saddle, and Einar wondered whose memories guided her to move so effortlessly with the surging beast, to cradle the reins with such confidence.

He'd made the mistake of thinking that someone so freshly born from the Dream must be naive. Untutored. In this moment, she seemed ancient, tapping into the primal knowledge of thousands of lives over a hundred generations.

Maybe he'd been wrong all along, and *he* was the one playing with fire. Maybe one night with her would leave *him* shattered on the rocks, utterly wrecked while the tide carried her out with the dawn.

The ground began to rise ahead of them. Another blast from a horn slowed their breakneck pace as they approached the top of a bluff. The wind across his face carried the acrid smell of burning wood now, and the sound of voices raised in panic.

Then they reached the top of the hill, and Einar saw the smoke.

Naia was gone before their mount had come to a full stop, springing as gracefully from the reindeer's back as she'd swung up onto it. Einar scrambled to follow her, striding to the edge of the cliff to stare down at the village.

In flames.

Time seemed to unravel. Einar had a lifetime between stately beats of his heart to take in the dire situation below them.

Jamyskar was burning. Fire curled up from the steeply pitched thatch roofs of too many buildings, its source not immediately apparent. Screams rose from within. Villagers scrambled in all directions, some trying to douse the flames, others fighting their way into the burning homes in an attempt at rescue.

More villagers carried weapons, charging toward the rocky beach where a trio of longboats rode the final wave onto the shore. At least a dozen well-armed and armored soldiers spilled from each one, their battle cries rising harshly over the chaos.

A familiar boom sounded with his next heartbeat, dragging his gaze out to the ocean. Three massive battleships floated just offshore, their cannons still smoking. Dark smudges resolved into projectiles that slammed into buildings, people, and earth alike with uncaring unanimity.

His blood chilled further as his gaze slid up, to the dark sails snapping in the morning breeze, and the distinctive flag flying proudly from the tallest mast of every ship.

The sigil of the Kraken.

Chapter Fourteen

The goddess once told me that death is not the enemy. I waited for her to elaborate, but she did not. Finally, unable to stop myself, I asked.

She told me there are many enemies. I asked for their names, and she gave me several.

"Greed. Fear. Anger." Her eyes met mine. "Pain."

from the unpublished papers of Rahvekyan High Priestess Omira

At first, the chaotic attack playing out before him filled Aleksi mainly with concern. These were civilians, for the Huntress's sake. Villagers who had sought no quarrel with anyone.

Then he spotted the Kraken's sigil blacked onto the marauding ships' oilcloth sails, and his worry froze over, turning to solid, icy fury in the span of a heartbeat.

Someone was trying to blame this gratuitous violence on *Einar*, and they weren't even doing a decent job of it. There was nothing elegant or believable about this. If Einar wanted to attack Gwynira right now, of all times, he knew better than to do it under his own colors. The rogue pirate was many things, some harsh and some beautiful, but sloppy did not rank among his traits.

And he would never, *ever* use a crew that was not his own.

Gwynira's mount pawed at the stony ground, lowing and grunting as she slid from the saddle. "You," she snapped at Naia, "with me." She turned without waiting for a response, heading for higher ground.

Naia started after her, but stopped short when Einar grasped her arm.

"Be careful," he rasped.

"To war again, Captain." She smiled a little, as if sharing a private joke, then pulled free and hurried after Gwynira, toward a promontory that jutted out over the bay.

From there, they would have an excellent vantage point over the battlefield below. With Naia's command of water combined with Gwynira's mastery of ice, they would make short work of the vessels firing on the village.

Good.

Arktikos pulled a fur-wrapped bundle from the reindeer's saddle pack. "You're going to need this, my lord." He tossed it to Aleksi.

The furs fell to the ground, revealing Aleksi's sword as it sailed through the air. He caught it, his fingers wrapping around the hilt as if it had always been in his hand. "You have my thanks."

"Don't thank me," the man growled through a smile. "Just fight well."

Then he hefted a battle-axe that looked too large for any man to wield, let out a primal cry of fury, and charged down the hill.

Blood pounded in Aleksi's ears as he and Einar ran after him, joining the rest of Gwynira's guard in a frantic thundering of boots. Villagers scattered out of their path, and Einar bent to sweep up a long spike tipped with a wicked hook. Steel met steel with a chorus of mighty clangs as they clashed with the invaders.

Aleksi swung his sword, channeling more might than skill into each blow. Another volley of cannon fire split the pale gray of the morning sky, and Aleksi gritted his teeth. The attackers didn't *care* that their landing parties were already ashore and were just as likely to be hit as anyone else. It was expedient to keep up their attack by sea, and nothing else mattered.

He slid one of the pirates off his sword and watched as a projectile sailed overhead, only to bank sharply, head in a different direction entirely, and slam into a small shack with an enormous crash.

Magic.

They would not risk such an asset on land, where any rusty blade could kill it stone dead with a single lucky blow. No, their magic user—assuming there was but one—would be secreted away on one of those ships, lashing out with the safety of distance.

Up on the bluff, Naia and Gwynira stood side by side, their arms outstretched as they wielded their respective powers over water and ice to neutralize the magically directed attacks. Gwynira had taken a blunt approach, wrapping the heavy lead cannonballs in layers of ice until they lost momentum and dropped to the ground. Naia was more precise. She whipped tendrils of water into the air to block the projectiles, turning them back toward the sea.

Her hair undulated around her, drifting as if she were floating in the depths of the ocean instead of standing on dry land. The water danced for her, alternating between the soft intercession of defense and the hard thrust of attack. It bent to her will, giving her whatever she needed as she coaxed it to spinning, swirling life.

She was absolutely glorious.

Power filled Aleksi, and the world bloomed into sudden, vivid color. No longer was the blood that painted his blade dull and muted, like burnt mahogany. It was *red*, hot and burning bright. Time slowed *and* sped, the battle around him whirling and crawling, all at once. This was the sole exception to his determination never to pry into the souls of others. He would not sacrifice innocent lives to protect his principles. If he would do such a thing, he might as well not have any in the first place.

No, necessity would always override his comfortable scruples. Here, he would do what Naia was doing—fight their magic with his own.

A shudder rocked him as minds and hearts opened to him. He could sense the villagers, the invaders, those still on the ships out in the bay. If all was quiet instead of explosions and screams, he could have heard the secret whispers of their innermost desires, tracked them all by feel alone.

He spun just in time to block an attack aimed at his unprotected back. Disappointed frustration exploded from his opponent, though it quickly gave way to shock, fear . . . and pain.

Aleksi embraced that pain. He had caused it; he *should* feel it. He drank it in along with all the other emotions curling up with the smoke from the wrecked village. There were hints of distasteful glee and even pleasure lurking amidst the anger and agony, but most of the invaders were flat, emotionless.

Professionals.

Aleksi swung his sword again, and an arm still clutching a deadly mace hit the sandy rock beneath his feet. Deep pride and determination joined the mélange of emotions surrounding him—the villagers, armed mostly with tools and other weapons of opportunity. They were availing themselves well, fighting with a ferocity matched only by their bravery as they used gutting knives and huge hooks to defend their homes.

An old man cried out. He cowered against the side of a small shack, shielding his head with his arms, as two men bore down on him, their gory blades raised. Aleksi interrupted them, deflecting their daggers with the flat of his blade before shoving them back.

"Run," he urged the old man, who did not linger.

One of the pirates stumbled and fell. Aleksi focused on the other, who kept his footing and launched an immediate counterattack. He shimmered in a cloud of deep, aggressive red as he drew a second blade from his belt and charged, bending low as if to come in beneath Aleksi's guard.

Daughter of Tides

But the deep red gave him away. This man was too hostile for subtlety—he wanted death, but he also wanted *pain*. To get close, to stare into someone's eyes while the life slowly drained from them. So when he reared up at the last moment for a headbutt, Aleksi sidestepped the attempt. His attacker hit the wall hard and reeled wildly back.

Aleksi ran him through.

Though it had taken only moments to dispatch the angry man, his companion had already recovered. Aleksi pulled his sword free and faced his second opponent.

Out of nowhere, a spear whistled through the air and skewered the man. Its momentum carried him forward, pinning him to the side of the shack like a missive nailed to a door.

Einar stood there, his chest heaving. "Are you all right?"

For a heartbeat, Aleksi's vision blurred. It was as if he was seeing double, only *worse*, his brain scrambling to process a million images, all superimposed over one another.

He blinked, and the blur cleared. Einar turned, swept up an abandoned oar, and bashed another pirate across the back of the head with it. He continued swinging until the oar had been obliterated, then grabbed another weapon of opportunity.

He fought as fiercely as the villagers. In fact, he could have been one of them. He throbbed with the same energy, a ferocious pulse of righteous anger streaked with something unexpected.

Sheer, unadulterated hope.

A deafening explosion cut through the cacophony of the battle. The ships had stopped firing their cannons on the village . . . and had turned them toward the bluff where Naia and Gwynira had taken up position.

Einar breathed a choked sound of protest and started forward, as if the need to go to her overwhelmed everything else. Aleksi caught him, held him back, even though the same urge gripped him, too.

"This is her fight," he rasped. "Our little nymph isn't about to let a handful of pretenders defeat her. You know this."

Einar shuddered and nodded, his gaze still fixed on Naia's distant form.

A huge wave lifted as it receded from shore, rising ten, twenty, then *fifty* feet high. It held for an interminable moment, shaking just like Naia's arms, then dissolved even as it froze. The ice shattered into projectiles, some wickedly sharp and others large and round like cannonballs themselves. Gwynira screamed, a primal sound of fury that carried over the shore like a vengeful wail, and the bits of ice flew toward one of the ships.

The destructive volley tore through sailcloth and wood, flesh and bone, as it hit the ship broadside. Bits of wood and cannons and even crew members exploded from the deck as the vessel began to list. Its stern dipped under the bubbling water, and the entire front of the ship rose before sliding down into the depths of the bay.

A roar shook the ground beneath Aleksi's feet. He nearly jumped back as a massive polar bear bounded past him. It charged toward a cluster of pirates who were attacking as a group, swiped at them with a gargantuan paw, then closed its jaws on one invader's head with a sickening crunch.

"What the *fuck*?" Einar growled.

The bear raked its claws through another group of pirates, and Aleksi looked—really looked, beyond the shaggy white fur and the impossibly large teeth to the familiar aura that wreathed the animal.

"It's Arktikos," he told Einar.

"What?"

Naia cried out, drawing Aleksi's gaze back to the bluff. She was raising another wave, this one even higher than the first, absolutely *colossal*, tall enough to dwarf the attacking ships. It arched over the nearest one, forming a perfect cresting curl over the vessel's bulk. As it crashed down, it solidified. Instead of rushing off the deck, washing away armaments and crew, it sat, heavy and deadly. The hull of the ship creaked and popped, then imploded under the weight of the ice.

The crew of the third ship raised sail to beat a hasty retreat, leaving their comrades stranded on land. The few that remained fought even more viciously. Aleksi's blade dripped with blood. Arktikos stampeded across the village, his roar scattering the attackers before him. Einar used a fishing net to snag a battle-axe and rip it from a pirate's hands, then turned the man's own weapon against him.

Then it was over.

But the emotions lingered. Aleksi closed his eyes against the riotous color and fought to steady his breathing. Everything was so *loud*, the sound so thick he could touch it, curl his fingers through it and squeeze it in his fists.

When he opened his eyes once more, Arktikos had resumed his human form. He was dressed in the clothes he'd been wearing before, much as Ulric always was when he let the Wolf slip away after a battle.

Arktikos nudged a fallen invader with the toe of his boot and scoffed in disgust. "I recognize mercenaries when I fight them."

"I suppose they likely do have a distinctive taste," Aleksi observed blandly. "You'll be picking hired killer out of your teeth for a week."

The bear eyed Aleksi, squinting in assessment, as if trying to determine whether a member of the High Court was mocking him. Finally, a smile curved his lips. "At least. But it's a small price to pay for victory."

Gwynira and Naia joined them, both a little dusty and disheveled. Sir Jaspar accompanied them, his armor pristine. Untouched by the battle.

"See to the survivors, Jaspar," Gwynira ordered. "Find out what they need, and give it to them."

Aleksi allowed his gaze to roam over Naia, but he saw no injuries. No clouds of pain hung around her, just an almost feral triumph that glowed even in the midmorning sun.

Einar did not content himself with merely looking. He slid his hands up her arms and tilted her head from side to side, until she clasped his hands in hers to still their frantic searching.

"I'm fine." Her voice was hot. "You and Aleksi?"

"Not a scratch, darling." Aleksi turned to Gwynira, whose brow was creased by a troubled frown, and pulled her aside, lowering his voice. "You must realize that Einar was not responsible for this attack."

"I *do*, my lord. Captain Einar is considered many things across this Empire, but he is not known to be a fool." Her frown deepened. "No. This was an attempt to drive a wedge between me and the High Court."

"Which means you have a noble problem."

She sighed. "When do I not?"

Naia gasped and rushed toward Aleksi. "You're bleeding!"

Someone had managed to land a knife across his ribs. The slice was shallow, but it had not yet healed, and Aleksi intercepted Naia's questing hands.

"It's nothing, little nymph," he assured her. "Already a memory."

A lie, but only a little one, and he offered it gladly as the pain began to rise and the color receded from his vision, casting the world into the same muted shades he'd already come to know. In fact, everything seemed just a tiny bit dimmer than before.

Everything but Naia and Einar.

Chapter Fifteen

Many who look upon this frozen island have wondered at the source of Grand Duchess Gwynira's unusual wealth. The truth is in the tundra cotton that grows effortlessly across the plains on the northeast part of the island. As mentioned in the introduction, the unique fibers naturally grow in prized shades of vivid teal, aquamarine, and green. The color of fabric woven from this cotton never fades—and is highly prized in the Empire.

Akeisa: A Study of Flora and Fauna
by Guildmaster Klement

Naia couldn't sleep, and this time, it had nothing to do with being assailed by too-vivid dreams every time she closed her eyes.

She hadn't been able to settle down since the fight earlier. Her heart still pounded, and her skin prickled with . . . *something*. It wasn't fear or even adrenaline, but a strange sort of nervous elation that no amount of deep breathing and meditation seemed to soothe.

She'd never won a battle before.

Oh, she'd been there when the High Court had vanquished Sorin and his forces. The Huntress had told her afterward, with full sincerity, that she'd fought well, and that her assistance had been indispensable.

But that was just it—she'd *helped*. She hadn't stood as the vanguard against an onslaught. She hadn't sunk any enemy vessels.

But, by the Dream, she had today.

Her entire body thrummed as she slipped from her useless bed. She didn't bother replacing the nightgown the servants had insisted on helping her don, simply shoved her feet into her waiting slippers and threw a fur-lined cloak over it all.

She couldn't go to the library again. It would only trouble the servants, and she'd done enough of that during her stay. She'd have to find someplace less obtrusive to spend her time. Perhaps one of the higher balconies of the palace. She could watch the stars twinkle, and draw the cool, salty night air into her lungs until it had washed away the edgy excitement that suffused her now.

She drifted past Aleksi's door, only to pause when she saw that the ornate metal knocker had been wrapped in velvet. A flash of someone else's memory supplied the reason for the quaint tradition—the Lover did not wish to be disturbed tonight.

Naia ended up at Einar's door.

She raised her hand and tapped the far less ornate knocker against its metal plate. The door swung open several moments later, and Einar stood there. He wasn't dressed. Of course he wasn't—it was late, and the day had been long and arduous. He had every reason to be barefoot and rumpled, with his shirt half open.

In that moment, Naia was forced to reassess the truth of why she'd come here. Had she expected this sort of vulnerability? *Wanted* it, even? It was an intimacy she craved, but did she have any right to it, especially when she was wound this tight, like a spring? And would she let that stop her?

Could she?

Daughter of Tides

A book dangled from one strong hand. The other swept his dark hair back as concern furrowed his brow. "Naia? Are you well?"

"Very," she answered automatically, then gestured into the room. "May I?"

Einar stepped aside silently. His chamber was much like hers, though a bit more utilitarian. There was a sitting area arranged around a large stone fireplace. A low fire burned within, the kind that cast out as much shadow as light, and the bed had been made up with a thickly woven but plain coverlet.

Naia swallowed and looked away.

He clearly had not been offered the most sumptuous accommodations available, but this room suited him. It had been designed for a purpose, and it performed its function well, without distractions or frippery.

Einar closed the door and turned, waving a hand toward the plush seats in invitation. "I think I have some wine, if you'd like some?"

"Thank you, but no," she demurred. Drinking with him could only lead down one path, and Naia refused to be out of her wits when she finally went *there*. "What are you reading?"

His fingers reverently stroked the book's aged spine . . . but his gaze never left Naia's face. "I found it in the library. It was written a few generations after the Empire invaded."

Curious, she moved closer and peered at the volume. "Is it a history of Rahvekya before its occupation?"

"Mmm. I'm surprised that Gwynira ever let such a thing survive, much less that she sees fit to own a copy." His breath stirred her hair as he leaned in, his voice a low murmur. "Petya has told me some of the stories, of course. But there are so many things I never knew."

"Like what?"

"How many things the people here did besides fish, for one. They were apparently famous for their weaving." He lifted his free hand to the gifted sea glass pendant necklace that nestled between her breasts, then traced the deep vee of her neckline. His knuckles burned her skin

137

through the sumptuous blue fabric. "I knew Gwynira got rich from exporting these textiles, but I never understood why. It's a tundra cotton that only grows here. It's prized because it never fades. They don't have to dye it, because it grows in the colors of the sea."

Naia suppressed a shudder at his touch, but it was his words that truly held her. They were hypnotic, rising and falling gently like the low waves far out in the midst of the ocean. Quiet but insistent, inviting you to let them wash over you.

Instead of shuddering, she drew in a sharp breath. She wasn't ready to take her leave of him, but if they stayed here, like this, they would absolutely end up in his bed.

So she held out a hand, one eyebrow raised, and waited until he laid the old, creased book on her palm. Then she placed it carefully on the nearest flat surface and reached out again, this time to take his hand.

"Let's go," she whispered. "Now is not the time to learn about your homeland from a book, not when you can see it instead."

He paused only long enough to pull on his boots and shrug into his long coat before following her out the door. But once they stood in the hallway, he hesitated. "Should we tell Aleksi where we're going?"

"He doesn't wish to be disturbed." Naia glanced back at Einar, a sudden twist of mischief making her smile. "Are you worried that Father will be cross if we sneak out?"

A choked laugh rattled his chest as he caught up to her. "I'd like to see you say that to his face."

"You think I wouldn't? Don't forget, I sank two ships today." Her voice dropped an octave, and her next words came out sounding far more suggestive than she'd intended. "I can handle Aleksi."

Einar's eyes flashed, but he only bowed his head and gestured for her to lead the way.

Naia avoided the main hall and headed instead for the areas that seemed to bustle with domestic activity. She'd watched the servants come and go, always to and from this corner of the palace. She was

Daughter of Tides

rewarded with an exit near the kitchens, one that spilled out into a small courtyard framed by long, low greenhouses.

She supposed those were necessary in such a place as this. Considering the amount of food the palace must go through, it couldn't be practical to have it all shipped in from the mainland.

A mountain loomed behind Gwynira's palace. It was a hill, really, nothing so grand as the craggy peaks of the Burning Hills, or even the majestic caldera that sheltered Dragon's Keep. But it was beautiful and mysterious, and Naia could just see a path winding up its side, lit here and there with glimpses of warm amber light.

"What do you suppose that is?" she asked softly.

He shrugged, his gaze following the twists of the path. "Maybe there's a good view at the top? Should we find out?"

"An adventure," Naia breathed, and tugged him toward the path.

It was a gentle slope at first, enclosed by gnarled branches free of foliage. They reached out and curved over the trail, almost as if protecting it from the elements. She and Einar passed the first light, which turned out to be a lantern of hammered metal with cutouts that cast fanciful patterns of light dancing across the path.

It was then that Naia realized this truly *was* a path, lined with flat, hand-chiseled stones worn smooth by the passage of time and many thousands of footsteps. Clumps of brush had grown up around the path, and the stone had crumbled away in places, but it was *there*. And someone was clearly still tending these lanterns with dedication, lighting them and trimming the wicks and refilling the whale oil when it ran low.

Soon, the path grew steep, and she and Einar continued to climb it without speaking. Something about this place, this ancient but remembered path winding up the side of a dark mountain, felt almost sacred. Deserving of their reverent silence.

Then they reached the top, a little plateau that had obviously been carved out of the mountain itself. The stones blossomed into a shattered floor, along with broken, sagging columns that ringed the area like soldiers who had fallen asleep during an endless watch.

Einar stepped up to the closest column and ran his fingers over the weathered stone until he found a raised spiral. "I think I know where we are."

The stone almost seemed to hum beneath Naia's feet, the same sensation she'd felt in snatches of other people's memories, recollections of consecrated lands and other hallowed spots. "It's a place of worship."

Instead of answering, he held out his hand for hers. His fingers were warm and gentle as he pressed her fingertips to the worn pattern and guided them in a slowly tightening spiral. "Like the necklaces they gave you," he murmured, his breath stirring the hair above her ear. "A seashell, to honor the goddess. This was her temple."

The ridges of stone were rough beneath her fingers, but she barely felt them. "What do you know about her?"

He hummed, the vibration rolling through her. "They say she walked this island for centuries beyond counting. And that when she lived here, it wasn't frozen like it is now. It was a paradise. Green, rolling hills. Flowers in every color you can imagine."

The description was nothing like the island now, but Naia could see that rainbow of blooms scattered across verdant hillsides, and all of it surrounded by lush turquoise waters. "How long ago was this?"

"Hundreds of years before I was born. Maybe a thousand." His fingers trailed up Naia's arm. "When she left, the island froze."

"Where did she go?"

A chill breeze swept through the shattered pillars just then, stirring Naia's hair. Einar moved closer, as if to shield her with the warmth of his body. "According to the stories, there was a terrible, cataclysmic storm. The seas went wild. The earth trembled, and waves as high as the mountains rose in the bay."

Einar coaxed Naia deeper into the temple, into the center of the ruined space, and turned her with gentle hands on her shoulders. This spot, situated as it was on the edge of a sheer cliff face, offered a breathtaking view of the sheltered harbor bay, as well as of the ocean beyond it.

Naia stared out at the water, her body hot wherever Einar touched her, despite the cool breeze sifting through her hair. Her toes curled in her slippers. She could almost feel the raging storm of which he spoke, angry waters pounding desperately against the rocks below until the mountain itself seemed to vibrate with their fury.

"Supposedly, this is exactly where she stood." Einar's lips grazed Naia's temple. "They say the goddess raised a wall of water that surrounded the entire island. She held it, day after day, as the sea raged and the earth shook. When the wall of water finally fell, the ocean beyond had calmed."

"And the goddess?"

"According to Petya? Dead. But a piece of her remained."

Startled, Naia turned to face him. "What does that mean?"

His lips curved in a soft smile. "I don't know. As a boy, I used to demand that she explain it to me. All she ever said was that the goddess may have died, but her heart still slumbers here."

It was a story Naia had never heard, but she knew the rhythms of it like her own name. The people had watched their goddess die, and their gorgeous island paradise had frozen over along with their bitter tears. Now, they waited in futility for the impossible return of everything they'd lost.

No wonder they kept bringing Naia gifts. To have survived this long, their hope had to be a beating thing, slamming against the walls of their chests in sheer agony. "The only difference between death and sleep is waking up. To say she slumbers, they must expect her to return someday."

"Yes." Einar touched the leather at Naia's throat again, stroking his finger down to the sea glass nestled against her skin. "Have you figured it out yet? Why the seas roiled and the earth quaked?"

There was only one event she'd heard about that might possibly have carried that sort of destructive power. "The War of the Gods?"

"It must have been." His knuckle grazed her collarbone, gentle and warm. "Petya didn't know about it when she first told me the stories. But after we met the Siren and learned about the sundering of the continents? A mountain range rose in the span of heartbeats. It would have caused chaos far beyond the confines of the Sheltered Lands. And the timing seems right."

Naia gazed out at the calm, cold waters of the bay, caught between Einar's very real warmth and the frigid tragedy of history. She tilted her head, inviting the exploration of his touch to continue. "How horrible for their goddess. To stand alone, and then to die the same way."

Einar hesitated, seemingly balanced on the edge of some vast emotion. When he finally spoke, his voice rolled over her, dark as the ocean depths. "She wasn't alone."

Naia held her breath and waited.

The warmth of his hand vanished abruptly. He reached into his pocket and pulled out something that glinted bronze in the moonlight—a charm, similar to the ones the servants had gifted her, but in the shape of the kraken sigil that flew above his ship.

"I grew up on stories of the Kraken," he whispered, his gaze finding hers. "In the legends Petya told me, he was a protector. Guardian of this island *and* of its goddess."

Naia's heart ached at the revelation. Einar had grown up hearing the stories of his homeland, of a hero who had protected his people. One so strong he had been tasked with guarding the well-being of another god. She imagined him, an orphaned little boy sitting cross-legged on the swaying deck of a ship, listening intently, needing to believe.

And the story could have ended there . . . except that theirs was a world built on belief. It could make things true. Make them *real*.

Smiling, she touched the charm. "And so you became the hero you needed. The one your people once had."

He closed his fingers over hers, his dark eyes intent. "Here, the Kraken is a hero, yes. But out there? To everyone else? He's . . ."

A monster. Naia could already hear the words, so she trapped them with her finger over his lips. "Also a hero. That's what I see, Einar. What I've always seen."

He leaned into her touch so that his next words fell against her fingertip like a kiss. "Maybe that's what the goddess saw, too. Because the Kraken wasn't just her protector."

"Oh?"

His gaze burned into hers. "He was also her lover."

Naia felt dizzy with sensation. There was that soft word again, whispered this time against her flesh, so different from the sudden hardness of cool stone against her back. Everything else had grown warm, as if the night breeze echoed with a hint of the tropical breezes that had once blown through this temple.

And then she heard him. Really *heard* him, and she thought she understood. "Is that why you look at me the way you do? Because I remind you of the goddess of your legends?"

His laugh was warm, too, curling around her as one hand ghosted up her side, the touch electric even through the layers of her clothing. He turned his face into her hand without releasing her gaze and brushed a kiss to her palm. "I've never looked at the Siren like this."

It wasn't exactly a denial. "Speak plainly, Einar. What are you saying?" Her words fell into the scant space between them, barely audible but louder than cracking ice.

"That you're different." The hand at her waist glided higher, up her arm and across the fur collar of her cape until his fingers found her chin. "That I've never looked at *anyone* like this before."

It held the ring of absolute truth—but Einar had always been honest with her. *Painfully* honest. Nothing about this declaration nullified his prior insistence that he wanted her, but only for a night or two. And, as tempted as she was to experience those nights, whatever their limited number, Naia was more convinced than ever that she would not survive watching him walk away.

Where does that leave us? The question hovered on her tongue and died there, because Einar was leaning even closer. Or perhaps *she* was the one doing that, stretching up on her toes. His hand was still on her face, and her fingers had wound into his hair, and every tiny moment that passed felt exactly like the inexorable push and pull of the tides.

Their lips met, and the electric shock of it startled Naia into a laugh that swiftly turned into a moan. Einar echoed the sound, the rumble of it as deep as the warning of an approaching storm. For endless moments, that was the entirety of her world—warm, firm lips on hers, gentle. Exploring.

Then the storm within him broke. With a hungry growl, he hoisted her up against the pillar, pressing into her with the hard length of his body as his head tilted. His tongue swept over her lips, demanding, and she opened to him, utterly and completely lost.

Yes.

Her head was spinning by the time Einar broke away with a groan that coalesced into her name. A frigid breeze whipped between them, but she barely felt it as his lips found her cheek. "Naia." Another kiss, this one on her jaw, and then another. His open mouth grazed her ear, and she felt the teasing sting of teeth before he rasped, "I've dreamt about tasting you every night since I met you."

It hit her like a bolt of lightning forking down to the churning surface of the ocean, and she knew. It didn't matter if this . . . *thing* between them lasted for a single night or a thousand years.

It would happen.

Naia laid her hand on his face and leaned back just enough to hold his gaze. "Of course you have. I remind you of your goddess." She curled her fingers, raking her nails slowly across his cheek. "So why have you never knelt for me?"

His eyes sparked at the challenge. Then his clever fingers found the clasp at her throat, and her cloak fell away, baring her neck to the icy wind. Einar was there a moment later, dropping a line of taunting kisses all the way to where her pulse fluttered rapidly in the hollow of her throat. The rasp of his stubbled cheek against sensitive flesh was lost beneath the sudden heat of his mouth—and the renewed sting of his teeth.

She only had time to gasp his name before he moved, sliding down her body until he was kneeling before her. "We *are* in the goddess's temple." His fingers slipped beneath her long skirt to trace over her ankle. "Should I worship you?"

"Yes." She touched the tip of one finger to his lower lip. "You've promised me untold pleasure, Captain. I want it."

He caught her finger between his teeth, his gaze still locked on hers. His tongue swept over the pad of her finger, tracing in a teasing circle that his eyes dared her to imagine as even more intimate contact.

Naia happily complied as he slipped his hands under her nightgown. They were hot against her chilled skin, and they seemed to grow hotter with every passing moment.

He hesitated when he reached the tops of her thighs, his fingers stroking up and down in minute increments. Waiting.

Naia exhaled sharply and met his questioning gaze. "*Now*, Einar."

The corner of his mouth kicked up in a wicked half smile, and he finally—*finally*—touched her. His thumb rubbed circles on her clit, each stroke firmer than the last, until she had to reclaim that sharp exhalation with an even sharper gasp.

She gripped the pillar behind her, fingernails scratching the pitted stone. In that moment, she knew that by the time Einar was finished with her, she'd be just as shattered as the rest of the ruins.

And if she let him take his time, it would be *so good*. So she tried to remain perfectly still, resisting the nearly overwhelming urge to seek deeper contact by arching her hips into his touch. But her body only wanted more, faster, and her hips jerked against his hand.

In that instant, Einar pulled away. Naia bit back a protest that melted into a moan when he pushed her gown higher . . . and licked the inside of her leg. That alone was enough to weaken her knees, but he kept going, drawing his tongue up her thigh.

Lightning flashed, inside her and out, and Naia whimpered. A moment later, a crack of thunder drowned out the sound of Einar's growl against her inner thigh. But she didn't need to hear it, because she felt it, reverberating through her like a promise.

Then he put his mouth on her, fulfilling that promise. He nudged her clit with his tongue, then slipped away to explore, over and over. Naia drove her fingers into his hair and clutched his head, trying to chase the sensation.

But she knew that Einar—damn him, *bless* him—would make her wait until he'd had his fill.

She wound up with her feet off the stone, her legs over his shoulders, riding his mouth. Her hair and her filmy gown caught on the rough stone behind her, but she didn't care. Because the storm was building again, and this time—

This time—

Another bolt of lightning lit the sky. Naia came with a hoarse cry that was swallowed by the blinding crash of thunder. The sheer, melting pleasure of it arched her back off the pillar and curled her toes in her slippers. Einar held her as she shook, but he did not stop. Not until she was pleading, gasping words that barely sounded like words at all, even to her own ears.

Naia was floating when her feet touched the stone once more, and Einar stood before her. He cupped her cheek with one hand and rubbed his thumb over her parted lips, catching every rough gasp that escaped her.

"Are you with me, sweet goddess?"

"I think so." Naia laughed at her own wobbly voice, then drew him close and kissed him.

He returned the caress, hot and hungry, and she could taste herself on his tongue. Too soon, he gently pulled away. "While I would love nothing more than to continue this, we should return to the castle before this storm grows any worse. We are on *very* high ground here."

"Right." Naia blinked tiny flakes of snow from her lashes. As reluctant as she was to leave his arms for even a moment, a warm fire and an even warmer bed seemed like a much better idea than a lightning strike. "We can go to my chamber."

He stared down at her, the heat in his gaze joined by regret. "It has been a long day, and tomorrow is likely to be more of the same. You should return to your bed, and hopefully to sweet dreams."

There was enough reluctance in his voice to temper the sting of rejection, but Naia caught his hand in hers anyway. "Another time. Promise me."

"Count on it." Einar raised her hand to his lips for a lingering kiss. "In a nice, soft bed, with all the time in the world to enjoy it."

Joy suffused Naia, bubbling through her veins like the fizzy, intoxicating wine she'd had at the Witchwood Ball. She didn't know what this meant—if it meant anything at all—but it didn't matter anymore.

She'd been thoroughly swept away by this riptide, and wherever she washed ashore, it would be worth it. Even if all she had left of Einar was a sweet memory.

Chapter Sixteen

I remember a day when a young girl asked for the goddess's blessing. She was sick, her father said, and would not linger for much longer.

The goddess denied this. She kissed the girl's brow, held her hands, and told her that she would be strong and lucky, and would live many years yet.

And so she did. Hers was a charmed life, that first goddess-touched child of Rahvekya.

from the unpublished papers of Rahvekyan High Priestess Omira

Aleksi had taken to spending most of his waking hours in quiet conversation with Gwynira. It was his mission, after all, to get to know the Grand Duchess, and to let her know him. True diplomacy always stemmed from finding common ground, and there was but one way to do that. It was a time-intensive process, but he was glad of it.

It meant that he could avoid Naia.

Not that he *wanted* to avoid her. Things were just simpler this way. She had been so concerned about the wound he'd suffered while defending the village from invasion that he didn't want to see her again until it was healed. Which would thankfully be soon—the process was still far more sluggish than it should have been, but much faster than for a human.

It seemed he still had *some* power left.

But the delayed nature of his healing would, at best, prompt uncomfortable questions. At worst, it could shift all her tender concern into far more dangerous territory.

He should not have flirted with her the night he'd found her in the library. But he'd been a bit tipsy, and so *pleased* that he'd been able to protect Einar and once again secure Gwynira's good will. At the time, it had seemed harmless. A bit of casual late-night conversation between friends.

Naia had been so *lonely*. The emotion had filled the room in icy, pale-green pulses that mimicked the beat of a heart, and he'd had only one thought: to bring her whatever comfort he could. So he'd spoken of his own difficulties, and how he'd overcome them.

And, eventually, he'd spoken of Alysaia.

That had been a mistake; he could see that now, in hindsight. Before that night, sitting in front of that hushed fire, Naia had looked at him as most others did. He was the Lover—sincere but distant, caring but inaccessible. A force as constant as gravity, and just as unlikely to be considered except for moments in extremis.

Now, when she looked at him, she truly *saw* him. What's more, she seemed interested in what she saw.

And that posed a problem.

Aleksi had no doubt whatsoever that Naia was in love with Einar. She had been strongly drawn to the pirate lord from their first meeting, and Aleksi had watched that interest deepen over time into a regard whose strength he could feel in his bones. But monogamy had never been particularly prized by Dreamers—their lives were too long for their hearts to be so tightly bound. Love came in many shades, and it was possible to feel them all. Naia's two closest friends were living proof of that.

The freedom to love however and whomever one chose was all Naia had ever seen, and her attachment to Einar did not preclude her developing feelings for Aleksi, as well. And that simply would not do. His failing health had made that much perfectly clear. He might not be *dying*, as he'd initially suspected—at least not anytime dreadfully soon—but there was something wrong with him. And he wouldn't be a fit partner for anyone, not until he figured that out.

No. If he could remove himself from Naia's notice, the sparks between her and Einar would have time to combust. And the resulting conflagration would leave the little nymph far too busy to think about Aleksi anymore.

The realization *hurt*, sharp and aching all at once, like falling and skidding over rough stone. But he had never resented watching love flourish from the outside, and he could not start now.

He *would* not.

A knock at the door pulled him from his reverie. So far, everyone had respected the wrapped knocker as a signal to leave him be . . . but emergencies *did* happen.

He hauled open the door, his heart in his throat. Einar stood on the other side, tight with nerves but otherwise calm.

Aleksi stepped back. He could not hide from everyone, not for long, and Einar was far from likely to accidentally fall in love with him. "Come in."

"Aleksi." Einar nodded his thanks as he entered, but wasted no more time on pleasantries or small talk. "You've been making yourself scarce of late."

"Diplomacy is hard work, and there is much to learn about the island." The truth, such as it was, just not the whole truth. He had immersed himself in learning about the island's people—Einar's people, the natives of Rahvekya, not the Imperial colonizers. He gestured toward a stack of books on the low table in his sitting area. "Your parents were fascinating people. I regret that I never had the chance to meet them."

"So do I." Einar hesitated, as if reluctant to go on. Finally, he did. "Do the people here truly remember them so well?"

"Yes, it seems they do." The volumes he'd borrowed from Gwynira's personal collection invariably spoke of the enduring respect for Rahvekya's last reigning queen and her king consort, regardless of when the books had been written. "What can I do for you, Einar?"

Einar heaved a conflicted sigh. "It's about the ball Gwynira is holding tomorrow. I don't know if I should attend."

"Whyever not?" Naia was almost certainly looking forward to it, and it was unlike Einar to willingly disappoint her.

He began to pace like a big cat in a too-small cage. "Most of the Imperial Court fears me. At best, I will be a distraction we can ill afford. At worst, it will be that disastrous dinner all over again."

"Most of Gwynira's court isn't worth considering, and she'd be the first to tell you so. In fact, she *has*." Aleksi tilted his head. Einar was far too upset for this to be about any of the Imperial Court's horrible, self-centered nobles. "What's wrong? The truth, if you please."

Einar stopped abruptly and ran a hand through his hair. Defiance clashed with the clear thread of self-consciousness that vibrated through the room. "I haven't spent my time in ballrooms and palaces. But Naia went on progress with Princess Sachielle. She knows about fancy parties."

It was a bit of a stretch, describing the consort's progress as *fancy*. Mostly, the journey involved living in tents or ancient rustic cabins for weeks on end. Most of the formal festivities happened at the various seats of the High Court, and Einar had spent plenty of his time visiting those.

But that wasn't really the point, was it? Aleksi dug past the surface of Einar's words and into the sentiment that motivated them. He was unsure of himself, intimidated by the foreign customs of the Akeisan court . . . and worried about looking a fool in front of Naia.

Only one thing mattered to Aleksi. "Do you *want* to go to the ball?"

Einar didn't answer. He frowned, his unease deepening into something that bordered on vexation. "Would Naia be disappointed if I didn't?"

"Honestly? Yes, probably. I imagine she would very much like to put on a lovely dress and dance with you again."

It was clearly the answer that Einar wanted and feared in equal measure. His momentary delight was quickly supplanted by what Aleksi could only identify as *dread*. "I don't even know how to dance. Not the kind you do in a ballroom," he clarified.

That, at least, was easily remedied. "I can teach you. Enough to get by, anyway." Aleksi winked, hoping to ease some of Einar's discomfort. "You'll have to rely on your relentless charm to do the rest."

Einar huffed out a wry laugh. When Aleksi did not join him, he raised one eyebrow. "What, you mean right now?"

"Well, the ball *is* tomorrow."

Einar stared at him for several long moments, reluctance warring with his dawning gratitude. Then he shrugged out of his heavy jacket, tossed it aside, and stood there in leather pants and a loose shirt of finely woven black cotton.

"All right." He held both arms out at his sides. "I am in your hands."

Aleksi circled him slowly, admiring his form even as he made minute corrections to it. Einar cut a fine figure, as always—his back straight, his stance relaxed, his shoulders thrown back with confidence. He was as beautiful as he was rugged, a devastating combination.

Here was Aleksi's chance to tip the scales and solidify the Kraken's seduction of his chosen lover. His heart ached, but the pain was tempered by his resolve. This was the right thing to do, so he would do it, and peace of mind would surely follow.

He moved to the corner, where the music player, an ornate cage-like machine made of finely wrought silver, rested on a carved stone table, wound and ready to play. Aleksi flicked the switch, and the crystal cylinder seated in the middle began to spin.

Music filled the room as he returned to circle Einar once again. "You don't have to learn all the most popular court dances. Naia won't know them, either. But that does not mean you cannot dance with her properly." He stopped in front of him. "One classic step, with a little added flourish. You can master that."

"And if I can't?"

"Sheer nonsense. If you can keep your feet while your ship bucks through a storm, you can do this." Aleksi took one of Einar's hands in his, then guided the other to his hip. "Step forward with your right foot, then simply follow what I do."

Aleksi moved with the music, coaxing Einar through a basic box step followed by a half turn. It was simple but effective, beautiful if executed well. His pupil moved haltingly at first, gazing down at their feet, but after a few repetitions, his steps smoothed, and he looked up once more.

"Excellent," Aleksi praised. "Now, it is imperative that you remember what a dance *is*—a physical expression of what we discussed previously. Consideration."

Einar's brow furrowed. "I don't see how wanting to make Naia happy will keep me from stepping on her feet."

"Think of it like sex, then. I *know* you're good at that."

Einar almost stumbled, but he recovered quickly. He eyed Aleksi arrogantly, though a hint of a blush colored his cheeks and the tops of his ears. "That was over two thousand years ago."

Einar had been human then, brash and fearless, with a reputation for fishing treacherous waters no other captain dared to sail. He'd brought that same arrogance to bear when visiting Seahold and Blade's Rest, showing true deference only to Dianthe and Elevia. He'd mingled with the High Court as blithely as only a secret prince in exile could have.

But what Aleksi remembered best were the small moments, the ones he imagined no one had been meant to witness. Einar's solicitous care for Petya, whom he treated like a mother rather than a first mate.

His crew distributing the Imperial goods they had plundered, without any particular regard for enriching their captain or themselves. The clear summer afternoon that Einar had spent repairing a tiny, battered boat, as meticulously as he'd ever maintained the Kraken, for a family that could not pay him for his labor.

These were the things that had caught Aleksi's attention, but it had not taken him long to realize that Einar's heart could not be touched. The man guarded it zealously, a dragon with his proverbial hoard of gold. So Aleksi had taken the considerable pleasure that Einar had offered freely, and then he'd moved on.

But he still remembered.

"It has been a while," he allowed, "but few people put in as much practice as you have only to get *worse* at something."

A hint of a smile curved Einar's lips, though it quickly faded. "True. But it's been so long since I had to *try*." He grimaced. "That sounds terrible, but you know how it is."

"How what is?"

They danced in silence for several moments before Einar answered. "Once people began to see me as a god, *they* chased *me*." He shook his head and corrected himself. "No, not me. They chased the Kraken."

"Ah. Now that, I do understand." How many potential lovers had Aleksi been obliged to turn away because they fancied themselves in love with him, when what they really wanted was some vague ideal rather than *him*? "It can be difficult, being seen as an idea. But . . . that does make it all the more intoxicating, doesn't it!"

"What?" Einar asked, puzzled.

"Having someone truly *see* you. Not the god, but the man."

"Intoxicating, perhaps, but also terrifying."

It was so unexpected that Aleksi was the one who almost stumbled this time. "Why would that frighten you?"

"Because I *haven't* been trying. They've chased me for centuries now. And I've never let them catch me unless I knew they wanted only what I had to offer—a night of pleasure. It's all I've ever given." Einar growled, low in his throat. "Maybe all I have to give."

Baffled, Aleksi shook his head. "Why would you think that?"

Magic surged through the room, and Einar's eyes began to glow a luminescent teal. "Because, Aleksi," he said gently. "Even in my human skin, I *am* the Kraken now. A creature of the deep. My blood runs cold."

"Not when you look at Naia," Aleksi countered.

"No. I want her. I crave her like I've never craved anything else, until it's an ache in my bones. She sings in the sea and in my dreams. I could drown in her." Einar shuddered, his glowing eyes haunted. "And I could break her."

So *that* was the part that truly terrified him.

"The ones who came before, they wanted to fuck the warrior or the pirate or the monster. I couldn't hurt them, not really." Einar closed his eyes and sighed. When he opened them again, they were their usual brown. "But I've never had gentleness inside me. Only lust and rage."

It was so far removed from what Aleksi saw that he barely managed to quell a snort. "You have lust and rage in you, certainly. But it's not all you have, Einar."

"How can you be so sure?"

The insecurity and fear in his voice threatened to break Aleksi's heart, but he smiled through it. "Because I happen to be an excruciatingly good judge of character."

Einar stopped dancing, his expression one of grave intensity. "You can see into a person's heart."

It wasn't a question, but Aleksi answered anyway, a knot forming in his gut. "If I must."

"Do it." He caught Aleksi's hands and pulled them to his face. "Tell me there's something inside me that's worthy of her. That there's a chance I won't shatter her."

Aleksi's first instinct was to yank his hands away, but he couldn't. Not with Einar staring at him with such desperate determination. But neither could he do what the man asked—no, demanded.

He shook his head. "Einar, trust me—the fact that you worry about that is answer enough."

"I am not afraid of what you might see," he insisted fiercely, holding Aleksi's gaze. "Only of what you might not."

"Only a fool would not be afraid." Aleksi had to make him understand. "You don't know what you're asking. Your entire soul would be laid bare to me. Nothing hidden, nothing kept sacred. Men have cried like babies, Einar, knowing all that I have seen."

Einar's answer was short and resolute. "Better my tears than hers."

So brave, almost to the point of foolhardiness. Here was the undaunted pirate who sailed into ferocious, icy seas without a second thought. He might claim that the notion of having someone see him was frightening, but it would not stop him from opening himself. And not just to mortal examination, either, but to having a god peer into his very soul.

Einar would do it—for Naia.

As would Aleksi.

"For her," Aleksi agreed in a whisper followed by a warning. "Breathe. And try not to fight it."

Einar didn't flinch, even when Aleksi gripped his face tighter and leaned closer, staring into his eyes. Beyond the rich brown flecked with gold, into the darkness of his pupils.

The rest of the world fell away.

Aleksi's breath bubbled out around him as he plunged into that darkness. It was cold and deep, the blackest depths of the ocean at night. It pressed in on him from all sides, the chilly pressure threatening to crush his very bones.

Then, a light.

Aleksi swam toward the wavering glow, closer and closer, his lungs burning, until the light resolved into a scene playing out in the dark water before him.

A woman and a man cradled a swaddled child between them. They were both dressed in royal finery. The woman wore a hammered metal crown, and the man resembled Einar so strongly that, had he been able, Aleksi would have gasped. These could only be his parents. They bent over their infant son, whispering all their hopes and dreams for his future.

It could have been a memory, a tiny scene that had once played out right where Aleksi stood. But it had the hazy, too-bright quality that he associated with longing.

This was Einar's hope, his vision of the past.

The heartwarming, heartbreaking scene dissolved before Aleksi, swept away by a warm eddy that swirled and then settled, forming a more vivid image. In this one, Einar sat at the captain's table on his ship, surrounded by his crew. This one had the familiar, lived-in feeling of memory, only crisper. Something exactly like this had happened hundreds of times before, and this was its distillation.

Einar's present.

Then it, too, dissipated. Aleksi blinked in the pitch black, until a song reached his ears, lilting and gentle and beckoning.

The ocean's song.

Flashes of light pierced the darkness, images that came and went as quickly as Aleksi could process them. Naia, her golden skin and dark hair spread across a pillow. Her lips curving against Einar's hand. A kiss scored by the soft sounds of waves lapping at the shore.

Einar, reaching out to Naia, desperate to close the distance between them. Water spun up between them, keeping them apart even as they strained toward one another. Finally, their fingers touched, twined, and a brilliant light washed everything away.

This was Einar's future, one he did not yet know how to grasp, and the thwarted yearning of it threatened to break Aleksi's heart.

He didn't know how long he stood in his borrowed bedchamber, his hands trembling on Einar's face, only that he could see Einar's worry even through the unshed tears veiling his vision.

Finally, Einar shook him gently. "Aleksi?"

He blinked, and the tears fell.

Einar brushed a thumb over Aleksi's wet cheek and grimaced. "Is it that bad?"

In that moment, still awash in Einar's reflected emotions, all Aleksi wanted was to taste that yearning. He moved without thinking, slid his hand to the back of Einar's head, drew him close, and captured his open mouth in a kiss.

Shock held Einar still, but only for a heartbeat. Then he moaned and slipped his fingers into Aleksi's hair, pulling at the short strands.

It had been *centuries* since their last embrace. Einar kissed with more skill but less polish, somehow, as if raw desire lent a hard edge to the caress. His tongue stroked over Aleksi's, pleading and commanding all at once.

It was mere steps to the bed. Aleksi burned to close the distance, to fall onto the soft surface and into all the other ways Einar had changed over the past two thousand years. But this was the opposite of what he'd intended, to remove himself from the situation as a potential complication.

Conscience—and no small amount of shame—led him to break the kiss and take a step back. "My apologies," he rasped. "I should not have done that."

Einar moved slowly, as if in a daze. He rubbed his thumb over his lower lip, then licked the spot. An absent gesture, quickly supplanted by sheer curiosity. "Why did you?"

Fuck. It was a complicated question, with an even more complicated answer. *Because I'm lonely, and I'm scared. Because you need her so much, and I know what that's like. And because I wanted to feel it, too, just for a moment.*

Because I could have loved you once.

But Aleksi could not say those impossible things, so he settled for a simpler answer. "I got carried away. It will not happen again."

Einar seemed to accept that. "As long as you weren't trying to distract me so you don't have to tell me that I'm hopeless."

"Not in the least. You can love her." *You* do *love her.* "All that is left now is to show her."

Some of the tension melted out of Einar, and he closed his eyes in vulnerable, unguarded relief. Then he opened his eyes once more, and the cocky, arrogant Kraken had returned. "I suppose that's where the dancing comes in."

"Don't try too hard," Aleksi advised. "Remember that she doesn't want you for who you aren't, but who you are."

Einar nodded solemnly. "Thank you, Aleksi."

He had to bite back an automatic denial, which was madness. He *had* helped, and he was happy to do so. But as he murmured words to that effect around the lump in his throat, he could not quell the feeling that he'd done something irrevocable. That his world had shifted off its axis.

He shook away the thought and clapped his hands together. "Well, are you ready to continue? You need to practice until you can hold a conversation instead of counting off the beats."

Another cocky grin. "Do your worst."

"I would not dream of it."

And yet, somehow, Aleksi suspected that perhaps he just had.

Chapter Seventeen

Primitive though they may be considered, one must respect the cunning of a people who would send the avatar of love as a diplomat. Few seem immune to his charm. Even I find myself drawn to him, almost enough to abandon my current work. An authoritative history of the war between the former Emperor and the High Court would be groundbreaking.

Untitled Manuscript in Progress
by Guildmaster Klement

The ball wasn't nearly as torturous as Einar had expected. Not because Gwynira's court had polished their manners, or because the seneschal had stopped his subtle campaign of sabotage. No, the formal outfit the servants had delivered for Einar had been the worst yet. It had been a glaring shade of orange that Einar could not imagine flattering *anyone's* skin tone, and at least two sizes too small. He'd shunned the offering in favor of another of his simple but meticulously tailored pirate prince outfits.

He'd attracted a flurry of whispers upon his arrival, but Einar doubted that the furtive mutters and sidelong glances were entirely due to his choice of attire. Gwynira might have expressed her belief that Einar was not behind the recent attacks against her duchy, but her court did not share her confidence.

Just as well. It kept him from having to make small talk with them.

Five of the more gullible-looking ones had gathered around Sir Jaspar, who was no doubt taking great liberties with the truth as he recounted the battle to save Jamyskar. Every lull in the music allowed a few words to drift to where Einar stood. Judging by those bits and pieces, the seneschal had single-handedly saved half the villagers while barely avoiding Einar's repeated attempts at treacherous sabotage.

A woman whose towering curls sparkled with enough diamonds to buy a palace gasped at Sir Jaspar's latest comment and shot Einar a look of delighted terror. The urge to bare his teeth in a snarl nearly overwhelmed him, but the woman had a glint in her eye that told him she would only relish it.

The fools of this court had lived too long under Gwynira's indifferent neglect. They might fear Einar, might even hate him, but they lived soft lives of unquestioned safety. Fear wasn't *real* to them. It did not settle in their bones and remind them of their own mortality. Fear had become a *hobby* for them, a thrill they sought out in order to feel alive, a bit of spice for their otherwise intolerably easy days of repetitive luxury.

In Gwynira's shoes, he would have packed the whole lot of them onto a ship and hoped the ocean saw fit to swallow it whole before they ever set foot on land again.

The thought drew Einar's attention to the low dais on the far side of the ballroom, where Gwynira reigned over her court while that enormous bear of a bodyguard lurked behind her. She was earning her fair share of sidelong looks tonight, as well—perhaps because she was actually smiling. It was startling to see the expression on her usually chilly face, even though the smile failed to entirely thaw her eyes. But Einar supposed that if anyone had a chance of doing so, it was Aleksi, who reclined easily on the ornate throne that had been placed next to hers.

The Lover looked as elegant as ever, his light-brown skin flawless, his dark hair artfully mussed, and his elegant body displayed to perfection in the Imperial clothing Einar had scorned. He didn't look stiff in the ornately embroidered jacket, the way so many other men of the court did. Aleksi's grace transcended whatever he put on his body to the point where the man would undoubtedly look handsome in a grain sack.

Einar doubted that physical perfection was what had softened Gwynira's demeanor, though. On the dais, Aleksi leaned in and whispered something to her, and his sudden smile could have eclipsed the sun. Gwynira's lips quirked, as if she was fighting the urge to return that smile.

She wouldn't last. No one did. Einar figured that was the point of sending Aleksi when you wanted to make friends—no one could know him for long and not end up wanting to earn one of those smiles.

As if the Lover could hear his thoughts, Aleksi's gaze swept toward him. Einar found himself on the receiving end of one of those devastating smiles, and the force of it nearly stole his breath. His lips tingled, as if he could still feel the other man's kiss, and the subtle crinkle around Aleksi's eyes made it clear the Lover knew *exactly* where Einar's thoughts had drifted.

Then Aleksi looked back to Gwynira, breaking the moment, and Einar exhaled roughly. A hardened pirate warrior who had seen over two thousand years of life was *certainly* too old to blush just because a man smiled at him—even if that man *was* the manifestation of desire and passion. *Especially* if that man was also wholeheartedly playing matchmaker. Only the Lover could half seduce a man while throwing him at someone else with both hands.

At least Einar knew better than to take it personally. Aleksi half seduced everyone.

The welcome thought of seduction had him surveying the vast ballroom again, but Naia was nowhere to be found. Not that he'd had to look to be sure. Her presence prickled over his skin now whenever she was near, as if their moment of passion in the ruins of the goddess's temple had bound them together with invisible ties. Naia's absence was a tangible ache, and not only because she was the only reason he'd wished to attend this cursed party to begin with. It was as if those ties had stretched too tight, threatening to snap.

He knew in his head the strings weren't real, but his heart dreaded the loss all the same.

His gaze swept over the seneschal just as the man shot him another withering look. Einar simply stared at him, letting his utter disregard gather behind his eyes in an unmistakable challenge.

Sir Jaspar blanched and looked hastily away.

A man stepped up next to Einar, a wry smile curving his lips. "Sir Jaspar has a terrible habit of picking fights he's too cowardly to win."

Einar turned to face him more fully. He'd seen him around the palace, and had come away with only the vague impression of a scholarly man with an easy smile. Nothing he saw now dissuaded him from that initial opinion. The man was of middling height, with black hair beginning to silver at the temples and ink stains on the first two fingers of his left hand.

He wore the same tunic and long jacket popular in Gwynira's court, but the embroidery on his was scant. His only true ornamentation came from a gold medallion as wide as Einar's palm. It hung from an equally ostentatious chain, and was stamped with scrolls and a quill.

A guild token. Einar had seen half a dozen of them over the centuries, usually cast in silver or bronze. Rumor claimed that few people of each generation earned the right to wear a golden master's medallion in their chosen field. Those fortunate or hardworking enough to be so honored were rarely parted from them.

The man noticed the path of Einar's gaze and beamed at him. "Never met a guildmaster before, have you?"

"I can't say I run across many in my line of work," he replied dryly, earning a hearty laugh from the other man.

"No, I can't imagine you would!" He inclined his head. "Allow me to introduce myself. I'm Guildmaster Klement, of the Scholar's Guild in Kasther. When young Jaspar was blustering about studying there, he meant he studied under *me*. It pains me to say he was a mediocre student."

Surprisingly, the name sounded vaguely familiar. It was no surprise, however, to find that Jaspar had overstated his scholastic achievements as generously as he had his martial ones. Einar bit back the urge to say as much, and responded only with a short nod. "I'm Captain Einar."

"Oh, I know." Smile lines crinkled around Klement's eyes as he beamed at Einar. "I've been so hoping for a chance to get you alone."

That sounded ominous, another observation that was undoubtedly unfit to make aloud. He cast another furtive glance around the room, but Aleksi was deep in conversation, and Naia *still* hadn't arrived.

There would be no rescue, then. He made what he hoped sounded like a polite noise of interest. It came out more like a low, rumbling growl.

"Oh, nothing nefarious, I promise." The master lifted a finger, and a servant rushed over with a tray full of chilled glasses filled with bubbling deep-amber liquid. "You must try the ice cider." Klement picked up a glass and handed it to Einar. When the servant had vanished, he raised his own glass in a toast and savored the first sip.

At his expectant look, Einar reluctantly tasted it as well. It was sweeter than he'd expected, almost cloyingly so, and unfortunately far too weak to get him as drunk as he needed to be if he was going to have to continue speaking with curious Imperials. "It's very good," he managed.

"Yes, a specialty of this island." Klement drank again, his fascinated gaze fixed on Einar's face in a way that was almost unnerving. "The precolonial history and culture of this island is a bit of a passion project for me, in fact. I've written several books on the subject."

Was that why the name sounded familiar? Had it been on one of the books Einar had found in the library? For the first time, honest interest in the man before him stirred. "Have you?"

"Indeed." Klement tilted his head. "You look surprised, Captain."

"Perhaps more . . . curious." Einar gestured with the glass in his hand to the little clusters of Imperial nobility, most of whom were still casting him sidelong glances. "In my experience, the Empire prefers to erase what came before. They rarely allow it to be preserved, and they certainly do not celebrate it."

"True enough," the man agreed readily. "Our former Emperor had his reasons for that, I suppose. The stability of the Empire, and his wish that the people focus on the wonders and glories of our promised future."

For all their blandness, there was an acidic edge to the words. Einar arched one eyebrow. "You didn't agree with those reasons?"

With a tight smile, Klement waved a hand, taking in the palace and the island beyond. "I am here, am I not?"

He said the words as if they were answer enough, and Einar frowned. "I don't understand."

The guildmaster huffed out a laugh, then lowered his voice. "I assume you know that Grand Duchess Gwynira was never the Emperor's—no, you call him the Betrayer, I believe. Either way, she was never one of his favorites."

It was a polite way of putting it. Einar had heard stories of Princess Sachielle's time spent as the Betrayer's prisoner. Gwynira had been the only member of Sorin's court to treat Sachielle with anything approaching kindness, and even that had been chilly at best, and almost certainly self-serving. But Gwynira had given Sachielle a knife meant to slay the Emperor, which was presumably the reason they were here to begin with.

Einar had never believed in making common cause with people simply because you shared an enemy, but there was no doubt Gwynira had viewed the Betrayer as exactly that—an enemy. But that still didn't answer his question. "What does that have to do with you being here?"

"Roughly a thousand years ago, Gwynira did something to enrage Sorin. This?" Klement gestured around again. "This was her punishment. Exile to a frozen island. He thought it clever, I imagine, given her affinity for ice. The rumor is that she was only meant to rule here until she had learned some humility. And yet, one thousand years later, here she remains, cut off from all the comforts of Imperial civilization."

It grated to hear rulership of his ancestral home referred to as *punishment*, but Einar supposed that to those accustomed to the sleek technology of the Empire, a place like this would seem barbaric.

"As for her so-called court . . ." The man gave a self-deprecating smile. "The Emperor has spent every generation since sending people like Sir Jaspar to serve here, just to irritate her."

So the whole lot of them were odious *by design*. People whose mere presences were meant to be punitive. It explained a lot about the atmosphere of this place.

And Gwynira's perpetually foul mood.

It did raise an interesting question, though. Einar studied the cheerful older man, wondering if he would actually answer it. When the man simply smiled and sipped his drink, Einar gave in. "So what did you do to get exiled here?"

"The greatest sin you could commit in the Empire without dying for it," Klement replied easily. "I liked to look backwards instead of forwards. I suspect I had come close to the line once or twice before, but after I wrote a book about the people who had called Kasther home before the Emperor's arrival, he stripped me of my estates and banished me here to live out my days with"—his voice changed, and for a moment it was an almost uncanny echo of the Betrayer's smoothly distinctive tone—"*the rustics and primitives you find so fascinating.*"

From everything Einar knew about the Betrayer, that *would* enrage the man. He wouldn't have liked the reminder that his glorious, benevolent Empire was steeped in blood and built on the bones of a hundred cultures he'd conquered. "You must have known it was a risk. So why did you do it?"

"I got complacent." Klement smiled and patted the heavy gold medallion on his chest. "I was the first scholar of history in five

Daughter of Tides

hundred years to become a guildmaster. In the Empire, a master is all but untouchable. I learned that day that *all but untouchable* means very little when you anger a god."

He wasn't the only one in this room who needed to learn that lesson. Einar might not have the power of a member of the High Court, but he had still walked this world for over two thousand years. Enduring the disrespect of the Imperial Court grated, political necessity or no.

"But I didn't mind coming here," the master continued. "I had already considered making Akeisa the focus of my next scholarly work. In Kasther, one might struggle for weeks to unearth a single half-remembered legend. Here, the culture still thrives. While I do miss my ancestral manor, it's possible he did me a favor. I get to spend my days in my research, and I no longer have to waste my time trying to educate people like Sir Jaspar." He beamed at Einar. "I should love to hear *your* stories sometime, Captain."

Einar could imagine nothing he wanted less than to have his childhood pain made into this man's next scholarly treatise. But the master *had* at least been friendly, so Einar made a noncommittal noise.

Klement clearly took it as agreement, because he lifted his glass in another toast before draining it. "Wonderful! Not tonight, though, of course. Perhaps in a less . . . confining situation. The local village will be holding their Flame of Life Festival tomorrow night. It's a charming celebration with a fascinating history."

An honest smile came to Einar's lips for the first time. "I've heard of it. Petya told me stories—"

"Petya?" Klement cut in excitedly, his eyes suddenly feverishly bright. "Petya of Stenyar? Captain of the Queen's Guard? So it's true, then? You were raised by her?"

"Yes, I—"

"*Amazing.*" The guildmaster clapped his hands together. "Oh, you and your friends simply must attend tomorrow. Tell me that you will."

The intensity of the scholar's interest was almost uncomfortable, but Einar sensed nothing beyond earnest fascination beneath the words.

167

He opened his mouth to answer, but in that moment a hush fell over the ballroom. One single stringed instrument wailed a solitary note before it, too, fell silent.

Heads turned, one by one. Einar followed their gaze to the doorway.

Naia stood there, framed perfectly in the archway, the light from a dozen crystal lamps catching the bits of glass sewn onto her gown. Every breath made her shimmer.

Einar didn't know where she'd gotten the dress, but it certainly wasn't Imperial in design. The wide skirt started at the bottom with the indigo of the deepest ocean, churning up into the navy of the North Sea, and the vivid teal of the Siren's own waters around Seahold. The tight bodice bled into the gentlest aqua, a color only seen around the distant Summer Isles, and was cut so low between her breasts that his fingers itched to trace the soft skin revealed there.

Naia took a single step forward, and the tiny bits of glass sparkled. She looked like a vision rising up out of the sea again, every shade of the ocean swirling around her as she shone like sunlight refracting through tiny drops of water. A siren in truth, ethereal and deadly, luring sailors to wreck themselves on whatever rocks she desired.

The ballroom was still frozen. Einar didn't think the assembled Imperials were even *breathing* anymore. They might not feel the sea in their bones the way those born to this island did—the way *Einar* did— but even the most ignorant of them recognized a goddess in their midst.

Every gaze in the room was fixed on her. And she only had eyes for Einar.

She swept toward him, her heels clicking softly and her skirts rustling as they swayed around her. The rest of the ballroom seemed to vanish in a swirl of mist, like the fog rolling in off the cliffs north of the Lover's Villa.

Einar's first step toward her felt like destiny, pulling him to where he had always been meant to be. The song of her wove through his blood, more intoxicating than anything a mortal instrument could hope to match, and his magic rose to meet it. He knew from the assembled crowd's sudden, sharp inhalations and muffled gasps that his eyes had begun to glow as the Kraken rose, too, brushing against the inside of his skin, whispering its need to take her to the ocean and dive so deep that no one would ever find them again.

Someday, he promised that other-self as he extended his hand. Naia was almost close enough to touch, but he didn't. Not yet. Simply held out his hand and let the words roll out in a rumbling invitation that still held too much of the monster. "Dance with me?"

Instead of accepting his hand, she gathered her skirts and spread them wide as she swept a curtsy so elegant, one would think she had come straight from the Mortal Queen's court. She gazed up at him, her eyes sparkling as much as her dress, her smile so bright that it burned away the fog. "With pleasure, Captain."

As she slipped her fingers into his, Einar heard the familiar cadence of the Lover's voice, lowered in a whisper. He turned in time to see Aleksi settling back in his chair with an easy smile. The musicians, seated close enough to the dais to be able to respond to any requests the Grand Duchess might make, lifted their instruments with haste.

Music exploded through the room. The song Aleksi had used to teach him how to dance.

The Lover left very little to chance.

Naia's free hand settled on Einar's shoulder as he reached for her waist. He tugged her closer with a hand at the small of her back and savored her inhalation as their bodies touched. His senses were so full of her that he couldn't remember the first step, but his body knew. One step forward and they were moving, gliding across the floor in a sweeping arc as she mirrored his every step. Advance and retreat, forward and back, swaying as the music he heard with his ears twined with the melody he'd heard in his dreams.

"You dance very well," she said softly, her eyes shining.

Perhaps Aleksi had imparted some skill or grace unto him, like the Lover giving a blessing, because Einar didn't even falter as he spun her into a turn that made her dress flare out and the onlookers gasp again.

Let them gawk. Let them *envy*. In this moment, she was his, and he proved it by pulling her to him with a wicked smile. "Only with you."

"You flatter me." The hand on his shoulder drifted up until her fingertips brushed the back of his neck, a whispering caress that was more than enough to stir his hunger. "Perhaps it's simply that we know each other so well now."

The mischief in her eyes left very little doubt what she meant. That swiftly, he was back in that shattered temple, on his knees before her. Memory conjured the sounds she'd made all too readily—soft and breathy at first, then yearning, then desperate as he drove her toward bliss. She tasted every bit as sweet as he'd imagined, and even the fury of a storm hadn't been able to distract him from the pleasure of feeling her shake apart for him.

A reckless thing to be thinking about with the hostile eyes of the entire court on them, but he didn't care. He let *his* hand drift, sliding it from the small of her back to the curve of her hip, where a flex of his fingers drew her so tightly against him that she could feel how his body responded to her every touch. He dipped his head just enough to let a whisper rumble over her. "Did you dream about the way I felt, my sweet goddess? Because I dream about the way you taste."

She tilted her head until their lips were so close he could almost taste that mischievous little smile. "Even when I'm awake," she breathed.

He nearly kissed her right then and there, but her cheeks flushed and she ducked her head with a laugh, hiding her face against his shoulder. His blood pounded as they spun again . . .

And he saw Aleksi's expression.

The Lover watched them the way everyone was watching them, but there was none of the triumph or pleasure Einar had expected to see on the face of a man whose matchmaking plans were coming to fruition. Oh, he was smiling pleasantly enough, but it was less like one of the Lover's generous smiles and more like one of Gwynira's—perfect and precise, with none of the joy reaching his eyes.

His eyes didn't smile. They looked *sad*.

Their gazes locked across the ballroom, and Einar could feel the ghost of Aleksi's hands on his body, guiding him through the steps of this dance. His lips tingled with the memory of their kiss, and it didn't matter that the entire length of the ballroom separated them. For one moment, it was as if the Lover was *there*, a part of every swaying step, every glancing touch. As if the three of them danced together.

Maybe if they were dancing together, they could chase the sadness from Aleksi's eyes.

Then the steps of the dance spun them again, and the moment was broken. Einar turned his face into Naia's hair and inhaled her familiar scent. She felt *right* like this, folded in his arms. Aleksi had told him he was worthy of the treasure of her trust . . . but the look in the other man's eyes haunted him.

There would never be any question whether the Lover was worthy. Even Gwynira's heart had softened for Aleksi, and Einar knew that his own beat faster when the man fixed the full force of his regard upon him. Who wouldn't be swept away by knowing the elemental manifestation of love saw *you*? Wanted *you*?

Did Aleksi want what Einar now had? And if he did, was it fair to Naia for Einar to stand in the way?

In that moment of indecision, Naia lifted her head to smile up at him, and something dangerous stirred inside him at the thought of never touching her again. An ache formed in his chest, like the memory of a loss so deep it was carved in his very bones.

If she walked away, he would let her go. He could do nothing else. But he would *never* turn away from her first.

"So intense," she murmured, lifting a hand to rub the spot between his eyebrows. He tried to relax his brow, but the ache had not yet dissipated. "What are you thinking?"

He parted his lips, unsure of how to respond. Then the final notes of the song dwindled into silence, and a spatter of applause broke the spell.

"Oh, wonderful!" Guildmaster Klement appeared at their side, positively beaming. "Your grace puts the rest of us to shame," he gushed, bowing deeply to Naia. When he straightened, he swept his graying hair from his face and gave her a hopeful look. "I can hardly compete with Lord Einar, but would you consider granting me this next dance, my lady?"

"I would be honored," Naia replied graciously, and Einar released her with great reluctance so she could accept the old man's hand. Klement started to lead her back into the dancing, but Naia looked back over her shoulder and arched one suggestive brow in a look that promised she and Einar *would* dance again—be it at the ball, or someplace far more intimate.

Einar fervently hoped it would be the latter.

He watched the two of them dance for a few moments, relieved to see nothing but that same earnest curiosity in the scholar's gaze. He wasn't exactly graceful, but whatever he was saying prompted an honest laugh from Naia as they twirled awkwardly. Satisfied that she wasn't in any distress, Einar went in search of something stronger than ice cider to drink.

He found it at a table near the back, where some sort of punch flowed over an unmelting ice replica of Gwynira's palace. The bright-blue color of the liquid didn't seem promising, but the first sip kicked so hard that Einar considered finding out what it was so he could bring a few dozen bottles back to his ship.

"You're doing well," a familiar voice murmured at his shoulder. "With the dancing, I mean. No one would ever guess you'd had only one lesson."

Einar turned and raised his glass to Aleksi. "I had a good teacher."

Aleksi mirrored his salute and smiled. "Unearned praise. But I will take it."

There was that smile again—perfect and precise—but the tone of the words had a slight edge that was reflected in the Lover's usually

Daughter of Tides

dancing brown eyes. They looked almost wry, now, as if he had told himself a joke that wasn't even a little bit funny.

That ache throbbed in Einar's chest, and this time he knew the name of it.

Fear.

Einar had spent his youth fishing the most dangerous waters known to their people, fighting currents and the weather and the beasts themselves to haul in the elusive great swordfish off of Dead Man Shoals. When the Empire had attempted to invade the Sheltered Lands, he had invented naval combat while still a mortal. He'd plunged into stormy waters to swim beneath massive ships and hack open their hulls. He'd found a way to rain fire down on enemy sails and decks. He'd tasted death a thousand times before his power had swelled and the Kraken had exploded out of him, promising that death would have to patiently wait out millennia before it could finally embrace him.

Fear had never been a problem for him before. Not until Naia.

Not until he considered losing her.

But what could he do? Ask Aleksi if he regretted his meddling? Ask the Lover if *he* wanted to be the one Naia gazed at with trust and mischief?

And what would Einar do if he did? Fight the embodiment of love itself? Winning would mean losing, because surely passion could not thrive if it came at the cost of the Lover's broken heart.

Einar took another bracing sip of the punch, let it burn away the fear, and made an awkward attempt to change the subject. "Things seem to be going well with Gwynira. I didn't know she could smile."

Between one heartbeat and the next, that odd discordance in the Lover faded. His smile finally reached his eyes as he chuckled. "I think the Grand Duchess appreciates that I have no hidden motives. I don't imagine she encounters that often."

Einar couldn't hold back a huffing laugh of his own. "Not in this court. Her seneschal is over there taking credit for the hard work of others. By the end of the night, Sir Jaspar will be the sole hero who saved every person in Jamyskar."

The Lover's gaze settled on Jaspar, who didn't seem to have the temerity to glare at *him* the way he had at Einar. "I've known men like him before," Aleksi murmured. "They're all talk and posturing." He paused for a moment, before continuing, "Until they're not. We'd best keep an eye on him, just in case."

"Definitely," Einar grumbled. Jaspar was watching Naia now, and the naked desire in his eyes was far more upsetting than the open hostility he'd directed at Einar. The fact that the man would disrespect Naia by erasing her heroics at Jamyskar, but still look upon her with such acquisitive hunger made Einar's blood boil.

When the dance in progress wound to a close and the ass started toward her, his anger manifested in an audible growl that only deepened when he caught sight of Naia's face. Even from across the room, he could see the hesitation in her gaze. She wanted to be anywhere but where she was, but was not willing to cause a diplomatic incident.

Einar slammed his glass down on the table hard enough to crack the stem. *Fuck* diplomatic incidents. "If he lays one finger on her, I'm going to snap it off."

He started to move forward, but one strong hand landed in the center of his chest. Aleksi held him back with that simple pressure and a low hum. "Subtlety, Einar. Please, allow me."

Whispers and conjecture and covetous gazes followed the Lover's progress as he crossed the room to Naia. When he was close enough to make it seem casual, he called her name, drawing her attention so she turned away from Jaspar. When she saw Aleksi reaching out to her, her gaze lit with relief as she slid her hand into his.

It was neatly done, without even the possibility of confrontation. Sir Jaspar was left standing a few paces behind them, alone and fuming, but with no opportunity to press his suit. Einar savored the man's helpless fury as the musicians responded to Gwynira's raised finger with a sudden ripple of music.

It was a far more complex song, one of the court dances Einar had dreaded. If he'd been forced to learn the steps to *this*, he would still be in Aleksi's room, cursing in frustration. But the Lover made it seem effortless, his inhuman grace turning the advances and retreats and complex spins of the dance into a floating kind of beauty that drew all eyes.

And Naia kept perfect pace with him. Maybe a memory of this dance had drifted up in her as they so often did, granting her skills beyond her experience. But Einar doubted many sailors and fishermen of the past had found themselves in ballrooms like this, navigating the intricate steps of complicated dances.

No, this was Naia's own inborn grace, coupled with the Lover's skill. He subtly guided her until most of the other dancers had fallen away, transfixed by the two creatures of otherworldly beauty floating through their midst. The Imperials might scorn the idea of gods beyond their blighted Emperor and the parody of the High Court he'd created, but it was clear that some of them had finally begun to understand just who walked among them.

The Lover. The manifestation of passion and life, whose blessings gifted fertility to the land and people. Whose gentle mercy could be found in the bond between family and friends and anyone whose heart had ever made space for another.

Even Einar's frozen heart wasn't immune. The rest of them had never had a chance.

"She's delightful." Einar glanced over to see Klement watching the dance with that same look of fascinated wonder. "I've seen the tokens the servants have left for her. They're quite taken with her. Did Petya teach you enough to understand why?"

Einar watched Aleksi's head dip toward Naia's ear. He whispered something that made her laugh, the delighted music of it sliding under Einar's skin to settle as longing. "She reminds them of the goddess," he answered with only half his attention. Naia wasn't the only one laughing. Aleksi was, too, any shadows of pain swallowed by pure joy.

"Yes, the goddess. Of course, the stories about her paint a fairly clear picture of what she might have looked like, and Lady Naia shares very few of her more superficial features. But the power? The power is enough to give even a doubting man pause."

"Uh-huh." Einar couldn't tell what *this* feeling in his chest was. He'd never imagined himself capable of jealousy. The potential loss of a lover was hardly threatening when you had never intended to keep them in the first place. If anything, on the rare occasion a paramour had lingered beyond a few nights of shared pleasure, Einar had been greatly relieved to detect any sign that their attention was wavering. As a mortal, he had not always been careful with the hearts flung at his feet. As a god, he had tried to move with greater care. The last thing he had ever wanted was for anyone to fall in love with him.

"And then there's the matter of your sigil . . ." Klement droned on, the words fading to an incoherent buzz as Einar watched Aleksi and Naia twirl and laugh.

Jealousy would be foolish, in any case. Aleksi was all but throwing Naia at Einar. Why the Lover was so fixated on the two of them making a match, he couldn't begin to guess. Then again, perhaps that was simply one of Aleksi's hobbies, the way the Witch enjoyed cultivating strange new plants and the Huntress read every book she could put her hands on. Why would the god of love not entertain himself by playing matchmaker?

If only reasoning it away could soothe the ache. It was still there, lodged deep in Einar's chest. Like a yearning for something that felt out of reach, which was equally foolish when he knew Naia would return to him soon enough.

Naia would. But Aleksi would drift onward, back to duty, back to diplomacy and the mission.

His gaze sought out the Lover again, examining his long-familiar features as if for the first time. That perfectly sculpted face—how many times and in how many places had Einar seen it lovingly carved into stone or marble, cast into bronze or gold? Artists had been trying for centuries to capture the elegant angle of the Lover's jaw, the exquisite shape of his cheekbones, the full lips that always seemed a mere heartbeat away from a smile. Few had managed, because chill, unmoving stone and metal couldn't capture *his essence*, the warmth and the life and the unspoken promise of acceptance and compassion in every expression or gesture.

Einar knew his own features were pleasing enough. But when artists captured him in stone, it was inevitably far more charming than the real thing. Stone had a softness to it that Einar lacked. Softness had had no place in his life—not as a child on a mean little fishing boat, not as a sailor braving the frozen north, not as a pirate or a warrior, and certainly not as the Kraken.

The Lover was everything warm that the Kraken could never be. And the Kraken had hard edges that the Lover would always lack. They were nothing alike, which was undoubtedly why their paths had so rarely crossed in the past.

But as Aleksi twirled Naia through the final complicated spin of the dance, Einar caught a glimpse of the Lover's unguarded face.

They had one thing in common now. *Her.*

And maybe this new ache in his chest was so odd because it did not go with his fear. Einar didn't want to snatch Naia away from Aleksi.

He wanted to join them.

Polite applause broke out as the song ended. The collected nobles might spurn Einar, but they were as susceptible to Aleksi's charm as the mortal court in the Sheltered Lands had been. Naia's cheeks flushed as Aleksi acknowledged the acclaim with a dazzling smile, then tucked her hand through his elbow and murmured something to her as they headed back toward Einar.

That funny ache in his chest expanded as they came within earshot and Naia gazed up at the Lover, her eyes sparkling. "You did *not* say that to the king's envoy."

"No, I did not," Aleksi admitted. "But I thought it very hard in his direction."

Her laughter swept over Einar in a wave, obliterating that ache under the sheer pleasure of having her close again. Of having *them* close. Because this wasn't like watching her endure Jaspar's awkward flirting. Aleksi made her laugh with delight. He made her eyes sparkle, and Einar *liked* to see them sparkle.

And he liked that the smile had returned to Aleksi's eyes, the warmth of the Lover the same sweet caress he remembered.

"Excuse me," he said, cutting off whatever Klement had been saying. He managed a polite nod, then swept forward to meet Naia and Aleksi. Abruptly, feeling the weight of the gazes of the entire court upon them, Einar simply wanted to be gone from this cursed place. "How long do we have to stay to be polite?" he rumbled.

One of Aleksi's elegant eyebrows swept up. "Longer than this," he said dryly. But then he seemed to soften. "But not too much. Give it another quartermark, and you can sneak away." Aleksi raised Naia's hand to his lips for a kiss before releasing her. "I'll handle the party."

A tiny furrow of concern creased her brow. "Are you certain?"

"I could do this in my sleep, love," Aleksi assured her. Then he cocked his head and grinned. "Fairly sure I have, actually. The first King Dalvish's court never was very exciting."

Leaving would be a blessing. But leaving Aleksi behind, alone, surrounded by these sharks . . .

Protectiveness stirred—irrational, foolish protectiveness. Even if Gwynira and Arktikos were Dreamers, they were still children compared to Aleksi, barely past their first thousand years. The Lover had taken out another of the Betrayer's court with the lazy ease of swatting a bug. The man was devastatingly brutal with a sword in his hand.

Aleksi didn't need Einar to watch over him. This ballroom was the Lover's traditional battlefield, and he understood it in a way Einar never could. So he locked down his hesitation and nodded. "Thank you—"

But Aleksi was already turning away, melting back into the crowd.

A touch at Einar's elbow drew his attention. Naia was smiling up at him with a sweetness that almost stole his breath. He lifted a hand, shivering at the bliss when she slid her fingers trustingly into his. "One more dance, then?"

"Insolence!" she gasped, her eyes alight with teasing glee. "I dressed up for you. You owe me at least two."

Einar traced the plunging neckline of her dress with his other hand, letting his fingertips graze her collarbone just to see her flush again. "Are you saying you wore this for me?" he asked in a rumbling whisper.

"Of course," she replied simply. She stepped closer, and Einar set a hand at her waist and did his best to lead her into the dance already in progress. They turned—a little too swiftly, as Einar attempted *not* to dance them directly into another couple—and Naia smiled down at her skirts as they flared out. "It has all the colors of the ocean."

"It's beautiful," he said, and he meant it. The crafting was exquisite, and when she moved she looked like an ethereal creature of the depths rising up on a cresting wave to tempt a sailor to his doom. Which gave him the perfect idea of where to take her.

Perhaps he should feel bad about leaving Aleksi to do this on his own, but the Lover was the diplomat. And stealing Naia away would give him the chance to ask her one important question.

Hopefully Aleksi would like the answer.

Chapter Eighteen

The goddess changed the day she met the storm god.

The stories speak of a god so dazzled by her bravery that he lost his heart and followed her home. What they omit is that she took that heart in trembling hands, held it close to her breast like a treasure.

The stories never say that she fell in love with him, too.

from the unpublished papers of Rahvekyan High Priestess Omira

Naia thought they might make a quick escape from the glittering confines of the palace. But as the first quartermark drifted into a second, she realized they would not get away so easily.

First, a man approached them. He was dressed like a sailor, only his clothes were made of delicate, readily damaged fabrics that would never hold up to the rigors of actual work. He braved Einar's wrath to ask about the quality of the fishing beyond the Western Wall. Naia looked on in startled amusement . . . until an older woman dripping with jewels cornered her to invite her to her estate on the eastern coast of Linzen. She extolled its virtues before finally coming to the point: could Naia help her design and execute a water feature that could take advantage of the property's proximity to the waterfront?

These two encounters would have been just absurd enough to make for an entertaining story, only it *kept happening.* Half a dozen nobles were eager to demand Naia's help, press her for information . . . or beg formal introductions to the Lover.

On and on it went, with time only for her and Einar to share rueful smiles that inevitably gave way to looks of warm promise. By the time they managed to extricate themselves and head toward a somewhat sheltered exit to the side hall, Naia was almost giddy, breathless with . . . what? Nerves? Anticipation? Arousal?

All that, and more. Still, she paused, her hand on the door's latch, and sought out Aleksi one last time. He had insisted that he would be fine on his own, but she found herself strangely reluctant to leave him.

He was watching them, an inscrutable look darkening his eyes. Then he blinked and it was gone, replaced by a wink, a half smile, and a subtle nod toward the door. Einar opened it with a nod in return, and Naia left the dazzling lights of the ballroom behind.

Out in the darkened corridor, Naia slipped her hand into Einar's. "Shall we hide in my chamber with a bottle of wine?"

A wicked smile curved his lips, making his dark eyes sparkle even in the dim light. "I have a better idea."

He tugged at her hand, pulling her down the hall. Several turns later, Naia had no clue where they were, but Einar seemed to know the way. Finally, he shoved open a large, heavy door, spilling them directly out on the path to the docks.

Naia slowed to a stop. "You're taking me to your ship?"

Einar turned, his grin melting into an expression of earnest solemnity. "I'm taking you to my home."

Warmth curled through Naia. Einar wanted her in his bed—she understood the carnal truth of that now more than ever—but this was something else entirely. His crew, his family, was on that ship, and he was inviting her to spend time with them.

Whatever else, it was clear that Einar did not mean to keep Naia rigidly separated from his life, his *real* one, like he had with the rest of his temporary bedmates through the years.

She released his hand, but only to slide her arm through his and snuggle closer. "That sounds lovely."

The ship was docked at the end of one of the floating piers. With the tide in, the ramp to its berth was almost level, though it rose and fell gently with the waves in the sheltered harbor. Another ramp led up to the Kraken itself, wide enough for Naia to navigate it even in her voluminous dress. Einar kept a hand at the small of her back all the same, steadying her when the ramp moved. He whistled once, a short, sharp sound that brought shuffling footsteps running across the deck.

Jinevra appeared, a frown creasing her brow until she caught sight of them. "Good evening, Cap. Lady Naia." She helped Naia board the vessel. "Welcome home."

Several others called out greetings, and Petya emerged from belowdecks. "Well," she said, drawing out the word as she looked them over. "Aren't you two all fancied up?"

"There was a ball tonight," Naia explained.

"So I heard."

"I decided that we deserve a night away from the castle," Einar added.

"Good." She gestured over her shoulder. "Jinevra's on watch. Most everyone else is in the quarterdeck cabin. Gambling, I believe."

Einar raised a questioning eyebrow at Naia. "Would you like to join them?"

She couldn't quite smother a laugh. "You once warned me against gambling with your crew. Are you lifting that restriction?"

He leaned close enough to whisper in her ear. "Perhaps I'm learning not to underestimate you. And if they do . . . well. They can pay for it. Quite literally."

"Deal."

Conversation and laughter and light and even a bit of music drifted out of the quarterdeck cabin, where the doors had been thrown open to the cool night air. When they walked in, a cheer of welcome rose from the round table in the center of the room.

"You're back!" Arayda tossed a handful of cards into the middle of the table. "Does this mean we're *finally* pushing off?"

Einar shook his head. "Not yet. Diplomacy takes time."

Silvio fanned out a handful of cards, then nimbly flipped them back into a neat stack as he shuffled. "The game is Three Queens. Are you in?"

Borrowed memories supplied Naia with a vague notion of how to play. The goal was to be the first player to collect three queens from the specialized deck. Players could employ a number of tricks to steal a displayed queen from another, and the game involved no small amount of bluffing—and flat-out lying.

"Thank you," Naia demurred, "but I'd rather watch."

"Very well. Captain?"

"Of course."

A sailor whose name Naia did not know jumped out of his seat and offered it to her. Einar held it as she sat, then brushed a lingering caress over the back of her shoulder as he pushed in her chair. She shivered, almost missing the glare he flashed at Arayda, who sat beside Naia.

"What?" she exclaimed. "It's not *my* fault you put the pretty lady next to me." She winked at Naia. "But I'm not moving."

Einar growled. "You want me to tell your wife?"

"Not unless you want Jinevra down here, flirting with her, too."

Einar's growl turned into a grumble, and the person on Naia's other side hopped out of her chair. "Here, Cap. Take mine."

He slid into the seat, pulling it so close that his thigh pressed against Naia's, warm even through the many layers of her dress. Ceillie, Petya's cat, rose from her spot on the table, stretched, and waited politely for Naia to pick her up before settling into her lap as the game began.

Everyone tossed their coin into the center of the table, and Silvio dealt the first hand. Unlike most card games Naia had played, Three Queens did not pay out the pot until the very end of the game. Every hand had a higher buy-in than the one before, and running out of money to pay into the pot meant forfeiting the game. So even if you had a strategy for being the first to collect your three queens, you had to win as quickly as possible.

Einar retrieved his cards and began sorting them. It was a solid hand—no queens, but a jack and a king that could both be used to steal from another player. And that was all Naia had time to notice before his leg moved against hers.

She inhaled sharply.

Einar cleared his throat. "Has anyone been giving you a hard time since the attack on Jamyskar?"

Petya, who was still standing in the doorway, snorted. "A few Imperial brats with more bluster than sense came down to shout insults at us, but Gwynira's guards chased them off."

Bexi, who sat on the opposite side of the table, shook her head and clucked her tongue. "Too bad, too. I offered to come closer and let them say it again—with feeling, this time—but no takers."

Her husband chuckled. "They did seem ready to soil themselves." He paused and smiled. "It was beautiful."

"You're biased, Brynjar."

"Yes, I am."

Solorena, who wore her dark hair in intricate braids tonight, tossed down a queen with more force than was strictly necessary. "As if we would have attacked a village full of fishermen and old ladies. Or been so incompetent if we *had*."

Einar started the next round by throwing more coins into the center of the table. "Everything else has been quiet?"

"I'd say more odd than quiet," Arayda answered.

"Odd?"

"Jinevra and I went out for dinner one night," she explained, "and you'd have thought *we* were gods. No one would let us pay for anything, and they kept asking us questions."

"About what?" Naia asked.

"About the captain, mostly. But also about you, Lady Naia," Arayda admitted, tossing her coins into the pile.

It made sense that the people who lived around the castle had heard about Einar's return, and that they were curious about their fabled lost prince. But Naia was less certain about why they would be eager to hear about *her*.

Unless they'd bought into the idea that a god with an affinity for water—*any* god—must be their goddess, returned. The belief had to linger, or else who was keeping those lanterns up the hillside filled and burning?

Or perhaps Naia and Einar were simply so inextricably linked in the people's minds already that curiosity about their prince naturally extended to his lover.

Naia dipped her head to hide the blush the word elicited, even in the silence of her own mind. Ceillie stared up at her, her green eyes unblinking.

"I hope you were circumspect," Einar muttered.

"Don't worry. We kept our mouths shut."

Bexi laughed. "Oh, I doubt that. Ever since that night, the villagers have been leaving trinkets on the dock. Fresh fruit and little charms and all sorts of things. Almost like offerings."

Nusaiba rapped on the table. "Stop trying to delay your inevitable defeats and *play the damn game*."

The game went on. Cheers and protests alike went up all around the table as queens were stolen and then stolen again. With each hand, the pot slowly grew, while the much smaller stacks of coins in front of each player dwindled even further.

One by one, players began to fall. Cards were laid down, and still more were dealt. Einar lost his only queen, and soon after, the last of his coin. The others teased him mercilessly, always stopping short of saying straight out that he'd lost because most of his attention was focused on Naia.

The flurry of activity and the noisy, boisterous voices should have overwhelmed Naia. Instead, it felt like *home*. She could easily imagine whiling away the long evenings at sea like this, laughing over ale and cards until her sides ached.

And then retiring to the captain's cabin.

Another blush heated her cheeks, then deepened when Einar's hand brushed her thigh. Her gaze met his. His eyes were still brown, but a tiny hint of sea green and teal swirled near their centers, and Naia found herself leaning toward him.

She jerked back when Ceillie meowed a protest and jumped off her lap, having obviously decided that it wasn't a restful place to be, after all.

Arayda laid down a third queen and shouted in victory. The others grumbled as she began to rake the huge pile of coins in her direction, and Silvio held up the cards. "Another game?"

But Petya stepped in. "That's enough lazing about. Arayda, go buy your wife something pretty. Now, you all have duties, so be about them."

"But I need to win my money back," Solorena protested, only for Nusaiba to hustle her out of her seat with a grin and a murmur.

As Petya closed the doors behind them all, Naia stifled a laugh and began to gather the scattered cards. "Well."

Einar groaned. "I'd say they're usually more subtle than this, but they're not."

"Do they need to be?"

"Not on this ship. Not while I'm still captain." He looked down at the cards in her hands, and another wicked smile curved his lips. "Lady Naia, what do you intend to wager?"

"Who says I'll be gambling with you?"

"I was *hoping* you might consider it."

"No. I managed to capture your interest, and that is luck enough for me. I don't intend to push it." She set the cards aside, then pushed the table over just far enough to clear a bit of space in front of Einar's chair. Then she climbed in his lap. "I intend to focus on other things tonight."

His hands settled on her hips. "I do like this much better than cards."

With the endless layers of her skirt puffing up around them, it felt like they were surrounded by the sea and the sky. It felt right, and she wound her arms around his neck. "It must be nice for you, being back on your ship for a little while."

His fingers swept up her spine, light and teasing, past the fabric of her dress to bare skin. "Like I can finally take a full breath again. It's good to feel the rhythm of the waves."

This visit had been so hard on him. She and Aleksi had no personal pain tied up in this mission; for them, it was just that. But Einar's entire life had been shaped by the trauma of colonization, of losing his home, losing his parents. By the very circumstances that had led to Gwynira's rule.

"You could stay here, with your crew," she suggested softly. "I don't mind, and I'm sure Aleksi wouldn't."

"No." The word was hard and immediate, though his expression gentled a moment later. "I don't think I could rest easily away from the two of you. I know you don't need protection from mortals, and Aleksi can take care of himself, but . . ."

"I understand. But I had to offer, you know that, right?"

Einar caressed her cheek. "And I appreciate it, sweet goddess."

She brushed her lips over his, quick and light. It was sweeter than their first kiss in the temple ruins, but no less electrifying. "You're welcome."

He wound his hands in the hair she'd left down this evening, his thumbs grazing the back of her neck. "I may have been wrong before, when I said that all I can offer you is a single night of pleasure."

187

Naia shivered. "Oh?"

He moved his hands higher, to the pins that secured the rest of her hair. Slowly, he plucked one pin. "I can't offer you fancy castles or balls or any sort of proper life. But I could offer you this." He tossed the pin on the table and tugged another free, followed by another. "The sea. This ship. A crew that adores you." Her hair tumbled down around them as he liberated the final pin. "And me."

Pretty, meaningless words could not have moved her half as much as this simple declaration, spoken with a sincerity that made unshed tears burn her eyes.

For a man who claimed not even a passing acquaintance with romance, Einar managed quite well.

"What more could a water nymph want than a life at sea?" Naia smiled and framed his face with her hands. "And a dashing pirate."

But he did not return her smile. He remained solemn and serious. "That's the question, isn't it? *Would* you want more? Because the Lover can give you things I never can."

It was so unexpected that it shocked a laugh from her. "I can't imagine Aleksi wants to give me anything."

"Then perhaps you've not noticed the way he looks at you." Einar ran his fingers through her hair, taming the wild curls. "There were moments tonight when I thought I glimpsed envy in his eyes."

It seemed *impossible* . . . but Naia had made incorrect assumptions about Aleksi before. He had been pushing her and Einar together, that much was unassailably certain. In fact, his efforts had seemed to increase as the days passed, even as he himself seemed to pull away from them.

Naia had imagined that his matchmaking efforts had been driven by a desire to see them both happy—and she still fully believed that to be true. But she'd also thought his current emotional distance to be born of courtesy, a way to ensure that she and Einar were focused on one another instead of being distracted by the mission or Aleksi's presence.

Perhaps that was not it at all.

"I care about Aleksi," she said finally. "He deserves to be happy, maybe more so than most. He gives so much, yet expects so little. It doesn't quite seem fair, does it?"

"No," Einar whispered. "But I must confess something, Naia. I asked him to tutor me, so that I could dance with you at the ball. And, during the lesson, he kissed me."

"He *kissed* you?" She pulled back a little and studied Einar's face. In it, she found guilt, concern . . . and a tiny shred of guarded interest. "It sounds more like Aleksi might be envious of *me*."

Einar chuckled ruefully. "If the Lover yearned for me alone, he's had centuries in which to act."

"Timing can be everything."

"So can circumstance. Perhaps the god of love saw little to intrigue him in the Kraken's frozen heart." Einar lifted her chin gently. "But it isn't so frozen anymore."

Naia's heart shuddered, then resumed a faster beat. Here was everything she'd wanted, laid out before her—Einar, freely offering her his heart and his future. She and Einar could pretend they had not noticed Aleksi noticing *them* and move ahead together.

That path was safe . . . but it would mean ignoring the loneliness she had glimpsed in Aleksi. It would mean shutting a part of herself off, and potentially a part of Einar, as well.

Or.

She and Einar could make themselves vulnerable—not just to each other, but to Aleksi—and find out the full extent of what their hearts could hold.

In the end, there was only one thing she could say. One thing that mattered. "Do you love him? *Could* you?"

He considered that. "Not so many weeks ago, I would have said I couldn't love anyone." He pressed his lips to hers in a lingering kiss. "Now, I say that I would be a poor excuse for a pirate if I could not take a risk when the potential treasure to be won is so great."

"Then we take the leap," Naia whispered. "And no matter where we land, it will have been worth it."

Einar kissed her again, more deeply this time, his tongue begging entrance to her mouth even as his hand clenched in her hair demanded it. It went on and on until Naia was squirming on his lap, and he had to grip her hips to hold her still.

She gasped for breath. "How do we speak to Aleksi about this?"

"Leave it to me." Einar licked her lower lip one last time. "I know the perfect place."

Chapter Nineteen

> While each village seems to have its own spattering of important days scattered throughout the year (see Chapter Seven for as comprehensive a list as I was able to assemble), there is one day every local on the island celebrates: The Flame of Life Festival.
>
> Akeisa: Religious Figures and Rites
by Guildmaster Klement

Einar had grown up on stories of the Flame of Life Festival. It had been one of Petya's favorite days of the year, a vibrant celebration of life and devotion to the goddess. He'd even tried to convince her to attend this one, hoping that the knowledge that something so beloved had survived the centuries might banish some of the pain she carried. But Petya was unwavering—she would not set foot onto the shores of Rahvekya while an Imperial still sat on the throne.

So it was probably just as well that Guildmaster Klement had sent his regrets, pleading an unexpected obligation. Einar suspected that the man had been more interested in talking to Petya than him, anyway. There had been hints that an invitation to come to the ship and speak with her would be most welcome, but Einar had pretended not to understand.

Klement's fascination might be well-meant, but Petya had enough painful memories to deal with without some overly curious scholar mining the shards of her past.

Petya may not have joined them, but Einar knew she would still celebrate the day in private. For many years, he'd done the same thing, taking a moment to light a candle and spare a thought for those lost to him. He'd never imagined he'd get to actually attend the festival. Or that the ocean goddess most on his mind wouldn't be the one of ancient legend, but the one whose lips he could still taste.

The festivities here in Aynalka had spilled out onto the beach, where they'd cooked seafood in giant pits in the sand and opened cask upon cask of sweet wine and crisp cider. The people had feasted as the sun dipped low over distant waters, with music and laughter and drinks that flowed freely and heated the blood.

But that was only the first part of the celebration. The part where children danced and screamed in delight, and ate far too many of the sugar-glazed cakes baked with the spring's generous tealberry harvest. When the first stars lit the sky overhead, the children would be tucked safely into their beds, and the people would finally ignite the massive bonfire that waited on the beach.

Then the villagers would celebrate the more carnal side of life. Einar and Naia would celebrate it, too—and find out if the Lover cared to join them.

Naia was seated next to him at the table, her soft warmth pressed against his side making it impossible for him to focus on dinner. Even though Aleksi sat on her other side, he proved an equal distraction— Einar had spent centuries listening to the Lover's warm laughter and smoky voice, but anticipation had turned both into a newly pleasurable torment.

He'd spent much of his life navigating by the stars, but he had never craved a glimpse of them quite so much as he did now.

Daughter of Tides

Across the table, one of the village elders was telling Aleksi and Naia about the origins of the festival. Jenz was easily in his ninth decade but still had a full head of snow-white hair braided with leather strips and adorned with small chips of goddess-touched glass. His pale skin had been weathered by sun and sea, and his eyes were the perfect aqua of Siren's Bay. There was a look to the shape of his features—a heavy brow, strong jaw, a bold nose that angled sharply down to a mouth made for laughter—that was achingly familiar.

The old man reminded him of Petya.

"In these times, it isn't unusual to see a storm this late in the season." His voice was deep and easy, with the cadence of a practiced storyteller. "But in ancient days, when the goddess walked these shores and the island bloomed green even in winter, sailors felt safe enough venturing north to fish the waters of the Great Reef. So the whole island was shocked when a storm whipped through, blowing hard enough to tear the very roofs from their cottages. They knew this was no ordinary gale. Only the storm god in a temper could cause such destruction."

Naia propped her chin on her hands, her eyes alight with fascination. "And this is why you celebrate?"

The old man chuckled. "I won't say I've never lifted a bottle and spit into the teeth of a storm in my day, but that's a different kind of celebration. No, today we honor the goddess."

He lifted his glass as if toasting the goddess, but there was a look in his bright-blue eyes, one Einar had seen reflected back from every person who had shyly approached their table. A look that said maybe, tonight, they were also celebrating *Naia*. "The goddess knew the sailors would be lost without her aid. So she told the people to prepare a great feast, for their friends would surely be hungry upon their return. And then she walked into the sea."

"To spit into the teeth of the storm herself."

Jenz grinned at Naia, as if she'd answered a trick question. "The goddess would never allow the storm god to take what was hers. And every sailor who's ever drawn first breath on this island belongs to her."

193

Naia's eyes sparkled as she refilled the man's wine. "So what happened?"

The ancient sailor turned those piercing eyes on Einar, and it was *his* turn to be tested. "Well, boy? Do you know the legend?"

"Of course," Einar replied. "The villagers lit signal fires on the beaches to guide their sailors home. The fires burned for three days before they glimpsed the first of the sails."

Jenz beamed at him like a proud grandfather. "So they did. The goddess had met the storm god and demanded that he release her people and take his foul mood elsewhere. Not being used to such outright defiance, the storm god relented. All seventeen vessels made it back home, with the goddess at the helm of the flagship. They had taken such a beating that not a single ship was seaworthy, but they rode the waves sweet as can be until everyone was safely back on land."

Naia smiled, looking thoroughly enchanted. "That's beautiful."

"I've always thought so." The old storyteller reached across the table to pat her hand. "It's an honor to have another with us who can hear the moods of the sea, especially on this night."

Naia raised her glass. "To the sea," she murmured. "And to having good reasons to celebrate."

"To the sea," Jenz echoed, and finished his drink. Then he set his cup down. "Speaking of celebration, I'll let you three enjoy the sunset. Those of us with old bones and achy joints leave this night to the young." He grinned as he pushed himself to his feet. "Besides, someone has to keep the children tucked up in their beds."

As the old man took his leave, Aleksi observed, "I can't decide if that sounded promising or ominous."

"Probably depends on your mood." Einar propped one elbow on the table so he could have a clear view of Aleksi's face—and his reaction. It was hard to keep his voice casual when so much hope rode on his next words. "And on whether you're up for a little wicked revelry tonight."

"When am I not?"

Daughter of Tides

The words were flippant. Automatic. Which didn't mean they weren't true, but it almost certainly meant that the normally perceptive Lover had not guessed at their motivations for the evening.

Einar had tried to convince himself that it didn't matter. That there was no path tonight that ended in defeat, when Naia was already won. He'd told himself that Aleksi was a secondary goal—a gift for Naia, or a way to ensure that she lacked for nothing. Perhaps he simply wanted to share with her the joy of an experience deeply coveted by so many—few who were blessed with the Lover's touch ever forgot the experience, no matter how many centuries passed. Einar had not.

But the lies he had told himself were unraveling. The tension rising in him now was far too exquisite to be anything but deeply, painfully personal.

If he'd had a quiet moment alone, he might have been able to find the truth at the heart of his tangled feelings. But a priestess appeared out of the swirl of people, her status made clear by her flowing sea green robes and the bronze diadem that circled her forehead. "My lords. My lady." She inclined her head in a gesture of respect before sweeping her hair back over her shoulder. "I'm Riika, the Flame Bearer for Aynalka. Normally, it would be my duty to light the bonfire, but we all agreed. We would be honored if our lost prince would serve as Flame Bearer this year."

It was the first time Einar had ever heard the word *prince* applied to him without feeling the pinch of it. Perhaps it was because the *lost* part seemed so much more important to her. On this day of all days, those who celebrated would cherish the proof that, even if it took thousands of years, the goddess would always bring their loved ones home.

Well, *a* goddess would.

He glanced at Aleksi and Naia. The Lover only smiled in encouragement, and Naia touched his shoulder. "Go," she whispered. "It's all right."

Even knowing that it would only fuel the villagers' speculation, he couldn't stop himself from catching her hand and lifting it to his mouth

195

for a kiss. She smiled as his lips brushed the backs of her fingers, a sweet flush coming to her cheeks, and it was harder than he wanted to admit to make himself rise and follow the priestess.

At the edge of the festivities stood a polished table surrounded by a protective circle of white-haired elders. Seashells and tealberry blossoms lay strewn around a tall bronze lantern. Sigils had been hammered into it—the seashell of the goddess, the kraken that flew on his own banners, swooping lines that looked like the waves crashing against the shore. Delicate glass shielded a flame, the distinct teal color that came from oil harvested from the great swordfish that thrived only in the coldest seas.

"The Flame of Life," Riika said reverently. Two of the elders parted so she could pick up the lantern and cradle it in her hands. "Come."

As she turned, Einar realized that much of the laughter and chatter had ceased. Silence reigned, and it seemed as though every eye in the village was on them as they walked to where dirt and grass gave way to the rock and sand. Tiny wooden structures draped in colorful bits of fabric lined the high tide line in either direction, each with its own small fire pit in front of it where driftwood and kindling waited.

"For the night's revelries," Riika explained with a smile, following his gaze. "Not all celebrate in a carnal way, and many will choose to return to their own beds. But it is considered good fortune to pass the night beneath the stars. Each fire is a beacon, welcoming our lost loved ones home. And it's a celebration of new love."

Einar tore his gaze away from the little makeshift tents—and thoughts of all the ways he'd like to celebrate beneath the stars *this* night—and glanced at her. "New love?"

"Mmm." Riika's eyes were too bright, as if he'd walked into a trap. "When the goddess bargained with the storm god, she won more than her ships. He followed her back to this island, his heart already half in her keeping. So when lovers celebrate this night, they also give thanks that our goddess found someone who could cherish her, the way she always cherished us."

Einar had vague memories of that part of the story. As a young boy, the idea of braving a terrifying storm had been more interesting than the part about falling in love. But he remembered the tale . . . and he knew what Riika wanted from him.

"You know, don't you?" she said softly. "You know the storm god's real nature. His name."

Yes, he knew. He'd chosen his sigil for his ship, out of arrogance or ego or simply because, in his heart, he'd always wanted to be as fierce a protector as the man in Petya's stories. "The Kraken."

Satisfaction lit her eyes. "It will be good, to have the Kraken and the goddess celebrate their love tonight."

Einar opened his mouth to correct her, but she'd already turned to continue toward the massive tower of stacked driftwood. Riika stopped a dozen paces away, where a slender torch had been stabbed into the sand. The strips of cloth wrapped around it were soaked in more of that distinctive oil, the scent unmistakable as Einar obeyed her gesture and picked it up.

"Deep in the heart of the island lies a temple where our most devoted spend their lives guarding the original flame." Her voice rose, and Einar realized the entire village was spread out behind them, gazes fixed on the priestess as she lifted the lantern high.

"This is a bit of that fire, saved from the very ones our ancestors lit at the goddess's behest. Every year, all across this island, the Flame Bearers gather at the temple to bring a piece of that undying flame back to kindle our own sacred fires in memory of the goddess and her miracle. And every year we bring back the ashes, newly imbued with our hope and faith, to feed the original flame. And so it has burned in an unbroken line for longer than time has been counted."

Riika turned and twisted something at the bottom of the lantern. The glass opened on the side facing Einar, and she held it up, her gaze making it clear enough what she expected of him.

He lowered the torch, and the flame all but leapt to its head. Teal fire engulfed it, and Einar raised it high enough for the villagers to see before starting toward the waiting tower. The flames burned hotter than they should have, the heat of it curling around him and sinking into his bones.

This little spark of fire had existed for longer than he had. Perhaps even longer than Aleksi had. It had survived the sundering of the continents, along with the destruction that catastrophe had wreaked. These people had sheltered it as their world froze over, had protected it while the Empire waged war against them for generations. They'd held it safe when their queen and her king consort had fallen, cherished this flame even after their conquerors had sent a literal god of ice to rule over their lands.

Einar came from a people with stubborn determination and unyielding faith. Petya had raised him with their values, instilled in him their unfaltering love for the sea that gave them life and the land that they called home.

But, try as she might, she had never been able to teach him the final lesson—to love with an open heart. He knew affection and camaraderie. Though he had never been destined to take a throne, he'd learned the weight of responsibility—first to the small family Petya had made for him, and then to his crew.

He knew how to fight to protect what was his, but only from a distance. Only with warmth and hope and the expectation of anything more tucked firmly away.

The Kraken's heart might not have been gone, but it had certainly been frozen. A block of ice lodged in his chest, protecting him from loss. His entire world had been torn away from him as an infant.

He had not been willing to give anyone the power to do the same to him as a man.

As he lifted the torch and set the waiting tower alight, something within him sparked, too. It burned through him with a purifying fire both ancient and enduring, cracking the ice around his heart with a finality that hurt.

The first agonizing beat of his heart pushed that fire through his veins. He threw the torch onto the rising inferno and turned slowly, recognizing the final truth as his gaze sought and found the objects of his obsession.

He'd always thought the Kraken was the frozen one, a monster that protected itself with the chill safety of the deep. But the original Kraken had loved, and fiercely. Which meant that this ice had always come from the human in Einar, from a man who had lost so much that he was terrified of losing more. The ice had merely imprisoned the Kraken along with the man.

The bonfire roared behind him, flames licking toward the sky as the stars unfurled overhead like diamonds. The flickering light danced across Aleksi and Naia, caressing their faces in a way he envied.

After centuries of confinement, the monster was loose.

And it wanted to claim what was *his*.

Chapter Twenty

It is interesting to note that while early stories about the goddess refer to her lover as the storm god, over the centuries that identity is subsumed into the avatar of the Kraken, who is more frequently referred to as the goddess's protector than a god in his own right. One imagines that a nation built on fishing enjoyed the idea of their goddess literally taming the storm, as it were.

Akeisa: Religious Figures and Rites
by Guildmaster Klement

The festival really was a lovely party.

The bonfire raged, its flames reaching into the night sky. It shone down on the people clustered around Einar, vying for his attention. He could claim that this was not his home, that it never truly *had* been, but their devotion did not lie. They wanted him, their long-lost island prince who was now a god born of the sea, and he fit here.

Would Einar and Naia stay here when the mission was over? Make this their new home?

Aleksi flinched. The thought was a discordant note that tasted like biting on metal. Which was the height of folly. They had only done what had been inevitable, what he had frankly urged them to do. They'd fallen in love. That was no crime, but rather something to be celebrated, wherever and whenever it happened.

That he should think of their connection now with sadness was worse than folly. It wasn't jealousy, nothing so ugly as that. Aleksi was honestly happy for them, but he also felt vaguely wistful, as if something he might have cherished had just slipped from his grasp.

Heavy thoughts, unbefitting the revels, so he pushed them away and turned to Naia. She looked ethereal in the firelight, clad in a simple white dress and adorned with her gifts from the locals. "Well, you finally have your prince, little nymph. What will you do with him now?"

"I'm open to suggestions." There was a teasing lilt in Naia's words . . . and a spark of heat.

He arched an eyebrow at her, trying to decipher her inscrutable expression. Was she *flirting* with him?

But Naia did not play coy; it simply wasn't in her nature. So he wasn't completely shocked when she tilted her head and smiled up at him. "Are you interested?"

His heart thumped *hard*, and his pulse picked up speed. The cool night air between them seemed to radiate heat that didn't come from the fire.

The silence tasted like possibility.

His voice came out too low, too rough. "Does Einar know what sorts of offers you're making in his stead?"

"Einar and I have no secrets. Not from one another." The drums started up again, beating a tattoo that matched the uncontrolled thumping of his heart, and Naia took his hand. "Dance with me."

The music was ill-suited to the kinds of dancing that happened in ballrooms and at court functions. It was too fast, too *visceral*. They ended up pressed close together, the space between them reduced to nearly nothing, moving instinctively with the heavy beat.

Her lips were slightly parted. *Ready*, he thought, and immediately had to shake himself and focus on her eyes. But her gaze was no less inviting, and he had to do *something* with his mouth so he would not end up kissing her.

So he spoke. "No secrets. A bold claim for a new relationship."

"Yes, but true, nonetheless." Her legs brushed his. "Einar told me about the kiss."

Startled, Aleksi looked automatically over to where he'd last seen Einar. He was still trapped in a circle of villagers, but his approving gaze was locked on the two of them.

Aleksi hesitated, unsure if he craved or feared the direction of Naia's conversation. "It was a mistake—"

"Well, I certainly hope not." Her fingers brushed through the short hair at his nape. "That would make what I'm about to say to you very awkward, indeed."

"And what do you have to say?"

She stopped moving and gazed solemnly up at him. "I want you. Einar wants you. We're yours, if you'll have us."

Words had power, especially carnal demands masquerading as sweet confessions, and these almost brought Aleksi to his knees. Together, Einar and Naia burned brighter and hotter than the bonfire.

Hot enough to reflect some of that passion onto him.

The vague, wistful regret that lingered in his chest sharpened into pain. Could he accept one single night of unimaginable pleasure, knowing that was all he would ever have?

More to the point, could he turn it down, knowing the same?

"I . . ." He trailed off, unsure what he even meant to say.

In the end, it didn't matter. Einar joined them, his hand sliding protectively—instinctively—to the small of Naia's back as he studied Aleksi. "What did you say to put *that* look in his eyes?"

"I asked him if he'd like to be with us tonight." Naia lifted her chin in challenge. "He has yet to answer."

Heat flared in Einar's dark eyes, driving away any possibility that he might not be just as invested in that answer as Naia was. "You don't have to decide or make promises now. We can start with a dance."

He spoke as though he didn't want to pressure Aleksi, which was sweet but wholly unnecessary. Whether he wanted either of them had never been in doubt. The only question was if he could ever, ever have them.

But here they were, propositioning him. And it didn't matter whether they saw him as a good-natured conquest, an adventure they wanted to experience just once, or an earnest, friendly fuck.

He did not want to die without knowing this moment.

"No one makes any promises," he told them. "Not yet. But when the time comes, my answer will be yes."

Naia wrapped her arms around his waist and pressed her cheek to his chest. "Thank you."

"Save your thanks, little nymph." He tangled his fingers in her hair and pulled her head back. "You may no longer wish to offer them when you find out what I have planned for you and your lover."

A growl rumbled up in Einar's chest as he stepped behind Naia, leaving her cradled between him and Aleksi. His lips grazed her temple, but his eyes never left Aleksi's. "We both know we're playing with fire."

Aleksi reached out and caught his chin with his free hand. He held it with a firm grip, nothing gentle or careful about it. "Do you? Because you've never seen this side of me, Kraken."

The monster stirred. The air around them nearly crackled as Einar's eyes swirled with teal . . . and the heat of carnal recollection. "I still remember the first time."

So did Aleksi. But that had been different, all clutching hands and hungry mouths. Hard cocks and sweat-slicked skin. This would be just as lustful, but with an edge of tenderness *and* longing that Aleksi could no longer pretend did not exist.

And Einar deserved a warning. "That was simple fun."

Naia stifled a laugh against the loose fabric of Aleksi's shirt. "Then what is this?"

He tilted her head back. "Something else."

Einar held Aleksi's gaze for several heartbeats, then broke with a groan. He bent his head to the vulnerable curve of Naia's exposed throat and kissed her until she breathed his name on a helpless moan. Then he nipped at her, his wicked half smile inviting Aleksi to imagine the delicate silk of her skin under his tongue.

They began to move again, not a dance so much as a grind. Their bodies clashed and their hands roamed, a precursor to what would come, set to the throbbing drums and the more personal sounds of gasps and growls.

Then Naia pulled Aleksi's face to hers and kissed him.

It was a sweet kiss, despite being open and hungry, despite her tongue eagerly searching for his. But that was *Naia*—whether she was being fierce or irreverent or even a little bit cocky, she was always sweet.

Her hands found his chest, her nails pressing into his skin through his shirt as she broke the kiss and pushed him back a step. They were already at the edge of the throng of dancers, and the insistent pressure on his chest had them stepping out onto the rocky beach.

There were structures there, near the edge of the water, ancient-looking wooden frames hung with mismatched tapestries. Some already had those heavy fabrics drawn, shutting the world away from whatever was happening inside.

Naia walked to the nearest empty one, stood by it . . . and waited.

Einar was the first to go after her. He pulled her into its shadowed confines, filling the space until, even with the tapestries still held back, it seemed small and intimate. He smiled and turned Naia in his arms so that she could lean back against his chest as they both gazed at Aleksi.

"Well?" Einar asked, a tremor of anticipation sneaking into his voice. "What do you have planned for us?"

There were more tapestries on the ground inside the structure, as well as a scattering of cushions. Aleksi stepped into the midst of them and began pulling the ties on the heavy drapes. One by one, they fell, blocking out the lights of the moons and the bonfire.

But not the heat.

A single metal lantern hung from the middle of the frame, casting out shadows and light in equal measure, illuminating Naia and Einar—and their eager expressions.

The strategy formed in Aleksi's mind, easy as breathing. He would focus on Naia, because nothing would arouse Einar as much or as quickly as watching her find her pleasure. And by the time she was sated, spent, one look at Einar's trembling desire would be enough to set her aflame again.

Perfect.

He lowered his voice to a whisper as he reached for Naia's hand. "Don't move." Neither of them breathed as he tugged her hand to his lips, kissed the back of it, then turned it over and licked the inside of her wrist.

Her breathing resumed with a hitch. She reached for Einar with her free hand, and he guided her to wrap her arm around his neck. Then he stroked his fingers down her side, a slow glide over the thin fabric.

Aleksi kept hold of her as he raised his other hand to the wrapped and tied bodice of her dress. He'd seen her wear it before, and had tried in vain not to wonder about its construction. Were the ties decorative? Or would unraveling them bare her naked flesh, bit by torturous bit?

He was going to find out. "I'm glad you wore your own clothes tonight." He plucked at the first knot. "Imperial fashions are so fussy."

"Very difficult to remove," she agreed breathlessly.

"Or even . . . adjust." He eased one side of her plunging bodice over, just a little, revealing more of the curve of her breast.

Einar immediately caressed her bared skin, tracing over it with a featherlight touch. "He's more patient than I am," he rumbled against her temple. "I would have torn this dress open already."

"I don't think he's patient," Naia murmured. "I think he's *devious.*"

Aleksi knelt at her feet and eased his hands under her dress. Her legs were warm and smooth, and she inhaled sharply as his hands brushed past her knees to linger on her thighs.

She moved, parting her legs and arching her hips. But instead of lifting her skirt and burying his face between her thighs, Aleksi stood up in one powerful movement. He kept his hands locked under her thighs, and her skirt rucked up around her hips as she wrapped her legs around his waist.

"I *am* devious." He could almost feel how wet she was already through their clothes, and he ground against her. "But I did warn you, love."

"Yes." She wound her arm around his neck so that she was clinging to them both. "You did."

Another thrust, and this time the sweet pressure of her ass against his erection made Einar groan. He muffled the sound against her cheek, then licked the curve of her jaw. "She makes the sweetest noises."

"Tell me," Aleksi ordered.

Einar eased his hand between Naia and Aleksi and worked at the second knot on her bodice. "If you kiss her inner thigh, she gasps. But if you use your teeth . . ." He demonstrated by nipping her earlobe.

Naia shuddered.

The final tie unraveled, and Einar coaxed her bodice open, revealing her breasts, full and soft, with seashell-pink nipples. He stroked one reverently before lifting his gaze to Aleksi. "I haven't heard the sounds she makes if you put your mouth here."

"Such heresy." Aleksi ran one finger around the edge of Naia's nipple. It puckered with anticipation and arousal. "How could you neglect such perfect breasts?"

"We were interrupted before I could get there." He chased Aleksi's finger with his own. "As much as I wanted to taste them, even I have better manners than to strip her naked during a blizzard."

"No excuses." He hardened his voice. "Put your hands on her hips."

For a long moment, Einar only stared at him with the eyes of a dangerous predator. Then, ever so slowly, he lowered his hands and gripped Naia's hips.

"There, now." Aleksi grasped Einar's chin again. "You're not allowed to touch her anywhere else until she's had at least one orgasm. Possibly two."

Einar growled and bared his teeth in challenge, but only licked Aleksi's thumb.

Aleksi chased Einar's tongue back into his mouth, pressing down until another growl rumbled up in the pirate's chest. "Consider this another lesson. And next time, you'll take more care to properly worship your goddess."

Naia's shaky moan drowned out another muffled growl. So Aleksi freed his thumb and rubbed the wet pad around her nipple as he rocked his hips. Her mouth opened in a gasp, and he took advantage of her parted lips to kiss her again.

She was already trembling in their arms. It would not take much to set her ablaze.

He broke the kiss but kept his mouth against hers, breathing her in as he slid his arms around them both to grip Einar's ass. This time, when he ground against her, he tugged Einar closer in counterpoint.

Einar hissed out a breath, his muscles shaking with the effort it must have taken him not to move. "That's it, sweet goddess. Come for him so he'll let me taste you."

She whimpered. Her nails raked over Aleksi's shoulders, and she tore at his collar in her quest to reach skin. She held him tighter as he moved faster. They were all panting now, the sounds melding together into a color Aleksi had never seen before, precious and indescribable.

Naia didn't scream when she came, just bit her lower lip with a shocked noise that melted as she shook between them. Einar steadied her, whispering encouragement against her temple.

Desire rocked Aleksi. Einar was stretched to his limit, taut as a bowstring and ready to snap. But Naia still needed them both, so Aleksi staved off the inevitable explosion with a little mercy. He pulled Einar's hands from Naia's hips and settled them over her breasts instead.

His big hands trembled on her skin, and his eyes flared teal for just a moment.

Aleksi hummed in approval. "Do you feel how much your pirate prince wants you, little nymph?"

"I feel . . ." She was still breathing heavily. But she was smiling, too, though the smile turned to a squeal when Einar pinched and tugged at her nipples. *"Everything."*

"Good." Aleksi lifted her higher, high enough for him to lick one nipple where it peeked through Einar's fingers. Einar moved his hand, and Aleksi drew the stiff peak into his mouth.

Freed from Aleksi's restrictions, Einar cradled Naia's chin and tilted her head back while he toyed with her other nipple. "What do you like?" he whispered. "Soft? Or rough?" He pinched her again, this time twisting lightly.

She arched, setting off that rocking grind again, and her nipple hardened even further in Aleksi's mouth. Her voice was raspy, desperate. "More."

Einar shifted his hold from her chin to her throat—tender, with the lightest of pressure. "If we give you more, will you come for us again?"

With a frustrated groan, Naia scratched Aleksi's shoulder beneath his shirt. He lifted his head with a soothing sound, licked the corner of her mouth, and reminded her, "Remember—you're not to be trifled with."

She met his gaze, and something bold sparked in her eyes. Then she dropped her hand to cover Einar's.

In response, Einar rocked his hips forward, thrusting her against Aleksi's cock. "Show me, goddess," he rumbled. "Show me how hard you want it."

She squeezed his fingers together harder than Einar had dared, so hard that it had to *hurt*. But hunger and pleasure pulsed off of Naia in waves that slid up Aleksi's spine like a questing, knowing caress. Waves that he could see, waves that surrounded all three of them.

This time when she came, it was slow, the pulses growing harder and brighter until she cried out in relief and completion and sheer, unadulterated joy.

No, Aleksi could never regret this. Even if his heart was broken, he would gather every moment of this night close, keep it and treasure it, like a proverbial dragon hoarding his gold.

Chapter Twenty-One

No one fears a storm the way an islander does, so the people did not know what to make of the storm god, not at first.

But there was another aspect to this god, both monstrous and more familiar to the goddess's people: the Kraken. He took this form when he visited Rahvekya, which was often.

Eventually, the people forgot about the storms.

from the unpublished papers of Rahvekyan High Priestess Omira

Naia's head was spinning.

Her heart beat so fast that it hurt a little as it thumped against the wall of her chest, and she struggled to catch her breath, but it was worth it. Pleasure curled through her in lazy waves, aftershocks that seemed to go on and on and *on*. Perhaps that was part of being intimate with the Lover.

Or maybe the three of them fucking each other was just that good.

Aleksi unwrapped her legs from his hips and lowered her slowly to the ground. He and Einar still held her close, which was good, because her knees were definitely wobbling. Aleksi kissed her nose, then turned her to face Einar.

He smiled down at her, his eyes soft and gentle, as he smoothed a lock of hair from her cheek. "You're so beautiful."

Now her chest hurt for an entirely different reason. "So are you."

"Yes." Aleksi stroked his thumb over Einar's cheek. "Now . . . how will you show her?"

He smiled slowly. "Kiss every beautiful curve of her body?"

"You can do better than that." Aleksi slipped his hand beneath Naia's dress, running his hand up her thigh as he waited for another answer.

"It's a start, though." Einar kissed her jaw and tried to follow Aleksi's hand. "You were just chiding me for not worshipping our goddess thoroughly enough. And there are so many other places I have yet to taste."

"No." Aleksi slapped his hand.

Einar growled, more shock than desire this time, and glared at Aleksi. "No?"

"No."

Aleksi reached the juncture of Naia's thighs and cupped her, his fingers sliding over her wet flesh. Then he curled them, pushing inside her, and the aftershocks of pleasure rebounded, doubled. She breathed his name, swayed, and clutched his arm.

"Naia is too sweet to ever be mean to you," he crooned softly, right next to her ear. "So I'll have to do it for her."

Einar huffed out a protest, but Aleksi moved quickly. He freed his hand from Naia's body and the confines of her skirt and pushed his fingers into Einar's open mouth.

Einar's eyes flared with color again, the same teal as the unending flame. But he didn't pull away. His gaze simply sought Naia's as he licked and sucked Aleksi's fingers.

A helpless groan rose in the near darkness—from Aleksi. He grabbed the back of Einar's head with his wet hand and kissed him.

Naia was caught between them as they licked the taste of her off each other's tongues, and she took the opportunity to sink her teeth into the strong column of Einar's throat.

He moaned into Aleksi's mouth and reached for her, forcing the Lover to still his hands. Naia whimpered, torn between denial and arousal.

Aleksi broke the kiss and panted into Naia's ear, his voice vibrating with possibility. "What do *you* want, love?"

She wanted this, only more of it. She wanted mindless need and gentle laughter and warm desire. She wanted to be loved, cherished. Craved.

She brushed Einar's hands aside and reached for his shirt. The single tie at the neck had long since come undone, so she tugged at the loose fabric. He stripped it over his head, and she stared at his chest. Every hard line spoke of who he was—a pirate, a warrior.

Hers.

And *that* was what she really wanted, to tease Einar until he truly set the monster free. She wanted that *moment*, the flaring eyes and the rumbling violence of the sea.

She looked at Aleksi and found him watching her intently. "Will you help me?"

Sincerity shone from his eyes as he caressed her cheek. "Of course, darling."

Einar had enjoyed being bitten before, so Naia tried it again while she mapped the contours of his chest with her hands. This time, she scraped her teeth over the slope of his shoulder, just past the base of his neck.

He groaned, his hands flexing in Aleksi's grasp. "You can bite me anywhere you want, goddess."

"Still trying to control what happens?" Aleksi shook his head. "Not this time, Einar. This time, Naia decides."

Power suffused her. If she wanted, Aleksi would hold Einar still for her. She could kiss him for hours, touch every single spot she could reach, trace those same paths with her tongue.

She stretched up on her toes and kissed Einar lightly. "If you want anything to stop, just say so. Promise me?"

His eyes gentled. "I promise." His tone made it perfectly clear he did not anticipate asking her to stop, but that was fine.

As long as he knew he could.

Aleksi released his hands and turned his attention to Naia. He pulled her hair back and dropped little teasing kisses under her ear. Naia tilted her head, inviting more of those tiny kisses as she continued to explore Einar's bare chest. It was indulgent, but this was a night for indulgence, wasn't it?

She put her mouth on Einar next, looking for the spots that would elicit indrawn breaths and soft groans. Aleksi touched her in the same way, running his hands along every dip and curve of her body.

Finally, he whispered in her ear. "Take what you want, little nymph."

She hesitated, glancing at Einar. But he looked as eager to find out what would happen next as Aleksi did.

Einar lifted a hand to brush his thumb over her lips. "Everything I am is already yours. Take me."

She shuddered and, without thinking, wrapped her hand in the front of Aleksi's shirt and dragged him down to the cushions alongside her. They knelt before Einar, their hands clashing as they both reached for his pants. Aleksi's mouth grazed Naia's cheek, and she turned into his kiss as she pulled brass buttons free of warm leather.

Then, she found her prize. She freed Einar's cock and closed her hand around its hot, rigid length.

Einar groaned, his head falling back. "*Naia—*"

Aleksi stroked his tongue over hers, showing her the rhythm to use. But when Einar reached for her, his fingers just beginning to thread through the disheveled strands of Naia's hair, Aleksi broke the kiss.

And caught Einar's hand. "Not yet."

Einar growled, sending a rush of warmth cascading through Naia. She squeezed his cock harder out of reflex, and the warmth turned into another shudder when he growled again, deeper this time.

She nuzzled his bare hip and pulled Aleksi closer. "Show me."

"Lick him," he murmured. "Just like this." He traced his tongue delicately around the head of Einar's cock. It glistened in the lamplight, tempting her to taste, as well.

So she did. She followed Aleksi's instructions, then ran her tongue along the length of the pulsing shaft until she had to move her hand to explore the rest of him.

Aleksi praised her silently, humming as he caressed the sensitive skin between her breasts. "That's it. Make him nice and wet." His hand moved lower. "Make him think about being buried deep inside you. Make him think about your pussy clenching around his cock."

Naia *did* clench then—hungry, empty. But not for long. The moment she closed her mouth around the head of Einar's cock, Aleksi slipped his hand between her thighs.

He thrust his fingers into her, and the suddenness of it stole her breath. It was too much, too fast. But she was so *wet*, hot and aching with need, that it didn't hurt.

It only made her want more.

Aleksi finally released Einar, let him clutch the back of Naia's head with his trembling hand. "The deeper you take him, the harder I'll fuck you. Nod if you understand."

Naia nodded as much as she could with the heavy weight of Einar's cock on her tongue.

"Do you want to stop?"

No. She moaned the word. It was unintelligible, of course, but it vibrated around Einar. He hissed out a curse, his chest heaving, and clenched his hand in her hair.

The tiny hint of pain left her instinctively shifting her hips, seeking more sensation. Aleksi gave it to her, fucking her harder the moment she began sliding her lips down Einar's shaft to meet her hand.

Slick, needy sounds filled the tiny cabana. Naia's entire world had condensed to this dark, secluded corner, to the feel and taste of Einar's skin and the insistent stretch of Aleksi's fingers inside her.

"Deeper, Naia," Aleksi rasped.

She obeyed without thinking, dropping her hand and sucking harder. Einar choked out her name, but she barely heard it over the buzzing in her ears. Because Aleksi had curled his fingers, was stroking over a spot inside her that made pleasure zip up her spine and colors explode behind her closed eyelids.

For an endless moment, she existed in that space, defined only by these things. By the hot wave of bliss sweeping outward from her core. By Aleksi's soft whispers. By Einar's tortured groans of desire and ecstasy.

Then, something shifted, and the world *opened* to her. She could see . . . *everything*. The abiding sea just beyond the tapestries. It was calm now, but she could hear the whispers of a far-off storm brewing. Einar pulsed in her mouth, hot jets across her tongue, and she could see him, too. Deep blue and fiery teal, all around her and under her skin. And Aleksi blazed, pure light as he dropped his open mouth to her shoulder and groaned.

She felt those parted lips on and in every part of her. Her neck, her breasts. Her clit. The pleasure swelled and throbbed until it drove away all else. The orgasm that rocked her felt like flying, floating. Being a part of the world but somehow beyond it. Her head dropped back, and she thought she screamed, but she couldn't be sure.

And then it stopped, so abruptly that Naia swayed at the loss.

Aleksi steadied her, but he'd gone silent. Cold. "I . . ."

He never finished. Instead, he rose, looked at them both, and slipped through the tapestries and into the night.

Einar hissed out a curse. But in the next moment he was reaching for her, gathering her into his arms. He held her there against his chest, where she could feel his heart pounding as he smoothed her hair with trembling fingers. "Are you—?"

She shook her head. "What happened?"

"I have no idea." He started to ease her dress up, smoothing it over her shoulders. "Everything felt . . . *a lot*. And then it suddenly didn't."

"But why did he leave us?"

"I wish I knew." With her dress back in place, he stroked her cheek. "I'm sorry, sweet goddess. This isn't how I thought this would go."

Perhaps they had asked for too much. Naia wouldn't know—she *couldn't*—until she had a chance to ask Aleksi, and that would not happen tonight. She still felt raw, exposed. She needed comfort and safety, to retreat to her bedchamber and think about everything that had happened.

She caught Einar's face and kissed him. "No regrets?"

"No regrets," he said without hesitation.

That was enough. And whatever had driven Aleksi from their arms . . .

That was tomorrow's problem.

Chapter Twenty-Two

While Imperial history tends to consider King Vylanar the final ruler of the island, a more careful reading of the source material reveals that he was in fact merely the subordinate consort to his wife, Queen Talvia. She was what the locals referred to as "goddess-touched," a status that this scholar has been unable to absolutely define. (For more information on the goddess-touched, see my volume on Religious Figures and Rites.)

Akeisa: An Overview of Prominent Historical Figures
by Guildmaster Klement

Einar dreamt of the deep.

Not peaceful dreams, filled with that sweet melody he'd come to crave, but dreams of darkness and danger. He slid through the water as the Kraken, and instead of music there were only screams. Cries of terror churned the water until even his vast strength couldn't keep him from tumbling into the forbidding depths and into the crack at the bottom of the world, the one that had formed when the continents smashed together, raising the Western Wall. No one had ever seen the bottom. Maybe there *was* no bottom. Maybe he would fall forever, through the center of their world, until the pressure crushed him into dust.

His human heart throbbed in his ears, the only link that remained to his mortal body. It struggled to beat under the enormous pressure, every thump an angry drumbeat calling him to war, but the protective armor of ice around his heart was gone, and the ocean crashed in, crashed in, crashed in—

"Einar."

The screams were fading, one by one. No, not fading. Being extinguished. Water churned, crashing down, destroying those fragile human lives—

"Einar." The feverish whisper tickled his ears. Did he *have* ears? "Wake up."

He reached for that familiar voice, and he had human hands now, too. Hands that encountered warm skin and waves of unbound hair.

"Einar, *please*."

The sea shattered around him. Einar lurched up in bed, then grabbed for Naia as the movement almost knocked her over. She ended up sprawled across his lap, disheveled and wild-eyed. "Naia? What is it?"

Her chest heaved with the force of her breaths. "We have to go."

Her cheeks were flushed, and when he pressed one hand to her face, she felt feverish. Concern swept away any lingering sleep. "Go where? What is it?"

"Can you hear them?" She slipped from the bed and crossed the floor on silent, bare feet, heading for the window and its thin, impossible pane of delicate ice. He scrambled after her, struggling to listen as he pulled on pants and shoved his feet into his boots.

Some of the High Court had heightened senses, but his had never seemed all that much sharper than they had been as a mortal—especially while he stood on dry land. If he concentrated, he could hear the murmurs of an active castle, along with the distant, uneasy churning of the ocean. Nothing that would put that look in her eyes.

Daughter of Tides

Einar snatched a shirt off the back of a chair and tugged it over his head. "What do you hear?"

Her tousled hair and flushed cheeks might have been alluring under better circumstances, but combined with the wild glitter in her eyes, they were almost as alarming as her whispered words. "The drums."

He caught her shoulders, stilling her frantic pacing. "Naia . . . I don't hear any drums."

"They're . . ." She looked up at him and trailed off. For one moment, she seemed confused. She lifted a trembling hand to his face, tracing his cheek as if she hadn't seen him in centuries and couldn't quite believe he was there.

She dragged in an unsteady breath, and released it on a sob.

"Shh, shh." Einar folded his arms around her, whispering into her hair as he stroked it. "Come with me, and we'll fix this."

The short walk to Aleksi's room took longer than he would have liked. He rapped heavily when they reached it, but he didn't wait for a response before shoving the door open. Whatever mood was riding the man was immaterial with Naia trembling in his arms like she'd shake apart. "Aleksi!"

Aleksi wasn't in bed. He stood by the window, gazing out of it, and turned when they pushed through the door. "Einar?"

"Something's wrong." He tried to ease back, but Naia only clung to him harder, her body still shaking with silent sobs. "She says she hears drums."

Fear hit Einar hard enough to nearly double him over. Not his own; *that*, he knew the flavor of. This was different—deep and faceted, washing in on him from every direction. Just as quickly, it vanished, and Aleksi crossed the room with swift steps.

If he'd been the source of that terror, there was no sign of it. His hands were gentle and his movements slow as he coaxed Naia from the protective circle of Einar's arms and urged her to look up at him. Her trembling eased, as if she saw safety in the Lover's warm brown eyes. Her breathing calmed, and Aleksi spoke just as gently. "Tell me, love?"

219

She gazed up at him in silence for an endless moment. Then she shuddered. "The ones from earlier. From the celebration. They're still out there, beating like a heart."

Her panicked eyes all but screamed that she did not expect them to believe her. But Aleksi only nodded, his expression utterly serene. "Do you know where? We'll go find them."

Naia licked her lips. Nodded. "The temple."

Aleksi glanced at Einar. Of course he wouldn't know—he had been safe in his bed and sleeping when Naia and Einar had gone exploring. "There's a path out beyond the kitchen garden," he explained. "It leads to the top of the cliff above the castle. The goddess's ancient temple is there."

As if the words freed something in her, Naia spun and tore free of their hands. "We have to hurry," she muttered, starting for the door.

"Naia, wait—" Einar reached for the nearest covering he could see—a cloak Aleksi had tossed over a chair—but she was already gone. "Dammit, she'll freeze!"

Aleksi grabbed Einar's arm and pulled him into the hallway. "When did this start?"

"I don't know. I woke up, and she was on my bed, distraught. I brought her straight to you."

"She wasn't with you tonight?"

It was a neutral question, giving away none of the Lover's thoughts on what had happened at the beach—or how he felt knowing that Einar and Naia had retreated to their own beds in the aftermath. "I left her in her own room. She seemed fine then."

"She isn't now."

That was more than obvious. Naia's pace seemed to pick up with every step, until they were all but racing through the kitchen gardens and past the greenhouses. Einar tried to drape the cloak over her shoulders, but she shrugged it off as if she couldn't feel the frigid night air. All her attention was focused on the lights leading up the path.

There were more than there had been before, a steady march of lanterns winding up the side of the mountain.

The lanterns offered plenty of illumination. No wind stirred their flames to make the shadows dance, as if the entire island was still, holding its breath. Einar was stretched as taut as a bowstring, and every step up toward the temple only twisted that tension tighter.

And then, as they approached the peak, he *did* hear something. Not drums, but the heartbeat from his dream. It started soft, a feeling more than a sound, the vibrations of it shivering through his boots. It felt as if the island itself had a heartbeat, and he realized Naia's footsteps fell in perfect rhythm.

The candles seemed to burn higher at the top of the path. *These* danced wildly in spite of the stillness of the night. Shadows played across Naia's face as she searched frantically for something. Three stumbling steps forward, and she dropped to her knees in the exact center of the ruined temple, head tilted back and eyes half-closed, as if she was listening to something.

Then she slapped one hand against the shattered stone. Her nails scraped painfully as she clawed at it, as if she could dig through ancient rocks and reach what she sought. "It's here," she whispered, barely seeming to notice when one of her nails broke. "We just have to find it."

Einar caught her wrist, wincing when he saw her broken nails and scratched fingers. "Tell us what you're looking for, and we can help you—"

Aleksi knelt beside her. "Naia, darling. Help us understand."

"I *can't*." Her head jerked up as if she'd heard something, then she pulled her wrist from Einar's grasp and staggered to her feet. "It would be hidden. Someplace where no one could find it."

Aleksi reached out, but did not touch her. "Find what, love?"

She didn't even acknowledge them. The dirty hem of her nightgown swayed in a breeze that wasn't there as she walked through the ruins as if in a daze. For one moment, she stood framed between two shattered columns, nothing beyond her but an endless star-strewn sky and the moons reflected back from the restless ocean below.

Then she gathered her nightgown in her hands, hoisted it up, and bolted for the cliff's edge.

"Naia!" Her name tore from Einar's lips as he lunged, nearly smashing into Aleksi. The Lover was faster, reaching the edge just in time for Naia's nightgown to flutter through his fingers before she vanished over the edge.

Aleksi threw himself to the filthy rock as Einar reached the precipice, but the look on his face reflected more confusion than stomach-clenching terror.

Einar's heart wasn't beating. He wasn't sure how he managed to choke out a single word. "Aleksi?"

"There's a ledge," he rasped, already turning to drop off the edge. "And some sort of opening . . ."

Einar fell to his knees to see a ledge—horrifyingly narrow—and a sliver of darkness that must have been the mouth of a cave. Tangled vines covered most of it, which explained why no one could see it from below, and Aleksi disappeared through them as Einar lowered himself to the narrow outcropping.

The cave should have been utterly dark, but a faint glow came from somewhere up ahead. The passage walls started out roughly hewn but grew smoother as they followed the sloping path. The path ended abruptly in a set of perfectly carved steps that led deeper into the cave.

Aleksi was already halfway down, and Einar caught a glimpse of Naia's nightgown as she vanished through an opening suffused with light. He took the steps two at a time, catching up to the Lover as he approached the doorway.

They stepped through together into a perfectly round cavern with walls as smooth as glass. The source of the light was revealed to be a glowing ball of light that rested on a pedestal in the center of the room.

Every hair on Einar's body rose as he moved closer. Power whispered over him, the kind that roared with the waves of the fiercest storm

Daughter of Tides

and swirled into whirlpools that could swallow half the world. But something softer slid underneath and around it—the playful eddies that nurtured the undersea creatures and the sweet currents that carried the fishing boats home.

Magic throbbed in his veins, and it was only then that he realized the globe in the center of the room pulsed to the same tempo of the heartbeat he'd heard before.

Naia stood before it, unmoving, staring intently into its ethereal glow. "Someplace where no one could find it."

Then she reached out, and Aleksi hurried forward to intercept her hands. "Perhaps not, darling," he murmured. "We don't know what that is, except that it is absolutely *magic*."

She whispered something in response, too quiet to hear. Einar stepped forward and laid a gentle hand on her shoulder. "What did you say?"

"I know what it is," she repeated. "The Heart of the Island."

Petya had always told him stories about the heart of the island, but they'd been even more fantastical than the usual tales. The kinds of stories even a child suspected were more fancy than fact. "There are myths about it," he murmured. "That protecting this island from the final wave burned through the goddess's body, but not her power or her heart. Petya would tell me . . ."

He trailed off, his gaze finding Naia's. In that moment, she didn't look entirely of this world, though Einar couldn't say why. Surely her broken nails and the tattered hem of her nightgown should have given her an air of fragility. But the light from that pulsing orb illuminated her face, showing . . .

What? Einar had recognized the islanders' belief that Naia was their goddess, returned to them, but he'd given it little thought. A Dreamer with some power over the sea might seem like a singular miracle to those on Rahvekya, but Einar had walked Dianthe's court. He'd witnessed the Siren's power, met others who held sway over the waves or the creatures beneath.

Naia was a god. That didn't mean she was their goddess.

"She's dead," Naia whispered. "But a piece of her remains."

Naia reached out again, as if she couldn't help herself. Aleksi took half a step toward her, his voice tight with worry. "Naia . . ."

"It will be all right, Aleksi." She said it with serene confidence, as if she trusted in what was about to happen implicitly—and wanted *them* to trust *her*.

So Einar locked his muscles, forcing himself to stand unmoving as her fingers grew closer and closer to the shining globe. The ground seemed to tremble beneath his boots, as if the entire island *hummed* in anticipation.

The tip of one finger made contact. Light licked out from it, welcoming her.

For two agonizing heartbeats, nothing happened.

A hot wind whipped through the cave, carrying the scent of tropical flowers and sultry nights. It tugged at Einar's clothing and tangled Naia's nightgown around her legs. Her hair blew back in a sudden gust, and it wasn't just the ball of light that was glowing anymore.

Naia glowed, too. Brilliant, incandescent, coaxing stinging tears from Einar's eyes that he let flow down his cheeks, because he couldn't look away from her. He wanted to fall to his knees. To beg for the blessing of her touch. To be *worthy* of her as the wind brought her scent to him, somehow twined with the tropical world this island must have been before the continents had shattered it and time had frozen it.

As quickly as it had come, the wind vanished. The glow coming from Naia winked out, and her knees crumpled.

Einar dove toward her, barely catching her before her head hit the cold stone floor. "Naia!"

She didn't respond. Her body was limp in his arms, her head tipped against his shoulder. Einar's heart froze in his chest, only resuming a staccato beat when Aleksi knelt next to them. "She's breathing."

"What in the name of creation is that thing?" Einar demanded, hoisting Naia closer to his body. He didn't think cold could kill a creature of the ocean, but the chill of her skin still stirred the dangerous side of his protective nature.

"I don't know." A frown furrowed Aleksi's brow as he brushed the hair back from Naia's pale face. "This place has affected her strongly, though. She's been having such intense dreams."

Naia stirred, her eyelashes fluttering.

"Was I dreaming?" she mumbled.

Aleksi gave her a soft smile. "I think perhaps you were, little nymph."

Whatever the orb was, Einar wanted Naia far away from it. He rose, with Naia cradled close to his chest. "And now we're taking you back to your bed, which is a far safer place for dreams."

Getting her out of the cave was easy. Getting her back up over the cliff's edge without jarring her was more complicated. She stirred with a murmur as Einar adjusted his hold on her, tucking her close to one side. Grateful for the many lazy afternoons he'd spent cliff diving with the brazen youth of Dianthe's court, he found finger- and toe-holds just wide enough to allow him to scale the cliff with one hand. Naia's chilled fingers wrapped sleepily around his neck inspired him to haste, and he was grateful to pass her up into Aleksi's waiting arms before he hauled himself up and over the edge.

Aleksi arched an elegant brow but said nothing when Einar reclaimed Naia. He didn't care what he revealed to the Lover at this point. He was too concerned with the harsh bite of the winter wind this high on the mountain.

He held her close in his arms, her head tucked beneath his chin, and descended with as much speed as was safe in the uncertain darkness— and tried not to wonder if the wind that had whipped through the underground cavern was responsible for snuffing out the lanterns that usually guarded the path. They'd been lit even in the teeth of a storm the night he'd first tasted Naia in the temple, but tonight . . .

No. Tomorrow was soon enough to worry about the implications of all of this. Tonight, she simply needed to be safe and warm.

Naia seemed content to snuggle against his chest until they reached her rooms, where she suddenly turned stubborn. "I can walk," she insisted, pushing so weakly against his chest that Einar suspected she'd collapse to the floor if he agreed to set her feet on it.

Instead, he carried her to the connected bathing room. While Aleksi ran warm water in the basin, Einar set Naia on the edge of a pristine marble countertop and lifted one of her bare feet. The healing power of a Dreamer had ensured she took no serious harm from her frantic scramble up the cliff and through the temple. When he used a warm washcloth to wipe the dirt away, he found only the thin memory of scratches that had already healed.

Her hands were in worse shape. The cuts and bruises had faded to fine lines and faint shadows, but her nails were ragged and broken. Aleksi held her upright as Einar used a fresh cloth to tenderly clean her wrists and hands. The soft smile that curved her lips as he finished squeezed at his heart, even as the world dipped. He had the momentary, dizzying sensation that he had done this before—

It shattered when Aleksi lifted Naia into his arms and carried her to the bed. Einar followed, every step fraught on a floor that seemed to dip and sway with an uneasy rhythm. Lingering unease from the cave, perhaps, and the knowledge that the odd, pulsing power sat somewhere above them even now.

The next time it called out to Naia, she might not stop to tell one of them. He watched Aleksi tug the patterned quilt up to her chin and made a decision. "I'm going to stay here. To watch her."

Aleksi hesitated, then nodded once and began to turn away.

He stopped when Naia wrapped her fingers around his wrist. "Don't go."

It was less of a command than a plea, and Aleksi exhaled sharply, as if hit by a blow. "Of course."

They both removed their boots in silence. Naia looked small and alone in the generous bed, but it felt tiny once Einar had stretched out on one side of her, with Aleksi on the other. She snuggled down with

Daughter of Tides

a blissful smile, seeming oblivious to the way her hip brushing Aleksi's thigh made the Lover's breath hitch, or how her fingers trailing sleepily up Einar's chest made his entire body tense.

Her hand found its goal, and she grasped Einar's wrist and tugged his arm so it was draped over her. She did the same to Aleksi, urging one of his arms around her. Then she sighed in contentment. Einar's fingers brushed Aleksi's where they rested on the quilt, and he only hesitated a moment before twining their fingers together.

When her breathing finally evened out, Einar exhaled softly in relief. But he didn't dare move, not even to find a more comfortable position for their hands. When he spoke, it was barely a whisper, terrified he'd disturb her fragile rest. "Do you have any idea what that was? A dream, you said?"

Aleksi's gaze met his. "More like a memory, I suspect. That's what most of her dreams here seem to be, and it makes sense. Only a long-dead priestess of the local religion could have known about that place."

Einar let himself listen for the beat of Naia's heart, soothed by its steady, easy rhythm. "Is that why she hasn't been sleeping much?"

"Yes. She's been trying to conceal it, but being here has been difficult for her." Aleksi sighed. "This place has so much history. So many memories."

"They think she's their goddess," Einar said. "Word must have spread across the entire island by now."

"Mmm. It would seem the weight of that belief is starting to affect her."

Because dreams became reality in their world, and could there be any power more potent than the faith of a people who had resisted the Empire's attempts to annihilate their beliefs? "Can we help her?"

A faint smile curved Aleksi's lips, and he dropped his free hand from the pillows above their heads to smooth the furrow between Einar's brows. "We'll do what we can, love."

Einar felt his muscles relaxing, soothed by the Lover's magic. Not the flashfire of desire this time, but a warmth that seemed to spread out from Aleksi's touch in a gentle wave, leaving an odd sort of peace in its wake. Maybe that was love, in its purest form. "We have to finish this mission and get her off the island," he said softly. "Is Gwynira at least close to agreement?"

"It's hard to say," Aleksi admitted. "She trusts us more than she trusts her own court, but that's not saying a whole hell of a lot." He shook his head. "She needs something from me, but I don't yet know what it is."

"Would it help if I came with you tomorrow?"

"Oh, I think we'll all have to put in an appearance eventually."

Einar would do anything to convince Gwynira to lend her support and her knowledge to the fight ahead. Dealing with the court would be tedious, at best—and infuriating, at worst—but if he could hasten their departure, he would endure.

The only sure way to protect Naia was to take her away from this island, with its too-vivid memories, and whatever magic beat an ominous rhythm in the island's heart. He'd learned more than he could have imagined on this visit to the home he'd never known, but he could leave its shores with an easy heart if it meant protecting her.

It was one thing both the man and the monster could agree on— keeping Naia safe, no matter what.

Chapter Twenty-Three

The teal berry (or tealberry—locals seem to use both interchangeably, to this scholar's dismay) is comparable in taste to Kasther's popular gooseberry, but its vibrant green color gives its jams, juices, and pies a somewhat startling appearance. Don't be intimidated! The taste is worth it. However, it is wisest not to sample other berries on the island. Several have hallucinogenic or even toxic properties.

Akeisa: A Study of Flora and Fauna
by Guildmaster Klement

Naia woke up in bed in the room she'd been assigned, which was not unusual. But she wasn't alone in it, which was most certainly odd.

She opened her eyes. Einar lay in front of her, wide awake and facing her. "Good morning," she whispered.

He studied her, one hand coming up to touch her cheek. "How do you feel?"

She turned her cheek to his touch, a bit confused by the question. "I'm fine. Why wouldn't I be?"

"Because you had quite the adventure last night, little nymph."

Startled, Naia rolled onto her back. Aleksi lay there, as well, one eyebrow arched, a soft smile curving his lips.

The night before was a blur. She vaguely recalled the sensation of cold stone beneath her feet, bright light, and the sound of drums.

"What happened?" she asked. "What did I do?"

"You found a secret room beneath the ruined temple," Einar said, his brow still furrowed with concern. "There was some sort of glowing light in it, which you touched. And then you passed out."

"I'm sorry." She wasn't even sure why she apologized, except that sounded like a terrifying thing to witness.

"As long as you're all right." Aleksi kissed her bare shoulder. "That's all that matters."

"I am, honestly."

"Good. Then it's time we make our appearance at court."

He started to rise, but Naia caught his shirt. "Not until you explain what happened at the festival. Why you ran away from us. Was it—?" She could barely bring herself to ask the question. "Was it bad?"

"No." Aleksi sat up and ran his hands through his hair. "I ran because I put you both in danger. I lost control."

That certainly explained the mind-altering orgasms . . . but not why it would be dangerous, or why Aleksi seemed so upset. "But that's okay. I liked it. Einar?"

"The only danger was coming so hard I saw stars," Einar replied. "It was good, Aleksi."

Aleksi remained silent for a moment, then nodded and kissed Naia's forehead. "We've already missed the first meal."

Einar kissed her, as well, brushing his lips over hers as he stroked her hair. "And you should eat something."

Having their mouths on her just confirmed why she didn't particularly want to leave the room—or the bed, for that matter. But perhaps *they* were hungry. And the three of them really did have a job to do.

Daughter of Tides

"Fine." She sat up and cupped Aleksi's cheek. "There will be time for this later."

Something very much like grief flashed in his eyes, gone so quickly that Naia must have imagined it. Pain like that could not be so easily erased.

Then he smiled. "Of course."

"Count on it." Einar rolled from the bed. "I'll clean up and meet you both in the corridor."

Aleksi left, as well, and a stream of servants entered to help Naia prepare for the day. She considered dismissing them, as she had before, but it always seemed to hurt their feelings. So she let them run her bath, style her hair, and help her dress.

This time, she chose another Imperial fashion—a long split tunic over formfitting pants. With it, she donned a heavy collar of hammered metal set with irregular pearls in shades that ranged from cream to smoky gray.

Sachi would approve of the jewelry. And Zanya would almost certainly approve of the practical trousers.

Einar and Aleksi were both waiting in the hall. Aleksi was dressed in his typical clothes—tight black pants, tall boots, and a loose, flowing shirt. He looked perfect, not at all like he'd spent half the night chasing her around the island.

Einar wore a more casual version of his formal attire. He looked like exactly what he was: a pirate king, whiling away some time on land before returning to his beloved ship. He looked like *himself*, the way he did when he strode around the decks of the Kraken, and Naia loved it. He looked warmer, almost approachable.

Whatever had plagued Aleksi earlier, it was gone now. He lifted her hand and kissed the back of it. "Ready?"

"Of course."

They walked to the Grand Hall, where a luncheon had been set up along one wall. Some members of the court filled tiny plates with finger foods, while others milled about. Still others stood around the vast room, grouped up for conversations.

"There you are." Gwynira smiled, as if pleased to see them—or Aleksi, at the very least. "I was beginning to wonder if you'd sleep all day."

"You'll have to pardon my lax attentions." Aleksi bowed. "I had a bit too much fun at the bonfire celebration."

"The local customs *are* fascinating." She eyed Einar. "I heard you were fêted as a guest of great honor. Did you enjoy yourself?"

"I did," he answered pleasantly. "It's good to see that the old traditions live on."

"I imagine so. Still . . ." She smiled at Naia. "I'm surprised they didn't have *you* light the bonfire. You've been the talk of the island, water goddess."

Naia felt her cheeks grow warm. "That honor belonged to Einar, and I'm glad for him."

"But you had a good time, yes?"

Her face was blazing hot now, surely so red that Gwynira would know *exactly* what sort of time she'd had at the festival.

Aleksi stepped into the silence. "It was a charming event, Grand Duchess."

"Please—*Gwynira*."

"Gwynira," he repeated with a grin.

The convivial moment shattered as a younger member of the court, a man of about thirty years, stepped up and cleared his throat. He was dressed in military garb, the kind more suited to the parade grounds than actual battle. "I have a question for your guest, if you'll permit me, Grand Duchess."

"That depends," she answered evenly. "Is it a polite question, Sir Balian?"

"Of course," the young man replied, before inclining his head in Aleksi's direction. "One of great respect, in fact."

Daughter of Tides

Naia very much doubted it. Something about his pinched expression made it patently clear that he was about to be snide—or worse.

But Aleksi simply gestured with an open hand. "By all means."

Sir Balian gripped the hilt of his sword. "I have heard that you possess singular skill with a blade. In fact, there are rumors circulating here at court that you killed the Shapechanger in a duel."

"This is true," he confirmed, causing a chorus of gasps to rise from those gathered nearest them.

"Shocking. A fair fight, was it?"

"It was, though he did not deserve one. He had just tried to murder a fifteen-year-old girl by posing as her uncle."

A pleased smile overtook Sir Balian's feigned surprise. "He was considered one of the most accomplished swordsmen in the Empire. I would love to see a demonstration of skill from the man who defeated him. A friendly sparring match, perhaps?"

Arktikos coughed behind his hand, covering something that sounded suspiciously like a laugh.

Gwynira was more forthright. "Sir Balian, we've just established that Lord Aleksi felled a Grand Duke in single combat. *Why* would you wish this?"

"Is that not how we hone our skills?" he asked innocently. "By testing ourselves against the very best we can find?"

Naia barely quelled an astonished laugh. His innocence was as feigned as his shock; he did not wish to *better himself.*

He truly thought he would win.

"Very well, Sir Balian. You shall have your sparring match." Aleksi turned to face the others, the barest hint of a rueful smile on his lips. "But I am unarmed. Arktikos—a sword, if it pleases our hostess."

The man waited for Gwynira's nod, then removed his own from his belt and held it out. "May it serve you well."

"Thank you."

A prickle of warning raised the fine hairs on Naia's nape. "Aleksi, must you do this?"

He pitched his voice so low that only she and Einar had a chance of hearing it. "He's harmless, little nymph." He tilted her head up. "Still, may I have your favor?"

She leaned up and kissed his cheek, pausing to whisper, "Take care. Imperials aren't averse to fighting dirty."

"Neither am I." He winked at Einar. "What short memories you both have."

But Einar did not smile. "Some of us have long memories when it comes to Imperial treachery." Then he raised his voice. "Don't humiliate him *too* badly."

Aleksi faced Balian, who had drawn his weapon. Naia had expected something gaudy, jewel-encrusted, and useless, but his sword was of fine make, and he wielded it with ease.

Balian struck first, a bold lunge that Aleksi countered easily. He likewise deflected a second swing, but he did not counter.

"Your form is excellent, Sir Balian," he offered graciously.

Balian did not seem gratified. All of the bold arrogance of earlier had melted into a look of fierce determination. Instead of responding, he lunged again. Aleksi spun out of the way in a graceful move that looked almost like a dance.

Aleksi's face betrayed no worry, no fear, merely a hint of boredom. But Naia's heart pounded. She had no idea why, when Balian was so obviously outmatched . . . except that something slimy and acrid hung in the air. A film that Naia could taste on the back of her tongue.

She watched because she had to, though she barely registered the feints and evasions, the clanging of blades. She felt nauseated, almost sick with fear.

Aleksi finally struck, though he pulled the blade before it could cut through Balian's heavy quilted jacket.

"Point," Gwynira intoned, "to the Lover."

Aleksi inclined his head and circled the cleared area, sparing a glance and a wink for Naia and Einar. Balian advanced in a flurry of blows, but Aleksi parried each with lazy ease. He was much better than Balian, *so* much better.

So why was Naia about to hyperventilate?

"Naia?" A hand touched her shoulder, then slid down to support her back. Einar's voice was a low rumble by her ear. "What is it?"

"Something's wrong." She could barely rasp the words past the fear lodged in her throat. "Einar, make them stop—"

He didn't question her, only stepped forward. "Aleksi."

Aleksi immediately pulled his blade up in front of his chest, parallel to the floor, signaling a pause in the match. He glanced past Einar, and his brows drew together in a frown. "Naia?"

Balian struck.

No.

His blade flashed, slicing Aleksi's arm. Hot blood splashed on the polished stone floor, and Naia cried out in wordless protest. Gwynira rose from her throne, and Arktikos advanced on Balian, placing himself between Aleksi and the surprised-looking man.

Gwynira clenched her jaw. *"Sir Balian."*

The man blanched. "I—I'm sorry, Grand Duchess. I didn't mean— the heat of the moment, you see—"

Aleksi held up one hand. "An accident," he declared. "No harm done."

"He drew blood in my Grand Hall," Gwynira shot back. "While *sparring*. That is unacceptable."

"Grand Duchess, please—"

But Aleksi cut him off. "The fault is mine. Leveling one's sword is the customary way to pause a match in the Sheltered Lands. Of course Sir Balian would be unfamiliar with the meaning of the gesture."

Gwynira was still furious, and Naia selfishly wanted her to argue. But she did not, merely nodded to Arktikos. "See him out," she instructed, "and ensure that he remains in his chambers today."

"I will also excuse myself." Aleksi passed his borrowed sword back to Arktikos and bowed once more to Gwynira. "I should get cleaned up."

Naia followed him to the side exit on shaking legs, her pulse still pounding a hard, harsh beat in her veins.

"Aleksi, wait—"

It was all she managed to say before Aleksi collapsed against the stone wall of the corridor, giving life to her fear.

"Shit." Einar was there in a moment, shoving a shoulder under Aleksi's arm. "What is this? Void magic?"

"Oh, not at all." Aleksi had gone pale, and he sagged even with Einar's support. "A terribly standard poison, I imagine. Average, one could even say."

"But how?" Naia choked. "How can a simple poison do this to *you*?"

"Because, little nymph." He murmured the appellation in a tone so gentle it hurt to hear. "I'm dying."

Ice crackled through Naia. She wanted to deny it, even opened her mouth to do so, but the words wouldn't come. Because he had spoken with that damnable sincerity again.

Every excruciating syllable was true.

"Impossible," Einar bit out, his voice angry with denial. "You can't die. Not like this. You're of the High Court. You're eternal."

"Nothing is eternal, Einar. Even love itself can die." Aleksi's smile was slow and sad. "But cheer up. The two of you—" His voice cracked, and he swallowed hard. "You almost made me believe again."

His eyes rolled back, and he collapsed in Einar's embrace.

"Aleksi?" Naia shook him. *"Aleksi!"*

Einar swept the Lover up into his arms. *"Gwynira,"* he bellowed, hard enough to shake the frozen windows. "We need a healer!"

This was the feeling that Naia had not been able to shake, the impending doom that had made it seem like the entire world was about to end.

Except that was wrong, wasn't it? If Aleksi died, the world would not end. The sun and moons would rise and set, and the world would keep spinning somehow.

It would just leave Naia and Einar behind.

Chapter Twenty-Four

While many doubted the truth that a creature of love could have truly struck down the Grand Duke of Inavihs, this scholar can offer a firsthand report on the Lover's skill with a blade. He is perhaps one of the finest I have ever seen.

*Untitled Manuscript in Progress
by Guildmaster Klement*

Aleksi's world was on fire.

Pain was simple. Agony, facile. This was anything but. Gone was his faded, grayscale vision, and he almost missed it. Everything around him was awash in color, and every color had an accompanying sound that he did not understand.

Swords clashed in deep red. Green smelled like the flowers and trees that Inga grew in the depths of the Witchwood. Purple wine on his tongue.

The dull blue sensation of Naia's hands wrapped right around his, her soft voice pleading. The darker sound of Einar's quick, halting footfalls as he paced the room.

They were standing vigil, bless them. Did they mean to protect Aleksi from further attempts on his life? Or were they keeping up a deathwatch by his bed?

He did not know. But their mingled ocean song, the lilting one that tasted of sunlit shallows and the cold embrace of the deep, was muted now. Mournful.

Perhaps he *did* know, after all.

He longed to look at them, to fix their faces more firmly into his being so that he could carry the images with him into the unknown. But his body refused to cooperate. He managed to open his heavy lids only long enough to catch glimpses.

Naia's hair, long and lustrous, the dark curls spread over the coverlet.

A soft frown marring her brow as she dozed fitfully.

Her head on Einar's shoulder, her entire body heaving with silent sobs.

Einar's slumped form, his forehead pressed to Aleksi's hand.

His lips moving in silent prayer.

Everything hurt, and nothing did. Aleksi had tried so hard not to do this, not to break them. But he had wanted them both so fiercely, and his longing had made him careless.

No, worse than careless. Cruel, in a way, because now he was going to die. And he knew in all modesty that his death would devastate them. And what sort of person would weigh their own desires against that sort of pain, and still forge ahead?

Naia's voice. "I think he's waking up."

But he wasn't. He *couldn't*, because he wasn't asleep or unconscious. He was fading, and Dream help him, he did not know how to do this.

How to die.

He had failed in his mission. Ash and Sachi and Zanya had trusted him to win over Gwynira's friendship and allegiance in their stead, and he had not been able to do it. His work would remain unfinished, and who knew what the consequences of that would be?

Worse, who knew how the rest of the High Court would react to Aleksi being murdered on arguably hostile foreign soil?

Elevia would be *livid*, but would ultimately make the pragmatic decision. Without proof that Gwynira had killed him, the Huntress would stay her hand. And Ulric would follow her lead, as he usually did.

Ash's anger would be a living thing, as would Zanya's, but both could be allayed. Sachi would see to that. She would mourn Aleksi to the very depths of her soul, but she would not let his death lead to more. She would comfort her lovers, soothe their pain, keep it from manifesting in the pure, destructive violence of fire and the Void.

Inga and Dianthe were different. Nothing could prevent them from avenging him. And neither would stop until everyone who might possibly have had a hand in his murder was utterly destroyed.

That fact alone might be enough to put the High Court at odds, to shatter it for the second time. Inga and Dianthe *would* go to war, and the others would either have to join them . . . or break from them for good.

And, oh *fuck*, Anikke. The young queen fancied herself in love with him. Would her grief be enough to drive her to stand with Inga and Dianthe? Would she invade the island, even the rest of the Empire, bolstered by his followers' rage and loss?

Would Naia and Einar join them?

No.

Aleksi could not let that happen. He had to stop it. Somehow.

Energy gathered like static in a storm. It was the same feeling he'd had before, as if his iron control had deserted him, leaving him at the mercies of instinct. Pure animal drive.

Naia's voice again, alarmed this time. "Einar . . . ?"

And then the room wasn't just on fire or awash in color. It was spinning, twisted by magic. Aleksi opened his eyes easily, fueled by desperation and determination and *resolve.*

The very fabric of reality tore, and a hole opened up in the space past the foot of his bed. Through it, Aleksi could see the Dream and Void, mingling and swirling until they were inextricable. Two halves of the same whole.

Naia screamed. In his peripheral vision, Aleksi saw her dive for the bed moments before Einar caught her, dragged her to the floor, and covered her body with his.

The rift exploded, and a naked woman fell out of it. Her hair flew wildly around her as she dropped from the swirling, blinding vortex and to the floor, out of sight.

She sprang to her feet a moment later, her face pale and her eyes wide with fear and confusion. Her eyes met Aleksi's and, for what seemed an eternity, they simply stared at one another.

Then he laughed.

It was not the proper response, that much was certain, but he couldn't help it. He was wounded to his soul, a god slowly greeting his own demise, and . . . what? Strange women were falling out of nowhere next to his deathbed?

It was absurd. So he *laughed*.

The sound galvanized the woman. She snatched up Aleksi's sword from where he'd left it near his dressing table, slid it free of its scabbard in one fluid, practiced motion, and jumped onto the bed. Naia and Einar tried to intervene, but she flung out a hand, and a wall of shadows blocked their approach. They tried to push through the churning darkness, only to be flung back and onto the floor.

Aleksi stared up at the woman, heedless of the blade kissing his throat. But his voice was strong. "No need for that, now."

But the woman was unmoved. She glared at him with eyes the same steel-gray color as his blade, which was beginning to slice into flesh.

"Very well, love. You have the upper hand." It did not matter what happened to him, not at this point. Only one thing did. "I ask that you not hurt them."

His request seemed to confuse her. She frowned, opened her mouth—

The door crashed open. The woman sprang off the bed and into the far corner, brandishing Aleksi's sword in front of her.

Arktikos rushed in, similarly armed, and stopped short at the scene before him—the naked woman, Aleksi's bleeding throat, a sobbing Naia and frantic Einar being held at bay by a wall of shadows.

"The *fuck*?" he growled.

Gwynira ran in, her untied dressing gown flying around her, ice already forming at her fingertips. "What in the frozen—?" Her words cut off abruptly as she caught sight of the woman in the corner.

A woman who spoke now for the first time. "Gwyn?"

"It cannot be." Gwynira swayed and nearly sank to the floor. *"Isa?"*

The naked woman dropped Aleksi's sword with a clatter and scrambled over the bed in her haste to get to Gwynira. Arktikos made an enraged, wordless sound of protest, but Gwynira ignored him and caught the woman in a wild embrace.

The wall of shadows dissipated, and Einar and Naia rushed to the bed.

"Aleksi!" Naia pressed the hem of her sleeve to his throat. "You're bleeding."

"I'm fine." Whether the words were true or not, he did not know. All he could see was the *glow* that enveloped Gwynira and Isa, and everything made sense now.

A lost love, returned. *That* was what Gwynira had needed from him all along.

"How beautiful is that?" he mumbled.

Then everything went black.

Chapter Twenty-Five

The final person to hold the prestigious position as head of the Queen's Guard was Petya of Stenyar. Official Imperial history tells us that Petya perished with the rest of the castle defenders in foolhardy defiance of General Akeisa's offer of amnesty to those who threw down their swords. Local legends, however, attest that she escaped with the infant prince. Perhaps that is why Petya and its derivations remain one of the most popular names among locals even now, more than two thousand years later.

Akeisa: An Overview of Prominent Historical Figures
by Guildmaster Klement

Gwynira's study was a relatively small room, blessedly private and easy to secure. Naia sat in a large chair by the fireplace, Einar at her side, and gazed across the table at their host.

She was giving them her attention, of course, but only part of it. The rest was focused on the woman next to her on the settee, a lovely brunette with large, haunted eyes. Gwynira was ecstatic, her joy a tangible thing that curled through the room like the heat of the fire.

Apparently, Isa—the woman that Aleksi had summoned from . . . *somewhere*—had also been a member of Sorin's court. He had created her, and subsequently killed her. At least, that was what Gwynira had thought. But it seemed that she had not been dead, after all, merely trapped and out of Sorin's way, for hundreds of years.

Naia could not really entertain any other possibility. Because if Isa *had* truly been dead, that would mean that Aleksi had resurrected her.

By accident.

But she couldn't think about that, not now. She had favors to beg, and another god to save.

Gwynira's expression was grave. "Arktikos and I have questioned Sir Balian. At length."

"He says he did not know his blade had been poisoned," Arktikos added. "Swears it on pain of death."

"I believe him." Naia did not know why, but she did. Perhaps it was the man's obvious fear when he'd realized that he'd lost his fool temper and wounded a foreign diplomat, a member of the High Court.

Or maybe it was because of the poison. Gwynira's healers had identified it as the extract of a plant that grew only along the shores of a particular river in Rehes. But Rehesian foxflower was not exceptionally potent *or* deadly, and certainly not enough of either to threaten a god. So it would have been an odd choice, indeed, had someone truly meant to end Aleksi's life.

It seemed a case of the usual Imperial Court machinations, only this time, things had gone horribly wrong.

Another thing Naia did not have time to think about just now.

"I'm happy for you, Grand Duchess," she began. "No one deserves to lose what you lost." She glanced at Einar, who nodded his encouragement. "Which is why we need your help."

Gwynira's hand tightened around Isa's. "And you'll have it. Anything that is within my power to do for Aleksi, I will do. You have my sworn oath."

"He needs more help than you can provide here." Einar's voice was tight with worry. "And I do not believe he has the time for a lengthy voyage at sea."

"But there is no need for such a voyage, is there?" She tilted her head. "I once saw your ship emerge in a thoroughly landlocked lake, Captain. Can you not simply take him where he needs to be in an instant?"

Einar studied the woman for so long that Naia thought he might not answer. "I can only do that by taking the ship through the Heart of the Ocean," he admitted finally. "It's a piece of the Dream. But I'm afraid of what could happen to him there in this condition. Or if he has another . . . surge. If he interfered with the magic of my ship, everyone on it would die. Including him."

Which only meant that *Aleksi* could not go. "You could travel to the Witchwood and fetch Inga," she whispered. "I'll stay here—"

"*No.*" There was no compromise to be found in Einar's gaze. "There *was* still poison on that blade. There are enemies here, and they may be ours."

"I do not blame you for your caution," Gwynira told him. "I cannot, given all that has transpired. Can your ship travel through the Dream without you?"

"No." Another hesitation. "It can't even *sail* without me. If my crew tried, the ship would travel directly into the wind in order to return to me, if necessary." He shook his head. "And even if they could leave without me, it's three days' hard sail from the nearest coast to Witchwood Castle. We don't even know if Inga is in residence."

"Then sending a message won't help, either," Naia pointed out. "It would take her too long to arrive."

"So." Gwynira nodded. "You need Zanya, then. She could bring your witch here in a heartbeat."

"Zanya . . . or Sachi," Naia admitted. The secret was not hers to reveal, but Sachi would never prize it above Aleksi's life. "Sachi can move through the Dream just as Zanya moves through the Void."

245

"Now, *that* I did not know." Gwynira's gaze sharpened with assessment and then softened with amusement. "Once again, I find that Princess Sachielle is not as soft as she appears. Good."

"Can you get word to them on the mainland?" Naia asked anxiously.

"I will send several messages through our quickest relay channels, bearing instructions to bring the witch, and to hurry." She leaned forward, solemn and sincere. "They *will* come, Naia. Until then, all of my best healers will be at your disposal. They will care for Aleksi as they would for me."

Tears stung Naia's eyes. It would have been easy for Gwynira to wash her hands of Aleksi, of all of them—who was there to stop her?—but she seemed genuinely determined to help. "Thank you, Gwynira."

"Yes, thank you." Einar met Gwynira's gaze squarely. "You are not what I expected."

"Neither are you . . . Crown-Prince Einar of Rahvekya."

He inhaled sharply, shaken by the title . . . or perhaps by hearing it spoken with such respect. "Just Captain Einar," he corrected. "But, as the son of my parents . . . I acknowledge how lightly you have allowed the hand of the Empire to rest upon their people."

Gwynira bowed her head, then turned to her guard. "Arktikos, get Jaspar. I want these messages sent immediately."

The Empire was vast, this much Naia knew. They did not know where Sachi and Zanya were currently, but she had to trust that Gwynira would find them. They would bring Inga, who would know exactly what to do to help Aleksi recover.

Anything else was unacceptable.

Chapter Twenty-Six

The years after the arrival of the Kraken were idyllic for Rahvekya. Never had the island's goddess been more beautiful, more radiant, than she was with her heart full and cherished.

There were hardships, yes. But we learned the most valuable lesson: that there is no strength to equal that granted by loving and being loved.

from the unpublished papers of Rahvekyan High Priestess Omira

Ash had once told Einar that, if they concentrated, the High Court could see the glow around other Dreamers. The Dragon had been commenting on Einar himself at the time, and the moody midnight blue-and-green glow that supposedly trumpeted the Kraken's power for the High Court to see.

In two thousand years, Einar had never caught more than glimpses of the colors the others seemed to see so easily. The only exception had been Princess Sachielle, who sparkled in the sunlight like diamonds. He'd been there, on the Imperial battlefield, in the moment she'd come into her full power as the manifestation of the Dream itself.

She'd been radiant, shining with a glow that defied color and yet embraced them all.

But, even though he'd rarely seen the colors, there was still a *feeling* to the oldest Dreamers. Power that vast had a weight. When you drew close, you knew on some level that you were in the presence of someone whose hopes shaped worlds. The Lover's power had been subtler than some, but vast in a manner beyond comprehension. How could you measure the size of love?

Aleksi lay still on the bed in front of him, his light-brown skin pallid and his chest rising in breaths that seemed far too slow. Einar rested a hand on that chest, next to Naia's, and tried to feel the *presence* of a member of the High Court.

All he felt was feverishly warm skin beneath Naia's trembling hand, and a silence that was terribly wrong.

Love was dying right in front of them, and they didn't know how to stop it.

Naia drew in a shaking breath. "You heard him, didn't you? What he said right after he was poisoned?"

"When he said—" Einar felt his voice crack, and swallowed. The idea of the god of love having doubts was bad enough. That he might have doubted *them* . . . "We almost made him believe again. Almost."

She moved her hand in slow, pleading circles on Aleksi's chest. "He can't die now. We still have to make him *understand*."

"We will," Einar promised, hating that it sounded weak even to his own ears. Could Aleksi have truly not understood? How could a man who had peered into Einar's very heart not believe there was room there for him? That he and Naia might have only wanted to enjoy the thrill of dallying with the Lover before they moved on without him . . .

Einar's fingers clenched around the quilt, and he exhaled sharply. "How long can we wait for those messengers to find Zanya and Sachielle? What if they *don't*?"

"I don't know," she confessed. "But it can't be much longer. Gwynira's healers are trying, but . . . he won't make it, Einar."

He reached up to brush dark hair back from Aleksi's brow, fingers trembling when he felt the heat. The Lover's body was struggling to fight off the poison, but he was too weak now. "Sunset," he whispered. "If one of them hasn't arrived by sunset, I'm taking Aleksi through the Heart of the Ocean."

"What do you mean, *you?*"

"It's dangerous, Naia." He made his voice firm as he met her startled look. "I'm not risking the crew. Or you. If something happens down there, I'm the one with the best chance of surviving."

"It *is* dangerous," she agreed. "And you will not face it alone. Your crew can stay behind, but if you and Aleksi go, then I go, as well."

"Naia—"

"I've made up my mind, Einar. We go together."

If she had been emotional or furious, he might have been able to argue. But there was nothing in her face but calm, unrelenting resolve. In that moment, she *did* remind him of Dianthe. Those who only thought of the sea as moody and uncontrolled forgot that in its vast and icy depths lived an unshakable stillness that even the wildest storms could never touch.

Naia had made up her mind. Fighting against her now would be futile. "All right. We leave at—"

The door creaked, and his heart leapt with hope—and fell just as abruptly when he realized it wasn't Sachielle or Zanya, only the latest in an endless stream of quiet, robed healers. Naia released Aleksi's hand, and Einar sat back to give the healer room to work.

But the healer didn't step closer, and their focus was *not* on Aleksi.

"Hello." Elegant hands rose and pushed back her hood, revealing a woman with pale skin, honey-blonde hair, and sharp blue eyes. "This will only take a moment, and I would greatly appreciate your cooperation."

Something cruel lurked in the depths of those eyes, and Einar's instincts screamed in warning. He tried to rise to block her path to the bed—

His smallest finger twitched. Every muscle in his body felt encased in ice. He couldn't even fight whatever had frozen him in place—there was nothing to fight *against*. He told his body to move, and it simply did not obey.

He inhaled sharply—grateful that he could still do that much—but what he intended to be a roar of demand came out as a rasping whisper. "Who . . . are you?"

"Shh." The woman peeled off her gloves. "Be a dove and pick him up, would you? I don't imagine your water witch can carry him."

Out of the corner of his eye, Einar caught sight of Naia, equally frozen at Aleksi's other side. Futile, furious tears streamed down her cheeks.

No. He tried to say it, but this time his lips wouldn't even move. His body did, though, and without his permission. He fought the slow rise, a snarl of effort escaping his lips. But his arms moved—not jerky, as if controlled from outside his body, but with smooth grace.

They were being kidnapped, and Einar couldn't stop it.

In moments, he had gathered Aleksi in his arms and lifted him from the bed. He struggled against the first step, but it was useless. He was trapped within his own mind as his body pivoted neatly. Naia was already following the robed woman out the door, her movements casual but still *wrong*.

If Einar had seen her moving like that, he would have known. It wasn't her pace, wasn't her rhythm. But there was no hope that someone else would notice and raise the alarm. The only people who knew her well enough to realize something was wrong were Einar . . . and the unconscious man in his arms.

This woman could parade them out of the palace in broad daylight, with no one the wiser.

Once in the hallway, they made an abrupt turn through a small, nondescript door that led into a far less ornate passage. "The service corridors," the woman remarked casually. "Fewer opportunities for mischief, but I do know how these locals dote upon the two of you. So to make it clear that I'll tolerate no mischief . . ."

Ahead of him, Naia's steps faltered, and a gasp of pain escaped her. Fury raged through Einar, but nothing escaped his lips but a muted growl, and his fingers barely twitched.

"It's so easy, you know," the woman said conversationally as Naia's steps resumed. Einar couldn't see her face, but he could hear her panting breaths, and he raged for the pain in them. "To squeeze the heart. To pinch a little here, or there. The body is so delicate, and there are so many things that can go wrong. So if either of you attempts to cry out or signal the servants in any way, the other will die where they stand."

A new emotion slid through him, as frigid as the North Sea. They'd reached an obscure exit to the palace before Einar recognized it for what it was—an emotion he had not felt in over two thousand years.

Helplessness.

Einar had never heard of a Dreamer with the power to reach inside another's body and control their every movement, their every *breath*. But wasn't that why they were in Gwynira's palace to begin with? This island had been spared, but the shattering of the Betrayer's power had awoken new Dreamers all across the rest of his Empire. Many had been twisted by dreams that had been left to fester for the thousands of years he'd stolen the will from his people.

What was the power of a god in the face of a woman who could stop the heart in the chest of the woman you loved?

Step by unwilling step, held hostage by his own heart, Einar began to walk.

Chapter Twenty-Seven

"Someday, I will die." The goddess said this to me as casually as one might remark upon the weather. As if the notion did not bother her at all.

I vehemently denied the words, of course, but she would not be swayed. "Do not be troubled," she told me. "For every ending is a new beginning of sorts."

from the unpublished papers of Rahvekyan High Priestess Omira

The Kraken was riding the waves hard, rising and falling with stomach-churning regularity. Aleksi felt his guts tighten with nausea. Einar's ship usually cut smoothly through the water, even when sweet little Naia wasn't helping it along by sweet-talking the sea.

But *was* this the Kraken? There were no jovial shouts, no laughter drifting through the air. No lilting shanties ringing out to set the rhythms of work on a ship.

He opened his eyes. *Definitely* not the Kraken. Aleksi had been tied to the base of one of the masts, and his feet were bound, as well. Sailors milled about, but none that he recognized.

And Naia and Einar were tied up beside him.

"Well, fuck," Aleksi mumbled. "What have we gotten ourselves into now?"

Neither one answered, though they were not gagged. Aleksi looked closer, and he realized that they weren't moving, not even to blink. Their chests barely rose and fell with the force of their breathing, and their eyes were wide and full of fear.

Panic shot through him, and he began to struggle against his bonds.

"Stop that." The command came from a robed figure, a woman Aleksi recalled seeing a few times around Gwynira's palace. The early-afternoon sunlight glinted off her hair. She was pretty but cold, and he remembered thinking that her demeanor suited the frozen island. "Immobilizing you might kill you in your weakened state. I'd rather avoid that, but I will do what I must if you force my hand."

His head spun. Looking deeper revealed dark colors swirling around her, black and red and a sickly green. Not a single shade that he associated with anything pleasant. "You're a cruel one, aren't you?"

"You have no idea." The woman's cloak floated out around her as she knelt in front of Aleksi and studied him closely. "Funny. You don't look like a god."

"What do I look like?"

"A human," she answered flatly. "A fragile, breakable human. Just like I used to be, before the sky split open and the Empire imploded."

This must be one of Sorin's newly freed Dreamers. That explained the unhealthy colors that emanated from her, but Aleksi knew the core of what she was must have already existed before her awakening—pure evil, with no conscience.

Aleksi licked his dry lips and looked past the waves of color to focus on the woman's face. "Where are you taking us?"

"Us? No, no." She clucked her tongue and reached out. Her fingers felt like ice against Aleksi's feverish cheek. "Just you, Lover. You did something naughty, and now you're to be punished."

Naia and Einar had not moved a muscle. Now, as he glanced at them, he could see the same discolored light that oozed from this woman shrouding them like fog. She must have possessed some sort of ability that granted her physical hold over them.

A hold that Aleksi had to figure out how to break.

He turned his attention back to the blonde with her hand on his face. "I have done many things in my time that might offend someone like you. You'll have to be more specific."

"Hmm. No, actually, I won't." She rose with a sigh of absolute boredom. "It's time to get on with things and eliminate the others."

One of the sailors piped up proudly. "We're in the middle of nowhere, no land for miles. Might as well throw the pirate and the girl overboard."

The woman sighed again. "They're *creatures of the sea*. Do you honestly consider that a prudent course of action?"

He deflated a bit. "They *are* tied up."

A chorus of derisive laughter met his words.

"This is what I have to deal with," she said to Aleksi, the exasperation in her tone overlaid with violent anticipation. "Silly suggestions like that. As if there are not easier ways."

She thrust out one hand and slowly closed her fingers into a fist. For a moment, it seemed like nothing more than ridiculous theatricality.

Then Naia started turning blue, and veins bulged in Einar's neck.

"Stop," Aleksi demanded. "Stop it!"

But the woman simply smiled. Naia and Einar had both stopped breathing, and blood was beginning to leak from vessels in the whites of their eyes. It was as eerie as it was horrifying—they were so perfectly still, and Aleksi had never seen anyone not thrashing and struggling when—

When they were dying like this.

He didn't lose control this time. He flung it away and *willed* one of the wild surges of magic he'd previously experienced to overtake him.

His hands started to shake, and he welcomed the tremors. He was the god of the fields, of children and art and all things that grew. Of love . . .

Not of peace.

And he had *power*, unimaginable and dreadful. Power enough to see into souls, to judge intentions. To bring a god back from the realms of the dead.

Sending one there would be far, far easier.

"Stop." The word reverberated through him to shake the deck beneath them. *"Now."*

The sailors gasped and scattered, but the woman whirled on Aleksi. "What are you going to do?" she mocked lightly. "*Seduce me* into sparing their lives?" Her ugly laughter echoed off the rigging.

Then she stopped. Just stopped.

Aleksi did not look away. He stared into her eyes—beautiful eyes, save for their flinty hardness—and let her feel his pain. Naia's pain. Einar's.

Then he reached deeper, sifting through the woman's memories. Dredging up the sharpest ones, the ones that still vibrated with the force of the violence she'd inflicted.

And he let her feel those, too.

She clutched at her face, her chest heaving. Then she started to scream, and the clutching turned to clawing. When she broke, it was with a whimper and a snap that Aleksi felt in his soul.

Still, he did not relent.

So she turned and ran from him, as fast as she could, heedless of the tragic fact that there was nowhere to go. When she reached the railing, she tipped over it without hesitation. A series of thuds broke the sudden, shocked stillness, but the final, terrible sound of a distant splash thrust the stunned crew back into action.

They shouted and reached for weapons, but all of Aleksi's attention was on Naia and Einar. They were gasping in relief now, drawing in great lungfuls of air.

The relief was short-lived. It had to be, because they weren't out of danger yet. Einar caught Naia's gaze, and she nodded. The ship rumbled and rocked as a huge wave swept up the side of the hull and over the deck. The crew screamed, but the water carried only one person overboard.

Einar.

Malevolent amusement replaced the pirate crew's collective fear, and they continued to advance. Naia, who had freed herself from her bonds, rose to stand in front of Aleksi. A second wave, higher and more violent than the last, crashed over the deck, tearing several of the men off their feet. Instead of washing over the other side of the boat, the wall of water whipped around and struck again.

Aleksi watched in awe as Naia unleashed the true fury of the sea upon their kidnappers. The water swirled around them, lifting them from their feet, tightening around them like a giant fist. It covered their mouths, their noses . . . and *squeezed*.

The hull creaked ominously, and the ship did not merely rock. It *lurched*, and the tower of water dropped twitching and jerking bodies unceremoniously to the deck as Naia pulled Aleksi to his feet. "Quickly," she urged. "We have to hurry."

The words made no sense . . . until a huge purple tentacle reached up around the side of the ship. Screams drowned out the sound of splintering wood, but nothing could obscure the vessel's desperate, dying shudders.

Naia tore at Aleksi's bonds as the top half of the mast he'd been tied to snapped off, and she jerked him off his feet and dove into the water.

For a moment, it felt exactly like staring into Einar's heart—cold water rushing around them, the air bubbling out of Aleksi, his lungs burning—

Naia pressed her lips to his. Light flashed behind Aleksi's closed eyelids, the same light that had illuminated his visions of Einar's desires.

It was a curious choice, her kissing him at just this moment, but Aleksi wasn't about to argue. If he was going to die, no immediately preferable way came to mind than to drown in Naia's arms.

Then he realized he *wasn't* drowning.

She was breathing for him.

They drifted free of the chaos, down and away from the wrecked ship, into the deep.

Chapter Twenty-Eight

It is said that on the day the young prince was born of his goddess-touched mother, a tree in the heart of the temple bloomed, though it was the middle of winter. It was seen as an omen of good luck. And that is why this scholar cautions against belief in omens—within a month, the island had fallen and the prince was dead.

Akeisa: Religious Figures and Rites
by Guildmaster Klement

The ocean was safe, familiar. Naia and Aleksi floated in it, cushioned from the violence above. Bits of jagged wood floated down around them, some missing them by less than a handspan.

So she sent out a silent plea. *Protect us.*

A heartbeat later, tentacles wrapped around them, each one larger than a person, with a leashed strength that could destroy a ship—and just had.

But this was familiar, too. The Kraken's embrace. Naia relaxed into it and focused on breathing, on Aleksi's arms around her, on the Kraken's body surrounding them both as he pulled them through the water.

It was hours before they emerged into the shallows, rocks and sand abrading Naia's legs. The sun was low on the horizon when she burst out of the water and onto shore, using a wave to carry Aleksi fully onto land. He gasped and sputtered, and she calmed him with a hand on his pale, icy cheek.

Then she turned to scream at the water. *"Einar!"*

The dying light slanted over a massive body as it twisted in the water and vanished. The water churned, and Einar broke the surface, rising to his full height in the shallows as he strode naked from the waves.

He looked . . . different. Taller, broader. His hair was longer, *wild*, and his skin was a shade of silvered purple, with a texture that sang of sea creatures. His eyes blazed teal.

This was the Kraken. Not the man most people saw, or the tentacled creature who'd hauled them to this island.

This was *Einar*.

He dropped to his knees in the sand next to them, and she could feel the heat radiating off him as he reached for Aleksi. "The light is almost gone. We need shelter."

The beach was a cold, barren expanse of rock, driftwood, and dead seaweed. But Naia could just see the peak of a roof over one of the dunes, and they hurried toward it.

It was a tiny fishing cabin, set back from the shore. Though apparently abandoned and weathered by the passage of years, it was mostly sound. Einar carried Aleksi inside, and Naia shut the loose door to close out the worst of the wind.

"We have to get him out of his clothes." Naia's jaw was starting to hurt from clenching her teeth to prevent them from chattering. Aleksi was far worse off, nearly frozen, his skin tinged with blue. "Help me."

Together, they stripped off Aleksi's clothes. His wet, naked body steamed against the furnace-like heat of Einar's chest. Naia pulled the water from them both, drying their skin and hair so the heat would linger.

The narrow bedstead had been strung with ropes that had long since rotted away. But there was a hearth, and if they could get a fire going . . .

"Over here," she murmured.

She drew the water from Aleksi's clothes and spread the dry garments before the hearth. She made quick work of stripping off her clothes, dried them, and covered Einar and Aleksi with her dress and cloak. Then she dried herself and climbed under the cloak with them.

For a while, they simply lay there, recovering their strength. Aleksi warmed—slowly, but at least he no longer felt like ice to the touch.

"He's still shivering." She pressed closer to Aleksi's chest, sliding her arms around him until they met the blazing heat of Einar's body behind him. "What if it's not enough?"

Einar's hand found her hip, pulling both her and Aleksi closer. "It will be enough. We'll *make* it be enough."

He sounded torn between determination and despair. Naia stroked the back of his hand. It was bigger than what she was accustomed to, his skin still soft but thicker, almost like a hide. "I didn't realize that you could do this. *Be* this."

His thumb swept over her hip, his skin almost rasping against hers. "I couldn't, not at first. But I'm not like Dianthe. There's no place in the ocean that doesn't welcome her. But in the deep . . ."

The ocean was dark and cold, the pressure of the water immense. "Is that how you found out?"

"Mmm. There was a raid along the Western Wall . . . fifteen hundred years ago now, I think? Some Imperial general thought to make his name by slaying the Kraken. He'd had a giant speargun designed, and he managed to hit me before I crushed his ship." His thumb drifted higher, drawing gentle circles on her waist. "I sank too deep and lost control of my form. But I didn't regain my mortal body. Instead, I became this. And it saved me."

Naia shuddered at the thought that he could have died. But it was an intriguing notion, nonetheless, that his power could transform him into something new in order to save his immortal life.

If she lived that long, what would she learn about herself and her abilities?

But all she said was, "I'm glad."

"Me, too." The caress slowed, until it was a mere suggestive whisper. His lips curved into a wry smile. "Though I learned over the years that most people find it unsettling."

"I think it's beautiful. Because it's you."

He raised his hand to cup her cheek. "Thank you," he said. "For seeing me."

She had not always. She'd once thought Einar to be brash and abrasive, a cocky pirate who cared only for the glories of battle and bedding his conquests. But now she knew who he really was—a warrior and a prince, a man who pretended not to care because he cared too much.

No, she had not always seen. Not until Aleksi had taught her how to *look*.

She blinked back stinging tears. "What do we do now?"

"We survive." He tucked her hair behind her ear and resumed his soothing caresses. "Remember what I said about my ship?"

She sucked in a breath. "That the Kraken will always find its master."

"The crew knows the signs." Einar huffed a laugh. "Dianthe took me through the Heart of the Ocean once without giving me time to warn the crew. The anchor chain snapped, and the ship was at full sail out of the harbor before Petya managed to get her boots on. It may take a day or two, but they *will* come for us."

"And then what?" she asked softly, as if Aleksi wasn't unconscious but listening to them. "Aleksi may have been poisoned by accident, but someone *did* try to kill us, Einar. Someone at Gwynira's court."

261

"They tried to kill us," he agreed. "But they tried to *take* Aleksi. Someone wants to hurt him—or worse." She heard a hint of the deep in his voice. The monster, protective and vengeful. "We find them. And we destroy them."

The thought of someone harming either of them was the distillation of every nightmare Naia had ever had, brought to life. "I won't let them hurt you. And I *will not* let them take Aleksi."

"It's sweet of you to worry about me, little nymph."

"Aleksi!" Her tears would not be contained this time. She touched his face, his chest, reassuring herself with the warmth of his skin.

"Shh, don't cry. I'm all right."

"Let her cry," Einar rumbled. "Hell, *I* might cry. You scared the shit out of us."

"Fair enough." Aleksi reached up and brushed Naia's hair from her face. "Last I knew, we were underwater. Now we're dry and on land. How long have I been unconscious?"

"Not long," she assured him. "Or I'd be far more upset than I am right now."

"How do you feel?" Einar laid a hand against the Lover's forehead.

"I'm fine." The words seemed automatic, as the whole of his attention was focused on Naia's mouth.

"Aleksi . . ." she warned. "You were half-frozen not long ago."

"So warm me up." He bent his head and brushed a kiss over her parted lips. "So many words, little nymph, when all you have to do is *show me.*"

It was a request for contact more than sex, for the reassurance of intimacy. So she kissed him back, slow and soft, and twined her fingers with Einar's. He moved their joined hands over Aleksi and Naia both, soothing and warming them.

The gentle rasp was as arousing as it was comforting, and Naia sighed into Aleksi's mouth.

"That's right." Whispered words, but they held the weight of a command.

Even recovering from hypothermia, Aleksi still had to be in control. But Naia didn't mind, and she was fairly certain Einar liked it, as well.

But not right now.

She pushed Aleksi onto his back and climbed on top of him, straddling his thighs. She made a show of running her hands up to his shoulders, leaning close enough for her body to press against his. Her nipples brushed his cock, which twitched and strained beneath her.

She ran her hands back down just as slowly, lingering over his chest and stomach. Then she straightened and pulled Einar close to her side. "What shall we do with him?"

Einar's teeth grazed her jaw in a teasing nip before he twined their fingers together and drew her hand back to Aleksi's chest. "He wants us to warm him up," Einar rasped, guiding her fingers until they circled one nipple. "I know just how hot your mouth is. Show him, Naia."

She wiggled a little as she leaned forward this time, coaxing a groan from Aleksi. He arched up against her as she drew her tongue around his nipple, following the direction of Einar's touch.

Aleksi hissed in a breath and threaded his fingers through her hair, tugging gently as she traced a path up to the side of his throat, his jaw, his ear . . . and finally to his mouth.

But she did not kiss him. Instead, she looked at him, silently willing him to understand that this was about more than pleasure for her. That it had always been more, even if he had not realized it.

Aleksi smiled. "I know, love. I see it, all around you both. Steam rising from a hot bath. A waterfall rushing over stone."

"As long as you see it." She sat up again and turned her attention to his cock. It pulsed at her gaze, and she licked her lips as she ran her fingertips down its entire impressive length.

The noise that escaped Aleksi made her clench in reaction.

Einar stretched out beside him, clenched a hand in his hair, and licked his cheek. "Can you hold still and let her explore, Aleksi? You made me do it."

"No."

That was Aleksi, honest to a fault. Naia rewarded him for it with the mercy of her fingers around him. He thrust into her hand, then again—and harder—when she squeezed lightly.

Einar's amused rumble filled the room as he tugged on Aleksi's hair. "So impatient," he chided, his free hand skating down the Lover's chest . . . and lower. He wrapped his fingers over Naia's, hot and gently rasping as he guided her to stroke. "Should we take pity on him, sweet goddess?"

"Yes." She slid back to kneel between Aleksi's thighs and bent her head to his cock. The moment her tongue touched him, a shiver, almost like an electric current, jolted through her, leaving tingling pleasure in its wake.

Einar hissed in a breath, his fingers flexing. "*Fuck.* I forgot about that."

Naia gasped in a breath, her nipples aching. "What *was* that?"

"That's what happens when you please the Lover." Einar claimed Aleksi's mouth in a fierce, growling kiss. His hand still curled around Naia's, and he squeezed their hands tighter, eliciting another shock that left her moaning and shuddering.

A hot flush stole over her skin, and Naia braced her other hand on Aleksi's hip. A drop of moisture had pearled at the head of his cock, and she caught it with her tongue a moment before Einar's questing thumb would have rubbed it away.

Einar broke their kiss, panting as he stared down at Aleksi. "Has anyone ever made you come before they did?"

His answer was immediate. Sure. "No one has ever made me lose control."

"A challenge, then." Einar left Aleksi's side, kissing his way down his body. He joined Naia in her attentions, swirling his tongue around Aleksi's cock just as she did. Their tongues twined, parted, and twined again, meeting in a hot, open kiss around the head.

Aleksi groaned. This time, the sound melded with the quick jolt that was already becoming familiar. Necessary. She tightened her hand around the base of his cock and closed her mouth around him. Einar grasped her hand, guiding her to twist her grip lightly as she stroked. The electric rush surged through Naia again, more intense this time, leaving her dizzy.

Einar's lips found her ear. "Do you want to ride him, goddess? Do you want to know what it feels like when he comes inside you?"

To answer, she would have to lift her head, and she wasn't willing to lose the heavy weight of Aleksi's cock on her tongue. She grabbed Einar's arm instead, digging her nails into his rough-smooth skin.

His dark chuckle washed over her. With a last fleeting kiss to her cheek, he moved. Then she felt broad, hot fingers stroking down her spine. "The Lover's bounty is generous." Einar teased his fingertips over her hip, then lower to her inner thighs. "Should I get her ready to take you, Aleksi?"

Aleksi shifted beneath her, his chest heaving, his skin hot. *"Yes."*

Naia sucked in a breath as Einar's touch rasped over her clit. He lingered until she moaned shakily, then began to push, slowly and inexorably, into her.

"My fingers are bigger in this form." He dropped a kiss to the small of her back. "But you're so wet . . ."

She was ready to beg, was getting ready to raise her head to do just that. But before she could do more than moan around Aleksi's cock, he grabbed her hair and pulled, harder this time.

"She needs more," he rasped. "Now."

Einar fucked his finger deeper, stretching her. "Is that true, goddess? Do you need *more*?"

Naia tossed her head back with a moan that Aleksi immediately echoed. It was all the answer Einar needed, because he eased his finger from her body and returned with a second, fucking them into her faster than before.

The sensation of it overwhelmed Naia, but there was no pain. Only an insistent, unquenchable need that drove her to rock back, taking Einar's fingers deeper.

He growled against her hip. "That's it, sweetheart. Just like that. Do you like being full?"

Her legs shook, and she maintained only the most tenuous hold over her own body. Something else loomed before her, something earth-shattering, but so, so worth it.

"Look at Aleksi's face. Look at how much he loves watching you like this." Einar fucked her harder. "You can do it, goddess. You can make him lose control. Take him."

Desperate, she sucked Aleksi's cock into her mouth again, silently pleading with him to *understand*. To know what she needed, and to give it to her. She fluttered her tongue, met his gaze. His eyes were burning coals, and the heat enveloped her a heartbeat before he swelled and jerked in her mouth, spilling over her hungry tongue.

Every cell in Naia's body contracted and expanded at the same time, and she could not even scream as the orgasm swept through her. It was intense, inescapable, because it was *everywhere*, all at once, curling her toes and making her lungs burn.

And it did not stop.

Behind her, Einar groaned, and she felt a hot splash against her leg as he came on her thigh. "Fuck. *Fuck.*"

The pleasure melted into aftershocks that rocked her, and she knew this feeling now. It was the same thing that had happened at the festival, the sense that the world was open to her now in ways it had not been before. That she could see and hear and taste it all. Feel *everything*.

And what she felt was hunger. Not to have another orgasm, or even to give one. But to be a part of them both.

She climbed over Aleksi again, grinding against his wet, still erect cock. Then she shifted her hips and took him inside her in one claiming thrust. He was big, but the overwhelming sense of invasion was exactly what she needed to center her long enough to catch her breath.

She wanted this moment, wanted *them*.

And she was going to have everything.

Chapter Twenty-Nine

The goddess of Rahvekya and her protector, the Kraken, are swiftly turning into legends. Their shared power grows as stories about them proliferate, and I worry. Yes, they are gods, but they are also people.

What will happen if Rahvekya forgets that the way we forgot the storms?

from the unpublished papers of Rahvekyan High Priestess Omira

Aleksi's world was awash in color again, but this time nothing hurt. And the shades were *glorious*, every possible iteration of blue sliding over and around him like a lover's body.

Like *his* lovers' bodies.

Naia rocked over him, clasping his cock in a hot, wet embrace. He'd known she would be magnificent like this, bold and ravenous, and so, so responsive.

But she was more.

He grabbed her hips as Einar twisted a hand in her hair and lifted it, clearing the way for his tongue to slick over her throat. His other hand teased over her breasts, cupping their full weight and pinching her nipples.

She turned her head and dragged his mouth to hers. Their tongues flashed as they kissed, and every glimpse sent a pulse of desire racing down Aleksi's spine. Naia echoed each one by clenching around him, tighter and tighter.

Her rocking slowed when she broke the kiss and urged Einar's mouth lower, to her swollen nipples. As he sucked one into his mouth, her head dropped back on a low, throaty moan.

Aleksi figured he could probably die now—right here, in this little cabin—and regret nothing.

Except then he'd never get to do this again.

As if Naia could hear the thought, she went still. She tangled her fingers in Einar's hair—which was long now, flowing past his shoulders and no longer shaved on the sides—and pushed his head even lower.

Einar needed no more encouragement. His tongue blazed a hot path down between her hips, and she bit her lip and shuddered when he licked her clit.

But she did not relinquish Aleksi's gaze.

"You're not a good girl at all," he praised. "You're delicious and so, so bad."

"I know what I want," she breathed, her voice darkened with pleasure.

"You—" Aleksi choked on the words, because now Einar was licking them both, his agile tongue flicking over Aleksi's shaft and Naia's wet flesh in the spot where they were joined.

Then he forgot what he was going to say anyway, because Naia came again, her body convulsing around him. She began to move, fitful jerks of her hips, rocking against Aleksi's cock and Einar's mouth in a frantic bid to prolong her pleasure.

She was flushed and trembling by the time Einar stretched out next to Aleksi and kissed him. Aleksi could taste Naia on his tongue, could feel her permeating every pore of Einar's being.

Daughter of Tides

"She looks perfect when she's coming on your cock," Einar growled.

"She looks perfect anyway." Absolute truth.

Then Aleksi immediately had to revise his definition of perfection, because Naia leaned over, braced her hands on his chest, and started riding him in earnest. Every moan that fell from her lips sounded like a prayer, and Einar's dick twitched against Aleksi's hip.

Aleksi reached for him. His cock was twice the size in this form, the same silvered purple color as the rest of him. Curved and thick, with concentric ridges that circled the shaft.

"He's gorgeous, isn't he?" Naia panted.

"Always."

Einar sucked in a breath, his hips arching into Aleksi's touch. "I don't let most people see me like this. People understand the man and the monster. They don't understand that, in my heart, I'm always both."

But Aleksi understood. To him, this was the most *Einar* that Einar had ever looked.

"You never have to be anything else," he whispered.

"Not for us," Naia added. Then she leaned forward and nuzzled Aleksi's cheek. "You're thinking something delectable."

How did she know? Aleksi exhaled and stroked his hand over Einar. "I was thinking about watching him work his cock into you."

She closed the distance between them a little more, her hard nipples grazing his chest, and turned her head to watch Aleksi's caressing hand. "Tell me."

"Slowly, of course. And you'd have to be ready. So ready." Aleksi stopped moving his hand, instead rhythmically squeezing and releasing Einar's cock.

Einar growled, a sound of pure frustrated pleasure. So impatient, yet still enjoying himself.

"You'd be able to feel every single ridge, every curve. Bumping every sweet, hungry spot inside you." Aleksi lowered his voice so that his next words rumbled right into Naia's ear. "No matter how wet you were, the friction would drive you mad. How would you want it, little nymph? Slow and easy?"

She nipped at Aleksi's lower lip, quick and hard, like a viper's strike. And wrapped her hand around Einar's cock, too.

"No, you don't want easy, do you?" Aleksi gripped her hip with his free hand and shifted her slightly, changing the angle of every lazy rock into something that sparked fire in Naia's eyes. "You want him to drive into you, fast and hard, until you come all over him."

The glow of Einar's eyes was nearly incandescent. "She was so tight around two of my fingers. I wouldn't last long with her squeezing my cock."

He wouldn't last long *now*, with the image so clearly forming in his mind.

"You wouldn't have to," Aleksi whispered, spinning out the fantasy for them. "I'd use my mouth. Fuck her with my tongue until you were ready to take her again."

Naia whimpered.

"How many times," Einar growled. "How many times could she take me?"

"Do you truly think there's anything your goddess would not do for you?"

Einar's curse vanished in a moan as he thrust up and came on their joined hands.

Naia shuddered, then echoed his sharp growl as she lifted her hand to Aleksi's mouth. She traced his lips, then thrust her fingers past them and into his mouth.

Before Aleksi could lick them clean, Naia pulled them away and kissed him, an echo of what he'd done to Einar at the festival, when they'd shared a kiss along with the taste of Naia.

Aleksi spread a hand between her shoulder blades, holding her in place for that endless kiss, and began pumping up into her. His entire world was soft skin, wet heat, and the maddening rasp of Einar's voice as he whispered to them both.

"Tell me," Einar demanded against Aleksi's ear. "Tell me how it feels to be in her."

Like everything that had ever been wrong in the world had been put right. Like love was a thing that existed outside of him, a brand-new manifestation more dazzling than anything else he'd ever seen.

"Like coming home," he breathed.

Naia sighed, a sound that turned into a cry as Einar's hand twisted tight in her hair and pulled her head back. His teeth raked her throat, and she whispered something Aleksi could not hear.

But he understood. He dragged his fingernails over her damp, fevered skin, licked the arched column of her neck, and gave in.

Pleasure crashed through him with the intensity of a storm at sea, cresting and falling until his lungs burned and his muscles ached. It went on and on, ecstasy so sharp that it hurt. Naia screamed, and Einar buried his face in her hair, a groan of impossible release tearing free of his chest.

His hot seed jetted between their bodies, splashing Aleksi's chest and Naia's breasts. Naia shook in their arms, wracking tremors that went on forever.

Finally, she stilled.

This was nothing like Aleksi's usual dalliances. It wasn't that he didn't care, or that he didn't let himself get emotionally involved. He always cared, and he didn't know what distance truly was.

But this was something vital. Air. Water. Naia and Einar.

Naia murmured his name, holding on to him when he rolled over, depositing her between him and Einar. "Shh."

Einar's hand trembled as he smoothed it up her arm and gently gathered her hair from her face. *"Fuck."*

Aleksi would take the compliment.

He finally took a good look around. "Aside from the obvious, where are we?"

Einar laughed, his arm falling heavily over both of their waists. "Some ancient fishing shack in the North Sea. I didn't recognize the island, but there are dozens up here. Hundreds."

Naia and Einar had saved his life. And, in turn, perhaps he had saved theirs.

Their abductors should have known better than to underestimate any of them. "Your ship will come for us, I suppose?"

"It will," Naia answered in Einar's stead. Her face was still flushed, her hair damp with sweat, but her smile was soft and sated. "How do you feel?"

"I—" Aleksi paused, because he did not know. He felt stronger, with little lingering weakness from the poison or his dip in the ocean. He checked, and even the wound on his arm had healed.

But the colors around him were still a bit muted. They had saved his life, but he did not know how long this renewed health would last. *If* it would last.

Only time would tell.

"I feel . . . better," he said finally. "Much better. But that's all I can truthfully say. I don't know what it means, not yet."

Naia clutched at him. "*How* did this happen? Was it the battle? What Sorin's witch did to you?"

"Yes." He soothed her instinctively, slowly drawing his fingers through her hair, even though the danger seemed as if it had passed. "I had never been separated from the Dream before. A part of me died that day. I think . . . the rest of me is simply taking longer to follow."

"But you feel stronger, right?" Einar pressed, and even though he'd joined in stroking Naia's hair, he sounded in need of soothing himself.

"Stronger," he reassured them both. "In time, perhaps, even whole again."

"Good." Naia hid her face against Aleksi's chest. "Because you're not allowed to die. Not when we just found you."

It was sweet, both in word and gesture. Affection, pride, and longing mingled in his chest until it ached. They had not given up on him, and they would not, so Aleksi would return the favor.

He would not give up on himself.

"Get some rest," he told them. "It's been a long day."

Left unspoken was the reality that their ordeal was far from over.

And, when it was . . . they still had to return to Akeisa.

Chapter Thirty

Is there any grace in this world equal to that of love? Any mercy to rival the comfort of a generous heart?

If there is, I've yet to find it.

This is what the goddess teaches us.

from the unpublished papers of Rahvekyan High Priestess Omira

This mean shack on a mostly barren island would have been unlivable if not for Naia's gifts.

A more thorough survey of their temporary home had revealed fairly little of use. Einar found two rusty buckets—one that might still be able to hold water, and one that most certainly could not—a cobwebbed hip bath, a cast-iron pot meant to hang over the empty hearth, an assortment of broken ceramic dishes with one chipped cup still intact, and a stack of blankets so dusty, Einar had sneezed upon shaking out the first one.

He'd learned how to live rough as a child, thanks to Petya's relentless tutelage. But when he lifted the bucket and opened the door to fetch

Daughter of Tides

water, Naia had laid a hand on his arm with a gentle laugh. With a graceful crook of her fingers, power had swirled around him. Water started flowing uphill from the churning ocean, like a babbling brook that jumped when it reached the doorframe and turned into a glittering arc of water that abruptly began to steam.

Einar and Aleksi both watched in reverent awe as tiny flakes of salt drifted down into Naia's outstretched palm. The water splashed into the hip bath, circling it once to rinse it clean. The dirty water splashed back into the bucket, and soon the little tub was full of steaming water.

Naia cradled her handful of salt and smiled at him. "If you can find driftwood for a fire, I can dry it out. And perhaps some fish?"

So Einar fetched her driftwood and fish. Soon enough, there was a merry blaze going in the hearth that heated the place to mostly tolerable. Everyone got a chance to bathe while the fish—seasoned with Naia's salt—crisped over the fire.

Einar had lost his clothing when the Kraken ripped out of him, and Naia's dress had ended up torn in the battle on the ship. But when her skirts were spread out and topped with one of the newly washed blankets, they created a cozy nest in front of the fire. She shrugged into Aleksi's shirt, and they wrapped the other blankets around them. With the heat Einar gave off in this form, along with the crackling of the fire, Aleksi and Naia both finally seemed warm enough.

The three of them leaned against each other, trading sips of fresh water from the single ceramic cup as they filled their bellies with fire-seared fish and savored the quiet moment together. But as loath as he was to shatter it, Einar knew there were things that must be said.

"I got a look around while I was out there," he said as he handed the cup back to Naia. "I think we're on one of the islands in the archipelago northeast of Akeisa. It may be dawn before the Kraken can reach us here, even with fair winds."

Naia frowned at him over the chipped rim of the cup. "Northeast? Where were they taking us? Taking Aleksi, I mean."

Aleksi made a distressed noise, as if the reminder that they all weren't meant to reach their destination, whatever it had been, still upset him.

Einar freed his arm from the blanket to rub a soothing hand over the Lover's shoulder. "South from the island would have been the quickest route to the Empire—but Kasther is in chaos now. My guess is the Eastern Waste. All that empty land and no laws to speak of? Most of the smugglers and pirates I've dealt with came from there. These probably did, too."

"They were common pirates," Aleksi agreed. "But you heard that woman. Someone wanted me to pay for something they believe I've done."

"Another member of Sorin's former court?" Naia asked softly.

"Retribution," he confirmed. "For killing the Shapechanger. We know they've heard. Sir Balian taunted me about it in open court."

The map of the Empire formed in Einar's mind, and his breath hissed out. "The lands the Shapechanger ruled on the Betrayer's behalf border on the Eastern Waste."

"It doesn't matter." Naia placed the cup on the floor with a thump. "They will not have you."

Aleksi stroked her cheek. "Of course not, love."

Einar slid his hand up to Aleksi's chin, turning the man's head slightly so he could meet his eyes. "We mean it. You understand that now, don't you? You've seen inside my heart. Do you think I would allow anyone to take what is mine?"

"Of course not. And I will not take unnecessary risks," he allowed. "You know that is all I can promise."

Because the Lover would not lie. And as a member of the High Court, he would not shrink away from battle or confrontation. If there was one thing they all had in common—sometimes perhaps the *only* thing—it was the sense of responsibility they felt to this world and the people in it.

It had been easier for Einar to go to war when his heart was frozen. He knew grief for those he had lost, but not even Petya had ever inspired this bone-deep terror. For the first time in his life, he wanted to spirit someone away, to hide them somewhere safe until the violence and death had passed. The Lover was not meant for a bloody battlefield, and Naia . . .

Oh, she was fierce. She fought with the heart of a warrior. But for all of the ancient wisdom she'd brought with her from the Dream, that heart was so open, so *soft*. He didn't want to watch it harden in the face of the fight to come.

He wanted to protect them, and yet he knew he could not. Gods didn't hide from their enemies. Dreamers didn't turn away when the very world they walked was threatened by nightmares.

Einar traced his thumb over Aleksi's lower lip. "You bade me open my heart," he whispered, reaching with his other hand to find Naia. Her fingers were soft and welcoming, twining instantly with his in a way that made his heart hitch. "Don't break it, Lover."

"Einar, that isn't fair." Naia clung to his hand. "He will try, as will I. But no one can predict or avoid the vagaries of fate. Not even the ancient goddess of your homeland."

Because every small choice had ripples no one could foresee. Three thousand years ago, Aleksi's family had fought. The final battle between the Betrayer and the Dragon had shattered the very continents, separating the Sheltered Lands from the Empire forever and raising the dangerous underwater mountain range that Einar now called home.

As a result of that fight between brothers, terrible waves had traveled the ocean, smashing into an island those men had never heard of, causing the death of a goddess who had walked those shores since before the High Court had first heard the whispers of the Dream.

Because of that fight, the Betrayer had fled and begun a conquest that had laid siege to that unknown island and killed Einar's parents.

Because of that fight, Einar had been a fisherman in the right place at the right time to thwart the Betrayer's attempt to return to Aleksi's home and wreak vengeance.

Because of that fight, he had become a god.

One fight had changed everything that came after.

Perhaps one kiss could do the same.

He might never know what ripples would spread out from this moment. What lives would be changed, what nations might rise or fall. The union of three gods could not help but shake the foundations of their very world. Perhaps, knowing how much pain could come from one simple action, he should be cautious.

Or maybe the War Between the Gods had only caused such pain because it had been a sundering. Maybe this kiss could be a union that brought joy.

Tangling his fingers in the Lover's hair, Einar pulled him closer and seized his mouth. The Lover's lips parted instantly, a welcome that turned fierce as a jolt of sensation shivered down Einar's spine. He'd kissed Aleksi before, and with considerably more heat, but something about this felt *different*.

Perhaps it was simply that none of them were fighting it anymore. The distance caused by Einar's wounded heart and the Lover's wounded soul had collapsed. Aleksi wasn't pushing them away. Einar wasn't holding back.

This wasn't a last kiss, but a first.

Naia climbed halfway onto Einar's lap, wrapped her arms around them both, and buried her face in the hollow of Aleksi's shoulder. Einar savored Aleksi's kiss for another heartbeat before breaking away to rest his forehead against the other man's. Naia's hair was like silk under his fingers, and she murmured her pleasure as he stroked it.

There was no rush this time. No grasping. There was nowhere to go and nothing to do until the Kraken arrived with the dawn.

So they cuddled. They exchanged lazy kisses and touches, soft whispers. Einar closed his eyes and reveled in the intimacy of it, something that had been so rare in his encounters before. Affection had been common enough, and passion inevitable. But closeness like this only came with trust. And maybe with love.

Abruptly, Aleksi sucked in a sharp breath, and Einar looked over to see Naia's teeth set in the vulnerable skin at the base of his throat. At the same time, one of her hands crept beneath the blanket that Einar wore.

Clever fingers danced up his thigh, and he became intensely aware that he was still in his other form. For centuries, this had been the body he only inhabited in solitude, sliding through the deep for the joy or the peace of it. Most mortals who caught a glimpse of it shied back in terror. The monster, in all its terrifying glory, they could at least understand. This monstrous man, trapped between worlds—

But Naia didn't flinch away. She caressed his skin, as if relishing the changed texture of it. And Aleksi's slow smile held nothing but heat. Einar let his head fall back, savoring her curious touch and the Lover's easy acceptance.

For now, in this moment, he could simply *be*.

Naia lifted her head. Her hair was tousled, her face flushed. She leaned close, her mouth hovering over Einar's, but only a murmured confession kissed his lips. "I think I've always loved you."

Einar couldn't imagine *that* was a memory she had brought with her from the Dream. Many of those who made their living on the seas had respected or feared him over the years. No small number had desired him. But the kind of passionate love that shone from her eyes?

He'd known that only from the two people in this shack.

He licked her lower lip just to hear her gasp, and gave her back a confession every bit as raw. "I felt you in the sea before I met you. I was already on my way to Seahold when Dianthe summoned me. I had to know who was calling to me."

Her mouth crashed into his, frantic and hungry, but even the pleasure of her quick tongue stroking his vanished in a roaring wave when her fingers wrapped around his cock.

Aleksi's words came back to him—the taunting promise to Naia that she would be able to feel its length inside her. Einar hadn't been sure she truly wanted it—the size alone was enough to be intimidating, but the sensitive ridges—

He shuddered as she drew a finger along one, swallowed her whimper of longing, and he could have cursed Aleksi when he wrapped his fingers around Naia's wrist and pulled her hand away.

"Patience, love," Aleksi murmured, utterly in command. "If you want him inside you, it will take some time."

Einar broke their kiss. There was a dangerous light in the Lover's eyes, one that meant they'd end this night weak and wrung out from pleasure, if only they trusted him.

Einar did. Naia wasn't feeling so patient. "I don't *want* to wait," she shot back.

"No. But you want to be *ready*."

The thought of sliding inside her in any form was enough to break a stronger man's will. But like this? His truest self, held tight within her body as she writhed and moaned and squeezed him with every screaming climax?

He almost wrapped his own fingers around his cock just to soothe that ache.

Instead, he reached for Naia's chin and tilted her face to his. "Do as he says, sweet goddess," he crooned. "And you can be the first person to ride the Kraken's *real* cock."

"Don't tease me," she moaned.

"It isn't a tease." Aleksi pulled her from Einar's lap and spilled her to the floor. "It's a promise."

Firelight from the hearth danced over her skin as Aleksi revealed it one inch at a time. The Lover was clearly taking his time, making a show of it for Einar's benefit and exploring each revealed spot with his tongue for Naia's. But his satisfaction was impossible to ignore, each bolt of it shared through the magic that pulsed through the room as the shirt fell away, baring Naia's naked body.

She reached for them then, but Aleksi clucked his tongue and resumed his slow exploration. When his lips teased the underside of her breast, she gasped and arched, her fingers plunging into Aleksi's hair.

"So impatient," Einar murmured as he captured Naia's wandering hand again. He kissed her palm and nipped at the fingertips. "If we were on my ship, I'd have a cure for these restless hands. Silken ties the color of the sea. But in their absence . . ."

He caught the Lover's gaze, and saw only hot anticipation there as he straightened. "By all means." Aleksi captured her wrists in one hand and pinned them both above her head. "Does this meet with your approval?"

She was stretched out between them on her back like an ancient offering, the flushed skin and glowing eyes and eagerly arching hips turning her into a temptation he could never resist. Einar started at the adorable tip of her chin and traced one finger down her throat, pressing just hard enough for the rasp of his thicker skin to cause a delicious friction. "So many places I have yet to touch. Where do I even start?"

"You start . . . here." Aleksi circled one of her nipples with his fingertip.

Naia's gasp was gratifying, but not as delicious as the way she squirmed when Einar ducked his head to lick Aleksi's finger and her nipple. He let his fingers drift to the other one, and now he knew exactly how she liked it—a gentle tease and then a pinch hard enough to bring her hips off the floor.

"Beautiful." Aleksi dipped his head and joined him. Einar felt the slick glide of the Lover's tongue and gave way, letting him soothe her ravaged nipple. But a moment later, Aleksi gave her a hint of teeth, enough to force a pleading cry from her throat that Einar wanted to hear again. *Needed* to hear again.

So he closed his teeth gently around her other nipple, tightening until she moaned his name in a throaty voice that might as well have been a caress.

Their goddess didn't like things soft and easy. No surprise, given how desperate she had always been to *feel*. She'd feel all of Einar soon enough, filling her so completely there'd be room for nothing but the sensation of him.

But not until she was so hungry for it that she begged.

So Einar took his time, aided in his exploration by Aleksi. She liked it when they sucked and loved it when they bit, but her favorite was when their tongues battled over her nipple, an intimate kiss she couldn't tear her gaze from.

They teased her until she was whimpering, and only then did Einar trail his roughened fingertips down her body to the soft skin of her inner thigh. "I remember how your skin tasted here. And the noises you made when I licked you."

"Please," she rasped.

"No making him give in," Aleksi warned. "You know what to do if it's too much. Otherwise, trust us to make it good."

Naia swallowed another whimper and nodded quickly.

Part of him wanted to hurry, but the rest of him knew that for her to truly take him without pain, she needed to be weak with wanting him. He had no fear of harming her—a Dreamer's body was never so fragile—but Einar wanted nothing but her unalloyed ecstasy when he finally sank into her.

So he kissed her everywhere. Her arms, her chin, the vulnerable curve of her throat and the sweet curve of her belly. He let Aleksi murmur dark, filthy words of encouragement as he stroked and coaxed, coming closer and closer to the hips she thrust up in naked plea before skating away to kiss and touch some more.

When she was shaking, he drew the tip of his finger up the inside of one thigh. It was slick already with desire, her need so intense that he almost groaned when he slid his fingers against her and found her hot and wet. He lifted his hand, painted Aleksi's lips with her desire, and smiled. "Taste how much she wants us."

Daughter of Tides

Aleksi licked his lips with a slow smile. Then he winked, released Naia's wrists, and vanished down her body. Naia barely had a moment to understand what was happening before Aleksi's face was between her thighs, his hum of pleasure eclipsed by Naia's stark cry.

Einar caught both of her hands as they plunged toward Aleksi's hair and coaxed them back up above her head. She whimpered in protest, her hips bucking, but Einar simply stretched out at her side and stroked her cheek. "Breathe, goddess."

"I can't." She twisted beneath his hands and Aleksi's mouth. "His *tongue . . .*"

Sharp pleasure raced up his spine, a tingle as intense as he'd felt the first time Naia had closed her lips around the head of Aleksi's cock. *His* pleasure, spilling out over them both, and apparently the Lover found the taste of Naia every bit as intoxicating as thrusting up into her mouth.

Einar could understand that feeling all too well. He nuzzled her ear, whispering the words against it just to make her squirm. "Can you feel it? How much he loves fucking you with his tongue?"

"Yes." She was trembling, the tremors overtaken now and then by tiny shudders. Then she went rigid, her teeth sinking into her lower lip.

Aleksi raised his head. He'd replaced his tongue with his fingers—three already, sliding deep. Einar soothed her with a hand stroking down her body, gently holding her hips down when they twisted upward. "That's it, goddess. Take all the pleasure the Lover can give you."

"All *we* can give you," Aleksi corrected. "Help me, Einar."

Einar teased his fingers lower, watching her face as his roughened fingertip slicked over her clit. One of her wrists jerked beneath his grip, and he let her go. She plunged her fingers into his hair and dragged Einar down into a desperate kiss, moaning with every slow circle of his finger. Her hips tried to buck up, but Aleksi steadied her, his fingers plunging deep again with a liquid sound.

"Ride it, love," Aleksi murmured. "Let it happen."

She made a choked noise, her teeth suddenly closing on Einar's tongue. He savored the bite of pain, all the more thrilling when he pulled back to watch pleasure break over her face. "Scratch me up, sweetheart. Show me how good it is."

She took him at his word. Her fingernails found his chest, digging furrows that would have broken his mortal skin. The pain shivered over him, mixing with the increasing pulse of Aleksi's pleasure, and his own satisfaction at watching her throw her head back, entire body straining.

Release broke over her like a tidal wave. Judging by Aleksi's hiss, he knew she must be pulsing around his fingers. Her entire body shuddered, the frantic sounds escaping her throat breathless as she bucked and writhed. When her hips finally dropped back to the blankets, Einar lifted his hand and stroked his knuckles over her cheek. "Beautiful. But she's not ready yet, is she?"

"Not to be fucked the way she wants to be fucked."

Einar traced Naia's parted lips with his pleasure-slick finger. "Can you take more?"

She laughed, giddy and more than a little breathless. "From you and Aleksi? Anything."

Einar glanced briefly at the Lover and received a nod. So he slid his hand back down her body until he encountered Aleksi's slick fingers. Then he caught Naia's gaze again, holding it even though his words were for Aleksi. "Use me. Give her everything she wants."

Aleksi eased his fingers free of Naia's body and grasped Einar's wrist. His hand slid down, stroking Einar's first three fingers, making them wet before he guided them to Naia's body, and they should have been too big, too much, but the Lover knew what she could take.

Einar worked them halfway into her as she panted and writhed. Aleksi bit her inner thigh, then moved up so that he was lying against her other side. "Easy, little nymph," he soothed, stroking her cheek. But his eyes held a silent command for Einar.

Einar thrust his fingers deep.

Naia's head dug back against the blankets as her whole body arched. She was impossibly tight around his fingers, slick and hot and so, so *greedy*, already driving her hips up as if she wanted to take more of him. Einar's head spun as he fucked them into her again, and it only took the slightest brush of his thumb against her clit for her to scream her release into Aleksi's mouth.

The shock of it hit Einar harder this time—Aleksi's pleasure at Naia's climax, a shivery demand that was almost impossible to resist. And then there were fingers in his hair, a grip tight enough to hurt, and Einar lost track of who he was kissing. There was only heat, and lips, and tongues, and Naia's slick body accepting the strong thrust of three impossibly wide fingers, easier each time she came, and came, and *came*—

A glow seemed to suffuse the room. Einar pulled back from a dizzying kiss to see Aleksi's face, illuminated from within as he stroked Naia's hair back from her face and drank in her latest orgasm. That glow that Einar had always struggled to see—it was impossible to look away from now, with deep-violet eddies and the diamond sparkles he'd always seen around Sachielle, only in Aleksi they shone like gold.

Everyone had always claimed that sex made the Lover stronger, but as Aleksi brushed his thumb over Naia's cheek with a heartbreaking tenderness, Einar finally understood. It wasn't sex that gave Aleksi his power—it was the pleasure of his partners, the intimacy of being trusted with moments like this. Moments of deep connection and absolute surrender.

And his power made everything more intense, more immediate. More devastating. Even limp from an orgasm that had barely ended, Naia's body had already tensed against the rising wave of the next one. Einar took pity on her, plunging his fingers into her deep and hard as his thumb stroked circles over her clit, and her relieved cry was followed by a climax so hard, Einar almost came against her hip when Aleksi's pleased reaction crashed over him.

Maybe he shouldn't bother to hold back. With the Lover's power twining around them, he could spend himself against her hip a dozen times and still be hard enough to fuck her. Caught in this web of magic, there would be no end to the bliss and the orgasms—no end except Aleksi's mercy.

Einar eased his fingers from Naia's trembling body. Aleksi slid an arm under her shoulders, lifting her half-upright so that she would be able to see everything when Einar knelt between her thighs, and licked her lips. "Watch him take you."

She was flushed and disheveled but so eager, and Einar thought he had never seen anything so beautiful as the two of them, eyes glazed with pleasure, waiting for him.

He moved slowly, coaxing her knees apart with gentle hands so he could settle between them. His hand was still slick with her pleasure, and he stroked it over his ridged cock, letting her watch as he positioned the broad head at the entrance to her body.

Naia was panting, trembling, but there was no hesitation in her. She reached down with one hand, curling her fingers over his, and urged him to thrust forward.

They both moaned as he worked himself in—barely deeper than the width of his thumb, but it didn't matter. She was already so tight and hot, squeezing the head of his cock, and when he rocked a little deeper, she threw back her head with a shuddering gasp.

So close. It took only the slightest brush over her clit to send her flying, her body shaking in Aleksi's grip as she moaned helplessly.

Pleasure rocked through Einar—his own, first. Then Aleksi's. Maybe Naia's, too, for all he knew. At this point there was no separating them. Every muscle in his body clenched against the need to thrust deeper and spend himself inside her.

Aleksi wrapped his hand around the back of Einar's neck. "Don't you dare. Not yet."

An unyielding order. Einar shuddered and held to self-control by his fingernails as Naia's shaking slowed. His next shallow thrust nearly undid them both, but with Aleksi's fingers digging into Einar's neck in command, he gritted his teeth and used one hand to grip Naia's thigh, forcing her legs wider. He was halfway in her now, and he knew that the ridges and bumps along his shaft must be driving her to near madness with every slow thrust.

The way she was watching his cock work into her, dreamy-eyed and eager, was driving *him* to near madness. "Look at you," he groaned, as her trembling started again. The roughened pad of his thumb against her clit was enough to bring her hips up to meet him, driving him a little deeper. "Look at how you take me."

Naia opened her lips, gasping in a breath, but whatever words she meant to form never came. She panted, her eyes wild, teetering on the edge again, and this time Einar didn't have to push her over. Aleksi did it for him, ducking his head to scrape his teeth over her nipple. Naia moaned, and came.

He rode her orgasm, unsure where the bliss from the hot clench of her body ended and the shuddering pleasure of Aleksi's satisfaction began. She was so slick now, and he was sliding deeper without having to try, her body welcoming him. He withdrew most of the way and thrust back in, setting off another wave of ecstasy—or maybe it was all one orgasm at this point—and her cries twined with the music that had haunted his dreams, as if *this* was what he had been seeking for decades beyond imagining.

Not just the sweet clasp of her body, but *her*, begging for him with her whole heart, pleading for all of him. Not just the man, not just the thrill of conquest that came with bedding a god.

Him. Einar.

The Kraken.

He groaned as one last thrust took him all the way into her body, and he froze there, overwhelmed by the feeling that he'd somehow come home to a place he'd been yearning for since before he'd been born. Then the physical sensation crashed over him, and he snarled with the effort it took not to give in and come.

The Lover eased Naia gently to the floor as he rose, shifting her body around Einar's cock. He hissed in a breath, and exhaled it just as sharply when Aleksi knelt behind him and licked the spot between his shoulder blades.

"Good," the Lover whispered.

He felt Aleksi's cock, hot against his back, and struggled between the competing needs to push back in silent demand and thrust forward to reward Naia's pleas.

Aleksi's tongue drifted higher, grazing Einar's earlobe. "Say yes."

As if there could be any other answer. "Anything," he growled in response. "Everything. *Yes.*"

Power rippled through the room again as Aleksi's fingers drifted down his back, and Einar had seen *this* trick before—though he'd never experienced it. The Lover stroked the curve of his ass, and it felt like fire followed in his wake, flooding Einar with the impossible sensation of heat and slickness and an unbearable need that only the Lover could quench.

The Witch might enjoy brewing aphrodisiacs to thrill the senses and oils that eased the passage of even the largest cock, but the Lover had no need of such things. The echo of his pleasure made the strongest aphrodisiac seem feeble, and magic always readied his path.

And, for once, Aleksi didn't tease him. He paused after the head of his cock breached that tight ring of muscle, as if reassuring himself that Einar could take everything he was—but when Einar pushed back with an eager growl, Aleksi wrapped his hand in Einar's hair and thrust deep.

Friction. Pleasure. Impossible heat, as the movement pushed him deeper into Naia—and then Aleksi's pleasure hit them both. She was writhing and clenching, and Aleksi thrust into him again. It was too much. Naia's hoarse cry was lost in Einar's groan of surrender as he slammed into her again and came, and came, and *came* . . .

Colors exploded behind Einar's eyelids. But when he opened his eyes, they were still there. Aleksi's glow was so bright, it filled the cabin.

Not just violet now but a rainbow of glittering magic that danced with every thrust.

It sank into him. Washed through him.

For all the longing he'd felt for Naia and the bliss of that feeling of homecoming, this was new. The missing piece, the thing that changed the haunting melody that ghosted through his dreams to one of pure joy.

Einar heard the new song woven around the sound of his heart pounding—one of destiny, one of vitality and life.

The Lover. In love.

Something in the universe *shifted*. Bliss swallowed him whole.

And lasted an eternity.

Einar didn't know how they all ended up curled together under the blanket. Aleksi must have done it—proof that tiring out his lovers only made Aleksi stronger. Einar certainly couldn't find the strength in his body to do more than turn his face into Naia's hair, nuzzling her as she panted for breath and the Lover stroked soothing fingers over their cheeks, a quiet promise that they could rest, and he would take care of them.

Einar closed his eyes and fell into dreams of the sun, and the sea, and music that no longer yearned but instead twined around him as he swam deeper, promising that he would never be alone.

◆ ◆ ◆

The sea woke Einar.

He jerked awake, unsure what had pulled him from those sweet dreams, until a ripple in the distance tugged at something inside him.

His ship had arrived.

He disentangled himself from his sleeping lovers, tucking the blanket around them both before standing. One glance down his body revealed the silvery-purple skin, and for the first time reluctance stirred at the thought of resuming his mortal form.

No, now was not the time.

He closed his eyes and changed back into his human form, then swept up another blanket to wrap around his waist.

Outside, the sun was just topping the eastern horizon. The sky was alive with blushing pinks and fragile blues, and the reflection of light seemed to draw a line straight to the majestic ship floating just offshore. On the deck, Bexi gave a shout of relief that brought the rest of the crew running.

They'd already launched a dinghy. Brynjar worked the oars with impressive speed while Petya shielded her eyes with one hand. The worry on her face only receded when she caught sight of him.

Einar lifted an arm to wave, then turned back to the cabin. Inside, he knelt beside the nest of blankets, where Naia was already awake. She stared up at him, unmoving. "Are they here?"

"They're rowing ashore now." He touched Aleksi's forehead, brushing his hair back. "Time to go, lover."

Aleksi stretched lazily. "I think I'll live here now, thank you. It rather has everything I need." He nipped at Naia's bare shoulder.

She swatted him away with a laugh. But her amusement faded as she sat up. "What do we do now?"

"We go back to Akeisa," Aleksi answered simply. "And we find out who at Gwynira's court is a traitor."

"And we kill them," Einar said softly.

"Or worse." Aleksi grinned. "I'm shockingly open to the possibilities."

This was the other side of the Lover, a side Einar understood all too well. In him, the protective rage had always burned hot, but it had been motivated by hatred as much as anything else. Hatred for the Empire, for the Betrayer, for the pain they had caused. But in Aleksi . . .

Hatred was a fragile thing. When the object of your revenge was defeated, there was little left to fuel that fire. But love—love could not be so easily quenched.

When roused to protective fury, love could shatter worlds.

Chapter Thirty-One

I will not live much longer. My hand shakes now as I write, and my eyes can no longer decipher the faded script from my earlier papers. I am soon to choose my successor, the next priestess who will record the teachings of the goddess.

It seems that I will not live to see the goddess's end, the one she foretold so many years ago. I am glad of it. My heart would break to witness such light extinguished from this world.

from the unpublished papers of Rahvekyan High Priestess Omira

Aleksi rather liked the bed in the captain's cabin. It wasn't large, but he supposed that made sense. When Einar was on his ship, he slept alone. There was just enough room for the three of them, but only if they tangled together in their sleep.

Aleksi rather liked that, too.

Then the window above the bed blew open. A rage-filled wind burst through it, raising the fine hair on the back of Aleksi's neck.

Naia gasped in a breath and sat straight up. "What—what's happening?"

Beside her, Einar struggled to peer through the darkness. "Is it a storm?"

"No." The wind howled around them, and Aleksi heard the faint echoes of Dianthe in it. "I think it's—"

It was all he managed before he was sucked into the Dream.

Naia and Einar stood beside him, blessedly clothed but looking confused. Aleksi couldn't help them with that. This was not a place he'd seen before, the Heart of the Dream or one of Sachi's adorable, cozy little sitting rooms. This was a bare hall of sepulchral marble, huge and cavernous, enclosed only by massive pillars and otherwise open to the dark woods beyond. Dead leaves sighed through the pillars and across the floor.

This was a place of loss and guilt. The manifestation of something terrible.

Aleksi shivered.

A large table sat in the center of the hall. Around it stood the rest of the High Court, looking grave. All except for Dianthe, who literally seethed with rage. It undulated around her like turbulent water, stirring her hair and her clothes.

"Sachi! Zanya!" Naia rushed forward to embrace her friends. "You received our messages!"

Zanya merely frowned, but Sachi pulled back with a questioning look. "Messages? I don't understand."

"Gwynira sent for you," Naia explained. "After Aleksi was poisoned."

"Poisoned," Elevia repeated flatly.

"I'm fine now," he offered.

"But then we were kidnapped," Naia continued.

This time, it was Ash who echoed the word in disbelief. *"Kidnapped?"*

"Also fine now," Aleksi assured him.

Naia frowned. "Wait . . . you mean you haven't heard from Gwynira?"

"No." Sachi cast a troubled glance at Ash. "And we've been in easy reach."

Aleksi quelled another shiver. If that was true, it meant that Gwynira had sent no messages, even though she'd sworn to Einar and Naia that she would.

Einar growled, having obviously come to the same conclusion.

Then another, darker thought flickered to life in Aleksi's mind. "If you didn't know about the poisoning and the kidnapping, why are we *here*?"

Dianthe made an angry, incoherent sound, and Inga rubbed her back to soothe her.

Fear coalesced in Aleksi's middle, a hard knot that only grew when Elevia sighed heavily. "Sorin has escaped from custody. He destroyed his cell at Seahold and wounded several of Dianthe's people."

"Will they . . . ?" He couldn't bring himself to finish the question.

"They'll live," Ulric rasped.

Of course. If Sorin had killed any of her followers, Dianthe's rage would have boiled the seas. "Where is he now?" Aleksi asked.

Inga's eyes burned a vivid, angry pink. "We don't know."

Sachi choked on a sob. "I'm so sorry. I should have killed him when I had the chance."

"Sachi, *no*," Zanya said firmly. "This is not your fault. You couldn't have known this would happen."

"*You* did. You said he would—"

"Sachielle." Aleksi stepped forward, circled the table, and grasped her shoulders. "Look at me."

When she did, the remorse and shame that filled her blue eyes tore at him. If they didn't stop her, she would drown in blame and contrition, and the next time she had to make such a difficult decision, she would do it with less mercy, less compassion.

And they would all be lost.

"You showed him kindness, and offered him what everyone deserves, even the lowest among us. Something priceless," Aleksi murmured. "A second chance."

Her tears spilled over. "Do you truly believe that?"

"With all my heart." He folded her in his arms. "You did the right thing."

"Did Sorin have help with his escape?" Einar asked. "He must have, right? Someone from his former Empire?"

"It's likely," Elevia admitted. "We've been working on the assumption that he's headed back there to try and reestablish a base of power."

"Which means, Aleksi, that we can't come help you with the situation in Akeisa." Ash's expression was nothing short of tortured. "I'm sorry."

"Don't be." Aleksi released Sachi and dried the tears from her face, then wrapped his arm around Zanya in a quick hug. "You lot go and save the world again. Naia and Einar and I will handle Akeisa."

At some point, he'd have to tell them everything that had really happened—up to and including how he'd brought a woman, another *god*, back from the dead. For now, they were all too worried to press, and that bought him a reprieve.

How much of one remained to be seen. Because the Betrayer had not taken that second chance that Sachi had so generously offered him. And he was out there again, free to wreak havoc on the world and do his murderous will.

Fuck.

Chapter Thirty-Two

The goddess has a name.

In sixty-seven years of service, I have never heard it. But I know it, because I have seen the syllables take shape through the smile on the Kraken's lips when he whispers to his lover.

Her name is Naia.

from the unpublished papers of Rahvekyan High Priestess Omira

After half a candlemark in the man's company, Sorin remembered vividly why he had banished Guildmaster Klement.

". . . truly is fascinating. I did wonder at first, you know. If she might *actually* be their goddess. It's an interesting theoretical question, you must agree. If belief can bring about the birth of such a person to begin with, surely it can facilitate a *re*birth. But she seemed a rather simple creature, if you must know. Very sweet, with some raw power. But surely the goddess of this island's legends would not have been so easily dispatched. In any case . . ."

The only comfort in being forced to endure his company was thinking of how much he must have tormented Gwynira over his years in her court. She detested aimless chatter and had even less tolerance for self-important scholars.

Imagining long winters of tedious dinners with Gwynira resisting the urge to stab a fork through the man's throat entertained Sorin so much that he was in fairly good humor by the time they finally reached the base of the mountain. As distasteful as Sorin had always found Klement's obsession with the past, he had to admit that without it, this opportunity might never have presented itself. He could afford to be gracious . . . for a little while longer, at least.

He might even let the man live, after all.

"It's up this way," the man said, lifting the hems of his long robes as he started up a narrow path lined with lanterns. Sorin glanced back once toward Gwynira's icy palace, shrouded now in darkness except for the scant light of the moons. It was tempting to simply stride through her doors and take satisfying and immediate vengeance upon her for her betrayal.

It wasn't fear that turned him back toward the path up the mountain. Even diminished, he had no doubt he could end the very life he had given the frigid traitor. But it would be much more satisfying to do it after he'd claimed what was rightfully his.

His steps quickened with his eagerness, and soon the elderly scholar was struggling to keep up—a fact that didn't seem to interrupt his breathless string of chatter.

"I think you will agree I did everything as instructed," he said, with none of the deference Sorin was owed. The man had certainly let the honor of that heavy gold medallion around his neck go to his head. "I framed Einar for an attack on the island to drive a wedge between Gwynira and the Lover—"

"Which failed," Sorin pointed out.

"Yes, but we knew it might. So I progressed to the contingency plan. I poisoned young Balian's blade and planted enough stories in his head to convince him to challenge the Lover to a duel."

"Which also failed."

"It didn't—" At a sharp look, Klement tacked on a belated "Your Imperial Majesty. He *did* poison the Lover."

"Yes, and look how that turned out. Whatever you gave him was so unpredictable, he brought that Void-tainted traitor back from the dead. Now I have to kill her a second time."

Silence, while Klement regarded the depth of *that* failure.

Perhaps Sorin had underestimated Aleksi. To bring Isa back from the living death to which Sorin had condemned her so many centuries ago would have involved a power far beyond any the man had ever displayed. The Lover had never *seemed* particularly formidable, even during the War of the Gods. He was too easily distracted by his inclination to nurture and protect, too soft. Aleksi had never had the Huntress's brilliant strategic mind or the Wolf's ruthlessness, or the Siren's or Dragon's terrifying power over the raw elements. Even the Witch was more impressive when her temper was roused, and as for the Phoenix . . .

No. Sorin wouldn't think about the Phoenix.

Klement wrung his hands together as they reached the top of the hill. "Perhaps there were . . . missteps. But the agent you sent to neutralize them—she was successful in removing all three of them from the palace."

"And the so-called raiders you hired to transport them were so inept, all three of them ended up dead." For the Kraken and that newborn godling, Sorin had little concern. But Aleksi . . . "I'm sure you know our mutual acquaintance will be *very* displeased to learn that he received a quick death at sea instead of a fate befitting one who murdered a Grand Duke of the Empire."

That finally silenced the man, as well it should. In the Nine Kingdoms, few people could evoke more fear than the one Klement had disappointed with his failure.

They reached the top of the mountain and came out into a ruined temple. The unattractive mess of it scraped at Sorin's nerves, but Gwynira had never had a sense of order. When she had been dispatched, perhaps he would raze this place and build a proper memorial to the miracle which was about to occur.

"Down here," the old man said, gesturing to a cliff. He turned and began to back awkwardly off of it, dangling for a moment from the rock cliff by his fingertips before vanishing. When Sorin glanced over, he saw Klement on a narrow ledge mostly protected by cleverly nurtured greenery.

When Sorin had joined him, Klement twisted his hands together again. "Even with all of our . . . setbacks, I *did* find this place. And recognize its significance."

The one intelligent thing the man had done. "We'll see," Sorin murmured as he stepped into the cave. Power pulsed at the back of it, the kind he once would have considered trivial. But now . . .

Drawn by that quiet song, Sorin descended the stairs and stepped into a perfectly round chamber. A ball of shimmering light pulsed at its center, a piece of the Dream trapped here in the mortal world.

"Hello, beautiful," he whispered, circling it slowly. Oh, yes. This would do.

Guildmaster Klement cleared his throat. "About my request. I've considered it a great deal, and I feel the most practical way to harness the faith on this island would be to step into the role of one of their existing gods. If you could grant me power over storms—"

Sorin reached out a tentative hand toward the orb, not quite touching. The spark was electric. "I can grant you some limited power," he murmured. "I cannot control what form it takes."

Klement cleared his throat again. "Well, the sooner the better. If the Dream and the Void were to return here, to Akeisa—"

Sorin turned slowly to look at him, and the man snapped his teeth together hard. Mention of *her* was enough to put death in Sorin's heart and in his eyes, and he hoped that was all the man could see. Certainly not that unfamiliar flutter of fear that still stirred in his gut when he remembered the moment when Princess Sachielle had torn his connection to the Dream from him, rendering him a weakling. A *mortal.*

That was what he was here to change. This lovely bit of the Dream was ripe for the taking, and once his link had been restored . . . "You needn't worry about either of them, or the Dragon," he said evenly, turning back to consider his prize. "Our mutual acquaintance is keeping them quite distracted, and will continue to do so."

Klement swallowed audibly but wisely said nothing. Sorin smiled and reached out to that beautiful little bit of concentrated Dream magic, his fingers tingling as they grew close.

The orb trembled, shying away from his touch. Frowning, he thrust his hand forward, only to find it sliding against an invisible surface as smooth as glass but utterly impenetrable. Mere fingerspans away, the globe of magic trembled, as if it would flee from him if it could.

"What is happening?" Klement whispered.

Sorin ignored him.

It seemed this little slice of the Dream wasn't so unclaimed. Someone had formed a link with it, fouling its magic and entangling it with the dreams of their own heart. While that heart still beat, Sorin would not be able to claim what should have been his.

So. Sorin had some people to murder on Gwynira's island after all.

ACKNOWLEDGMENTS

Greetings from the past. We can only hope you are opening this time capsule in a glorious 2025 (or some years after) and that the world is chill and boring and you are living your very best life. We are writing this in late summer of 2024, a time which I expect will go down in political history as "pretty bonkers." Tuning out the noise every day in order to write was both difficult and a blessing. Especially when our third Romancing the Vote auction ended up launching the same day this book was due. (Uhm. Whoops?) Our first gratitude goes to all of our volunteers, who stepped up to help us bring our lifetime total raised for voting rights to over *one million dollars*. Special shout-outs to Akeisha and Lee-Sien, who became a spreadsheet-wrangling, email-writing, crime-fighting (I assume) power duo, without whose help this book probably wouldn't have been completed.

As always, our full gratitude goes to our team at Montlake Publishing, who have supported these books and been our best cheerleaders. Lauren, you are the editor of our dreams, and the Dream! Eternal gratitude also goes to Sarah Younger, whose powers to manifest encouragement, career advice, and money for her authors has probably earned her a place on the High Court by now. Thank you forever to Seher, who once again read parts of this book paragraphs at a time just to cheer us on! And as always, we get through the good days and the bad with the emotional and occasional financial support of our Discord.

We are proud of how much you help each other, and grateful for how often you have helped us!

Last, but always most, we thank our readers. Every single one of you holds an entire world of dreams in your heart. Your love for reading makes the words we write matter. Thank you for being part of *our* dream.

ABOUT THE AUTHOR

Kit Rocha is the pseudonym for cowriting team Donna Herren and Bree Bridges. After penning dozens of paranormal novels, novellas, and stories as Moira Rogers, they reinvented themselves by writing the nine-book, multiple-award-winning—and extremely steamy—Beyond series, which became an instant cult favorite. They followed it up with two spin-off series, including the popular Mercenary Librarians trilogy, published by Tor. Now they're leaping into sexy epic fantasy with happily-ever-afters.

    Their favorite stories are about messy worlds, strong women, and falling in love with the people who love you just the way you are. When they're not writing, they can be found crafting handmade jewelry, caring too much about video games, or freaking out about their favorite books or TV shows, all of which are chronicled on their various social media accounts. Learn more at www.kitrocha.com.